AMISH COUNTRY TOURS COLLECTION

RACHEL STOLTZFUS

ISBN: 1522978411
ISBN-13: 978-1522978411

TABLE OF CONTENTS

ACKNOWLEDGMENTS

I have to thank God first and foremost for the gift of my life and the life of my family. I also have to thank my family for putting up with my crazy hours and how stressed out I can get as I approach a deadline. In addition, I must thank the ladies at Global Grafx Press for working with me to help make my books the best they can be. And last, I thank you, for taking the time to read this book. God Bless!

AMISH COUNTRY TOURS 1

CHAPTER ONE

Thursday, March 26

I struggle to peddle my bicycle up the hill toward the post office as it starts to rain. This hasn't exactly been the best of days; the buggy has broken down, I have a custom-ordered crib quilt to ship, that I spent most of the night finishing, and today is the final day to mail my property taxes to avoid another penalty. Which would require more money – that I don't have.

Ordinarily, I love the rain, but it makes for a difficult uphill ride in a long, wet dress with cars speeding by. I say a prayer as another car passes, splattering me with mud. I suppose I could have borrowed Deacon Byler's buggy. But the Byler family comes from a strict, old-order community and I didn't want the shame of him finding out that I couldn't pay my taxes when they first became due and didn't ask the church for help.

God forgive me for my pride, but the farm was Jacob's dream long before we married and all five of my children were born there. I fear that if my family becomes too much of a burden on the community, we could be asked to sell the farm and then my children would *ne* longer have the legacy their *daed* intended for them to have.

As I continue up the hill I think about the uncertain futures of my children. When Jacob died, they didn't just lose a man who loved them. In many ways they also lost an entire family heritage and the foundation of who they might become.

My sons lost the man who would teach them to hunt and to work the land, to provide for their own families someday. Whether or not they ever choose to rely on those skills as a primary means of income, Jacob and I always agreed that they were fundamental necessities to surviving in any economy.

They also lost the role model who could teach them carpentry and cabinet making if any of them ever wanted to forge a different path. Jacob was good with horses too and dreamt of building stalls someday to train and breed them. My sons would have, at the very least, had options for their futures. Who will teach them now? How will they become good husbands?

I can't forget that my daughters have lost something irreplaceable too. They lost the one man in their lives who would set the bar for the men they would choose to marry someday, and the relativity of their own roles in a marriage.

Who would set the male example for any of my children now?

All that my family had lost in Jacob's death was bad enough without losing our home too! As a *mamm* I feel it's my God-given responsibility to do whatever I can to keep that from happening.

Lost in my thoughts, I'm startled by another passing motorist and react by swerving slightly. The front tire of my bicycle wedges itself into a rut along the outside edge of the pavement. It has been etched into the blacktop by the steel wheels of the many Amish buggies that travel this road into town. I struggle with the handlebars to steer myself out of it but the hem of my dress catches in the chain, and my bicycle and I, go toppling over into the muddy gravel on the side of the road.

'Pride goeth before a fall.' I can hear my *daed* say, just as if he were sitting on the wet ground next to me. The only difference being that *daed* would have been laughing at the situation and I'm much too frustrated to laugh at the moment.

I scoot myself over to retrieve my purse from the grass and my package which is now lying in a puddle, then struggle to free my dress from the steely jaws of the bike chain. It's my newest dress and I don't want to tear it because I don't have the spare time or the desire to make another. In just two more months I will *ne* longer be required to clad myself in black from head to toe as a symbol of mourning. In fact, I hope to never own another black dress for as long as I live.

I loved my husband dearly and I accept that it's my wifely duty to honor his memory by keeping with the traditions of our faith – but the mourning attire only seems to prolong my grief and sadness. It only honors his death, not his memory. Because in life, Jacob always preferred seeing me in lighter colors.

Just as I begin to pray for God's help, another car passes by and splashes me with muddy rainwater. I hang my head down and sigh. I realize that I'm probably going to have to give in and rip my dress free before someone runs me over. Just as I put my foot against the frame and begin to tug, I hear the rhythmic clop and prattle of a horse and buggy coming up behind me.

"Oh Lord, please let it be anyone but Deacon or Esther Byler," I pray, but as the words escape my lips, I'm too ashamed of myself to even turn around and look to see who it is.

"Are you okay?" a man's voice calls out to me.

I turn as the man climbs out of the buggy and steps towards me. "My dress got caught in the chain," I explain, squinting to look at him through the rain pelting my face.

He tries to rotate the wheel but it doesn't budge. "Hold on," he says over the pounding rain. He runs back to the buggy and returns with a pair of pliers.

"Your chain is jammed. I'll get you loose but you'll have to get it fixed before you can ride it again," he explains as he frees me from the bike. "Can I offer you a lift somewhere?"

"I've got to get to the post office in town but I live back in Hope Landing," I explain.

"I'm going near the post office now. If you don't mind an extra stop, I can take you home afterwards."

"I don't mind," I assure him, as he carefully pulls me to my feet.

He helps me onto the seat with my package, loads my bicycle to the buggy and steers us back onto the roadway headed for town.

"I'm Sarah Fisher."

"I'm John Troyer. "Your hand is bleeding, are you sure you're okay?"

"I'm fine; I must have scraped it on the pavement when I fell. I had hoped I could make it back home before the rain started." I wrap the front hem of my apron around my hand self-consciously.

"It must be a pretty important package to go to all of this trouble on a day like today."

"It's a crib quilt for an expectant *mamm*. I'm a quilter. The baby's due in a few days."

"Are those your quilts at Yoder's store?"

"I have a few quilts for sale there, but the ones on display were made by Deacon Byler's wife and daughter. I've been quilting since I was old enough to thread a needle but only started selling my quilts after my husband died last May."

John Troyer is a tall, handsome man in his middle thirties with a deep voice, a gentle smile, and kind, hazel eyes. His full head of dark brown hair is about the only physical feature that reminds me of Jacob. But he seems to carry that same purposed, thoughtful demeanor that I always admired in my husband, even in a crisis. "Where are you from Mr. Troyer?"

"Please, call me John."

I smile modestly.

"I bought the old Schwartz farm on the south end of Hope Landing."

"*Och*, how long have you been in the community?"

"Four months now but I still have a lot of family in Hopkinsville so I've still been attending church services there."

"That explains why we've never met. I knew the Schwartz property was for sale but I didn't realize anyone had moved in."

"I'm slowly making the transition from Hopkinsville. I'll be at the Lapp's barn raising coming up next Thursday. And I was thinking I might attend next month's community dinner."

"I'm sure Hope Landing will feel more like home once you get to know everyone."

He stops in front of the Post Office and comes around to help me out of the buggy. “If you’re going to be here for a few minutes, I can run over to the tractor supply and come back. I just need to pick up a part that I ordered.”

“*Ya*, that’s fine. I’ll probably have to make a new label and get a new box anyway; this one’s kind of soggy.”

“I’ll be as quick as I can.”

He leaves and I catch a glimpse of my reflection in the glass post office doors as I step inside. I look a fright, from shoes to bonnet, but there’s nothing I can do about it now. I pull the quilt out of the old box, still safe in the plastic bag I wrapped it in, and step up to the cashier when it’s my turn.

The postman helps me select the quickest shipping method, which also happens to be the least expensive, for the size and weight of the package. He gives me a new box and I fill out a new label before retrieving the property tax payment envelope from my purse. I pay the postage for both items and go back outside to wait for John.

It’s still raining and the temperature has dropped several degrees, but I feel more unnoticeable here than in the busy post office. I stay close to the building under the overhang of the roof to keep as warm and dry as possible. Had I been able to manage holding an umbrella and steering a bike at the same time, I would have brought one, but there was *ne* way I could have.

I turn my back to the glass to avoid looking at my reflection and making myself even more self-conscious about the wet fabric of my dress clinging to my figure. Even in the plain black mourning dress, I look immodest. Inconspicuously, I try to pull the fabric away from my body as Mr. Troyer pulls alongside the curb.

He hurries around to open the buggy door for me and helps me inside. I admire his gentlemanly resolve in spite of the rain.

"I hope I didn't keep you waiting long," he says kindly.

"*Ne*, I'm grateful for the ride," I assure him.

We get back on the road and I try to ignore the chill setting into my bones.

"So how long does it take to make a quilt?" he asks curiously.

"It depends on whether I have an existing pattern, how complicated the design is and how big the finished quilt needs to be. Some of the smaller quilts can be finished in two week's time and some of the larger ones take months to finish.

"Do you make them by yourself?"

"My eldest daughter Mary loves to help, just the way I did at her age. She helps me choose and cut the fabrics and I'm teaching her to plan the layout of the designs. She's very methodical for a ten year old. My youngest daughter Hannah is six. She counts pieces, sorts and fetches things - but like most six year olds, it's hard to get her to sit still for very long."

"Are they your only *kinner*?"

"*Ne* I have three boys too." I chuckle. "Mark is Mary's twin, they're ten years old. He's creative and studious like his sister, but he's an adventurer, that one. He'll try his hand at everything and loves to figure out how things work. Then there's Samuel, who's eight. He's small but mighty and he loves to entertain everyone with his stories. When his *daed* took him fishing last; he talked for two days, as if he'd harpooned a whale." I smile at the thought. "I think he's taken his *daed's* death the hardest in some ways. My youngest is five, his name is Joshua. He's a kind soul, but a little rambunctious and curious about everything." I pause, realizing that I've been going on and on about my family. "Do you have children?"

"My wife died several years back, she had been ill for a long time. We always wanted a big family but it just wasn't in God's plan for us."

"I'm sorry for your loss."

"And I for yours," he says thoughtfully, "I suppose that's one of the reasons I left Hopkinsville; it just felt like the longer I was there, the harder it was to move on with my life. My brothers are all married with families of their own and my parents are well cared for. It was just time for me to make a fresh start and try something else."

"I admire your independence."

"Was your husband a farmer?"

"*Ya*, he was raised as a cabinetmaker but he had a greater love for being outdoors and working the land; how about you?"

"*Och*, I'm a farmer at heart, and I suppose I will always keep up the tradition, but I guess I'm a lot like your son in that I love to try my hand at things and find out how they work. We were raised on a small farm but my *daed* and his brother started a construction company once all of the *kinner* were all out of school. I've done masonry, carpentry, roofing and just about anything involved with building houses.

"When my wife was ill, I took to working in a factory and learned a lot about heating and cooling systems and engines. After she died, I opened a small equipment and engine shop on the property and introduced my younger brother to the business. When he was able to manage it on his own, I sold it to him with the main house and the farm and I moved here."

"It's a rare gift to be skilled in so many trades. I'm sure you'll be a big help to the community."

"I guess never having children to raise afforded me the freedom to work as I pleased, and to explore different skills and hobbies. It's been useful, but I often wonder if it was as rewarding as a family would have been."

He stops the buggy in front of the old Schwartz farmhouse. "You're shivering, come inside the house and get warm for a minute while I give this part to my nephew so he can get the tractor running again. I could grab my tools, so I can fix your bike when I take you home, if you'd like. It should only take a few minutes."

"*Denki*, I appreciate that."

Lost in our conversation, I hadn't even noticed that the rain outside had slowed to a drizzle. He comes around, helps me out of the buggy and then shows me inside. The house is large but rather bare, even by plain standards. It could certainly use a woman's touch, I reflected, though I decide to keep that observation to myself.

He fetches a towel and a heavy blanket from a closet in the hallway and hands them to me, "I'll just find my nephew and come right back, he's probably in the barn."

I watch through the screen door for a moment as he walks toward the barn. He's a strapping sort of man, muscular and broad shouldered, but there's a gentle assuredness about him that puts me at ease and he's definitely *ne* stranger to a hard day's work.

I hurry to towel myself as dry as I can from my face to my stockings, then fold the towel neatly over the back of a kitchen chair before wrapping the blanket around my arms and shoulders. When he returns, he helps me into the buggy, puts his toolbox in the back and leads us down the driveway. On the way home, I think about all of the things I still need to accomplish today and how much worse it could have been if he hadn't stopped to help me.

"Do your *kinner* attend the parochial school?" he asks curiously.

"*Ya*, my four oldest do, my *mamm* keeps my youngest during the day so I can quilt when the chores are done."

"They probably already know my nephew Caleb then; he alternates with Eli Lapp to bring the *kinner* home from school when the weather is bad. He's been staying with me every two weeks since I moved here to help me get things going."

"I've never met him personally but it is a big help not to have to pick the children up in the rain or snow. Is that why you attend services in Hopkinsville?"

"*Ya*, I bring him here after church and he stays with me until the next time we go. He wants to try his hand at farming, and this gives him two weeks in each place, so he can learn without neglecting his family at home. My oldest brother still works in the construction business so Caleb never really learned to work the land. He's got quite a gift with kids and animals though. Even if he doesn't become a farmer, I think it's good for him to have the experience."

"That's what I want for my boys too. I don't mind if they farm or find some other trade; that's between them and the call God puts in their hearts, but I still want them to learn how to work the land and to know that they can always provide for their families."

I think of the fields that need to be planted in a couple of weeks as we approach the farm, "That's my property just ahead on the right."

He pulls onto the drive that leads to the main house, "*Och, ya*, someone told me this farm might be coming up for sale when I first started looking to buy in the area. I remember thinking what a nice property it is. I'm glad you decided to keep it."

I know deep down that some of the townspeople are still expecting and maybe even hoping that I'll sell the farm and find something smaller. I'm sure that some of the older community members feel that a 30 acre farm isn't a suitable home for a widow with five young children to look after. And I'm sure they have relatives that would jump at the chance to settle in my place, but I've never considered selling.

I say nothing, for fear of making him uncomfortable. He means *ne* harm in repeating what he was told and I don't want to stir up strife. I just thank God for his kindness and for putting John Troyer in my path today.

CHAPTER TWO

John parks in front of the barn. "Your bike probably won't take long to fix, the chain probably just slipped out of its track when your dress got caught. I might have a chain guard back at the shop in Hopkinsville – we work on a lot of bikes and buggies there. I'll check when I take my nephew back in a few days."

"*Denki*, you're very kind. I don't ride my bicycle that often but I was afraid to take the family buggy since the wheel has started to wobble like it's going to fly off. My husband used to take care of that sort of thing and I've been so busy this past week that I didn't have time to have anyone look at it."

"Most of my plans for the day will have to wait because of the rain. I'd be happy to take a look at it while I'm here."

"If you could fit it into your day, I'd be happy to pay you for your services."

"Let me see if it can be fixed here or whether it has to be taken to a shop."

I feel a little uncomfortable inviting a man into my home but I don't want to be unkind when he's been so helpful. "Come on in and warm yourself by the stove before you get started, your clothes must be as damp as mine. I'll make you a cup of coffee or some cocoa."

"A cup of coffee would be terrific," he says, rubbing his hands together to warm them.

I leave the kitchen door open, show him inside and offer him a seat at the table near the wood burning stove. Our church district is considered modern or New-Order Amish because we're permitted to have electric in the home but I grew up using a wood burning stove and continuing to do so doesn't bother me. I light the stove and fill the kettle before I put it on to boil.

"*Och*, your faucet's leaking; let me grab my wrenches and see if I can tighten it for you while we wait for the kettle.

Before I can dismiss the notion, he's halfway out the door to fetch his tools, "*Denki*," I call out as he closes the screen door. There are so many little reminders of Jacob's absence constantly creeping up around the house that I suppose I need to get used to the idea of letting others help me tend to them.

He returns with his wrenches and goes to work on the faucet as I pull the French press, two mugs and coffee from the cupboard. When John is satisfied that the leak has been fixed, he sits back down next to the warm stove.

"Do you prefer the wood stove for cooking?" he asks curiously.

"We bought the farm from an Old Order Amish family, so it came with the house. We intended to replace it someday but it wasn't as high on our list of priorities as my gas clothes dryer," I chuckle.

"It reminds me of when I was a kid, all of us huddling around the stove after being outside on a cold day to get warm. When my wife was ill, I converted most of our house to solar power thinking it might be easier for her if she ever recovered. My dad did the same at the family house, so my *mamm* uses electric now too – but she says it's not the same."

"It's certainly nice to have some modern conveniences. But sometimes the old ways are still the best. I've never really cooked much on an electric stove, so I really don't know."

"I've heard some of the women in Hopkinsville say they prefer electric stoves and some say they don't – but I've never heard any of the men say that they miss chopping all that wood."

We both laugh, "I suppose that's true."

"It's nice to sit by the fire again though."

I wash enough potatoes for dinner tonight and breakfast tomorrow, then set them aside as the kettle begins to whistle. I prepare the coffee and pour us both a cup.

He takes a few sips, "*Och*, that's *gut*. I forgot how much better it tastes when it's prepared properly," he smiles. "My wife used to use a French press, but I can never manage it without getting grounds into the coffee."

"It's difficult adjusting to some things alone isn't it?"

"It's the little things that seem the most challenging sometimes."

"I think it would have been much harder for me if it hadn't been for the children. In spite of how I felt on any given day, they still had to be nurtured and cared for. I remember being in the house on the day of the burial. It was crowded and bustling with people, when all I wanted was to be left alone. After the meal, I had gone upstairs to lie down and when I woke, I could hear my children laughing and playing with the *kinner* who were there. I felt so angry at how they could be laughing and enjoying time with friends when we just put their *daed* in the ground only a few hours before. I marched down the stairs to scold them discreetly and halfway down God said to me, *'Don't be angry Sarah; they're behaving exactly as they're supposed to be. Go and let your soul be comforted.'* It really helped me to see things differently."

I realized that I couldn't let Jacob's death keep me from being who I was supposed to be either. I had children who needed a strong and nurturing *mamm*, a *mamm* who needed a faithful daughter, friends who needed my kindness and maybe someday, there would be a man in need of a woman who is willing to stand firm and able to love again. I don't know what the future holds but I feel that neither God nor Jacob would approve of anything less."

I sigh self-consciously, "I'm sorry if I'm making you uncomfortable. Sometimes I think that as Amish people, we expect that shunning the dead from our thoughts and our conversations will make it easier to go on with life. But I don't think that's really possible and the more I try to forget, the more I feel tormented by his memory. One day, I finally just stopped trying. Jacob was a good man, loving him taught me a lot and helped me become who I am. I could *ne* more forget him than I could forget having a left arm. But as time passes and I and allow myself to have hope again, for my children and for my future, I feel less sorrow and more peace when I think about him."

I look down at my hands knowing the church probably wouldn't approve of my openness, especially with someone of the opposite sex, but it felt like something in my heart was leading me to share as the words seemed to spill from my mouth.

The Bible says in James 5:16 *'Confess your faults to one another and pray for one another, that ye may be healed.'*, so whether community tradition approves or not, I believe that God does. I imagine it's probably harder for our Amish men to find support and understanding in their grief from anyone, male or female.

"It sounds like you're handling it well."

"*Och*, I have an occasional bad day but it's getting easier. Would you like some more coffee?" I ask, taking his empty cup.

"Actually I think I'm warm enough to go back outside. I'd like to take a look at that buggy before it gets much later, in case we need a part from town."

Outside, he stops to unload my bike and carries it to the barn. I show him to the buggy with its wobbly wheel. "If you don't need me for anything, I'm going to go change into some dry clothes and start my afternoon chores."

"Go ahead, I'll be fine."

I return to the kitchen and tidy up, putting the French press in the dish drain to dry, before grabbing a bath towel and going into the bedroom to change. The rain is still drizzling outside but I feel much better after the coffee. I strip out of my rain soaked dress, stockings and underwear and suddenly feel ten pounds lighter. I swish my hair in the towel, to get it as dry as possible, then towel my damp skin from my face to my toes. By the time I'm fully dressed in fresh dry clothes, I feel ten degrees warmer too.

I gather the laundry which would normally be done by this hour, and head downstairs to the basement to begin the first load. With seven family members including *mamm* and six separate beds to change, I usually wash our clothes on

Mondays and Thursdays, saving the linens for Saturdays when the children are all home to help.

I still use the wringer washer my parents gave us as a wedding present but thankfully Jacob bought me a propane operated clothes dryer when we learned that I was pregnant with Josh. Whenever possible, to keep costs down, I will still use my wooden drying rack; but that dryer has saved me from getting behind more times than I care to admit. Today will have to be one of those days. I run the first load of washing through the wringer and start the dryer.

Back upstairs, I step inside the food pantry and immediately think of Jacob as I always do. It used to be the laundry room when we bought the house, but Jacob lined three entire walls with shelves and cupboards so that I could store the food I canned closer to the kitchen. We also planned to put an upright freezer on the wall next to the basement door someday but he died before we could make that happen.

We used to talk about being able to stock up on more of the meat he hunted, or the fish he caught as a failsafe for more difficult times. We could certainly have used it right about now.

Jacob was always a good provider but as I look at my dwindling food supply, I wonder again how my sons will learn to hunt or whether they'll even be interested in it without their *daed's* example and enthusiasm to rally them. With fewer and fewer people in the community relying on the land to survive, things were certainly changing in the Amish culture as a whole.

I grab some beef stock and vegetables that I canned in the fall, for the soup I plan to make for dinner. I sit everything on the kitchen counter and then grab some orzo and corn meal from what I refer to as my 'dry goods pantry'. Which is the original closet pantry that I use for things like rice, pasta, flour and oatmeal.

I stand over the sink and start to peel the potatoes that I washed earlier, when I realize that my hair is still down. I hurry into the bathroom, brush the tangles out and secure it under a fresh *kapp* before returning to the kitchen. I know many Amish women that only let their hair down to wash it or to sleep at night and they feel naked without their *kapps* – but I'm not one of them. We're only required to wear it outside the home or in mixed company, and by the time the evening chores are done I'm usually more than ready to take it down.

Once I peel and cube the potatoes, I decide to check on John.

***

In the barn, I assess the problem with the buggy and give it a once-over to see if anything else needs to be repaired while I'm here. I start by replacing the battery that operates her blinkers and check the single trees, bolts, straps and all of her harnessing snaps. I notice a cupboard above the work area near the buggy stall and look through it to see if there are any spare parts. Once I'm satisfied that I have everything needed to do the repair, I decide to work on the bicycle first before getting my hands greasy with the buggy.

I head back to the house, to grab the wrenches I was using to fix the kitchen faucet, but as I grab the handle to the screen door, Sarah emerges from the pantry with her hair down and her *kapp* off.

I take a step back and stop myself from entering for fear that I might embarrass her, but in those few seconds, I can't help but notice how beautiful she looks as the soft waves of chestnut hair fall around her face and over the narrow shoulders of her petite frame. I think about how open and honest she was with me about her beliefs and experiences with her grief. Though some in the community would admonish her for those thoughts, I find them incredibly refreshing, and I realize I don't want to dishonor her.

She may be small, but in the same way she described her middle son, I can tell that she's a mighty woman on the inside. She's loyal to God and strong in her faith without letting the community traditions close her mind to the way that life should be. It's a quality that I've rarely seen in Amish women over the years and I'm curious to know more about her.

I go back to the barn and make due with my pliers, resetting the chain on her bike before returning to the buggy wheel. Just about the time I get everything put back together, she comes into the barn.

***

"It's chilly out here this afternoon; would you like another cup of coffee? I can put some in a thermos," I politely offer to Mr. Troyer. I notice Jacob's metal toolbox on the workbench and the cupboard doors open just above it. He notices my momentary reaction.

"I hope you don't mind, I thought this might have been where your husband kept any spare parts for your riding equipment. It saved me from having to go back to my place or into town to fix the problem."

"*Ne*, I don't mind at all, did you find what you needed?" I don't know why I paid it any attention at all, except that I hadn't seen that old tool box sitting there since the morning Jacob died.

"*Ya*, I should have it all fixed up in just a few more minutes."

"I'll go back and put the kettle on, just come on in when you're done."

Inside the house, I collect my thoughts for a second before putting the kettle on the stove and going back down to check the laundry. I take the clothes out of the dryer, wring out the next load of wash and start the dryer again before carrying the laundry basket upstairs to fold.

A few minutes later, I hear him scruff his shoes on the door mat and step inside just before the kettle whistles. "I grab it and pour the water into the press as he washes his hands in the sink.

"Just let me know what I owe you, I can't tell you what a

relief it is to have everything working properly again." I say, filling our coffee mugs.

"Don't worry about it, they were just minor repairs."

"You have to let me pay you something," I insist, not wanting to take advantage of his kindness.

"If your cooking is as good as your coffee, you could invite me to dinner some night when it's convenient but I won't take your money," he says stubbornly.

I chuckle, "Okay, how about Saturday if you don't have any other plans? You can even bring your nephew if you'd like."

"Saturday would be great. I don't know what my nephew has planned, but if he's available I'm sure he'll jump at the chance for a home-cooked meal. Neither of us is anything to brag about in the kitchen."

I fold the laundry as we chat and finish our coffee. Fifteen minutes later, we say our goodbyes and I send him on his way with a full thermos and an extra quart of goat's milk I had in the refrigerator from this morning's milking. I wave as he climbs back in the buggy, looking forward to seeing them both at dinner on Saturday.

After he leaves, I dust, run a damp mop over the floor, mend some socks and let out the buttons on three pairs of Josh's pants that he's not wearing. He's getting a little pudgy for his height but I'm confident that it will correct itself naturally in the months to come when he can play outside more.

I go back downstairs to wring and dry the last load of laundry for the day, which includes the dress I muddied today. After that's done, it's just about time for the children to come home from school so I walk over to the Daadi Haus to fetch my *mamm* and Josh.

"Hi *mamm*," I smile, as I walk in the door. I can smell the pies she's baking. Josh rushes to me and gives me a big sticky hug and kiss.

"I smell cinnamon and apples. Has someone has been baking fruit pies?" I ask curiously, sniffing his chubby cheek.

"We have!" he tells me excitedly.

"*Och*, did you make one for me?"

"*Ya*, and *mammi*, and Mark, and Mary, and Samuel, and Hannah, and Ruth, and Dan, and Jesus, and *daed*, and *daadi*."

"My goodness that's a lot of pies," I chuckle, "I think you might have forgotten to mention one though."

He looks at his co-conspirator for help. My *mamm* and I always managed to get 13 hand pies out of a 12 pie yielding recipe so we could sample one together right as they came out of the oven.

"Would there happen to be half of a missing pie right here?!" I ask tickling his belly.

"*Mammi*," he sighs, throwing up his hands and blaming his grandmother.

She and I both laugh.

"Actually I made 36 pies, we have a ladies' frolic tomorrow and I thought we might be having visitors this weekend," she says with a knowing look.

"Ruth and Dan will probably come over Sunday after church but you know Ruth always brings dessert."

"I meant the tall young man who moved into the old Schwartz place right after Christmas."

If I didn't know that my *mamm* was devoted to her church and the Amish life, I would swear that she had internet access and spy cameras planted all over the community. For a sixty-four year old widow with failing eyesight and terrible arthritis that keeps her from getting out much, she seems to always know what's going on in the community long before I do. "He fixed my bicycle and the buggy wheel today but how did you know I invited him to dinner or who he is?"

"I raised you, I know you well," she says cleaning the flour off of the counter from rolling out her last batch of pies. "Him I met when he brought the *kinner* home from school in the snow one day while Eli Lapp's tractor was broken down. It was the day Hannah lost her mittens right after Christmas break. He found them in the wagon and brought them by the next day while you were gone. I talked to him for a few minutes. He seems like a good man. Did you know that he and one of the Lapp boys built the wagon they pull behind the tractor?"

I hear the children coming down the drive toward the house behind me. "*Ne*, he didn't mention it."

"*Och*, see he's humble too," she says casually.

"I need to get dinner started, are you coming?"

"We'll be right over when the pies are done, you go on ahead," she says taking Josh's hand and shooing me out the door.

My *mamm* is small and thin, much like me and I suppose I'll look like her when I'm older. Her body is weak from arthritis and a few injuries she's had over the years. She has always set a good example for me as a Godly wife but she has a big personality tucked in her small frame that hides behind her quiet, submissive demeanor.

Mamm's parents owned a tobacco farm with seven children. She worked the fields and helped take care of the family from the time she was a young girl until the day she married my *daed* at the age of nineteen. He died eleven years ago and I regret that my children never knew him but I'm eternally grateful for having her in our lives every day.

I have a brother too – but we rarely see him. He moved to Maryland a few years ago to take over my uncle's farm when he started having health problems. He's always been a big boy, taking more after my *daed's* side of the family. In fact, that's how he came to be named Sampson. There were complications during his birth and though they both survived, my *mamm* was never able to conceive again.

I go back inside the house and greet the children with a hug and a kiss as they change into their mud boots to go do their afternoon chores.

I prepare my grandmother's sweet cornbread recipe and put it in the oven before going back down to pull the last of the clean clothes from the dryer, which are mostly mine. I put them away while everyone comes in and washes their hands after chore time.

We all gather around the kitchen table and surrounded by the warmth radiating from the wood stove, the children tell me about their day. As I finish getting the soup on to simmer and take the cornbread out of the oven, I tell everyone about falling off the bike in the rain and the nice man who brought me home and fixed everything.

Mark agrees that inviting him for dinner was a good idea, Mary and Hannah decide to make him a thank you card, Samuel promises to show him his best magic trick and Josh decides to give him three pies because he fixed three things…apparently if Caleb comes he can have five. *Mamm* and I laugh at his rationale.

After dinner and a hand pie each, the children do their night time chores and then it's time for baths, pajamas, teeth brushing, prayers and bed. By the time they're all tucked in, I'm tuckered out. I go to the living room to sit with *mamm* for a little while.

"*Denki* for the pies *mamm*, they were delicious and they'll save me a lot of work Saturday."

"I've never met an Amish man who didn't like hand pies," she smiles.

"Do you regret never remarrying?" I ask curiously.

"At the time when I was faced with that decision, *ne* but things are much clearer in hindsight and sometimes I wonder what might have been if I had. Besides, I was 55 when *daed* died and you're 32, there's enough room for a whole lifetime of love in between the two."

"Still, I'm glad you didn't marry Deacon King," I chuckle, "You'd probably be getting up every morning at 4 a.m. to starch his underwear."

"Shame on you," she laughs.

"I think I'm going to turn in early, what time is the ladies' frolic tomorrow?"

"*Ya*, quilting and tea sandwiches at noon at the Stoltzfus farm…be there if you wanna be square," she teases as I shake my head in amusement.

A ladies' frolic is a time when groups of women in the community gather together to socialize and learn from one another as we work on different hobbies or projects. There are several different types of frolics like scrapbooking, soap making or crafting but the one we're going to is for the quilters.

We've been working on a quilt for Mrs. Stoltzfus' daughter's upcoming wedding in November.

Go on in to bed *liebchen*," my mom says, peering over her glasses as she tidies up her sewing box, "You've had a long day. I'll see myself home."

"Night *mamm*," I say, kissing her forehead, "See you in the morning."

CHAPTER THREE

Saturday, March 28

By 6:00 a.m., Saturday morning is already a buzz of activity as everyone makes their way to the breakfast table. I stayed up working on the layout for a new quilt order until after midnight last night, so I don't feel well rested this morning and I have a log day ahead. Fortunately there's *ne* rush on this latest quilt. But I do need to try to make up for the time I lost putting this one aside to complete the baby quilt in time. I finish frying the eggs in my griddle pan as my *maam* puts the potatoes and the last of the winter's bacon on the table.

"Can we have pies for dessert?" Hannah asks before she's even started breakfast.

"The rest of the pies are for after dinner; remember we have John and Caleb coming tonight?

"*Mammi* made some strawberry rhubarb jam you can have on your sandwich at lunch," *mamm* assures her.

"Mmmm, mmmm, my favorite," Samuel smiles.

"Did you two finish your thank you card?" I ask, putting eggs on everyone's plate.

"We just need to pick some leaves to glue on the edges," Mary informs me.

When the food is on the table and everyone is seated, we bow our heads in prayer before everyone digs in.

"What are you planning to make tonight?" *Mamm* asks curiously.

"Chicken and dumplings!" Samuel calls out.

"Taco pie!" Josh chimes in.

"I think you should make fried chicken with biscuits and gravy, green beans and mashed potatoes," Mary adds.

"Only *Mammi* should make the biscuits," Mark suggests.

"And just what is wrong with my biscuits?" I ask.

"Well, they're good but I like *Mammi's* biscuits better."

"Shame on you Mark Fisher," my *mamm* scolds.

"It's okay *mamm*, he speaks the truth, but I think Mark needs to help you make them next time," I chuckle.

"I wanna help," Hannah offers.

"A meatloaf would be nice and a lot easier than slaughtering a chicken," *mamm* suggests.

I give her a suspicious look. The only recipe I use for meatloaf is the one she passed down to me, which she has always referred to as her 'courtship meatloaf' because it's the recipe she prepared the night my *daed* asked to court her – and he swore for 36 years that it was the meatloaf that swayed him. The problem is that I can't serve it without my *mamm* telling that story and I'm not sure it would be appropriate in mixed company. I don't want to give the wrong impression.

"Eat your breakfast everyone, we have lots to do today. I'll consider your suggestions and give you my decision at lunch."

"Are we going to do the chore chart today?" Hannah asks.

"Uh, we haven't even done our morning chores yet Hannah," Mark says, rolling his eyes dismissively.

"Mark Fisher," I scold. I know that just calling him by his full name carries enough weight for him to know he's out of line. I'm not militant with my children and they're fairly well behaved. I know there will be disagreements and times when they'll get on each other's nerves, but the one thing they're not allowed to do is put each other down, and he's walking a fine line this morning.

"Sorry Hannah," he says

I look around the table and see that most everyone's finished eating. "Okay as soon as morning chores are done, we'll do the chore chart."

Mary carries her plate to the sink and starts the dish water, Mark gathers empty plates and silverware and Samuel starts gathering the trash. Hannah tries to cram her remaining half of a strip of bacon in her mouth at one time and Josh puts away the ketchup while *mamm* chuckles.

"I've got to hand it to you; the chore chart was a great idea."

When the dishes are cleared and stacked to wash, I call Mark aside before he goes outside to tend to the goats. "Are you having a bad morning?" I ask in a concerned voice.

"*Ne* it's just that she always wants to know what we're doing next instead of focusing on right now."

"Maybe, but did you ever stop to consider that she's not as mature as you? Maybe thinking ahead to the next reward helps motivate her as she goes along. If something's bothering you, let's talk about it but there's *ne* reason for you to be so critical of others today."

"Sorry *mamm*."

"Now go get your chores done. I think you have some points to tally if I'm not mistaken."

He smiles and runs in to get his mud boots on while my *mamm* takes Hannah and Josh to feed the chickens and gather and wash the eggs.

Our farm is considered small by farming standards but it takes time and money to build, which has only become more challenging since Jacob died. Still, with five children, six goats, three horses, 30 chickens and a *mamm* to look after, I have to be organized in order to accomplish everything that has to be done in one day.

In addition to the basic responsibilites of cleaning their rooms and picking up toys and games from the common areas every day, there are several, more complex, chores in our home that I've broken down into four categories and charted on a dry erase board that hangs in the food pantry:

Daily chores (inside and outside): which they know are routine chores that have to be done every day without fail at specific times; like feeding the animals or picking up their toys before bed. These chores teach them a sense of ownership and responsibility in our collective home.

Weekly chores(inside and outside): which are various duties that don't always have a rigid schedule, aren't done on Sundays or bad weather days and they're allowed to trade or take turns doing them as long as they all get done by the Saturday suppertime deadline; like washing the buggy or sweeping the porches. These chores teach them to work together as a team and to manage their time.

Assigned Chores: These teach different skills based on each *kinner's* level of maturity and help address areas they need to grow in. I believe these chores will help them become well-rounded, self-reliant men and women someday. Mary may do the dishes regularly because she enjoys it more than mucking the barn, but at some point, they will all be assigned to the task even if it's just for a month at a time.

Community Chores: These can be projects done individually or as a group, in the home or for others in the community; and I assign them point values, both individually and as a team for completing these chores.

Individual points can be redeemed for things they want like a toy or a candy bar or even a new dress or baseball glove. I don't tally their individual points openly because I don't want to encourage a spirit of competition between them but for every five hundred team points they earn, they get a group treat like a new game or a family picnic at the park or anything fun I can come up with for them to do together.

Of course the tallying of points has become something they look forward to every Saturday and I find it helps to keep them motivated all week. I usually try to work it in before lunch so that they'll have the rest of the day to accomplish anything they've forgotten or mismanaged throughout the week since tomorrow is the Sabbath, which we reserve for rest, church and fellowship.

I visit the pantry to collect my notes and to decide what I'm making for dinner. There are plusses and minuses to living in the Amish culture, much like I imagine there are in any society. Though I don't always agree wholeheartedly with some of the traditions I've been raised with, the sense of community among my Amish brothers and sisters is something I'm constantly grateful for.

For an entire year after Jacob's death, varying members of the community will take turns visiting my family on Sunday afternoons to offer fellowship and bring food, which feeds us that night and sometimes lasts a day or so after they've gone. Without this, I know there would have already been times where I wouldn't have had enough food to get my family through the week.

In two months, that support won't be expected anymore and as I look at my pantry, it worries me to see my provisions diminish day by day. I know that planting season is coming, with harvest to follow, but that's many hours of labor spent out in the field that can't be used for quilting, not to mention months away.

Of course it also doesn't offer much help with the mortgage, new shoes for the children, material for new clothes, the cost of feed for the animals we rely on to survive, doctor's expenses, repairs, toiletries and the list goes on. The money I've made from my quilts has afforded us the essentials so far but if I have to allocate more of that money toward feeding the family, we won't stay afloat long.

In the Amish community, there's a widow's fund that I can request money from in an emergency but I know that if I do, I will bring myself under greater scrutiny and it won't be long before I will be asked to sell the farm and to settle somewhere more "manageable," especially considering I have two widows in my household who threaten to drain the community's resources dry with just one misfortune; like a large hospital bill. It worries me because my *mamm* certainly hasn't been getting any healthier in recent years.

I can't blame the leaders of the community for taking those things into consideration and I hate the idea of ever being a burden to anyone. Maybe this *is* too much for me to handle but I just can't let my family be pushed out of our home and see all that Jacob and I have worked for be lost. It's all I have left to leave our children someday.

As I fight back the tears, Mark comes running through the house and into the pantry. "Mark, you're tracking in mud-,"

"*Mamm*, there's an *Englisch* family outside who saw our sign for eggs and they want to know if they can take a tour of the farm!" he says excitedly.

I wipe my tears. "I don't want you talking to strangers, especially the *Englisch*," I scold him. The English are often curious about the Amish people with our plain manner of dress, our buggies and funny hats. A lot of them say unkind things in front of the children or try to take pictures of us when we're in town, which is against our religion. I've had to hurry my children to the buggy on more than one occasion to get away from them.

"But *mamm* they promise not to take any pictures and they're willing to pay fifty bucks! They seem really nice and I think they're rich, they have a big fancy car and everything!"

I sigh, knowing I'm going to have to handle this myself but as I remove my kitchen apron and head toward the front door, it occurs to me that they could be dangerous. Who pays fifty dollars to look at a few goats and chickens?

When I step outside, Mary is talking to an *Englisch* girl a bit older than her while Samuel is telling the girl's parents and a young boy the story of Jonah and the whale named *Jaws*. He stops rambling when I walk up behind him and gently place my hand on his shoulder. I see my *mamm* returning from the chicken coop with Josh and Hannah who is holding her basket of fresh eggs.

"Hello, I'm Sarah Fisher," I say politely. My son says you wanted to tour the farm?"

"Yes, hi there, my name is Allen Ruby; this is my wife Georgia, my daughter Katie and my son Samuel," he offers his hand to shake mine.

I look down at his hand, "I'm sorry I-,"

He interrupts me before I finish. "Oh yes, I apologize that's probably against the rules. Well anyway, we're here on vacation visiting relatives and we were just talking to our kids last night about an Amish woman we saw in the drugstore.

"Such a pretty young girl, she had a hat like yours but it was white," Mrs. Ruby chimes in.

"Well anyway, Our kids didn't believe that there were people who actually live a happy life without cars and televisions and computers and cell phones, so when we were driving down the road toward my sister's place, we saw your sign for eggs and I just knew by the little picture of the buggy that the eggs were Amish and I thought maybe my kids could look and see that it's all true. We read on the internet that the Amish aren't allowed to have their picture taken but I'd be willing to pay you for your time if fifty dollars would be fair, I'd spend that much on dinner and this would be so much more meaningful."

"I'm afraid my faith does not permit me to invite you into my home, I-,"

He interrupts me again. "Oh, say no more, I understand, I know this must seem strange with us just barging in on you like this."

Maybe it wouldn't be so bad to show some *Englisch* children that it was possible to live a simpler, more peaceful life and we sure could use the money. "Mr. Ruby, I was just going to say that I'd be happy to give you a tour of the rest of the farm in the buggy and let everyone pet the goats, horses and chickens while we answer any questions they might have."

"Oh well that would be fantastic. What do you say kids?" he asks his family.

"I want to ride in the buggy!" the older girl says.

"Me too!" the younger boy agrees, "Mom, his name's Sam just like mine!" he says pointing to my son who looks up at me with a smile.

"This is my *mamm*, Miriam Miller, this is Mark, Mary, Samuel, Hannah and Josh," I say. The children wave when their name is called. "Come on into the barn and the children will let everyone pet the goats while my son and I get the horse and buggy ready."

Mamm gives me a nod of approval and follows the children and the Ruby family into the barn. Mark helps me harness the horses while Mary answers questions about the goats, what they eat, whether we milk them, if we drink the milk, and so on. Samuel tells them all of the goat's names while Josh encourages them to pet them and Hannah clings to mamm's leg, observing.

When the buggy is ready, Samuel introduces the horses. "This one's name is Waffles because she likes to eat them only we're not allowed to give her syrup." The Ruby family laughs as he pets the horse and then let's them pet her too.

"This one's name is Jonah because he's really stubborn sometimes like the guy I was telling you about."

They laugh again.

He shows them the horse still in his stall which we don't use for the buggy. "This horse's name is Jester because he likes to make people laugh. Smile Jester," he tells the horse. Jester bares his teeth and curls his lips, holding the pose while everyone laughs. "Hand Jester," Samuel says, as Jester lifts his hoof to Samuel's hand. The Ruby's clap and Jester shakes his head up and down with enthusiasm.

It had never occurred to me that we might possess enough excitement on our little family farm to entertain fancy tourists. My children also seem to be enjoying it...especially Samuel who I've been so worried about lately.

I climb into the buggy and take the reins.

"After you ma'am," Mark says helping Mrs. Ruby into the buggy first, then the rest of the family as he does with our own family. Once everyone is seated, I tell my *mamm* to meet us at the chicken coop after Mark and I take the Ruby's for a ride.

"How do you like our car?" Mark asks with a smile.

"Do you really drive this everywhere instead of a car?" the older girl asks.

"I've only ridden in a car two times in my whole life," he tells her.

"And you don't have an ipad or a cell phone?"

"What's an ipad?" he asks.

"It's a type of small computer," Mrs. Ruby explains.

Mark chuckles, "We don't have a computer. We're allowed to have a phone in the house but since we never use it, we just use the phone shack for emergencies. I'll show it to you on the way back," he assures them.

"This reminds me of the carriage ride we took on our first anniversary," Mrs. Ruby says. "It's so peaceful out here, and pretty too."

I smile, remembering the many buggy rides we took when Jacob was courting me, as Mark points out the corn fields we'll be planning in a couple of weeks, the windmill and the different trees we have.

Even after living here for all of these years, I begin to see the property from a different perspective, as my son orates the tour. It reminds me of things I take for granted at times; like the lush green grass that covers the ground dotted with blooms of White Splendor, or the *Glory-of-the-snow* I planted around the trees last fall with pretty blue flowers now in full bloom. I remember planting them to glorify God as I tried to get my mind off of my grief. But I imagine that to anyone driving by, it's rather picturesque.

I stop at the phone shack and Mark hops out of the buggy so that everyone can take a look inside. It's nothing more than the old wooden outhouse with a bench seat that I upholstered to cover the hole with a blue touch-tone phone wired inside, located about 200 yards from the barn. I never imagined the old crapper would be considered a tourist attraction but the *Englisch* seem to find it rather intriguing. I chuckle at the irony as Mark smiles knowingly at me.

We head back to the barn where Mark helps everyone out of the buggy and then walks them over to the chicken coop while

I unhitch the horses and put everything away. I join everyone outside where Hannah is petting a baby chick and answering a couple of questions about them as Josh carries his around for everyone to hold.

All of my children love animals and the outdoors but Hannah is a bit more timid than the others. My mamm supervises as she and Josh feed the chickens and gather the eggs in the morning, after school and again after dinner so the chicken coop is really their domain and it's nice to see them sharing their fondness for it with others.

"Would it be possible to buy a dozen eggs from you?" Mr. Ruby asks. "I think my sister would like them, she's into everything organic these days."

"You're welcome to take some with you free of charge Mr. Ruby; I hope your family enjoyed the tour." I watch as *mamm* whispers to Mary who promptly runs into the house with the basket of eggs.

"Oh we had a great time; it'll be something my family will remember for a long time to come."

"Your children are just wonderful Ms. Fisher, I'd love to do it again in the fall when the leaves turn, I bet it's just beautiful."

Mary tugs on my sleeve and asks me a question in *Deutsch*.

"*Ya*, okay," I tell her.

"Here are your eggs and a jar of homemade apple butter for

your family. We also make quilts that you can order from our friend's store. She has pictures of them in a book you can look at if you ever want one," she says handing Mrs. Ruby one of Theresa's business cards.

"Well, that is so sweet, thank you so much. Isn't she a doll?" Mrs. Ruby says to her husband.

"You have a lovely family Ms. Fisher, thank you so much for taking the time. Little lady, you give this to your mother when we leave," he says handing Mary some money as everyone returns from the coop.

"*Denki*, have a nice vacation," Mary calls out as they pile into the big fancy car.

We all wave as we watch them leave and then go inside the house together. The children are brewing over with enthusiasm and I plan to talk to them about it but right now, I need a moment to think about what just happened. I gather the children at the table as *mamm* puts a kettle on the stove to boil.

"Children, I know everyone is excited but we mustn't let our visit from the *Englisch* keep us from taking care of our home and cutting into our time together. Let me see your hand if you didn't finish morning chores." Mark, Mary and Samuel all raise their hands.

"You three go and finish your chores Hannah and Josh, I want you to work together as a team and go to all of the bedrooms and strip the sheets and pillowcases off the beds and throw them down over the basement steps like we usually do together. Make sure to fold the blankets in every room too."

"*Mammi's* bed too?" Hannah asks.

"I'll help you with *mammi's* when you're done," I tell her.

"Here's the money he gave us *mamm*," Mary says putting it in my hand as she kisses my cheek.

"*Denki liebchen*, we'll still try to finish the chore chart before lunch," I assure them.

They all return to chore time and *mamm* pours us both a cup of coffee. I count the money before putting it in the tin coffee can in the cupboard over the fridge that I call the 'cash can'.

I sigh and join *mamm* at the table, knowing she's waiting patiently for me to open the discussion. "That *Englisch* man just paid sixty dollars for one hour of looking around at the quirky Amish family." I say, still wrestling with it in my head, "Did I just make a harlot of my family?" I ask her.

"*Ne mei dochder*, I think you received a blessing from the Lord just for being faithful to who you already are. Nobody violated the *Ordnung* and I think the *kinner* pulled together as well as any frolic I've ever seen. This is the way of life we hope for them."

"They were pretty great weren't they? Mark was leading the way and talking about our Amish values, Samuel was my old Samuel again, telling stories and making people smile. Josh encouraged the children to pet the animals and even Hannah came out of her shell. Mary of course was as thoughtful as ever, but always thinking ahead to the next quilt order," I chuckle. "Did you tell her to give them the apple butter?"

"*Ne* I just told her to put the eggs in a carton so they wouldn't break, I was afraid you would give away my best egg basket."

We both laugh and it makes me feel a sense of relief. "I'm happy that I didn't disappoint you by deciding to give the tour."

"Our families must all learn to survive in changing times. Do you think the *Englisch* flock to Yoder's store in seasons because they have nowhere else to buy jams and jellies? They come because of the Amish hands that prepare them. In my eyes, this is *ne* different. You just pray and let God speak to your heart."

"*Denki mamm*, I will," I say, hugging her neck. "I'd better get busy on the chore chart; I don't want the visit from the *Englisch* to take that away from them."

"I'll make lunch while you do that. Don't forget about dinner," she reminds me.

"Actually I think I'm going to make that meatball casserole I made for the last barn frolic. It won't take long to put together and everyone seemed to really enjoy it. I froze two dozen meatballs the last time I made a 'courtship meatloaf' and I have some marinara sauce I canned when we harvested all of those tomatoes in the fall. Would you mind making two loaves of crusty bread this afternoon? I'll use one tonight and make a bread pudding later in the week with the other."

"*Ya*, I think that's a good idea. They've probably never had it before and the children love it. You tally the chore chart and I'll get started."

CHAPTER FOUR

I sit at the kitchen table with the chore chart; ticking off completed tasks for the week. In spite of a busy week for all of them, only a few items remain that still need to be accomplished today. Next I look at the notes I've made about the community chores each child completed and begin assigning points to each of them individually.

Hannah found a lost kitten for the little Zook girl, Mary and *mamm* baked Mrs. Zook a birthday cake because her *kinner* are both barely more than toddlers. Mary also volunteered to give up going to a singing to babysit for the Zooks while they visited Mr. Zook's *mamm* in the hospital. Mark, Samuel and Josh spent two afternoons doing chores for the widow Helmuth while her son was down with the flu.

I'm pleased with the way my children help the community *ne* matter how simple the task because I know it's in their hearts to glorify God in the good deeds that they do. It puts my mind at ease about today and strengthens my faith that the exposure to the *Englisch* won't change who they are inside.

I find myself wondering whether the *Englisch* family assigns chores or does anything to encourage their children to help others in their community. As I tally the points, it occurs to me that the curiosity I have about how they live is *ne* different from the curiosity that drove them to our doorstep. I suppose we can't set ourselves apart from the world and expect *ne* one to notice or ever be curious.

I note everyone's individual points and decide to award enough group points for them to reach 500 just for the way they worked together today and presented our culture in a way that both respected the rules of our faith and glorified God. I like for my children to have goals and work hard to achieve them, but it should be just as rewarding to them that they have the values I've worked so hard to instill in them.

Mary comes in from finishing her chores outside and offers to start the laundry.

"I'll get it later but you could go over to the *Daadi Haus* for me and change *mammi's* bedding, the boys should be finished by then," I tell her, kissing her cheek.

Once everyone has gathered around the table for lunch, I give them their individual point values on a slip of paper and announce that as a group, they have succeeded in reaching the 500 point goal. They cheer with enthusiasm and Mark and Mary high-five one another. I calm them down so that we can pray over the meal. I thank God for his generous blessing.

The children are still brewing with excitement from the tour as they eat the leftover vegetable soup and peanut butter sandwiches with strawberry rhubarb jam. "Does anyone have any feelings about giving the tour today?" I ask, curious to know their thoughts.

"I think we should do it again!" Mark says.

"Me too!" says Mary.

"Me three!" Samuel agrees.

"Me four," Hannah chimes in with a giggle.

"I'm five…I mean, me five," Josh laughs.

I look at my *mamm* who is fighting a smile and probably the urge to designate herself as number six. I chuckle at the thought.

"What are we having for dinner?" Hannah asks.

"I've decided to make," I pause to build the excitement, "Meatball casserole!"

The kids cheer and laugh excitedly and I can't help but laugh too.

"Now listen, there are just a few things that need to be finished today. The porches need to be swept-,"

"Nope, I just did it," Mark informs me.

"The water troughs need to be scrubbed-,"

"That's what we were doing when the *Englischers* came," Samuel says.

"*Och*, I see," I say, pleased with their responsible behavior.

"Then here's what I want everyone to do this afternoon," I say as they all look at me intently, expecting a random addition to the chore list. "In the next thirty minutes, Hannah and Mary finish your card for our guests, Josh, you help Samuel work on his magic trick, Mark, you can help me put fresh linens on the beds upstairs and then all of you can have fun and play together for a few hours," I smile.

They cheer again as *mamm* and I chuckle knowingly. Hard work is a part of Amish life. Children learn early on to have fun while doing their chores and most of the time they'd just as soon be helping as playing but I think it's good for them to be told every once in a while to just enjoy themselves.

Mammi starts tidying the kitchen as Mark and I head upstairs. We grab a stack of sheets and pillow cases from the linen closet and start in the first bedroom.

"*Mamm* do you think it was wrong to do the tour?" he asks curiously.

"*Ne*, I gave it a lot of thought this morning and I don't thing we did anything that goes against God or the *Ordnung*."

He's quiet for a few moments and I can tell there's something else on his mind. "Is something troubling you?" I ask.

I smooth the first sheet on the bed while he shakes the pillow down into a fresh pillowcase. "I was just trying to figure out in my head how long it takes you to make one quilt."

"*Och*, it depends on what the customer orders and whether I already have a pattern for the design – it's hard to say. I think in the past ten months I've completed four. Why do you ask?"

"It just seems like it takes a really long time and I know you worry about money sometimes. I noticed the cash can was almost empty last week."

"*Ya*, but cooking, cleaning, gardening, quilting and taking care of my family are all I know. It might take a while to make a quilt but I'm fortunate that what I do to earn money doesn't take me away from my family."

"Do you think it will be enough now that *daed's* gone?"

"I pray that it will. You shouldn't be worrying about such things, Mark." I hug him. "Everything will be alright," I assure him. It's suddenly clear to me that this burden he's been carrying over our finances is why he's been so on edge these past few days.

"But I'm the man of the house now. I have to help look after my family," he informs me.

We finish the second bed and move to Samuel's room. "You already do, in many ways. I couldn't do it without you. The most important thing you can do to help with the finances right now is to just pray that God continues to bless us."

"I have been praying *mamm*, I prayed about it again last night and today, when the *Englisch* came, I felt like God was answering my prayers by sending them to us."

We move into the room that Josh and Hannah share. Considering that I was almost in tears the very minute they arrived, I have to agree that the timing seemed unmistakable as anything else but the grace of God.

"Are you surprised that God answered our prayers?" I ask, "He's done it many times."

"I'm not surprised but I think maybe He was also showing us a way we can make extra money using what we already have."

"*Ya*, but we have ne idea when the *Englischers* will come, it's great to have the extra money but we can't rely on it."

"We could put up a sign," he suggests.

"I don't know if-," he interrupts me.

"Remember when *daed* and I went to see his *daed* in the hospital in Marion?"

"*Ya*, I remember."

"Well at the bus station when we were waiting for Uncle Luke to come and get us, I saw a booklet about an Amish farm offering tours."

"What did your *daed* say?"

"He said that he knew the family and that they have nine children. He also said that sometimes it takes more than farming or cabinetmaking to support a large family."

"What else did he say?"

"That was it really; I just kept looking at the booklet until Uncle Luke came." We finish the last bed as I mull it over in my mind. "I know we can do it if we all work together and you would still have time to make quilts. Mary and I could supervise everything and make sure nobody wanders off or anything. Even if we only did it a few times a week, it could help a lot."

"I know you want what's best for us and I'm proud of the way you handled the tour today but I need to think it over and we have guests coming for dinner. You go and enjoy the afternoon with your brothers and sisters and we'll talk about it again after the Sabbath." I rumple his hair and kiss his forehead.

"Just let me know if you need any help," he sighs. "I'll go see what everyone's doing."

I chuckle as he hurries down the stairs and out the door. I worry sometimes that he's too serious for a ten year old but I suppose it's just part of who he is. I say a prayer asking God to guide me to the right decision and to keep the burden of my son's maturity tempered with the lighthearted joy of being a child.

CHAPTER FIVE

Hannah sprinkles the cheese on the casserole just before I put it in the oven to bake. I send her outside to join the rest of the children while I stir the creamed spinach and finish making the iced tea.

"Are you nervous," mamm asks, setting the table for nine.

"He's not courting me *mamm*, I'm just repaying him for his kindness. If he hadn't fixed the buggy for us, it certainly wouldn't have been much of a tour today."

I tell her about my discussion with Mark and the booklet he saw in Marion with his daed.

"That's *gut*, if they're already doing it in Marion, it will go a long way with Bishop Graber. I know he has family there and he's a wise man. I don't think he'll give you any trouble."

"I've prayed about it and I promised Mark that I would think it over," I say, sitting down to relax for a moment. "For now I think I'm just going to enjoy the evening with our guests."

I hear male voices and a happy commotion outside which I'm guessing is the sound of my children greeting John and Caleb.

"Don't forget to take off your cooking apron," *mamm* smiles, filling glasses with ice.

I toss the apron downstairs with the last of the unlaundered sheets and give the spinach a final stir before going to the door.

"*Wilkom*, it's nice to see you," I say to John as the younger children talk to Caleb excitedly.

"*Denki* for having us," he says, looking at me for a moment before stepping inside.

"This is my *mamm* Miriam,"

"*Ya* we've met," he says, nodding humbly in her direction, "This is my nephew Caleb."

We say hello as the children enter the room and I introduce them one by one. They all say hello then I send them to wash their hands.

John hands me large shopping bag, "I brought back your thermos and milk bottle. There's some fish in there too, it's already cleaned and wrapped. Caleb and I had quite a catch this morning."

"*Denki*, it was kind of you to think of us. Let me just put it in the fridge and we can eat." I glance at my *mamm* who is smiling contentedly.

Once we are all gathered at the table, we bow our heads in silent prayer before *mamm* and I start filling plates for everyone.

"It looks and smells delicious, what do you call it?" John asks.

"Meatball casserole!" Josh replies.

"And creamy spinach," Hannah adds, putting a spoonful in her mouth.

"It's really like a meatball bread pudding," Mary explains, "We cut up the crusty bread and put the meatballs on top then we cover it with sauce and cheese before we bake it."

"Did you help make it?" John asks, taking his first bite.

"Hannah and I both did," she smiles, watching expectantly.

"Mmmm, it's delicious," he tells her, "I might have to have a bite of yours later though, just to make sure."

She laughs, Hannah giggles and I can tell by the look on Josh's face that he's not quite sure if he's serious or not. He pulls his plate closer to him.

"How many fish did you catch today?" Mark asks John.

"We caught a baker's dozen," John chuckles.

“What’s a baker’s dozen?” Mark asks.

“It means thirteen!” Josh says excitedly.

“Why do they call it a baker’s dozen?” Samuel asks.

“When the baker needs to make twelve of something, she makes one extra to sample,” *mamm* explains.

“I guess that makes sense,” Samuel says with approval.

“Can Caleb take us for a ride on the tractor after we do our chores? John said it was okay if it’s okay with you *mamm*,” Mary asks.

“I don’t see a problem with it as long as you don’t go out on the main road,” I say decidedly.

John smiles at me and as I look around the table, I feel warm inside. It’s nice to have men in the community like John and Caleb who the kinner can still look up to now that their *daed* is gone. They all need a little fatherly encouragement at times and knowing how John wishes he had a family of his own, I think it will help him too.

“Will you two be at the frolic on Thursday?” *mamm* asks curiously.

“Caleb will be in Hopkinsville with his folks for the next two weeks but I try never to miss a good old fashioned barn raising,” John says enthusiastically.

“What if it rains and we’re at school?” Hannah asks Caleb.

"Eli Lapp will still bring you home and I'll be back in two weeks."

"They take turns Hannah," Mark assures her.

"I wish I could drive the tractor," Samuel says.

"Me too," Mark adds.

"When you're older boys," I remind them.

"But I already know how," Mark pleads.

"I promised we would talk about it when it comes time for fall planting," I say in a warning tone.

We've had the discussion before and his *daed* had given him his first lesson on the tractor before he died, but I'm not as comfortable with the idea yet.

"Can I show John my magic trick?" Samuel asks.

I look at his empty plate. "*Ya* okay."

He shows everyone his amazing, color-changing popsicle-stick trick and repeats it a few times while John and Caleb watch in amazement; the way I did when he first showed it to me.

"Can I tell John about dessert?" Josh asks, before putting the last bite of meatball in his mouth.

"*Ya*, okay," I smile, knowing he wants to get in on the fun.

"You made dessert too?" John asks.

"We made pies!" Josh says excitedly.

"Mmmm, I love pie, what kind?" John says.

"Um, apples and-," he looks over at *mamm* who whispers the answer to him, "Cinnabun."

Mamm and I chuckle. "*Och*, that sounds *gut*," John tells him.

"And since you fixed everything for us and came to dinner with Caleb, you can have six pies," Josh informs him. Apparently he's decided to up the count from five.

John and Caleb chuckle, "Wow six pies, I'm going to be in pie Heaven," John says.

"You have to share two with Caleb," he informs him.

John looks at Caleb, "I don't know if Caleb even likes pie." He waves his hand dismissively.

"He loves pie!" Josh says decidedly.

Everyone laughs. He's never met Caleb before tonight but I'm sure it's unthinkable to him to imagine anyone not loving pie.

"Maybe I should try one first and I can tell you if Caleb might like it," John suggests.

"You should let Caleb try it himself," Hannah giggles, defending Caleb.

I smile. At least she's not being quiet and shy like she

normally is with strangers.

"Can we just eat the pies already?! Talking about it is making me hungry!" Samuel pleads.

I look around the table and see nothing but empty plates and serving dishes. "*Ya*, I'll warm the pies and make some coffee while you children clear the table.

"*Denki* Sarah and everyone for a great dinner," John says.

"Can we give him our surprise too *mamm*?" Mary asks, putting her plate in the sink.

"*Ya*, go ahead," I tell her as Mark and Samuel mill about the kitchen.

"I feel like it's my birthday," John chuckles.

"*Ya*, the *kinner* wanted to do something nice for you for fixing the buggy," she tells him, "They're thoughtful children."

"We sure needed the buggy today, didn't we *mamm*?" Mark says.

I hesitate for a moment. I wasn't exactly planning to discuss it with anyone outside the family just yet but it would be nice to know how someone else in the community feels about it...especially if I decide to do it again. "*Ya*, we did, the *Englisch* loved it," I say, opening the discussion.

"What *Englisch*?" John asks.

Mark and Samuel tell him all about giving the tour, the horse tricks and how the whole *Englisch* family spent five minutes admiring the old crapper.

Everyone laughs as Josh and Hannah join the discussion, telling him about the goats and the baby chicks. Mary returns from downstairs and joins in, telling him about the man giving us sixty dollars for the tour, a dozen eggs and a jar of apple butter.

I pull the pies from the oven and everyone takes notice as the smell of apples and cinnamon fills the room. *Mamm* pours the coffee as Mary encourages Hannah to present their card.

"*Denki* John, it's for you," is all Hannah says before handing him the card. I step over to get a look as he reads it aloud: '*Thank you for being a nice neighbor and helping our family'*. He gives them both a hug and admires the artwork. Mary drew a picture of a buggy on the back with a bunch of happy-face Amish, stick-people in it. I can tell they're Amish because they're all wearing hats or bonnets with stick arms waving out of the windows. The horses are black, the buggy is colored in purple and the front of the card has a border of leaves glued around the edges with a big, orange smiley face in the center.

"I'm going to keep this forever," he assures them. Hannah hugs his neck.

We all begin eating our hand pies and John raves about them to Josh which makes him blush and giggle while mamm tells about the mess they created while making them.

"Dinner was great Mrs. Fisher. Could I get the recipe for my *mamm* if it's not too much trouble?" Caleb asks, "She makes baked spaghetti and puts meatballs in it but I like your recipe better."

"*Denki*, I'll be happy to write it down for her."

As soon as Caleb finishes his pie, the children ask to go do their night time chores, rushing eagerly out the door as soon as I agree. "I'll go help with the horses," Caleb says, excusing himself from the table as *mamm* takes Josh and Hannah to the coop.

Mary busies herself with the dishes and I take a seat at the table to write down the recipe while John has a second pie.

"You have some really great kids," he says with a handsome smile.

"I'm kind of fond of them," I chuckle.

"Dinner was great too." He holds eye contact with me again for just a moment before I look back down at my recipe card. His hazel eyes look green today. "*Denki*, I wanted to make something you had never tried before."

"It's a pretty serious compliment when Caleb starts asking for recipes," he chuckles.

"I'll have to think of something good to bring to the frolic next week."

"*Mamm*, can I leave the clean dishes in the drain to dry and put them away later?" Mary asks.

"*Ya*, go ahead but watch the little ones on the tractor for me," I remind her.

"Okay!" she calls out, halfway through the screen door.

"They seem to like Caleb," I chuckle. I start drying the dishes for Mary as we talk to keep my hands busy.

"*Ya*, he's good with children, He's the oldest of six."

"How old is he?"

"He's eighteen, my brother gave him the choice to go through *Rumspringa* when he was sixteen but other than getting a driver's license, he never really strayed too far from home. He really doesn't enjoy working construction though. He's debating going to college or getting baptized into the church and working the land."

"It's a big decision."

"He's a good kid; he'll be okay in whatever he chooses."

I pour us both another cup of coffee as *mamm* returns with Josh and Hannah. She sends them to wash their hands and I offer to pour her another cup too.

"*Ne*, I think I'm going to go on over to the *Daadi Haus* and write a letter to Sampson and Leah before I turn in. The children can walk me over, you enjoy your visit."

I hug her goodnight. "See you in the morning *mamm*."

"It was nice having you John, I hope to see you again soon," she says as the children return.

"*Denki*, I look forward to it," he smiles.

"Come children, walk *mammi* home before you go for a ride with Caleb." She walks them outside just as I finish drying the dishes.

"It's a lovely night, would you like to go out on the porch and drink our coffee?" he asks.

I laugh, "I was going to ask you the same thing; I've been stuck inside most of the day. Let me just grab a shawl."

***

We sit side-by-side in the two rocking chairs on the front porch, looking at the stars as we talk. I can hear the kinner giggling and singing in the distance as Caleb pulls them in the wagon hitched to the tractor around the property. The crickets are buzzing around us and the earthy smell of the grass after the rain fills the air. It's peaceful and I feel more relaxed than I have all week.

"Have you started a new quilt?"

"*Ya*, I started one for a customer yesterday and worked on it a little more last night."

"How do you get your orders?"

"I made a crib quilt for an *Englisch* friend right before Jacob died. When she came to visit me, to see how I was getting along, she convinced me that I could sell them. She and her husband own a restaurant and store near the army base, so I gave her a quilt I had recently finished to see if she was right. It sold the following week. She takes photographs of each one I complete and puts them in a book for her customers to look through or they can bring her a picture of a design they want and I can make it from that. She stops by to visit and to give me the orders as she gets them."

"Do other women in the community help with the quilting?"

"Usually when we get together for a quilting frolic, it's to make a quilt for someone in the community, not to sell. Aside from the girl's help, my *mamm* helps me stitch when she can but her eyesight is poor and her arthritis bothers her after a while. She helps with the cooking and the children though. It gives me a little more time to devote to my quilting and that's probably the biggest help of all. "What makes you so interested in quilting John Troyer?" she asks with a chuckle.

"Well to tell you the truth I had never given it much thought. My *mamm* only sewed clothes and things when we were growing up. But before my wife died, I was walking around in the hospital one day and they had these big colorful quilts hanging on the walls. Some of the squares had names of loved ones stitched into them and to pass the time, I looked for Amish names. I was there every day for weeks so eventually I just started to notice more and more detail in the quilts, as I would stop and admire them, and it just took my mind off of everything for a while. It was comforting."

"Did your wife quilt?"

"Elizabeth couldn't sew a potholder," I laugh, "But she was a great teacher, the students at the school all loved her. I guess that's why I have a hard time discouraging Caleb from going to college, even though I know what a big decision he's facing. Liz and I had many discussions about education and higher learning; it's hard not to want more opportunities for someone in my family."

"I always kind of hope in the back of my mind, that things will change by the time my children have to face that decision. I worry about Mark especially."

I can see the worry in her delicate face and I find myself wanting to reach over and comfort her. "He seems like a bright boy; I'm sure he'll do what's right for him when the time comes."

"What do you think about the tour we did with the *Englisch* today?" she asks casually.

I think about it for a moment before I speak. "I think that change is forged by the brave and you certainly are that Sarah Fisher," I smile. "I guess I understand why some people are against it but it's inevitable really. We spend our lives setting ourselves apart from worldly things but we still have to live in the world and operate on the same currency. As the Amish community grows, we're going to have to start accepting some new ideas. Some communities out there already thrive on tourism."

"But do you think it's wrong?"

I know there are some old traditionalists in the community who'll criticize her for it if they ever find out but I'm glad she did what she needed to do for her family. "I don't think it's wrong if it's done in a sincere way that honors who we are and I'm sure you handled it with integrity."

"What if I decided to do it on a regular basis?"

"Then I would ask you what I could do to help," Again, I have to resist the urge to comfort her as I see her struggling with the idea. "I don't see it as being any different from selling Amish butter, Amish furniture or Amish quilts. It's part of the way our families have survived for hundreds of years whether we like to admit it or not."

"*Och*, you should have seen the children today," she says looking over at me with a smile, "Mark lead the tour and talked about our customs; Mary looked after them and told them about my quilts; Samuel told Bible stories and showed them horse tricks; Hannah was her gentle, loving self and Josh rallied them to participate. I haven't seen my *kinner* so excited in months. They want to do it again and even Mark pointed out to me today that I can only complete so many quilts a year. I need to be thinking of some options." She smiles as she looks up at the sky but I can tell she's concerned for her family.

"Enough about what's going on with me, how's your farm coming?" she asks curiously.

"We've been working more on the shop than the land for the past two weeks but when Caleb returns from his folks' we're going to start plowing. I've got some wild pigs on the property I need to catch first. We built a corral-trap this week and they've already started rooting around in it. If you need any fresh pork, I'll probably be over-run with it in about two weeks."

She chuckles. "*Denki*, that's very kind of you, but if you keep bringing food, you're going to have to eat here a lot."

"I'll catch it if you'll cook it, that sounds like the perfect partnership to me," I smile.

"Even with five *kinner* clamoring for your attention?"

"*Och*, that's one of the best things about it."

"I'm glad you feel that way because here they come and I think they've taken Caleb captive," she laughs.

Caleb is walking toward the porch with Josh on his shoulders and Hannah on his hip as Mark, Mary and Samuel follow along.

"*Mamm*, can we get a jar to capture some fireflies?" Hannah asks.

"It's too early for fireflies, they don't usually come out until summer," Sarah explains.

“We saw a rabbit out by the garden; we tried to catch him but he hopped away,” Samuel tells us.

“We’re going to catch some pigs soon, we set up a big trap down by the creek at John’s place,” Caleb tells them.

“Oooh, can we come and see?” Mark asks.

“*Ya, ya, ya*,” Samuel agrees, jumping up and down.

“Me too, Josh says.

“Maybe we could all go,” Mary adds.

“If it’s okay with your *mamm*,” I tell them.

“It’s fine with me,” she says.

“I’ll come and get all of you in the wagon when it’s time, it might take a couple of weeks though,” I tell them.

“Speaking of time, children it’s time for baths, don’t forget we have church in the morning, Sarah announces.

“I’ll put Josh and Samuel in the tub, Mary you take care of Hannah,” Mark says.

“Actually, we should probably go too, I need to get this one to Hopkinsville in the morning,” I tell them, “*Denki* children for the dinner, the magic show, and the card and the delicious pie. I’ll see you all next week,” I assure them.

The children all say goodnight to Caleb and me before reluctantly going inside to take their baths. Caleb pulls the tractor around as I walk Sarah to the kitchen door. "*Denki* for a really nice evening," I tell her.

"It's the least I could do," she says, putting the extra pies and the hand-written meatball casserole recipe in a bag for us to take home. "Do you need any eggs or milk to take with you?" she asks.

"I might next week, I'll let you know." I linger for a moment to gaze into those pretty blue eyes as I take the bag from her hand. She smiles timidly, "Good night Sarah," I say.

"Good night," she replies.

***

After John and Caleb leave and the children are bathed I tuck them into bed and soak in a nice hot bath myself. As I close my eyes and let the soapy lavender water sooth my tired body and my troubled mind, I think of how much fun everyone had today, including me.

It was nice to have a male figure to talk to again, just as I know it was for my *kinner*. The day that Jacob died, he was busy working on the tractor when I went inside the house and lying dead on the floor of the barn when I took him his lunch ten minutes later. There was *ne* warning, *ne* illness or pain that I was aware of in the days before it happened, he was just gone. I ran to the phone shack and called for help but deep down I knew by the look on their faces when they loaded him in the ambulance that he was never coming back.

The doctors said that that he had a heart condition that he had probably been born with and that it just stopped suddenly.

I think of John and the way he had to watch his wife suffer as she slowly died right before his eyes. I can't help but wonder how much harder that would have been to cope with but at the same time, I regret not being able to say goodbye or to prepare my children in some small way.

I remember the first day that the children went back to school. Mark got into a fight with Deacon Byler's grandson at recess because he said that Jacob must have been a really bad man for God to strike him down like that. I was so angry when he told me that if I had been there, I probably would have been tempted to slap the child myself, but I realize now that he's just a product of the judgment he hears and sees in his own home. Still, it wasn't easy to explain to my children once the concept had caused them to question it. The truth is that I was questioning it too.

I think about how sick I was of people referring to Jacob's death as part of God's mysterious plan. Whether it was true or not, I didn't find any comfort in it at the time and neither did they. Now that some time has passed and some measure of faith and happiness has returned to my home, I wonder.

I think about the prayers God has answered for me lately, and the kindness of friends and even strangers like John, that He seems to send our way at just the right time.

If God's infinite plan could be so unfathomable that it could include the unexpected death of my husband one sunny afternoon in May, then maybe it could also include the curiosity of *Englischers* to help support the wife and five children he left behind. I remember a passage in **James 1:17** that says: *'Every good gift and every perfect gift is from above, and cometh down from the Father of lights, with whom is no variableness, neither shadow of turning.*

I want to find out what God has in store for me and my family with the tour business idea. I feel a sense of peace as I step out of the bath and dry myself off. It lingers in my heart as I put on my nightgown, brush my hair and climb into bed. For the first time in a very long time, I fall asleep peacefully as soon as my head hits the pillow.

CHAPTER SIX

Sunday, March 29

I awake Sunday morning, put on my robe and join the whole family already gathered in the kitchen. Josh and Hannah run up to me and hug my legs as soon as they hear me come in.

"Why didn't anyone wake me?"

"We thought you must need the rest. You're usually the first one awake," *mamm* says, pouring me a cup of coffee.

"*Denki, mamm*," I say kissing her cheek.

"We wanted to let you sleep so we could surprise you by making breakfast for you," Mary explains.

"I hug her, "I think God has blessed me with the best *mamm* and *kinner* in the world." I lean over and kiss both Mark and then Samuel on the forehead. "What are you boys working on this morning?" I ask, glancing at the notebook lying on the table in front of them.

"I'm making a list of all the tricks I know how to do and all of the tricks that Joker can do," Samuel says cheerfully.

"I'm telling Mark about games I like to play with my friends," Josh adds.

"I'm coloring a picture of my favorite animals," Hannah says.

"And what about you Miss Mary? What are you doing?"

"I was just thinking of some of the things we like to make together like hand pies, banana bread, muffins and strawberry rhubarb jam," she smiles innocently.

"How about you *mamm*?" I chuckle.

"Me? *Och*, I'm just making breakfast. How do you want your eggs this morning *liebchen*?" she asks with a guilty smile.

"Whatever you're making for yourself is fine but you might want to check your pancake," I tell her, looking at the stove, "I think it's burning." Let's hope that's not a sign from God.

I raise my eyebrows at Mark, knowing where all of this is going, "And how about you Mark Fisher? What are you doing this morning?"

"I'm just thinking of interesting things you could do or see on a farm," he smiles, "Like a pumpkin patch or a tire swing or maybe a wagon for hay rides or pony rides."

"Or a phone shack?" I tease, knowingly. Everyone looks at

each other and laughs.

"I just thought maybe if we showed you that we could come up with ideas that wouldn't be too much trouble it might help you decide," Mark explains.

"What about chores? The animals still have to eat on the Sabbath you know."

"We finished them already," Mary smiles, "I just have to do the dishes after breakfast and we all have to get dressed for church."

Sunday chores are always cut back to just the morning and evening basics so that the family can enjoy a day of rest together. The older boys tend to the goats and horses. Mary does the dishes and the milking while *mamm* and the younger children feed the chickens and gather the eggs.

"Also, we were thinking that for the points we earned on the chore chart, maybe we could get some supplies for the business instead…that is, if you decide to do it," he says.

"Like a bunny cage!" Hannah giggles.

"People like to pet bunnies because they're really cuddly and soft," Josh informs me.

"Okay children, that'll be enough for now, let's eat our breakfast and give your *mamm* some time to think about it," *mamm* says, sitting the large plate of pancakes on the table.

As the children put away their things, grab their plates and sit at the table, I think about my *daed* growing up. Any time he was wrestling with a big decision, he would always quote a passage from 2 Corinthians 13:1 which says that *'In the mouth of two or three witnesses shall every word be established'*.

It always seemed to help him in times of uncertainty and I look for those confirmations in my own life even now. If the tour is the starting point, I certainly count the support of my entire family as one confirmation and the support of John is significant too, but I'd like to have one more witness before making an official decision or announcing it to anyone.

As we bow our heads in silent prayer. I thank God for my *mamm*, my children and the people He has sent to help and encourage us, and ask Him to give me a final sign today that the decision I'm about to make is truly His will for us.

After breakfast, *mamm*, Mary and I do the dishes together before we all get dressed and leave for church. Services begin at 9:00 a.m. and last for almost three hours. It's filled with singing, praying, listening to a passage from the Bible and a prayer from the *Christenplict*, followed by sermons from Bishop Graber and Deacon Byler about living a Godly life. The passage that Bishop Graber reads today is the *Parable of Talents* in Matthew 25:14-30.

I know that the term *'talents'* refers to an ancient form of currency but I believe that it also refers literally to the gifts and abilities that make us who we are. I feel like God is saying to me: *'Use the talents I've given you to glorify Me instead of hiding them away and I will bless you.'* His message leaves me feeling encouraged and full of hope.

After a silent prayer, the first official sermon of the day is delivered by Minister Paul Oyer. He's a thin, wiry man in his early sixties who has worked as a blacksmith for as long as I can remember. He's a kind man and many of the people in the community look up to him, often coming to him for advice and support.

His message is on Matthew 22:36-38 in which Jesus tells a lawyer that the greatest commandment is to love God with all of his heart, all of his soul and all of his mind. The sermon is only about twenty minutes long but he delivers it passionately to the point of tears as he too, urges the congregation to seek to love and honor God in all we do.

The final sermon of the day is given by Deacon Byler. He's a short, round man with a salt-and-pepper beard, ruddy cheeks, wire-rimmed glasses and the gruff, stubborn demeanor of a Billy goat. He's in his early sixties and clings to the traditions of his former Old Order Amish community in spite of living in Hope Landing for the past twenty years.

Deacon Byler is the first person I expect to object to my decision and I'm a bit afraid of his disapproval because his opinion carries a lot of weight in our community. If I'm honest with myself, I don't feel I've ever met with his approval *ne* matter what I've done or haven't done.

The first summer he lived in Hope Landing, he had a barn

raising. I was playing softball with some other children after the noon meal and accidentally hit a foul ball that broke a bedroom window. My parents offered to pay for the window, he refused. I even offered to work it off by doing chores but he still refused and called me an insolent girl.

Even back then, I figured it would eventually pass but in spite of his outward politeness, I can still sense his unspoken disdain for me every time I interact with him. It didn't help that the comment his grandson made to Mark about Jacob's death, only served as confirmation in my mind that I hadn't been imagining it all of these years. I guess I'm still avoiding him like a twelve year old whenever I can, always reminding myself that he's an elder in the community and a Deacon in the church, which deserves to be respected in spite of feeling that he has been unfair with me.

He reads from the *Martyr's Mirror* and talks about living by faith, separating ourselves from the world and being willing to suffer persecution as the martyrs did for religious freedom all those years ago. He reads from the *Sermon on the Mount* found in the fifth chapter of Matthew but instead of stopping at verse 12 as he always does when preaching about persecution; he continues on through verse 16, which reads:

13 Ye are the salt of the earth: but if the salt have lost his savour, wherewith shall it be salted? It is thenceforth good for nothing, but to be cast out, and to be trodden under foot of men.

14 Ye are the light of the world. A city that is set on a hill cannot be hid.

[15] Neither do men light a candle, and put it under a bushel, but on a candlestick; and it giveth light unto all that are in the house.

[16] Let your light so shine before men, that they may see your good works, and glorify your Father which is in heaven.

I bow my head and close my eyes as *mamm* puts her hand on mine. It's ironic that Deacon Byler would be the voice to confirm my decision but in my heart it only proves to me that God is showing me His will via the least likely person to be swayed out of any kind of personal fondness or compassion for me.

I mark the passage in my Bible to read again later. During silent prayer, I pray for Deacon Byler, forgiving him and asking God to forgive me for any part that I've had in perpetuating any ill will between us.

Sometimes, when church services are over, we also have to attend a Members' Meeting where issues in the church district are addressed. But today, we go right from services to enjoying a light lunch, as we socialize with friends both new and old.

CHAPTER SEVEN

As the children join the other youth to play and sing songs together, *mamm* joins the ladies in the kitchen, while I look for my friend Ruth. I spot her with her husband Dan talking to Bishop Graber and wait casually outside the kitchen for her.

To look at the two of us, one would never imagine that we had anything more in common than being close in age and the Amish clothing we both wear; but I love her like my very own sister. Ruth Sutter is tall and pleasantly plump with bright auburn hair, fair skin, a light dusting of cinnamon colored freckles across her nose and cheerful eyes that remind me of green jasper.

The corners of her mouth turn down slightly so when she's concentrating on something, she looks angry without meaning to. The irony of this is that Ruth is generally a very pleasant, happy person who's always seeking the positive in whatever life throws her way. She is my dearest friend and we've been there for one another through thick and thin for twenty years.

We met the summer after I turned twelve and spent our last year in school together. She was tall for her age even then and in spite of being the runt of the girls my age, I struck up a conversation with her – and we've never looked back.

Her parents bought the bakery in town when they moved to Hope Landing. They just officially retired to an even more progressive Amish community in Florida, though they're both still in their late fifties. Ruth went with them to help them get settled while Dan stayed behind to run the bakery. So I haven't seen her in over a month.

She finishes her conversation with Bishop Graber and comes over to greet me with a hug. "It's so good to see you, how have you been?" she asks.

"I'm doing good, I've missed you though, I can't wait until we go to my house," I tell her.

"Me too, we brought plenty of food for dinner, I have a little gift for everyone and so much to tell you about Florida," she smiles excitedly.

"I have some news for you too," I tell her.

"I want to say hello to Ms. Helmut, the Eichers and the Zooks but I could ask Dan to bring your *mamm* and the *kinner* home when he's done so you and I can take your buggy and sneak off to the house."

"Okay, I'll come with you, I need to let *mamm* know anyway." I don't want to be rude by leaving but at the same time, I long to have some girl time with Ruth to just relax and catch up on everything – without having to worry about who's listening. It's her week to visit me anyway and as a widow, one afternoon with my closest friend was more consoling and uplifting than any other fellowship could provide.

We make our way into the kitchen and greet Mrs. Eicher whose family hosted this Sunday's church service and luncheon. She insists on sending some sandwiches home with me, so I thank her and make my way through the crowd saying hello to Ms. Helmut, Mrs. Oyer and Mrs. Zook as I come across them. Next I locate my *mamm* and tell her the plan.

"*Ya*, go spend some time with Ruth, I'll look after the *kinner* and find Dan when we're done," she assures me.

I hitch the buggy outside as Ruth arranges everything with Dan before heading to the house. She climbs into the buggy with a giggle.

"What did he say?"

"He said not to be surprised if he gives *mamm* and Mary his half of the bakery on the way home," she laughs.

"He probably just misses you," I chuckle.

"I think in the past two weeks without having me at home or at the bakery, he's realized just how much I really take care of that he never has to worry about. I'm glad I decided to go though, it's good to walk a mile in each other's shoes sometimes."

"How do your *mamm* and *daed* like Florida so far?"

"Aside from the sunburns they love it," she chuckles "We all went out to the beach the second afternoon we were there and even in March we all ended up sunburned before dinner time. We spent the whole evening unpacking boxes in pain. "Dan says it was God's little way of reminding me of my modesty but it was like 90 degrees outside and it's like a steam bath down there."

"What did you wear on the beach?" I ask, disbelieving.

"*Och ya*, let me first say, the Amish down there are allowed to wear swimsuits on the beach," she laughs, "But I just wore a tank top and shorts."

"Like real bathing suits with *ne* shorts or t-shirts over them…in public?"

"They sure do. I mean granted, a lot of Amish just go there on vacation to see the ocean so I did see some groups of Amish men and women fully dressed on the beach but the Amish from the community either wear shorts and t-shirts out of personal preference or real swimsuits."

"I guess they really are the *'Beachy'* Amish," I chuckle. Beachy is actually an Amish family surname but it seems fitting that they would be predominant in Florida. I pull into the barn and we unhitch the buggy before going inside.

"The Amish there have cell phones too, at least some of them do."

"I don't even want to imagine needing a phone that regularly," I chuckle. "I see *Englisch* children in town with cell phones, some of them ne older than Mark and Mary. Can you imagine five *kinner* calling me all day? I'd never get anything done!"

"*Och*, I know I see it at the bakery all the time. I do know one thing they do in Florida you'd love though," she says with a smile.

"What's that?"

"Golf carts," she giggles, "They ride them everywhere just zipping around in *ne* time."

"Did you ride in one?"

"*Och, ya*, they're pretty smooth and comfortable too."

"You're right; I would love to drive one."

"I also rode a pink bicycle that had over 20 giant plastic pink flamingos on it," she laughs.

"*Verruckt*!" I laugh. "But then you've always had a fondness for quirky things." I pour us both a glass of iced tea while she unwraps the peanut butter and marshmallow crème sandwiches Mrs. Eicher gave us. We go out on the porch to enjoy the beautiful spring weather as we eat and chat.

"So tell me your news, it must be good," she says expectantly.

"How do you know it's good news?" I chuckle.

"Sarah," she scolds, "I've known you for twenty years, even in your mourning clothes I know you well enough to recognize that little twinkle glowing in your eyes, now don't keep me waiting, I've been worried about you."

I tell her about falling off my bike and meeting John Troyer,"

"Wait he bought the old Schwartz farm?"

"*Ya* right after Christmas. He's going to farm some of the land but he's opening a small engine repair shop in the bigger barn closest to the road."

"Okay, go on," she smiles.

I tell her about him fixing the faucet, the bike and the wheel, and about staring at the pantry in tears, worrying about being asked to sell the farm.

"I told if you ever need anything, Dan and I will do whatever we can to help and nobody would ever have to know," she assures me.

"You're my dearest friend Ruth and I know you mean that, but two widows and five children can't survive off of the kindness of others indefinitely, I need income, I need my own plan."

"*Ya* I understand," she says rubbing my shoulder to comfort me.

So I go on to tell her about the *Englisch* showing up at the very moment I was praying in the pantry and about giving the tour in the buggy that had just been repaired and how the children all took part in their own special way according to their talents and how well it all turned out.

"Your kids are pretty incredible, I bet they loved it," she smiles.

"*Och ya*, they told me at dinner they wanted to do it again but I just brushed it off at first. Then Mark and I talked about it and I found out that he too had been praying about our finances the morning before the tour. I haven't even told him about my fears or praying in the pantry but he also felt like the visit from the *Englisch* had been a sign from God."

"He's quite the little man now isn't he?"

"I worry that he's too mature at times but he made a good point; I can only complete a handful of quilt orders per year, we need to have another source of income."

"So you're going to do tours of the farm?" she asks enthusiastically.

"Well, I prayed about it, I talked to *mamm* about it, of course the kids are already trying to come up with ideas and things we can do like baking banana bread or getting some bunnies for children to pet but I was still wrestling with the decision until this morning in church."

"What did Miriam say?"

"She was perfectly fine with the idea, even encouraging…she and John basically said the same thing; that people are naturally curious about our culture and that giving the tours would be *ne* more exploitive than selling Amish jams or quilts."

"Wait, so you talked about this with John too?" she asks curiously.

"*Ya*, he wouldn't let me pay him anything for the repairs, so I invited him to dinner on Saturday and Mark was sort of hinting around about the tour idea – so I decided it would be nice to get an outside opinion."

"How did the *kinner* react to him being here?"

"They couldn't get enough of his attention," I chuckle. "He brought his nephew Caleb who picks them up from school sometimes when the weather's bad."

"Even Hannah?" she asked curiously.

"*Och ya*, it surprised me too but she was hugging him and talking to him and she's really fond of Caleb." I know that it's surprising to her because after Jacob died, even Dan, who has known Hannah all her life couldn't hold her or even talk to her much without her bursting into tears. She wouldn't even talk to the Bishop. She told me once when I asked her what was wrong that she missed her *daed*.

"Wow, so what does Miriam think about this John Troyer?" she asks curiously.

"What does she think or what has she said?" I ask for clarification.

"Both," she chuckles.

"She says he's a good man and seems to like him. When I was trying to decide what to make for dinner Saturday night, she suggested 'courtship meatloaf,' so I'm not completely sure her intentions for us are exactly platonic, she takes that meatloaf seriously. When Deacon King wanted to court her after *daed* died, he came to dinner one night with his sister. I remember asking my mom what she was making and she said *'anything but 'courtship meatloaf'*!"

We both laugh. Deacon King was a decent man but he was very meticulous and always correcting every little thing. He eventually moved to Ohio.

"I'm sure she just wants to see you happy again. What do you think?"

"It's getting easier to find some happiness with each passing day and I'm open to marrying again someday but let's be honest, I don't know too many men who are willing to raise another man's five children."

"*Ne* silly, what do you think of John?"

"*Och*, he's a good man and I really think God put him in my path that day in the rain. Here I was worrying about how long our provisions were going to last and he brings a dozen fish to a thank you dinner, already cleaned and wrapped."

She raises her eyebrows knowing how impressive this is since we always did the cleaning and wrapping when our husbands would go fishing together.

"He offered to help with the tours too. Except for the ham I saved for Easter Sunday, we had just eaten the last of the pork that Mr. Rupp had slaughtered for us at breakfast. Well of course I hadn't mentioned that to John but later that night he tells me that he's trapping some wild pigs on his property and offers to bring us some fresh pork once they're caught in a couple of weeks."

"Sounds like he likes you too," she smiles.

"He's definitely been a blessing. I think there's a kinship there because we both understand having to pick up the pieces after losing a spouse and trying to figure out how to manage everything on our own. I just hope in some way I can help him as much as he helps me."

"Well I think the whole tour thing is a great idea and I'd like to help too, I'd be happy to bake some things for you to sell." Her eyes widened with excitement, "You know, I still have that gas oven from our old house that I offered you once before; you can bake a lot more in it at one time than your wood stove and we have an older bakery case that my parents kept after the remodel too. They're both just sitting in the back room taking up space. We're never going to need them now that my parents are in Florida; neither Dan nor I want the hassle of two shops."

Her parents had remodeled the store and debated opening a

second location when Dan joined the family business; but Ruth was pregnant at the time and the bakery was doing so well that everyone decided not to take on the added responsibility. Now, six years later, her parents are retired and the business is just enough for them to manage while still being able to enjoy life.

"I think it would be a great idea to have the case and I know the stove makes more sense if we're going to bake my quick breads but you have enough work to do just keeping the bakery running, I couldn't ask you to bake for us too."

"*Och*, don't worry. It really doesn't take more than a few minutes longer to make sixty whoopie pies when you're already making fifty. Now that my parents are gone, I can implement some changes I've wanted to make for a long time to cut down on costs so it won't be a financial burden either. If your business takes off and it gets to be too cumbersome, Mary can come to the bakery and help out. It won't be long until she's out of school for summer…or for good."

"She'd certainly love that," I chuckle.

Mary loves to bake and she's been itching to go work with Ruth in the "real bakery" since she was Hannah's age. Even when she spends a couple of hours helping out, she raves about the fun she had for days. "I can't believe I'm actually going to do this. How do you think this will be received in the community?" I ask her.

"You know, I think God has been preparing my heart for this because I've been thinking a lot about change and the economy and even tourism this past two weeks. If you had told me all of this before I went to Florida, I would have been more concerned than excited," she eats the last bite of her sandwich before finishing.

"We grew up in this community together and I know some of the more conservative people aren't going to approve of this because they'll think it will corrupt our community. But every morning when we open the bakery, I pull the items that didn't sell the day before to make way for fresh inventory and there is almost always someone from our community waiting to collect the day old breads and cakes just so their families can survive. I'm more than happy to give it to them, don't get me wrong but I see first hand how some families are struggling to live, even with two parents."

She fights back the tears and I know it's because she's a deeply caring person who hates to see anyone struggle.

"Anyway, my point is that some things in our Amish culture just have to change and I'd rather cope with everything that tourism brings than to cope with watching people I love go hungry or lose their homes."

I get her a tissue.

"In Florida, tourism is a way of life and the Amish people seem to be handling it pretty well…in spite of the swimsuits and cell phones," she chuckles. "I think we all tend to fear the unknown but my trip really opened my eyes and I'll stand behind you one hundred percent."

I fight back the tears too but I've decided that I'm done crying. "I can't tell you how much it means to me to know that I have your blessing. I don't know if this will solve everything, but with Jacob gone, I've worried what will become of my sons. We always imagined that he would teach them all the skills and hobbies he knew so they'd have some options growing up. Now, I'd be grateful to just give them a home with love, faith in God, enough food to eat and clothes to wear."

"From the way everything has happened with this tour idea, I'm sure that God's hand is in it and I know He has a plan for your whole family, not just the *kinner*. Maybe it's even bigger than you can accept right now so He's only revealing it to you bit by bit.

"Remember when you cried for a whole afternoon because we burnt those cookies we made for your *mamm* and you swore you never, ever wanted to be a 'dumb old baker'?" I smile reminiscently.

"Remember? I still have the cookie sheet with a dented corner where I threw it on the porch. My *mamm* passed it down to me when Dan and I got married," she giggles.

"How do you think Dan will feel about all of this?" I ask curiously.

"I think he'll like it, not to mention that he'll probably be ticking off the days until Mary gets out of school. He always says that having her around makes him twice as productive because she watches Ben *and* helps with the baking. I told him that makes *her* twice as productive, not him," she laughs.

"Well I'll make sure to give you credit for any of the items you bake so that maybe it'll drive some repeat customers to the bakery."

"That's a great idea. *Och*, that reminds me, you know the display area to the left of the door when you walk in where the greeting cards and handmade dolls were?"

"*Ya*, did you get rid of them?"

"We decided not to keep the greeting card display because it seemed like most people would rather pick up a card at the discount store and the dolls weren't selling either, so the lady who made them took them all back last week so she could try selling them at the flea market. That means we have that whole little corner waiting to be filled. Dan suggested yesterday that we put one of your quilts on the wall and then fill the display case with some of Miriam's jams, preserves or whatever you want. People do look at that stuff while they're waiting in line."

"That's sweet, *denki*. I'm sure she'll love the idea. We'll put our heads together and see what we can come up with."

"It was all Dan's idea, I was going to put an Amish cupboard there and fill it with nostalgic tins or something but I'd rather the space be used to help you if you want it."

"It all seems to be falling into place doesn't it?"

"All in God's perfect timing, she smiles.

We visit a little longer on the porch before going inside to look over the design for the quilt I'm working on. She helps me solve a problem with the layout that I had been struggling with and I show her the fabric I plan to use.

"I can't wait to see it all come together. It's going to be really pretty."

"I love quilting but I'm pretty excited about the tour business too," I smile, "My head is spinning with ideas but I'm trying to set a good example for the *kinner* and not spend the Sabbath focusing on work related things. They were all up before me this morning making lists as it is."

She giggles, "What were they making lists of?"

"*Och*, things we can bake or sell, interesting things to tell about Amish culture, Samuel even plans to get the horses to do tricks for people, Josh was coming up with games to play and Hannah was drawing pictures of the bunnies she wants to get so people can pet them."

"Those are some pretty good ideas you have to admit," she chuckles.

"I know, I just don't want them to get so wrapped up in organizing and planning that they forget to just be kids sometimes. They even told me that they want to allocate their chore chart award towards something for the business."

"*Ya*, well take a look at that chore chart in your pantry and tell me who in the world they got the organizing and planning gene from," she laughs.

"*Ya*, maybe," I chuckle knowingly. "I guess I like to plan and organize."

"You guess?" she giggles, "Do you remember when my *mamm* asked us to sort the recipe file to get us out of her hair one Saturday afternoon?"

I laugh, "*Ya*, I remember."

"Four days! It took us a whole month of Saturdays to sort and label it all and to hand copy all those jumbled up index cards onto paper the way you wanted to. My fingers cramped for like two weeks afterward!"

"I know but you have to admit, you're still using the binder we put together seventeen years later and that box of index cards was destined for disaster."

Ruth starts laughing which makes me laugh and it goes on until we're both so tickled that tears are streaming down our cheeks. Right in the middle of it all, Dan, my *mamm* and all six children show up. By this time we're both laughing so hard we can't control ourselves, let alone speak. The *kinner* start laughing too. This goes on for what seems like a really long time and just as Ruth starts to catch her breath, Dan asks with a serious look, "Have you two been drinking?"

We burst into simultaneous laughter again until she drags me outside so we can catch our breath. My sides hurt and I can't even look at her without giggling.

"Ooooooh, I haven't laughed that hard in a really long time," she says fighting back the giggles. "It's so good to laugh with you again."

"I agree, we have to do this more often; now don't look at me or it'll just start all over again," I warn.

We take a few seconds to sober ourselves up and head back into the house where *mamm* already has the stove going and the kettle on for coffee. Dan and the children entertain one another in the living room and Ruth and I unpack the cooler full of food they brought for dinner.

It contains of a large casserole dish of baked macaroni and cheese, a casserole dish of green beans with pieces of ham and new potatoes, three grocery store fried chickens, two homemade strawberry pies and a big box of doughnut holes for tomorrow's breakfast. "It looks delicious."

"I had too much unpacking and catching up to do after my trip that I didn't have time to fry the chickens myself but these are pretty tasty."

"*Och*, trust me it's fine and more than enough. I could have helped you know."

"*Ya*, but the whole purpose of this visitation thing is to relieve you of some of the pressures of looking after the family alone and I just wanted us to enjoy the fellowship."

Dan comes into the kitchen and sits at the table while Ruth pours him some coffee. *Mamm* takes the younger children to the chicken coop while I send the older children out to do their chores. We tell him about the tour business as Ruth heats up dinner and I set the table.

He likes the idea too, so when everyone's chores are done and hands are washed, I gather them around the table to officially announce my decision. I know they're all anxious to know and I want Ruth and Dan to be there when I do. I figure this will also give the *kinner* time to quell their excitement before bed so they can get a good night's rest before the real work begins.

"Children, I've prayed about it, I've sought the counsel of *mamm*, John, Aunt Ruthie and Uncle Dan and I've decided," I pause and watch their eyes all get wide with anticipation as they look around the table at one another, "That we're going into the tour business!"

Everyone at the table claps as the children cheer and squeal with excitement. I manage to calm them down as we bow our heads in prayer and I take the quiet moment to thank God for the support of my friends and family.

We all enjoy the delicious food and good fellowship as the children share their ideas and Ruth tells them about her visit to Florida. I don't know if they've ever even seen a golf cart but I'd love to have one someday.

When dinner's over, we open the gifts she's brought which include Florida-themed puzzles and a big book about Florida for the children; a seashell stationary set and a tin of my *mamm's* favorite fudge handmade for her by Ruth's *mamm*; a journal set for me with a silver and mother-of-pearl writing pen and a Florida recipe collection cookbook. I can't wait to use them.

I hug them both as *mamm* and the children crowd around to thank them too. *Mamm*, Ruth and I tidy up the kitchen as Dan reads to the *kinner* from the Florida book, letting them all take turns to marvel at the pictures while he reads aloud about alligators.

At 8:00 p.m., the visit comes to an end. The children do their nightly baths and prayers and I tuck them all into bed before turning in for the night.

***

After church services in Hopkinsville, I spend time visiting family and old friends in the community but my thoughts keep drifting to Sarah and her *kinner*. As I sit at the long picnic table surrounded by people, I find myself wondering if she's doing the same. I think about the *kinner* singing and playing with friends while Sarah socializes with the women, maybe talking about quilting or the flowers in bloom. I think about her small, delicate hands that labor for her family and the tidy vegetable garden I saw out behind the barn. I feel a longing to see her again.

I get up from the table and join my eldest brother to redirect my thoughts as he tells Deacon Wyse about taking my 14 year old nephew Micah turkey hunting at daybreak on Saturday.

"I didn't think turkey season opened for two more weeks," I comment curiously.

"For adults *ya*, but they have a youth-only opening for two days. Boys under 16 can bag one turkey during that time. It's a good time for them to learn. Why don't you come with us so Joseph can come too? You can keep the turkey and he won't have to be left out, it'll be like old times when we used to hunt together as boys."

My brother Aaron and his wife Lydia have four sons and two daughters. Of the boys in the family, Caleb is the oldest, Micah is about to turn 15, Joseph is 13 and Saul is nine.

"I'm going to be at your house for Good Friday anyway, so I could probably spare a few hours Saturday morning before I head back to Hope Landing."

"Great, we'll tell the boys tonight."

Growing up, my family had two major turkey dinner celebrations each year; one at Thanksgiving and one at Easter, mainly because both holidays coincide with turkey season. Of course there were other times when we would have meals that included turkey but canned turkey is never quite as festive or exciting as seeing a plump, fresh turkey, roasted to a golden brown and laid out on the table with a feast of colorful side dishes.

Those were certainly fond memories and I can't think of a better way to share the occasion with Sarah and the *kinner* than to bring them a fresh turkey on Easter weekend, I think to myself.

As one of the ladies goes around refilling glasses of iced tea, Deacon Wyse puts his hand on my shoulder "How's the transition to Hope Landing going John?" My brother wanders off to talk to someone else.

"It's coming along, I've met some people in the community and I'm getting the shop set up. Caleb and I will be plowing in a couple of weeks so I imagine that I'll be going back and forth a little less in the months to come."

"I know it must be difficult with one foot in both communities at the same time. Everyone will certainly miss having you here but it's important for you to settle down and establish yourself in your new home. I have to be honest John, I've been worried about you these past few years. I hope you'll forgive me for being forward but I feel like the Lord has put it in my heart to talk to you."

I know that he's referring to the almost six years since Elizabeth died and I suppose it's obvious that I haven't handled it all that well.

"I appreciate your concern; it's been a rough few years but I think starting over in a new community is doing me a lot of good. It's tiresome but as things start coming together, I'm enjoying my work again and even starting to see things a little differently."

"You're a hard worker John, a Godly man and a respected member of this community. You've always been willing to lend a helping hand to others with little concern for how you will be paid – or even if you will be paid, and I think the good Lord has prospered you because of your generous heart, but God says in Genesis 2:18 that *'It is not good that the man should be alone.'* I worry that you give so much but have *ne* help-mate to comfort you and encourage you. Even my wife often mentions you in prayer with *ne* prompting from me."

We walk along under the shade trees as he continues.

"I want to encourage you in this new beginning of your life to open your heart again and let God send someone to share the burden with you. In the past couple of months, as I've watched you go back and forth from here to there, I feel like the Lord keeps urging me to share Romans 8:18 with you which says: *'For I reckon that the sufferings of this present time [are] not worthy [to be compared] with the glory which shall be revealed in us.'* I believe that God is telling you that whatever your sufferings are, they are nothing compared to the joy that He still has in store for you.

He stops and rests his hand on my shoulder again. "I don't think this is limited to the glory that God has for you in Heaven. I think He wants you to know that it waits for you even now."

I can see the heartfelt concern in his eyes. He's a mild-mannered man in his early sixties who I've been acquainted with most of my life and he's never pulled me aside like this before. He let's go of my shoulder and continues walking.

"*Denki* Deacon Wyse, for your encouragement, what you've said is truly a comfort to me and I know you don't come to me with this frivolously."

"I suppose I hesitated to talk to you sooner because I was afraid of making you feel judged or pressured but I wanted to be obedient to the Lord and to let you know that I'm here for you if you ever need me."

My younger brother Isaac jogs over to where we are, "The game's about to start if you want in."

There's often an adult softball game in our community after the Sunday luncheon. "Go ahead, enjoy your day, that's all I wanted to say" Deacon Wyse smiles kindly.

"Thanks again, I promise to keep you posted," I smile, shaking his hand.

CHAPTER EIGHT

Just before midnight I awake from a dreamy half-sleep with ideas and images of the farm tour business reeling through my mind. I get out of bed and make my way to the kitchen. The house is dark and quiet with the children tucked safely in their beds. Though I went to bed myself hours ago, I don't feel as if I've rested at all, yet I'm too invigorated to go back to sleep.

I pour myself a glass of milk hoping that will help and sit down at the desk in the living room with my new journal and pen. I turn on the small reading lamp and attempt to sort the jumble of thoughts rolling around in my mind, so I can put them onto the page for safekeeping.

There's a picture of the farm in my head but I can't describe it with the written word. I start doodling crosses on my page but decide that I don't want to scribble up my nice new journal.

I open the drawer to grab one of the children's spiral notebooks to doodle on instead. As I pull the notebook from the desk, a loose page falls out. I lean over to pick it up and realize that it's almost exactly what I'm seeing in my mind, only in reverse. It's the backside of a baby animals coloring page that Hannah had torn from her activity book this morning.

On the coloring side are her fluffy, baby bunnies shaded in gray with pink ears and noses but on the backside, is a picture of a maze in the shape of a cross.

"*Ya*, a corn maze, I say to myself…a maze that leads to the cross. I can see it now as if I were flying over the fields like a bird. It's a cross with mazes in each surrounding quadrant, leading to the center pathway.

I think of the Bible passage in John 14:4-6 where Jesus says:

4 And whither I go ye know, and the way ye know.

5 Thomas saith unto him, Lord, we know not whither thou goest; and how can we know the way?

6 Jesus saith unto him, I am the way, the truth, and the life: no man cometh unto the Father, but by me.

I know in my heart that this is from God.

I suppose that laying out a corn maze in a field couldn't be much different from laying out a design for a quilt but I still might need some help to make it work. I try to think of experienced farmers in the community who might be able to advise me but the only person I can really imagine confiding in about my plan at the moment is John.

Afraid to lose my train of thought, I decide to start writing it all down in my journal dividing the pages into three columns with ideas on the left, the person best suited for that part of the tour in the center and notes on the right, including who to ask for help or tasks that need to be done to make it happen.

Once I've gotten the majority of my thoughts on paper, I start to feel sleepy. At 2:00a.m., I tuck the picture of the maze into my journal and go back to bed for a few hours of rest.

***

Sunday night I wake around 12:00 a.m. out of a sound sleep. I was dreaming about plowing the corn fields but as I neared the fence line, I realized that I wasn't on my own property. It wasn't my farm in Hopkinsville either, because the fence that bordered the property in my dream was still a natural wood color and both of my fences have been painted white.

I go into the kitchen and pour myself a glass of milk and grab a slice of cornbread to help me get back to sleep. Instinctively, I know that I was dreaming of plowing the field on Sarah Fisher's property. I suppose it doesn't surprise me much because I've been thinking about her since I left Hope Landing this morning. Actually, I've been thinking about her since the day I met her in the rain. I close my eyes and try to go back to sleep but this strange longing that I feel for a woman I barely know is making it difficult.

I keep seeing her deep-set blue eyes framed by dark brows and thick lashes that seem to draw me to her. I think about her lips and how her top one turns up slightly at the corners whether she's smiling intentionally or not. *Ne* matter how plainly she dresses or how modestly she wears her hair, it does little to obscure her beauty.

I think about the kind of *mamm* she is and how her sense of duty to the people she loves seems to have been a driving force in helping her overcome her grief. She's dedicated without smothering, kind and loving yet steadfast in her role as a teacher. She reminds me a little of Elizabeth in that way. She's progressive without being rebellious and it doesn't take long to see the commitment to God that she strives to uphold in her life. I feel inspired by her determination and how openhearted she seems to be.

I know that the death of a spouse is difficult for anyone and that there are millions of people in the world who have survived the loss without losing themselves in the process but it's been a struggle for me.

Looking back, there really was nothing particularly extraordinary about my marriage to Elizabeth, we just loved one another the best we knew how at that age. We met in Hopkinsville, which was an even smaller community thirteen years ago. She was nineteen and had moved to the area with her parents who were looking for a more progressive community. She volunteered in the afternoons as a teacher's assistant and had done so well with the children that she was offered the full-time, paid position when the teacher retired the following summer.

I was twenty-one at the time and working with my *daed's* construction company. I went to repair a window in the school building one afternoon after the *kinner* had all gone home and there she was, working on her lesson plan. I thought she was pretty so I spoke to her the following Sunday after church. We socialized at community gatherings until I began officially courting her the day of the fall harvest celebration. We were married two years later.

It was exciting at first but it eventually settled into a routine that resembled any young Amish couple. My days were split between tending to the farm and working for my *daed* often into evening. Her days were spent managing the home, teaching, gardening and cooking.

We shared the same beliefs in God and the Amish culture though I was a bit more conservative back then. Still, we got along well in spite of the occasional lively discussion. We were both devoted to the friends and family in the community that took up most of our social time and we both hoped to have a house full of children someday.

We made a rigorous effort to conceive in the first two years of our marriage, which only resulted in a miscarriage. After that, I convinced her to stop putting so much concentrated emphasis on getting pregnant and to just leave the situation up to God.

Later that year she started complaining of headaches. At first, we didn't think much of it; blaming it on sinuses and the changing weather. After school started again, she was tired a lot with a few dizzy spells, which she didn't mention to me until later. When her symptoms continued into the spring with added bouts of blurry vision, causing her to bump into things, she finally came to me about it and I insisted that she see a doctor.

The family doctor ordered a CT scan and on the way to the appointment, she had a seizure in the buggy. I was terrified to say the least. I ran into a dollar store across the street from where we were and a cashier called 911 for me on her cell phone.

By the time paramedics arrived, she was sitting up and refusing to be taken to the emergency room alone in the ambulance. Even if they allowed me to ride with her, we were seven miles from home and I had nowhere to leave two horses and a buggy. The diagnostic center was only a mile away, so I took her there, called the doctor and the construction foreman to notify my dad to come and get the buggy.

After the CT scan and a needle biopsy, she was diagnosed with grade III Anaplastic Astrocytoma. In simpler terms, it was a malignant brain tumor that needed to be removed immediately. After almost three years of battling back and forth between periods of sickness and recovery, brain surgeries, radiation, chemo, debilitating side effects, MRI's, oncologists, neurosurgeons and hospitals, she passed away quietly in her sleep. Toward the end, she was only a shell of the woman I once knew and the real grieving had begun long before her death.

In the first couple of years that followed, I couldn't have slowed down if I wanted to. I had a farm to run, a job to go to and a ton of medical bills to pay. I told myself that staying busy was the key to overcoming my grief, anger and sadness. In fact, when my family would tell me to take some time off, I would flippantly reply, *'If the Good Lord wanted me to take time off, He wouldn't have invented medical bills.'*

I know now that I was just delaying the agony like sweeping dust under a rug. I looked up one day and four years had passed and in spite of any good things happening in my life, I felt like I was just going through the motions. I was lonely and becoming bitter to the point of making excuses to keep from spending time with my family...especially the *kinner*.

Then one day my niece Eve got kicked in the face by a horse. She was only six at the time and lucky that the doctors didn't expect any long term damage. When I stopped by her hospital room that night after a long day in the machine shop, I took one look at her tiny swollen and bruised face and thought about her sweet little angelic voice calling me *'Uncle John-John'* just that morning at breakfast, asking me to put her on my shoulders. The memory of seeing Elizabeth lying that same way with her face all swollen just came rushing back to me like I was standing waist deep in river rapids.

I felt my knees buckle and my brother had to take me home. I locked myself in the house for three days crying and screaming at God and finally praying. When I emerged again, I vowed that I was going to find new meaning for my life and *ne* longer let my grief rob me of who I was or spending time with the people I love. That was almost two years ago.

I suppose that's why it made such an impression on me to hear how Sarah had come to the same conclusion in her own grief. The only difference is that in less than ten months, she had accomplished what took me over four years to figure out.

There's just a certain fire in her belly that makes me admire her and respect what a woman and *mamm* she is. The more time I spend with her, the more I find myself wanting to see her again even though I know the timing is all wrong. It wouldn't be respectable to ask a woman to court while she wears the dress of mourning but I hope that I can find favor with her in the meantime.

CHAPTER NINE

Thursday, April 2

I awake just before daylight, say my morning prayers, get dressed and head into the kitchen.

I light the stove for the day and go downstairs to start the load of laundry leftover from yesterday. We've spent the last two days getting ahead our chores for the week because we have a barn raising to attend today and Easter coming this weekend.

Barn raisings, which we often refer to as *'frolics,'* are rather festive occasions in the community and we all look forward to them days in advance. They usually begin at 7:00 a.m. and last until around 5:00 p.m., involving hundreds of people gathered together for a single purpose.

The most valuable thing about a barn raising is that our sense of community spirit is built as solidly as the barn itself, and in one day, the whole community is reminded of what the

Amish culture is all about. This particular barn raising is for the Rocke family, who moved here in the fall from Michigan.

The whole family spent most of our free time preparing for it yesterday. The boys handled all of the outside chores before and after school while *mamm*, Mary and I made 5 gallons of tea, baked sixteen loaves of banana bread, four at a time; peeled, cut and mashed twenty pounds of potatoes and prepared two large chicken, rice and broccoli casseroles; one of which I'll bake before we leave. It sounds like a lot of food and it is, but the things we've prepared pale in comparison to the copious amounts of food that will be there.

Normally at a barn raising, the hosting family will supply as much of the food as possible which is often cooked right on-site. They might bake 10 pies, slaughter 40 chickens and dig up all of their leftover potatoes from the last planting in preparation for the crowd of hungry workers. But once this particular frolic was already planned, the foundation poured and the materials paid for, 11 year old Jude Rocke fell from a tree while playing with his brother.

Thankfully, he survived the eight foot drop but he was hospitalized with a broken arm and a spinal concussion, with partial loss of his motor functions. After hundreds of prayers, two weeks later, his prognosis is good, with *ne* signs of paralysis. Although in the beginning, the doctors didn't know whether or not he would ever make a full recovery. The Rocke family spent every possible moment at the hospital, by his side, in the days that followed.

Mr. Rocke went to the Bishop ready to postpone, even though like most Amish families, he needed the barn to survive. We had a Member's Meeting after church that Sunday and everyone agreed to pitch in and make the preparations for them. From having the meal "potluck" style, to helping Mrs. Rocke clean and overseeing the laying of the cement block so that the build could still take place.

We agreed that each family in attendance would bring enough food to feed their own household plus two or three others, in order to accommodate the men who didn't have wives to cook for them. Though everything will be shared, it ensures that there's enough food to go around without the preparation and expense being too much of a burden on any one family.

What I'm bringing will feed ten people a hearty lunch, not counting the mashed potatoes and banana bread but I'll still set aside a few of the things we prepared to feed my family for dinner without much effort.

Once the laundry is washed, wrung and in the dryer, I go back upstairs with an empty box, put the casserole in the oven and start packing the items to take with us.

I grab two quart jars of pickled okra and a quart of pickled baby corn with green beans and peppers. None of us really like okra at all but it was one of Jacob's favorite snacks. This is the perfect time to share it with people who might enjoy it and it will free up my canning jars for the peas I need to can.

I put aside eight loaves of banana bread and pack the rest in the box. Three loaves will be for the family; I'll give two loaves to John when I ask him to help us build a 'rabbitat' and pick his brain about planting the corn maze. I also plan to give one loaf to Bishop Graber when I talk to him about advertising and signs, and I know the other two loaves will probably come in handy over the upcoming Easter weekend.

I put the kettle on for coffee as *mamm* walks over from the *Daadi Haus* and the children begin coming downstairs for breakfast. Hannah sets the table with paper plates while I slice a loaf of banana bread and lay it on a cookie sheet, on top of the casserole dish, to toast for five minutes. I pour two cups cup of coffee while Mary pours everyone else a glass of milk.

"*Mamm* this banana bread is so good I bet the *Englisch* are going to love it," Mark says.

"Maybe we can give out some samples like they do at the grocery store," Mary adds.

"That's a great idea," *mamm* says.

"Remember when we made those caramel apples for the harvest festival? We could make those too, that was fun!" Samuel chimes in.

"They're both great ideas and I'll add everything to the plan but let's all remember not to talk about the tour business at the frolic today. It wouldn't be right for people to start talking about it before I've had a chance to clear a few things with

Bishop Graber," I warn. "We'll just keep putting our ideas together and making preparations until I can meet with him after the Easter holiday."

"*Mamm* are we going to color eggs this year?"

"*Ya* we're going to color lots of them," I assure her.

"Are you going to hide them too?" Josh asks.

"*Ya, mamm* and I will hide them for all of my little hunters to find."

"Does anyone remember what today is?" *mamm* asks.

"*Och,* I do!" Samuel says excitedly, "*Gruna Dunaschdawk.*"

"What's that?" Josh asks.

"It's Green Thursday, it means it's the day before Good Friday," Mark informs him.

"Why do they call it Green Thursday?" Josh asks.

"Because you have to eat something green today so you will have good health all year," Mary explains.

"*Mamm* are we having anything green to eat today?" Hannah asks.

"*Ya*, I put a few bullfrogs in the banana bread," I tease.

"Ewwww," she protests.

"I can't taste any frogs in here," Josh smiles taking another bite.

"I think my banana bread just croaked," Samuel laughs.

Mark belches which sounds like a bullfrog and they all follow along. I chuckle at *mamm*, shaking my head.

"You started it," she laughs.

After breakfast, everyone finishes their chores while I fold the laundry from the dryer and pull the casserole out of the oven to cool for a minute while Mark hitches the buggy. As I walk outside with the large stock-pot in my hand that contains over half of the mashed potatoes we prepared, I see John and Caleb coming up the drive on the tractor, pulling the wagon behind it.

The children cheer excitedly as I load the potatoes in the buggy and watch as they pull up in front of the barn.

John has a broad smile on his face as they approach, "I heard there was a frolic going on today and I wondered if any of the Fishers wanted to come," he chuckles.

Mark's eyes widen, "Ooohh, can we ride to the frolic in the wagon?" followed by Josh cheering "Take me too!"

"Can we *mamm*?" Mary asks me.

"John did you know that today is *Gruna Dunaschdawk*?" Samuel asks him.

"*Ya*, and *mamm* put green frogs in our banana bread," Hannah informs him.

"*Och* she did?!" he chuckles, smiling at me. He steps off of the tractor and leans down close to her and pokes her tummy. "I don't hear any frogs in there."

Hannah giggles.

"Buuurrriibbit" Samuel belches.

"*Och* Hannah I think Samuel must have eaten your banana bread too!" John says.

The children all laugh at his playfulness.

"I really just stopped by to see if you needed any help getting anything to the frolic since you were on our way," he says to me.

"Actually I've got a five-gallon cooler jug of iced tea you could load for me," I tell him.

"I'd be happy to drive you and Miriam in the buggy so the *kinner* can ride in the wagon with Caleb," he offers as he steps into the kitchen to grab the cooler.

"If you're sure you don't mind," I tell him, "I know they would really enjoy it."

"Climb in everyone!" he calls out to them.

Mamm and I chuckle as we listen to them squeal and cheer excitedly.

He loads the tea onto the wagon with them and then carries the box with the banana bread out to the buggy. He helps *mamm* inside and then me. I lay a towel across my legs and sit the warm casserole dish in my lap.

Caleb waits for us to get the horses moving before he leads the way to the Rocke farm.

"I found three of those chain guards I mentioned at the shop Monday. I thought I could put one on your, Mary's and Hannah's bikes, since dresses are more likely to get caught in the chain than pant legs. Caleb and I could put them on when we come back this afternoon if you want."

"*Denki*, actually, I have a couple of things I want to get your advice on for the tour business if you and Caleb feel like staying for dinner afterwards. I have another chicken, broccoli and rice casserole ready to pop in the oven and I could throw together some bread pudding for dessert while you're working on the bikes.

I think about how hard they'll probably work today and the fact that he probably has his own chores waiting for him at home, "Of course, it can wait if you have other things you need to do," I add.

"You don't have to ask me to dinner twice," he chuckles, "Well you could, I wouldn't object," he smiles as *mamm* chuckles. "I'll send Caleb to tend to the animals at my place while I fix the bikes, and we should both be ready by the time you set the table."

"*Gut*, it's settled then," I say with a smile, watching the scenery as we trot along.

We arrive at the Rocke farm where the *kinner* are already meeting up with their friends as people arrive. John helps *mamm* and I out of the buggy and then carries the iced tea up to the patio just outside of the kitchen. It's a beautiful day, so Mrs. Rocke has the patio doors open creating a huge space that encompasses the kitchen, dining area and patio.

"*Och*! Hello Mrs. Fisher, hello John, thanks for coming," Mr. Rocke says, shaking his hand. "Men, in case you haven't met him yet, this is John Troyer from Hopkinsville. Like me, he's fairly new to the community but he's already been a big help to my family and he's here to help again today – so please make him feel welcome."

I smile knowingly at John as some of the other men step over to shake hands and introduce themselves. I know he's not the kind of man who likes public attention, but I think it's good that he gets acquainted with more people in the community.

The younger *kinner* mostly spend their day at the barn raising watching or playing with their friends, away from the construction and kitchen areas, so that they're not underfoot. Once I check to make sure that Josh and Hannah are situated, I send Mark and Mary to get the mashed potatoes and banana bread box from the buggy, then step into the kitchen to join *mamm* and the other ladies. Over the lively chatter of women puttering around the kitchen, Mrs. Rocke thanks me for coming

When Mark returns, he hands me the stock pot and joins John and Caleb outside as the foreman doles out instructions to coordinate the workers. Usually at a barn raising, the men who are able-bodied will do the actual raising of walls and all of the climbing work. The older men work on the ground level, keeping things moving by passing materials up to the men doing the actual framework. The younger boys, ranging anywhere from ages nine to fifteen, are put to work fetching and carrying things and running tools back and forth as needed.

Mark was just eight years old at his last frolic, so I know he's excited to get to work alongside the men this time. I watch as John gives him a hammer and shows him how to beat the nails out of a board so it can be reused.

It's hard not to notice what a sturdy, handsome man John is, but I'm even more impressed by the fact that he's taking the time to give my son this patient instruction to help him feel like part of the team. Though I know that nobody will ever really replace his *daed*, I thank God for sending someone to help fill that void in his life, even if it's only for a few moments at a time.

"Would you like me to put that on the dining room table with the other dishes to be warmed?" *mamm* asks.

I'm so lost in my thoughts that I'm not even aware of how long I've been standing in the patio doorway, still holding the stock pot of mashed potatoes in my hand.

"*Ne*, I'll get it," I tell her.

She looks at me with a knowing look and I avert my eyes as I head for the dining room.

Even though most everyone has prepared for the occasion, there's still plenty going on in the kitchen as the women socialize while they work. I make small talk while I watch through the open doorway as some of the older men begin setting up the long tables and benches that we use for church, to double as seating for the noon meal. Before I know it, the patio looks like a cafeteria and I find myself trying to catch a glimpse of Mark and John in the distance.

As noon approaches, the women in the kitchen begin rushing about, some carrying dishes of food to the table, some preparing plates for the men, some filling glasses with tea or lemonade.

Because of the large number of people in attendance, the noon meal is usually eaten in shifts, starting with the older men down to the youngest, while the women serve. They eat until they're satisfied. Some indulging more than others, but there's *ne* question that they'll need the energy to finish the day as they begin the roof and siding work. When they return to their work, the women gather at the same tables, the eldest to the youngest until everyone has had their fill.

Once the mountain of dishes are all washed and dried, we begin packing away the things we *ne* longer need and start preparing the late afternoon snack which consists of cake, apple pie or banana bread served with iced tea or coffee usually around 3:00 p.m.

After everyone has enjoyed their choice of snacks, the dishes are done and most everything is packed away, the women begin to gather and watch as the last of the siding and galvanized steel roof are secured into place.

The men congregate between the porch and the completed barn, admiring the finished project as they socialize for a few minutes longer. Once everyone has said their goodbyes; each family gathers the last of their things and starts heading home by the buggy full, until only the Rocke family remains.

CHAPTER TEN

By 5:30 p.m., *mamm* and the children are busy doing afternoon chores and tending to the animals, as John works on the bikes in the barn. I busy myself in the kitchen washing out the empty cooler, putting away the clean dishes and cutting *mamm's* crusty bread for the bread pudding. I mix my spices and wet ingredients in a separate bowl as *mamm* joins me in the kitchen with a basket full of washed eggs. "The *kinner* are in the barn watching John work on the bikes," she says. "He seems to have quite a way with the children."

"*Ya*, I'm surprised they seem to have taken to him so easily, especially Hannah, but I think it's good." I crack and stir the eggs into the wet ingredients and sit the bowl in the fridge until I'm ready to bake it – but first I need to bake the casserole.

"Maybe he and Caleb could help you pick up the oven and the bakery case in the wagon," she suggests.

I know Dan offered to hire someone with a truck, but I hate to have them go to the expense.

"You don't think it's too much to ask? I'm already planning to enlist his help building a bunny habitat and I need to find out what he knows about corn mazes."

"Something tells me he won't mind," she smiles. "It'll give you a good excuse to invite him for dinner over the Easter weekend since he doesn't have any local family to celebrate with."

I have to admit that she makes a good point. "I'll ask him at dinner; they may be spending the whole weekend or at least Easter day with his family in Hopkinsville. If not, I'll invite them," I assure her as I put the casserole in the oven.

I run a damp mop over the floors as the casserole bakes. By the time Caleb returns from tending to the animals, John has finished with the bikes. Mary and Hannah test the new chain guards by riding around in circles in front of the barn. As *mamm* sets the table, I pull the casserole from the oven, pour my egg mixture over the bread and put it in the oven to bake before calling everyone inside to wash their hands.

The *kinner* dash into the house and I have to warn them to slow down as they line up at the bathroom door. Caleb and John come inside a little more slowly but not by much. *Mamm* chuckles but I resist the urge to call attention to it.

I finish pouring tea as everyone is seated and we bow our heads in prayer. I fill everyone's plate as they pass them around the table and then we all dig in.

"*Mamm* did you put trees in this because I think I see some trees." Hannah asks.

"Ya, but only little ones," I assure her.

"Will you and Caleb be in Hope Landing over the Easter holiday John?" I ask casually.

"Well, I'm taking Caleb home in the morning so I'll be at my brother's for Good Friday but I need to be here Saturday to look after the farm. I promised my *mamm* I'd be at the big family gathering on Sunday so I'll be back and forth. I'm going turkey hunting early Saturday morning and I hope to bring a fresh turkey back with me if you know anyone who might be interested in cooking one," he smiles.

Easter in the Amish community is a significant time of celebration, usually lasting for several days. Good Friday is treated a lot like the Sabbath, usually spent fasting in the morning and reading from the Bible with minimal chores or focus on work throughout the day. Aside from the time spent boiling and coloring Easter eggs, the day is usually quiet and rather solemn in commemoration of the crucifixion of Christ. The fast is broken at dinner time and is usually a big meal.

Saturday is spent getting ready for holiday visitors, catching up on chores and cleaning throughout the day, with a lot of cooking in preparation for the next two days. Saturday evening's dinner usually involves a big gathering of friends and family. Since Ruth's parents are in Florida now, she and Dan will join us for the Saturday dinner and spend Easter

Sunday and Monday at his family's farm.

Easter Sunday and the Monday that follows are also treated a lot like any other Sabbath in that chores and work are kept to a minimum. The days are spent relaxing and fellowshipping with friends and family, and end with a big dinner celebration to commemorate the resurrection of Christ.

My Sunday widow's visitation this week will be from the Zook family which we've all become a lot closer to as a result. Since there's *ne* church service this Sunday, we'll be able to relax and enjoy a quiet morning together and then I'll hide the Easter eggs for all of the children to hunt when the Zooks arrive in the afternoon. While the children play, *mamm*, Catherine Zook and I will warm food and put the final touches on the dishes we've prepared the day before.

"Well whether you get a turkey or not, we would love to have you over for dinner Saturday and Monday."

"*Ya* John there's *ne* reason for you to spend the holiday alone when you could be with friends," *mamm* agrees.

"I'm baking a ham for Saturday's dinner but on Monday I can roast the turkey if you catch one and if you don't I can fry the fish you and Caleb brought us. Either way there will be plenty of food with dressing and mashed potatoes and whatever else we end up making on Saturday."

"And eggs?" Hannah asks.

"*Ya*, and eggs," I assure her.

"You could help us color the Easter eggs on Saturday too," Josh offers.

"Well I don't know how to color Easter eggs but I'd love to come to dinner," he smiles.

"It's easy, we can teach you," Hannah assures him.

Caleb laughs but doesn't say anything as he watches his uncle wriggle out of this one.

"Look at those hands," *mamm* says, "I think John's hands might be just a bit too big to color eggs without dropping them.

"How about if you guys color the eggs and I'll help your *mamm* hide them?" he says.

"*Ya* Josh, he probably knows all the good hiding places," Mark offers.

"Okay but don't hide them up too high because I'm only this tall," Josh says, standing up and raising his arms to demonstrate.

Mamm and I laugh as Mary shakes her head with a smile.

"*Mamm* what smells so good?" Samuel asks curiously as the aroma of the bread pudding baking in the oven begins to fill the room.

"The first one to guess the dessert or one of the two main ingredients gets the first piece," I tell them.

"Mmmm, I bet I know," John says.

"Go ahead and guess," Mary encourages.

"It just wouldn't be fair; your *mamm* already told me one ingredient," he says.

"I think it's cinnabum," Josh decides. We all chuckle at his pronunciation but he has a pretty good nose for a five year old.

"Ooooh, I think I know, is it pear crisp?" Mark asks.

"I'll give you one hint…it's orange," I tell them.

"Pumpkin!" Caleb chimes in.

"*Ya*, I think it's pumpkin too," Mary adds.

"What can I say, the boy loves pumpkin," John chuckles.

We laugh and chatter along as we finish dinner. When everyone has cleared their plates, Mary starts washing the dishes as *mamm* puts the kettle on. The boys show John and Caleb the Florida book while I prepare the glaze to pour over the bread pudding. I can hear Samuel telling them everything he's already learned about alligators as Mark fills him in on all the things Ruth did while she was there.

After everyone finishes dessert, it's almost 8:00 p.m. The *kinner* do their evening chores and I give them another thirty minutes to play with Caleb before going upstairs to take their baths and get ready for bed. John, *mamm* and I sit around the table as I share some of our ideas with him for the tour business out of my journal.

"When I saw the corn maze in my dream, the maze wound around in all four quadrants surrounding the cross and then leading into it; but on the activity page, the maze is inside the cross. I know the design in my mind might be a little too complicated to start out with on the first try but that's the vision I want to work toward."

When I finish telling him all about the corn maze, he's silent for a minute but I can tell he's going through it in his mind. "What do you think?" I ask curiously. I'm eager to hear his opinion on the whole thing.

"I'm impressed. I can tell you've put some serious thought into your whole plan and I think it will go over really well with both kids and adults."

"Do you know if there are any special preparations we need to make to plant a corn maze?" *mamm* asks curiously.

"I've never done it myself but I've been through one and I certainly know how to grow corn. I'll give it some thought this weekend. I'm sure I can figure it out. Whatever we try, there will be a maze. If the design doesn't work out quite the way we want, we'll just learn to do a better job of it next season. That's the nice thing about working with living, growing things."

"You mean you'll help us with the layout?" I ask with a hopeful smile.

"Of course, I'd be happy to help. Can I take Hannah's coloring page with me?"

I gladly give him the coloring page but decide to wait to ask for his help with the stove, bakery case and the rabbitat until after Easter. There won't be any work done before then anyway and I'll have a whole week until planting season to figure everything out. I'd rather we all just enjoy the long weekend of fellowship ahead without making him feel overwhelmed or obligated with projects if he doesn't have the time. I'm just grateful that he's going to help with the maze.

CHAPTER ELEVEN

Saturday April 4

As I ride the tractor home from Hopkinsville after the turkey hunt Saturday morning, I realize how excited I am to be bringing a nice big turkey back with me. I love a good turkey dinner but the idea of sharing it with Sarah and the *kinner* is really what I'm looking forward to the most. I thank God for having met her and for the way He's helping me to be a blessing to them. I feel a greater sense of purpose and closeness with Him that I really haven't ever experienced before.

I think about how He showed her the maze and showed me how I would be plowing her corn fields simultaneously, in two different places, in the middle of the night. I don't know why all this is happening, all I know is that I'm starting to enjoy life again and looking forward to being a part of it as it unfolds.

As the crow flies, Hopkinsville is only about sixteen miles from Hope Landing. By buggy it takes about two hours to drive and by tractor, around 40 minutes depending on how fast you can go and what route you take. The biggest challenge with either mode of transportation is staying out of the way of impatient automobile drivers. This usually means driving the back roads and staying off of busy highways that are often the most direct route.

On a whim, I decide to try a different route today, to see if I can avoid one of the hills I usually have to navigate. I veer left at the cutoff and down the country road past several homesteads before coming upon a wooded area full of picturesque sugar maple trees. Just beyond that, I see an older man walking along the side of the road. He's tall and thin with stringy gray hair that falls just over his shirt-collar. He's wearing denim overalls and a plaid shirt.

'*Stop,'* I hear that still, small voice say to me.

I pull past him and out of the roadway before coming to a stop. I don't really know what to say so I ask him if he needs any help.

"My truck broke down a couple of miles back and I couldn't get ahold of anyone to come and get me so I just decided to walk.

"I can take a look at it if you'd like." I don't drive a car but I know enough about engines that I might be able to help.

"I just need to get to my son's place, he'll help me get it runnin' again when he gets home; he's about four miles down the road."

"Hop on," I tell him.

"I sure appreciate it, I can't walk for long distances like I used to," he says.

He climbs onto the tractor next to me and leans against the fender over the back wheel. He must be a farmer because most people would have opted to ride in the wagon. It's safer in the wagon as a general rule but harder to hear anyone give directions over the sound of the engine. I suspect he knows this.

We continue on down the road and he has me take a left and then a right before pulling onto an old dirt road. There's a wooden pole on the corner just beyond the street sign. And nailed to the pole is a yellow cardboard sign with hand-printed, black letters that simply read: *'Free Bunnies.'* I chuckle to myself as I realize that I'm not here by accident.

We drive down the road about three quarters of a mile and then turn into a long driveway leading to a two-acre lot with a trailer on it. There's another yellow sign tied to the fence. I can hear children playing as I shut off the engine at the end of the drive.

"I haven't been on a tractor like that in a long time," he chuckles, stepping down onto the ground. "Say are you one of those Ame-ish people?"

"*Ya*, sir, I am."

"Lot's of good, kind folks the Ame-ish. I sure do appreciate the ride.

"You said this was your son's place?" I ask curiously.

"Yeah, he should be along any time now. His wife's probably out back with my grandkids and can't hear the phone. Come on up to the house and I'll give you a little something for your trouble," he offers.

"That's not necessary, I'm just glad I could help. I would like to ask about the bunnies though."

"Well I'm sure my daughter-in-law will be glad to help you, they got one for each of the kids last year and now they've got so many they can't give 'em away fast enough. Come on, we'll go find her and she can tell you all about 'em."

We walk around to the back of the property behind the trailer where a handful of kids are jumping on a trampoline. It occurs to me that the *kinner* might enjoy something like that. There are three wooden structures in the backyard. There's a wooden shed with a double door, probably where they keep their mower, a small chicken coop big enough for maybe ten chickens and a large wooden rabbit hutch with a woman standing in front of it.

"Deanna, this man wants some bunnies," he calls out to her as we cross the lawn.

"Hey pop, when did you get here?" she asks.

“My truck broke down just before the turnoff, I tried to call Tom but he didn’t answer and nobody answered the house phone. I started walking and this man gave me a ride. He was the only one who even bothered to stop.”

“Oh I’m so sorry, Kayla must’ve left the cordless in the house, Tom should be home any minute,” she tells him. “Thank you for giving him a ride. You’re interested in some bunnies?” she asks, wiping a lock of bright red hair from her eyes.

“*Ya* I noticed your sign, I’d like maybe five or seven, depending on how many you have to give,” I tell her.

“Hon, I have about twenty right now, countin’ the original four we have in the house, you can take any of them you want and as many as you want. I would recommend you get them spayed or neutered in the next few months though if you don’t want to end up in the same boat,” she laughs. “They’re great pets; we just didn’t realize how quickly we would end up with so many.”

“We had some when I was a boy. How old are they?”

“These here on this side are all nine weeks old and the ones on the other side are ten. They’re from two different litters from two different mama’s but they’re all weaned and healthy. They’re called Holland Lops.

“If I took seven, would you have something I could transport them in?” I ask. “I didn’t expect to find bunnies today but I know a family that would love to have some.”

"If you'll take nine, I'll throw in a big wire cage and enough pellets to get you by for a few days. We bought the cage when the first mama had her litter and the following week the second mama had hers so my husband just gave up and built the outdoor hutch for them. If you take nine I can move the four my kids are keeping out here with the others and get them out of my house," she chuckles.

"You've got yourself a deal," I smile.

"I'll go get the cage Deanna," the old man says, heading toward the shed.

I peer into the hutch at all the cute little lop-eared bunnies wondering which ones to choose. Since they're supposed to be for petting, I just decide to reach out my hands inside the hutch and see if any of them come to me.

The first one comes to me and I take off my hat and put him inside while I repeat the process. The second one comes and I put him in my hat too as the old man puts the cage on the ground next to me. I put the two from my hat inside the cage as he fills the bottom with some hay for me.

I stick my hands in again and wait for another bunny as they watch.

"Are ya' lettin' the good Lord pick 'em for ya'?" the old man asks.

"*Ya* I guess I am," I chuckle. It hadn't even occurred to me but I suppose if God brought me here to get them in the first place, He probably knows better than anyone which ones he wants the *kinner* to have. Once I have eight rabbits in the cage, I put my hands in for the last time but none of them come to me like the others did.

I peer into the hutch, looking over the remaining bunnies and I see a little white one with gray ears and a patch of gray around her nose crouching over in the corner, eyeing me curiously. "You must be Hannah's," I say to the bunny. I reach in and grab her by the fur of the neck, adding her to my litter.

The old man carries the food to the tractor for me as I load the cage and thanks me again for the ride as I climb into the seat. I give him a handshake, "*Ne* sir, thank you!" I smile and wave goodbye as I start the engine.

"Happy Easter!" I hear him call out as I drive away.

I can't stop grinning as I drive the remaining five miles or so to Hope Landing, where I stop at my house first to store the turkey in the fridge until Monday because I know Sarah probably won't have room in hers with the ham and all the other food she'll be cooking. I'm going to have to find her a good working freezer by the time I start butchering pigs. Mine's already half full and she's going to need a lot more space than what she has now. "Lord, you led me to the rabbits, I know you can lead me to a freezer too," I say out loud.

I eat the roast beef sandwich my sister-in-law sent with me from our Good Friday dinner leftovers and down a glass of milk; wash out the cooler I transported the turkey in and take a few minutes to start the list of supplies that I'll need to build the rabbit hutch.

I know it's going to be a busy week after Easter Monday and I need to try to have my materials ready so that I can get it built in one day. That will leave me four working days to finish my own work and figure out this corn maze before I shift my focus to planting season the following week.

I go into the barn and load the eight sheets of leftover plywood I have leaning against a wall along with some chicken wire leftover from the pig corral, my toolbox, a saw and four leftover 2x4's. Once all of that's loaded, I feed and water the animals, check the pig corral then go inside to take a quick shower and change into some clean clothes before heading to Sarah's.

I pull into the drive and am relieved that the *kinner* are all still inside so I can surprise them. I park behind the barn and knock on Sarah's kitchen door.

"Come on in John," Miriam says, opening the screen door. The children are upstairs making sure their rooms are clean and Sarah went downstairs to get their blankets out of the dryer. Would you like some coffee?

"I'd love some thank you. I hope I'm not too early."

"*Och ne*, we just had lunch but I could make you something if you're hungry."

"I already had lunch too, I just came early because I have a surprise," I whisper.

"You're a good man John Troyer," she says with a smile.

"Hey John," Sarah says as she steps into the kitchen, "How did your turkey hunting go?"

"My nephew is a pretty good shot for a thirteen year old, so I brought back a nice fat one for you.. It was a two day youth-only season event and my brother wanted to take both of his younger sons, since the oldest one will be too old next year."

"These are Caleb's brothers?"

"*Ya* Joseph and Micah. I put the turkey in the fridge at my house because I didn't think you'd have room. I can bring it by Monday morning."

"It's cleaned and plucked already?" she asks.

"*Ya*, my brother's wife and daughter went ahead and cleaned both turkeys when we got back from the hunt so I would have time to look at their tractor before I left. It was just a short in a wire so I think I got the better end of the deal," I look at Miriam and chuckle.

"*Och*, that's so nice of them! And you're right, that was a good idea, since my fridge will be full by the time we finish cooking."

"How about an egg salad sandwich?" she offers.

"I already ate, I wanted to talk to you and Miriam alone

outside for a minute without the *kinner* showing up."

"Okay, let's go outside. I'm surprised they're not already down here wondering who's come to visit."

We step outside and I lead them through to the other side of the barn near the tractor.

"What is going on?" Sarah chuckles.

"I brought a little surprise for everyone but I wanted to make sure you were okay with it first." I tell her.

"You brought wood?" she asks curiously looking at the plywood standing up in the back of the wagon, blocking the side view of the bunny cage.

"Well *ya*," I chuckle. "I thought maybe the boys could help me build a hutch," I tease. I'm starting to enjoy prolonging the suspense.

"Like for dishes?" she asks, still confused.

I look at Miriam who I'm pretty sure has already figured it out. She laughs.

"*Och*, I've kept you in suspense long enough," I chuckle. I wish could kiss her right then and there but I take a deep breath and walk around to the back of the wagon as she follows behind.

She takes one look at the cage and gasps with her eyes wide and a big surprised smile on her face, *Och*, John they're adorable!" she says as her eyes well with tears.

"Wait until you hear the story of how I got them," I tell her, "But first let's figure out how we're going to surprise the *kinner*."

Miriam hugs her as she wipes her tears. "Let's tell them we're doing a practice Easter egg hunt," she says.

"How about if I sit the cage on that pile of hay for them to find?"

"*Ya*, okay," she smiles.

"Sarah let's go inside; John come to the door when you finish getting everything ready and we'll all send them out," Miriam says.

Sarah and Miriam go inside while I fluff the hay and sit the cage full of cuddly bunnies in the center. Back in the house I sit down at the table to drink my coffee as the children start coming down the stairs.

"I told you John was here," Josh says.

"*Mamm* you said you would tell us when John got here," Samuel says.

I chuckle. "I had something important to do."

"Is everyone's room nice and clean?" Sarah asks.

They all reply '*ya mamm.*'

"Well since John doesn't have any children, this is his first time hiding Easter eggs and he was a little nervous, so we thought we would let him practice one time before Aunt Ruthie and Uncle Dan get here," she tells them.

"You mean we get to hunt for eggs two times?" Samuel asks excitedly.

"*Ya*," she tells them, "But since this is just practice, they're all hidden somewhere between here and the barn.

"Ooooh this will be easy," Mark says.

"Yay!" Josh cheers.

"It's okay John, I'm sue you did a good job of hiding them," Mary smiles.

I chuckle knowingly. "*Och*, thank you Mary."

"When can we go? Hannah asks.

"Right…now!" Sarah says.

The *kinner* squeal and cheer and hurry outside as Sarah, Miriam and I trail behind them to watch. We stop nonchalantly near the edge of the house as the children go off looking high and low. Mark is forging his own path while Samuel and Josh kind of stay close to one another. Mary huddles with Hannah and then takes off behind the house while Hannah heads toward the barn.

My heart is beating like a drum in my chest, partly because

I'm so excited to see the children's reaction and partly because Sarah put her hand in the bend of my arm for a moment; when we hear the scream.

The other children rush to the barn to see what's happening as we step inside behind them. Hannah is sitting on the ground petting her rabbit through the cage as the other *kinner* gather around.

"*Och* mamm they're so cute can we all pet them?" Mary asks.

"Do you all want to hear the story of how God brought you the rabbits?" I ask.

"I thought you brought them," Samuel says.

"*Och ya*, I delivered them but God picked these very rabbits especially for each and every one of you. Everyone gather around and I'll tell you the story while we pet them."

I move the cage to the center of the barn and we all gather around it. I tell them the story of going the different route and picking up the old *Englisch* man; about seeing the sign for the bunnies and how I knew God had meant for me to be there. I told them about how I chose the bunnies and what the old man said and then told them about Hanna's shy bunny and how that's the very one she was petting right now. "So, now you have to decide, do you want to choose your own bunnies or do you want to see which one comes to you? Let's start with Josh and Hannah."

"I like all of them! I want to see if one will come to me," Josh decides.

"Okay but you have to name it too so everyone knows their names."

"I want the shy one you said was mine and I want to name it *Lammie* because it looks like a little lamb.

I chuckle, "That's very good, she does look like a little lamb," I reach into the cage, grab her bunny and put it in her lap. Okay Josh, open your hands and stick them right outside the door of the cage and see if one comes to you."

He puts his open hands in the cage and a reddish-brown bunny with white circles under its chin and around its eyes comes to the edge of the cage and sniffs his hands.

He giggles and I show him how to pick her up gently. "Her name is *Cinnabum*," he declares.

Everyone chuckles. "*Och ya*, her fur looks like cinnamon doesn't it?" I smile, ruffling his hair.

"Okay Samuel, what will it be?"

"I want to see if it will come to me," he smiles.

"Me too," Mary and Mark both agree at the same time.

"Me four," Sarah says.

"Me five," Miriam agrees.

I laugh, "Okay Samuel, go for it," I tell him.

His bunny sniffs the edge of the cage curiously, "It's coming to me!" he says excitedly. "I'm going to name him *Shadow* because he's gray."

I look up at Sarah's beautiful smile as she watches intently.

"Very nice Samuel, okay Mary, your turn," I say, turning the cage toward her.

She holds out her hands and her bunny comes to the edge of the cage, but its ears are too long to poke its head over the edge. She giggles, "I think I'm going to call her *Ora* because she has the longest ears."

We all laugh, "*Ora* it is!" Let's see which one likes Mark."

He scoots closer to the cage and puts his hands out. We all wait patiently for several moments until a white bunny with big black spots comes right to him. "Awww he's so cute, I'm going to name him *Patches* after my *daed's* old cow because he looks just like her."

"*Och*, that's a fine name," I tell him. "Okay Sarah, your turn," I smile, turning the opening of the cage toward her.

We all watch as the rabbit comes to her, it's a goldish brown color, not as red as Josh's bunny, with a white nose and a long white patch down the center of her head and her belly. "I'm going to call her *Cookie* because she looks like a vanilla sandwich crème," she laughs.

"She does *mamm*," Mary giggles.

"Okay Miriam, your turn."

She holds out her hands and one of the last three remaining rabbits comes to her rather quickly. This one looks a lot like Samuel's and Hannah's, mostly white with smaller gray patches scattered around it's back half and solid gray ears.

"I'm going to call this one *Smoky* because of his gray spots," she chuckles.

"That only leaves two. John you should name one," Sarah says with a smile.

"I think I want to call the black one *Midnight*," I say decidedly. "He's the only one that's entirely black."

"Well what should we do about the last bunny?" Sarah asks.

"We could vote on a name," Mary suggests.

The last bunny is mostly white too with big patches like Mark's but in the orangey-brown color of Josh's.

"Ooooh I know," Mark says. "We could call her Pumpkin Pie because of her spots."

"We could give her to Caleb," Hannah suggests.

"Yeah then when he comes over he will have one too," Samuel agrees.

"Caleb loves pumpkin," Mary sighs.

We all laugh, “Pumpkin pie it is,” I chuckle.

“Okay children. I know you are all very excited and you’ll be able to pet the bunnies with Ben later, but we still have a few things to do before they get here and afternoon chores to do.”

“John, what if Ben wants a bunny to, can God give him one?” Josh asks.

“If Ben’s *mamm* and *dead* say it’s okay, you can give *Midnight* to Ben, how’s that?”

“Okay,” he sighs, “You can still share my bunny if you need one to pet.”

“*Denki*, that’s very nice of you.”

“Children what do you all say?” Miriam asks.

They all thank me with a hug for the bunnies and we put them back into the cage. I feel so blessed to have been a part of their joy.

CHAPTER TWELVE

I pull my buggy in front of Yoder's store, climb out and go inside. My wife needs sage and I want to get my grandson a treat for Easter morning. I find the sage on the shelf with the spices and step to the middle aisle of the store where the candies are. I hear the bell jingle again as someone enters.

"Um, yes hello," An *Englisch* woman says to Levi.

"Yes ma'am how can I help you?" Levi asks.

Levi Yoder just recently turned seventeen and is at that crossroads in his life wrought with temptation. I listen quietly to see how this young man handles himself with an *Englischer*. I have the sanctity of his good family name and a community to protect and I've been appointed by God for this duty.

"Well, last Saturday, my brother and his family we're visiting from out of town and they brought me some eggs from a local farm. I think she was a widow woman, well anyway she gave my brother and his kids a tour of her farm and they had such a good time that I wanted to take my kids too but I couldn't find the place. He said her name was Mrs. Fisher and she had a little sign out in front of her farm advertising eggs for sale not more than a mile from here.

I'm shocked and appalled by what I've just heard. That insolent Sarah Fisher is going to corrupt our settlement with her foolish ways.

"I think the Fisher farm is about a mile and a half down the road. Actually, it might even be two. Just take a right out of the parking lot and go straight down, you'll see the egg sign on the fence by the road, just keep watching on your right."

"Thank you so much, ya'll have a happy Easter now."

I grab a bag of chocolate-covered, crème filled Easter eggs for my grandson and make my way to the register.

"*Och*, uh, hello Deacon Byler," Levi says to me almost tripping over his tongue, "I didn't see you there."

"Hello Levi, how is your *mamm* doing?" I ask politely even though my blood is boiling.

"Um she's great she'll be back in the store on Tuesday. Is that all for you sir?" he asks.

"*Ya*, that will be all Levi."

"That'll be six fifty-five."

I hand him the money and get back in my buggy, sneaking

one of the Easter egg candies from the bag.

I'm the Deacon in this settlement and Sarah Fisher should have never let *Englischers* on her farm. Especially without permission, let alone for a cheap tour. I'm not going to let her make a mockery of our community. I want to know exactly what's happening down on that farm before this gets any further out of hand.

I drive my buggy just past her place and see the *Englischer's* fancy, flashy, bright red car parked in front of her barn. I wait and watch but even after sitting in my buggy for twenty minutes and polishing off the candy-crème eggs, the *Englisch* are still nowhere in sight.

Maybe she's letting them in her home too. She must be doing something she knows is wrong; why else would she feel the need to keep it hidden from the Bishop and me for the past week?

The Bishop is certainly going to hear about this, I will not have her shaming this settlement and I'll do whatever it takes to stop her foolishness!

The End

AUTHORS NOTE: AMISH COUNTRY TOUR IDEAS

Dear Reader,

Since this series is titled Amish Country Tours, I thought it might be a good idea to start gathering a list of places where one can visit and learn about Amish culture throughout the United States. This is not a comprehensive list, and in fact, if you have taken a tour or have a recommendation to add to this list, please drop me a line at Rachel.stoltzfus@globalgrafxpress.com and I will add your recommendation to this list. Or if you've tried one of these tours and have a review, please let me know so I can add it and inform the folks on our mailing list.

Amish Country, Lancaster County, PA

Official Visitors Guide:

http://www.discoverlancaster.com/index.asp

Amish Country Tours at Plain & Fancy Farm: http://amishexperience.com/

From their website: *For over 50 years the Amish Experience has remained the definitive interpretive center for guided tours of the Amish Farmlands, tours of Lancaster County's only officially designated "Heritage Site" Amish House & One-Room School, and the spectacular Amish Experience Theater F/X production of Jacob's Choice.*

Abe's Buggy Rides: http://www.abesbuggyrides.com/

From their website: *We have been in business since 1968 because we have kept our rides to what our customers want, which is private rides through the countryside in authentic Amish buggies. We have larger buggies that can hold seven average sized adults if your family is of a larger number. We look forward to serving you and hope you will allow us to make your visit to Lancaster County a better experience. And after your ride with us you will leave with a small gift to remember your visit with us.*

Amish Country, Ohio

Official Visitors Guide:

http://www.ohiosamishcountry.com/

.

Amish Heartland Tours:

http://www.amishheartlandtours.com/

From their website: *Amish Heartland Tours is the original back road tour company, offering various packages Monday thru Saturday, year around. See Amish country like never before with one of our scenic back road tours!*

Amish Country, Indiana

Official Visitors Guide: http://www.amishcountry.org/

Miller's Buggy Line Company: http://www.buggyline.com/

From their website: *We offer buggy rides, farm trips, 2-3 hour sight seeing adventures,and Step-on guide service that showcases the Shipshewana Amish area. Several of our trips will end the day or evening at an Amish Home for lunch/dinner. This is served in their home and we call it a Thrasher's Meal but you will call it* ***unforgettable****!*

I live in Pennsylvania, so I have more information about Pennsylvania Amish attractions than those in other places, but I hope this provides a good starter list for anyone who is looking to take a tour of Amish Country.

All the best,

Rachel

AMISH COUNTRY TOURS 2

CHAPTER ONE

Saturday, April 4

As Miriam and the *kinner* start tending to their afternoon chores, talking excitedly about the new bunnies, Sarah and I stand out behind the barn talking for a moment.

"John, did you buy all of this wood just to build us a rabbit hutch?" she asks curiously.

"Don't you worry; the wood and supplies I brought are all just leftovers from projects at my place. I'm not even sure if they'll be enough to finish the project. I need to get an idea of where you'd like it built and then I'll draw up a plan and calculate how much we'll need to be sure. I figured I would design it today and try to get it built on Tuesday. Maybe the boys could even help after they get home from school."

"That would be wonderful, the boys will be thrilled to help and there's *ne* school next week, it's their spring break. We'll make a whole day of it! We'll call it a *'rabbitat frolic,'* you men can build the hutch and we'll make lunch and cook that fish you brought us for dinner. That way the girls can help too," she chuckles.

"A rabbitat frolic, I like that," I smile.

She shows me to the spot where she'd like the hutch built. "I think this is a *gut* spot. It'll be close to the barn and the chicken coop with room for people to gather around without trampling my garden."

"That makes sense; I'll have Mark help me move the supplies from the wagon into the barn. Will I be in the way if I work on the plans while you're cooking this afternoon?"

"*Och, ne*. I'll find a notebook and pencil for you, just come on inside when you're ready," she smiles.

As we walk back toward the house a shiny red car pulls down the drive, stopping in front of us. A blonde-haired woman wearing big sunglasses pokes her head out of the driver's window, "I hope I'm in the right place, are you Ms. Fisher?" she asks.

"*Ya*, I'm Sarah Fisher," Sarah says looking over at me a little nervously.

The woman gets out of the car, "Hi there, my name's Melissa Callan, my brother and his family were visiting last week and took a tour of your farm? Well the whole family just raved about it and my kids and I were wondering if we could take the tour too. I know tomorrow's Easter but we drove thirty miles to see it," she smiles. "He said the tour was fifty dollars plus whatever else we buy. I would like so much for my kids to see a real farm."

"I'd be happy to give you a tour Mrs. Callan. Would you mind waiting just a few minutes? My *kinner* are just finishing up their chores."

"Would you mind if we got out and stretched our legs while we wait?" she asks.

"*Ya* go ahead," Sarah tells her.

"I'll let the *kinner* know," I tell her as I head back to the barn.

"Are those people here for a tour?" Mark asks curiously.

I chuckle, "*Ya*, they're waiting for you to finish your chores."

"I'm finished with mine, I'll hitch up the buggy," he informs me. "You could come with us this time; maybe you'll have some new ideas."

"That sounds like a *gut* idea," I smile.

I walk around to the chicken coop and let Miriam know that the *Englischers* are here, before joining Sarah out front. Apparently the *Englisch* woman is a single *mamm* of three and she's admiring Sarah's ability to manage five *kinner* on her own.

"Mark is getting the buggy ready, Miriam and the girls will be right out."

"This is such a beautiful place, my sister-in-law said it reminded her of a pretty postcard and she was right," the *Englisch* woman says looking around. "I just don't know how you do all of this; five children, canning and baking too. I just fell in love with your apple butter! You don't happen to have any more for sale do you?"

"I think I have a few more jars. I also have some pear honey made from the pears we grow and homemade banana bread if you're interested in either of those."

I'm impressed with her salesmanship for being so new to the whole tour idea.

"I'm watching my carbs, but the pear honey sounds delicious. I'll take another dozen eggs, a jar of pear honey and two jars of apple butter if you have it."

By the time she finishes conveying her order, the *kinner* have all gathered around. "I'll get everything ready for you while you take the tour. These are my *kinner*," Sarah says, pointing out each of the children and introducing them by name.

"My goodness they're adorable," the English woman marvels, "This is Trevor, Marcus and Taylor; and I'm

Melissa," she says to the *kinner*.

"I'll help Mark give the tour while you get their order ready," I assure Sarah, sensing her nervousness.

"First we'll go for a buggy ride and then you can pet the animals," Mark informs the *Englisch* woman.

"And we have some brand new bunnies too," Josh adds excitedly.

The *Englisch* children are all excited to hear about that.

"Follow me," Samuel says, leading them to the buggy.

Mark helps everyone inside as I climb in and take the reins.

***

The whole tour from start to finish lasts approximately an hour and the *Englisch* woman pays us sixty-five dollars, including the cost of the extra items she purchased. I realize that her brother had given her the price, which was probably generously based on the fact that they showed up without being invited. But it reminds me that I need to figure out what to charge in the future. For now, I'm just grateful for the blessing.

John and Mark stay behind to unload the supplies from the wagon as *mamm* and the *kinner* all come inside with me. "Okay, show me your hands if your room is clean and your afternoon chores are finished," I say to the four of them.

They all raise their hands and I go over the chore chart with them before assigning them a few enjoyable tasks. "Mary, would you and Hannah find a nice bunny or two that you can trace in one of the coloring books? You'll need to trace enough of them so that you can color one to look like each bunny with the bunny's name on it so we can have them for the tours."

"You mean like they have at the zoo where it tells about the animals?"

"*Ya* very *gut*, I think the *Englisch* children would like to know the name of the bunnies they pet."

"We could hang them on a sign and decorate it too!" she says excitedly.

"Can Samuel and I do some for the horses, *mamm*?" Josh asks.

"I don't like to color, you can make them Josh," Samuel tells him. "I want to see if I can teach Joker any more tricks, can I *mamm*?"

"*Ya* go ahead," I chuckle.

"I want to go with you," Josh pleads.

"It's okay Josh, we'll make the pictures of the horses too," Mary assures him.

The girls start getting out their coloring supplies and both boys take off for the barn as John and Mark return.

"Leave some room for John at the table girls, he's going to

design your rabbitat," I chuckle.

"What's a rabbitat John?" Mark asks.

"It's a word your *mamm* invented for rabbit-habitat," he laughs, "Pretty catchy isn't it?"

"That's so silly *mamm*," Hannah decides.

"Ooooh I want to help," Mark smiles excitedly.

"I'm glad because I'm going to need some *gut* strong men on Tuesday when we build it," John tells him, "We're going to have a whole rabbitat frolic day and since you're the oldest, you're going to be my right-hand man."

"I won't let you down," he assures him, "You already showed me how to use the hammer, I could probably even hammer all of the nails for you," he smiles enthusiastically.

"Well before you build anything, you should always have a plan with all of your measurements written down. As we work out the plan, you'll have the important task of managing our supply list. There's nothing worse than being in the middle of a job and finding out you don't have enough materials," John explains.

"I'm really *gut* at planning. You can tell me anything you need me to write down," Mark informs him, while getting some paper and pencil.

I look over at my *mamm* who hasn't even started to chop the onions in front of her, but I can tell that her eyes are already starting to water. I can't say that I blame her; it's touching to see John work with Mark and the way he just soaks up the male attention.

As everyone goes about working on their various projects, I make the cornbread batter for the stuffing. I put the first two large pans in to bake and realize what a blessing it will be to have more oven space since I'll probably need four pans of cornbread to make enough stuffing for the holiday weekend.

As soon as the last two pans of cornbread are in the oven, John carries the ham over to the *Daadi Haus* to put in *mamm*'s oven to bake before he and Mark see what other materials they can round up from Jacob's woodshop. *Mamm* rolls out her pie crusts and I make a pea salad for Monday; minus the eggs that I'll add after the *kinner* hunt them tomorrow.

After they've finished their bunny tracings and coloring the horses, Mary and Hannah take their coloring pages out to the barn so that they can color each bunny more accurately.

Mamm chuckles, "John sure made the *kinner* happy today" she smiles, pinching the edges of her pie dough around the pan. "It's easy to see God's hand in all of this."

"Ruth said the same thing. I have to admit that whatever fears I may have been hanging onto about making the right decision sure disappeared when he showed up with those rabbits and the supplies for the hutch," I chuckle. "Now I'm just excited to watch it all come together."

Mamm puts all four pies in the oven just as someone knocks on the front door.

"I'll get it," *mamm* says as I put the kettle on for coffee. I peek out the screen door and recognize Deacon Byler's buggy parked in front of the house. I step into the living room where they're standing near the door. "Happy Easter Deacon Byler, may I offer you a cup of coffee?"

"I came to speak to you about a serious matter Sarah Fisher," he says in a gruff voice, "I hear you're giving tours of your farm to *Englisch*ers," he says in an accusatory tone with a red face.

"Well ya but we only gave them a buggy ride around the property and let them pet the animals, it's harmless I assure you."

"That's what you say now but soon you will have *Englisch*ers all over our community, disrupting our lives, going wherever they please and taking pictures everywhere we go. I'll not have it and I'll be talking to the bishop about this."

"I'm sorry you feel that way, I meant *ne*-,"

"*Gut* day Sarah Fisher," he says dismissively and walks away.

Mamm and I look at one another and I can see the concern on her face. "I wonder how he found out," I sigh.

"Sarah, you've done nothing wrong, just go and talk with

the bishop like you planned. I'm sure that even Deacon Byler won't make a fuss over the holiday."

"I was planning to go on Tuesday but maybe I should try to talk to him before Deacon Byler does. The bishop's always been fond of my banana bread and I wanted to take him a loaf anyway. I think I'll go Monday and see if he won't mind discussing it in spite of the holiday."

"*Ya* I think that's a *gut* idea," she says hugging me, "Just try not to let it spoil your evening."

"Don't worry, I'm not letting him discourage me. But I'd better get started on the stuffing and the green bean casserole. Ruth and Dan will be here in an hour" I smile reassuringly.

The kettle starts to whistle. "I'll go over and baste the ham," she says, patting me on the shoulder as we head back toward the kitchen.

I wrap two pans of cornbread for Monday and put them in the fridge with half of the diced celery and onions then pull the pies from the oven. I put the half full stock pot of mashed potatoes on the stove to warm, prepare the green bean casserole and the stuffing mixture for tonight, and put both pans in the oven while I double check to make sure I haven't forgotten anything.

Mamm comes back from the *Daadi Haus* with John and Mark right behind her. She prepares three cups of coffee while John and Mark huddle at the table.

"Was that Deacon Byler's buggy *mamm*?" Mark asks curiously.

"*Ya*, it was," I say, glancing at *mamm* and then at John.

"So tell your *mamm* the *gut* news," John says, changing the subject.

"*Och* ya, well between the stuff that John brought and the materials we found in the woodshop, we're only going to need one more sheet of plywood to build the rabbitat," he smiles enthusiastically, "We've got it all planned out with measurements and everything."

"I was thinking I would stop in town and pick one up on the way over on Tuesday morning," John explains.

"Did you happen to see any smaller pieces of wood we could use to make a few signs while you were out there? We might need some paint too."

"If you could use barn red and white, I have some left over from painting the barn at my place."

"*Ya* that would be fine, *danki*," I tell him. Mark why don't you go check on your brothers and see if they need any help, you still have about thirty minutes before Ruth and Dan get here," I say.

"Okay, I wanted to visit the rabbits anyway," he says, heading out the door.

"It's none of my business but I'm guessing Deacon Byler

wasn't here to wish you a Happy Easter," John says tactfully.

"He didn't say anything to you or the *kinner* did he?" I ask, stirring the potatoes.

"*Ne*, Mark and I were coming out of the shed just as he was leaving but he doesn't strike me as the kind of man who keeps anyone guessing about his emotions."

Mamm chuckles, "You're a very perceptive man John."

"He found out about the tours somehow and says he's going to report me to the bishop."

"He probably saw the *Englisch*ers here earlier; it was bound to happen sooner or later. There will always be people that don't agree with what you're doing Sarah but that doesn't make them right."

"It's not me that I'm worried about; it's you and the *kinner* and anyone else who gets involved. I don't want you to be resented by members of the community when you're just starting to get settled here."

"Every community has people who just aren't satisfied unless they have someone to criticize; even Jesus was criticized and resented. Something like this just separates the wheat from the chaff as far as I'm concerned. I'm not worried and don't you be worried for me. I made my own decision about getting involved and I don't plan on backing down just because someone disapproves."

I study his expression as his words steep inside of me. His voice is calm but his eyes are lit with a fiery determination I've never seen before. It isn't defiance, rebellion, or even stubbornness lurking beneath his gaze, it's something else and I'm comforted by it.

Mamm's voice startles me from my thoughts, "You're a wise man too John Troyer," she says patting him on the arm. "I'm going to go take the ham out so it can rest."

"*Danki* John, your support means a lot to me."

"So what are you going to do?" he asks curiously.

"I'm going to pack up some banana bread and some goat cheese and pay a visit to bishop Graber on Monday myself."

"That's certainly a *gut* way to get his attention. I don't have much influence in the community yet but I've met the bishop, I'd be happy to come with you if you think it will help."

"As much as I would like the moral support, I think I need to do this on my own," I smile, "I have a feeling I'm going to need the practice."

He chuckles and tucks his plans for the rabbitat in his pocket. "I'll go help Miriam bring the ham over, let me know if you change your mind."

***

As Miriam and I make our way back to the house, I see a buggy coming down the drive. I take the ham inside and let

Sarah know her guests are here before stepping back outside with her to greet them. Sarah introduces me to Ruth and Dan as their son Ben joins the *kinner* in the barn to see the bunnies. Dan and I walk toward the barn and chat as the women make their way into the kitchen.

"I think we met at the frolic on Thursday," I say.

"We did, I had to help my wife open the bakery so I was a little late but I hate to miss a barn raising, it's the only chance I get to build something these days," he chuckles.

"Do you own the bakery in town by the shoe store?"

"That's us, Kauffman's Bakery. I'm a brick mason by trade and I never imagined that I would be a baker. But I started helping out on rainy days while we were courting and it just grew on me. Her parents just retired to Florida so there's *ne* turning back now."

"Courtship makes a man do crazy things sometimes," I chuckle.

"Isn't that the truth," he laughs.

Inside the barn, the *kinner* are all raving about the bunnies, telling Ben their names as he pets Midnight.

"Don't look now but I think you're about to get a new addition to the family," I tell him under my breath.

"*Daed* can I get a bunny?" Ben asks.

"We'll have to check with *mamm*, you know she's allergic to furry creatures," he smiles.

"He could still be your bunny Ben but he can live here with his friends," Mary tells him."

"But I want to name him," Ben says with a frown.

"How about if you choose a name for the one you're holding and you can visit him any time you come over?" I ask him.

"I want to name him Licorice because I love licorice and I love him," he smiles.

"Licorice it is," I chuckle.

"*Danki* for the save, he'd be asking to sleep with it every night," Dan laughs, "Hey is that your tractor and wagon?" he asks curiously.

"*Ya*, I brought some plywood and supplies for the bunny hutch we're building on Tuesday. Sarah's calling it a rabbitat frolic," I chuckle.

"Ruthie told me you've been a big help to Sarah in the past couple of weeks, do you need any help?"

"It would sure make it go a lot faster, are you interested in joining us?"

"Well I've got a gas stove and a bakery case we were going to give Sarah for the tour business. It's just taking up room at the bakery and Ruth thought it would help her to have more oven space and some way to display her baked goods. I was going to try to find someone to deliver it to her next week but if we could use your wagon, maybe we could get both projects done in one day."

"That sounds like a great idea to me; it might even encourage her a little. Deacon Byler paid her a visit today threatening to go to the bishop about the tours. She hasn't waivered from her decision but I think it upset her to run into a little opposition this early on."

"Yeah well, he's got that old-order mentality that's for sure. I can't believe he would do that on Easter weekend though."

"She was planning to go to the bishop on Tuesday but I think she's decided to go on Monday instead so that he doesn't hear about it from someone else first."

"I see it hasn't deterred you," he smiles knowingly.

"I told her I'd help her and that's what I intend to do."

"That sure sounds crazy to me," he chuckles.

Dan, the *kinner* and I join the ladies inside and wash up for dinner. The house is filled with delicious aromas and my mouth waters with one look at the spread on the table. We join in silent prayer and dig in as the *kinner* tell Dan and Ruth about the bunnies and how I happened upon them. Ben saves the day by telling Ruth about his bunny and thankfully, I'm out of the spotlight.

As I look around the table, I can't help but notice Sarah's beautiful smile and how her eyes light up when she's just happily enjoying the moment, forgetting her troubles and the responsibility of taking care of everyone else. It's so infectious that a man could devote his life to provoking that kind of joy in her on a daily basis and never feel cheated. Miriam catches me staring with a smile glued to my face. I grab another spoonful of stuffing to distract myself.

As we talk around the table, eating our fill, Dan tells everyone about our plan for Tuesday. "I'll bring Ben here with me so he can spend a little time with the boys."

"I'm still going to help right John?" Mark asks.

"You're still my right hand man but since Dan's a little taller, he can help us with those big sheets of plywood," I assure him.

"Well it sounds like lots of fun," Ruth smiles, "I wish I could come but somebody's got to run the bakery."

"Maybe I could help you Aunt Ruthie," Mary offers, "We don't have school for a whole week."

"Personally I would love it but your mom might need you here," Ruth says, not wanting to put her on the spot.

"*Mamm* and I can manage, Mary can help you at the bakery if you want," Sarah smiles.

"What about me?" Hannah asks curiously.

Ruth looks at Sarah and gives her a little nod indicating that Hannah can go too if Sarah agrees.

"Do you want to go to the bakery with Ruth and Mary or stay here with *mamm* and me?" Sarah asks curiously.

"I wanna go to the bakery!" she smiles.

"Well *mamm* I guess it's just you, me and the boys on Tuesday," Sarah chuckles.

We all laugh and talk as we enjoy the rest of the meal and I can't help but notice how *gut* it feels. When I'm at dinner with family in Hopkinsville, I always feel like something's missing and for the past several years, I blamed that empty feeling on Elizabeth's death but I've never felt that way here, not once.

***

After dessert, *mamm* decides to help Mary wash dishes while Ben helps the rest of the *kinner* tend to their night time chores. The rest of us go out on the front porch to enjoy the night air. Ruth and Dan settle in the porch swing while John and I sit back in the rocking chairs.

"I hear you had a visit from Deacon Byler today," Dan says casually.

"*Ya*, I pretty much expected him to disapprove of me giving the tours, I just didn't expect him to do it so confrontationally or so soon," I sigh.

"He came today?" Ruth asks, disbelieving.

“About an hour before you guys got here,” John explains, “He threatened to go to the bishop.”

“I don’t think you have anything to fear from Bishop Graber, he’s a *gut* man and he’s a lot more open minded than Deacon Byler,” Dan adds.

“I know, I just prefer to talk to him before anyone else does. I don’t want him to think I intentionally went behind anyone’s back. The *Englisch*er who came today was the sister of the family I gave the original tour to. I didn’t tell them to come but they drove thirty miles to get here. It didn’t seem right to turn them away.”

“I understand if you feel a little discouraged after being confronted like that but the fact that you’re already getting some interest is definitely a *gut* sign,” Ruth says encouragingly.

“I hope this goes without saying Sarah but Ruth and I will stand by you even if Deacon Byler tries to make trouble for you. He’s stuck in that old-order mindset and most of the community isn’t going to support that either.” Dan assures me.

“You already know where I stand,” John says reassuringly.

“Well I sure hope it doesn’t come to that, but I’m blessed to have all of you,” I smile fondly.

The *kinner* come looking for us on the porch, “*Mamm* do you want to come and meet Licorice?” Ben asks Ruth, “Mary says the bunnies have to go to sleep soon.”

"I know a little boy that needs to go to sleep soon too if you want to hunt Easter eggs at *mammi*'s tomorrow," she says, straightening his hair. "I guess we should get going, I still have lots to do before we leave in the morning," Ruth explains.

"My *kinner* all need to take their baths and get ready for bed too," I say looking them over.

"C'mon, guys, I'll say goodnight to Licorice while I'm at it," Ruth chuckles.

We all say our goodbyes as the men firm up their arrangements for Tuesday. I send the *kinner* upstairs to take their baths and stand outside to say goodnight to John.

"I need to get on back to the house and do a few chores myself but I promised to help hide Easter eggs," he chuckles.

"How about hiding one for each of the *kinner* and we'll take care of the rest, I don't want to keep you," I chuckle.

"*Danki*, I have a feeling they'd suspect if I didn't," he smiles, following me back into the kitchen.

I go inside and pull five eggs and the banana bread I set aside for him to take home, and then walk outside with him as he chooses his hiding places. "I really enjoyed being here all afternoon, and dinner was great. *Danki* for having me," he says, leaning over my shoulder to place an egg on the window sill. He holds my gaze for a moment and I'm curious to know what he's thinking. "You're not going to tell where all of my eggs are hidden are you?" he laughs.

"Well John Troyer, I can't believe you would ask me such a thing," I giggle.

"I don't know," he smiles, eyeing me suspiciously, "Something tells me you'd be too worried about letting them rot if they're not found."

"Okay that might actually be true but I assure you, those *kinner* will not stop until the last egg is accounted for without any prompting from me," I laugh.

"Just be sure to save some deviled eggs for me tomorrow," he chuckles.

"That won't be a problem, trust me."

"Great, then I guess I'll see you when I get back from Hopkinsville Monday morning." He says, climbing onto his tractor.

"*Gut* night John," I smile.

CHAPTER TWO

Monday, April 6

Easter Sunday with the Zook family was enjoyed by the whole family. The *kinner* hunted Easter eggs soon after they arrived. And as expected, the bunnies were a big hit with their three and five year old daughters. The *kinner* spent most of the afternoon playing outside with Thomas Zook while *Mamm*, Catherine Zook and I spent most of the day visiting and putting the finishing touches on the food we had prepared.

It was relaxing to have a day set aside to celebrate the resurrection of our Lord with friends and family. I didn't want to spoil the happy occasion by talking about Deacon Byler's visit, but I did tell them about doing the tour business and they encouraged me in my decision. Aside from Ruth, Dan, John and bishop Graber, I suppose the Zooks' opinion is the only other one that really matters to me.

Today, while most of the community is still in holiday

mode, my mind is fixed on intercepting the seeds of ill will that I believe Deacon Byler intends to plant in the bishop's mind. He may still think of me as a twelve year old girl who cowers at the very sound of his voice, but I'm through acting like one. Once the morning chores are finished and everyone's had breakfast, I decide that it's time to head for Bishop Graber's house.

Though I still haven't told the *kinner* of Deacon Byler's unpleasant visit, they all know that I'm on my way to get permission for the business.

"Want me to go with you *mamm*? I can tell him all about the tours?" Mark asks.

I kiss him on the forehead, "I need to do this on my own today liebchen; just pray that God's will be done."

"Okay," he sighs.

"I'll be back in a few hours," I assure him, clicking the reigns.

As I pull out of the drive, I'm a bundle of nerves, anxious and even afraid of what the bishop might say. As the horse's hooves clop against the road, I think about my *kinner* and our home. I think about how devastated they would be to have to leave the only home they've ever known, the place that holds every memory they've ever had.

I think about how impossible it would be for a plain woman who makes four or five quilts a year to ever be able to buy another place for them with room for them to run and play and to grow a garden or ride a horse.

By the time I reach the turn-off to Bishop Graber's farm, some twenty minutes later, my fears are overcome by my determination and my anxiousness quelled by my sense of duty to my family.

As I turn onto the long drive that leads to the house, I keep repeating a verse in my head from Philippians 4:13 which says: 'I can do all things through Christ which strengtheneth me.' It's the same verse that I used to recite to myself so that I could drag myself out of bed in the days immediately following Jacob's death and it is the verse that will give me the courage that I need today.

I park the buggy in front of the barn, climb out and take a moment to gather my courage before walking up to the house. Just as I am about to ring the doorbell, I remember the banana bread and goat cheese I brought for the occasion and run back to get it. As I turn to head for the door again, Bishop Graber steps out from inside the barn.

"Sarah Fisher is that you?" he asks putting on his glasses.

"*Ya*, Bishop Graber, Happy Easter," I smile nervously, "I brought you some banana bread and goat cheese for the holiday."

"I was just checking on a foal. Come on inside the house and have some tea. Mrs. Graber, Ms. Helmut and my granddaughter Abby are all inside; they'll be delighted to see you."

"Actually Bishop Graber, I was wondering if I might speak with you for a moment first if you aren't too busy."

I don't know what possesses me to just plunge right into the discussion except that I can't imagine it would be polite to have the conversation in front of his guests.

"I suppose the tea can wait, what's on your mind?" he asks, closing the barn door.

"I'm sorry to bother you with my problems on the holiday weekend but I didn't want you to hear it from anyone else before we had a chance to speak."

As we walk around the property, I tell him everything, from standing in the pantry wondering how I'm going to support my family, to giving the first tour and the *kinner*'s enthusiasm. I tell him about Mark reading the brochures for the tours in Marion. About praying for guidance and how God seems to be answering those prayers in providing a means for some of the ideas we've had for the tours. I tell him how the first tour led to the most recent tour on Saturday and my plans to come to him now that I've decided that I want to pursue the idea. By the time I'm finished, I feel like a weight has been lifted from my shoulders, *ne* matter the outcome.

"The reason I came to you today instead of waiting is because Deacon Byler came by to express his disapproval of the tour we gave on Saturday and I wanted you to hear it from me first. I'm sorry if I'm wrong in doing so, I'm just concerned for my family. I don't want to be a burden to the community or for my *kinner* to lose the only home they've ever known." I try to fight the tears welling in my eyes.

"There, there," he says offering me his handkerchief. "You can always come to me, think nothing of it," he says, trying to put me at ease.

"I don't think I've violated the *Ordnung,* Bishop Graber, I love my community and I didn't want you to think that I was trying to hide it from you but I can't support my family indefinitely on four or five quilts a year."

"These are difficult times for many families. We've been taught to be self-sufficient and to live off of the land for generations but as Amish communities grow and affordable land becomes scarce, I'm afraid we're going to have to open our minds to other sources of income to keep our communities thriving. I know many of the old-order Amish are opposed to the idea of tourism but I don't see how we can avoid it much longer."

"Then you don't disapprove of making a living off of the curiosities of the *Englisch*?"

"We're all curious. Why there are museums all over the world and libraries full of history books designed to give people a glimpse into other eras and other cultures. Even the Bible is studied for this purpose. If the children of Israel were giving a tour, I would like to go and see the manna fall from Heaven, the Ark of the Covenant and even the way the women prepared a meal in the hot, dry desert. It's just human nature and the communities who refuse to participate may avoid it for a while but it's impossible to escape entirely."

He stops walking as we approach the house and turns to face me.

"It's never easy being the first one to initiate change and I'm sure there will be some criticism but there are already Amish communities who thrive on tourism and based on the ideas you've proposed, I don't see anything wrong with it. Who knows, it might even help bring paying customers to other Amish businesses in the community."

"Bishop Graber, I can't tell you how much it means to me and my family to have your blessing," I sigh with relief.

"I'll be curious to see how things progress, now come inside and have a cup of tea before your journey home," he smiles.

We go inside and sit at the dining room table to enjoy our tea and a slice of banana bread. Ms. Helmut and the bishop rave over my recipe as we chat about how the *kinner* are doing and catch up on the latest news in their lives. As I make my way home, giving thanks to God for His blessings, I feel a strange sense of independence that I wasn't quite convinced I was capable of before today.

By the time I arrive at the house, John's tractor is there and the *kinner* are all playing in a clearing between two trees on the far side of the property. I pull into the barn to unhitch the horses when he comes in to help me.

"I hope you don't mind, I brought some metal stakes and some horseshoes for the *kinner*. I told them if you didn't like the location we chose, we would move it."

"I think the location is fine, it's out of the way and still close enough to the house that I can keep an eye on them," I say, trying to contain my excitement.

"Are you going to tell me how the meeting went or just keep me in suspense all day?" he chuckles.

Although keeping him in suspense sounds like fun, I'm bursting at the seams to tell someone. "He gave me his blessing!" I giggle, excitedly.

He puts his arms around me, picks me up and spins me around before letting my feet touch the ground, "That's wonderful, I'm so happy for you!" he says with a big smile.

I feel so small in his arms and I'm almost stunned by his reaction, but it feels so *gut* to see his joy. I can sense the same overwhelming relief in him that I'm feeling myself and it only confirms that he was worried for me. I look up at his face for a moment and smile. "Be sure to bring your appetite to dinner, I think we need to celebrate."

"*Och*! I brought a couple of surprises I think you'll enjoy," he smiles.

"You mean besides the turkey and the horseshoes?" I chuckle.

"Well the horseshoes were just lying around at my brother's place in Hopkinsville but I did find a leftover piece of plywood there too and the turkey wasn't exactly a surprise. I've sworn your *mamm* to secrecy though so don't even try to get it out of her," he smiles.

"I'm grateful for your generosity John Troyer," I smile.

"I'm just resourceful," he blushes modestly, "And a terrible cook," he laughs.

"How are you at horseshoes?" I goad.

"I thought I was pretty *gut* but I think Mary has me beat," he sighs.

"Maybe she'll give you a chance to redeem yourself later," I chuckle, "I'd better get inside and make some lunch, we're just having ham sandwiches and leftovers but you're *wilkom* to stay."

"If you're sure it's *ne* trouble."

"I'm sure," I smile. "I'll call everyone when it's ready."

Inside, the house smells of fresh baked bread and *Mamm* is sitting at the table, reading her Bible with a cup of coffee.

"Hi *mamm*," I say, kissing her cheek.

"It must've gone well with the bishop," she smiles casually.

“You’ve always read me like a book,” I chuckle. “What’s this? I ask, eyeing the picnic basket on the kitchen counter.

“I thought that it was such a beautiful day outside that you might want to have lunch outdoors under the trees where the *kinner* are playing, maybe we could even join them in a game of horseshoes.”

“I was going to make some more deviled eggs and some fresh iced tea for tonight.”

“Mary and I made two gallons of tea, filled two dozen eggs besides the ones we put in the pea salad and baked four loaves of bread so that you would have enough for tomorrow too…she’s practicing for the bakery,” she chuckles. “The turkey won’t need to go into the oven until about 2:00 p.m. Why not take the next couple of hours to enjoy the outdoors and tonight, we’ll feast and celebrate the new beginning,” she smiles, closing her Bible.

“You managed to do all of that while I was gone?”

“You forget that I’ve been raising a family most of my life,” she says, looking over her reading glasses at me.”

“I guess we’d better pack some sandwiches then,” I smile.

Mamm slices a loaf of bread, while I dress the sandwiches in true assembly line fashion. We pack half of the eggs, along with some pickled vegetables and the box of Easter cookies that Catherine Zook baked for us. I dump the ice into a cooler and grab the *kinner*’s wagon to haul it all so that we can surprise everyone. *Mamm* grabs the picnic blanket and off we go across the lawn. By the time we get about seventy feet from where the *kinner* are playing, Samuel is onto us.

"We're having a picnic!" he yells excitedly as the other *kinner* join in, cheering excitedly.

John comes over and grabs the wagon handle, "I would have helped you carry everything," he chuckles as the wagon bobs and jostles over the grass.

"We wanted to surprise everyone," I laugh, "Besides, *mamm*'s the horseshoe champ in the family and we couldn't let her title go undefended.

"Great, there's nothing like spending the day getting beat by a bunch of girls," he chuckles.

We all laugh except for Hannah who does her best to console him, "You just need to practice but you can come over whenever you want and we'll teach you," she smiles innocently.

"Is that so?" he says, swooping her into the air over his head. She giggles until he puts her down.

"I wanna go next!" Josh chimes in.

He gives Josh a turn and then Samuel, while Mark helps me spread out the blanket. *Mamm* and Mary lay out the food while I fill plastic cups with tea, as everyone settles down.

We enjoy our lunch in the shade under the willow tree as

John raves about the homemade bread and deviled eggs. When the sandwiches are gone, he teases Josh about eating all of the cookies and takes off running with the entire box. The *kinner* chase after him and he makes a *gut* start but he's *ne* match for cookie-crazed *kinner*; ambushing him from five different directions.

They tackle him to the ground in a heap of giggling laughter as mom and I watch the scene unfold. How he managed to save the box of cookies from scattering across the lawn in the struggle, I'll never know. Mark commandeers the cookies and the rest of the *kinner* huddle around him as John catches his breath and joins us on the blanket.

"You think they're plotting against me?" he asks as they whisper amongst themselves.

"Don't worry we've still got pie at the house if this doesn't go well for you," *mamm* assures him.

Mary makes the announcement, "Normally you're only supposed to get two cookies for dessert but we can each have three because there are 24 cookies and there are eight people," she explains diplomatically.

"Eight times three is twenty four," Samuel informs him.

John looks at me with a curious smile, as I realize the underlying motive of their delegations.

"Can we *mamm*?" Josh asks.

My *kinner* are generally hard workers and I know they'll burn off the extra sugar between chores and playing outside. "Since the bishop has given us his blessing for the tour business, I guess we could call this is a three-cookie occasion," I announce excitedly.

"I knew you could do it *mamm*," Mark says hugging me and I have to admit that I feel pretty satisfied with myself for facing my fears to forge a future for my family.

The *kinner* cheer excitedly as Mary passes the cookies around. I nibble on a cookie and look around feeling so blessed for what we have and the *gut* people that God has put in our lives to share it with.

We spend the next hour or so tossing horseshoes and enjoying one another's company as John teaches Josh and *mamm* teaches Hannah to throw in a game of doubles. I don't know what it is about my *mamm* and horseshoes but she really is tough to beat and today is *ne* exception.

"It's okay John, you'll get better," Hannah assures him putting her tiny arm around John's broad shoulder to comfort him.

Mamm and I chuckle as we pack up the remains of the picnic. John says goodbye to the *kinner* to tend to his animals at home, promising to be back in time for dinner.

"They really are fond of him," I say to *mamm* as we stroll along behind the *kinner* toward the house.

"I'd say we're all pretty fond of him," she smiles.

"I see you didn't let that stop you from winning," I tease.

"*Och ne*, it keeps a man humble," she laughs.

CHAPTER THREE

As I tend to the horses and the pig corral, I find my thoughts drifting to Sarah and how *gut* she felt in my arms today. I didn't intend to sweep her off of her feet when I heard the news, nor did I mean to embarrass her. I was just caught up in the moment, overwhelmed with relief and intoxicated by her beautiful smile. The more time I spend with her, the harder it is to keep my distance, even while she wears the dress of mourning.

Though I would never do anything to disgrace her, it's a challenge not to tell her how I feel – let alone hide the fact that I want to hold her in my arms and to kiss her lips. When I'm with her I'm whole again and it's like I can feel the Lord drawing us together. It's as if He has prepared her especially for me, uniquely equipped with the strengths and qualities needed to tear down the walls around my heart. From her cooking, to her faithful determination, to her fine *kinner* and her first-hand experience with overcoming the grief of losing a spouse. Even just the fact that she's here, in Hope Landing, the place where I found my new home, is a miracle in itself.

I'm even more confounded that the things she needs seem to just fall into my lap; from the ride home in the rain and fixing her buggy, to the turkey, the bunnies and just enough supplies to build the rabbitat. I chuckle to myself at the thought. I remember Deacon Wyse's exact words to me last Sunday about the joys God has in store for me, 'He wants you to know that it waits for you even now.' *Ya*, God is certainly drawing us together and the excitement I feel when I'm with her is only further proof of that.

I think about the various women that friends and family have introduced me to or tried to encourage me to spend time with back in Hopkinsville in the last few years. I've never felt the least little romantic spark for any of them, which even had me questioning my own brokenness. I'm pretty sure that even my brothers and their wives have given up on the idea of me ever getting married again. And I can't say that I blame them.

I pull the tractor back around to the barn just as I spot someone coming down the drive. I sigh discontentedly as I recognize the Old-Order style buggy, tacked all in black with roll-up side curtains, made of heavy canvas instead of doors. I wait patiently as the short, aging man with the rotund belly and wire-rimmed glasses crawls out of the buggy and approaches me.

"Are you John Troyer?"

"*Ya*, I am."

"Deacon Amos Byler, pleased to meet you," he says, offering his hand.

I shake his hand, curious as to why he's here.

"I heard you had bought the old Schwartz farm and I wanted to stop by to say hello. I thought we would meet at church services but I haven't seen you there. I hope you had a *gut* holiday," he says in a slightly condemning tone.

"*Ya* well I still have a few things to tend to in Hopkinsville so I've been attending church services there with my family."

"Ah, ya I see. It's not easy moving away from a place where you have spent most of your life. I've been here for twenty years but I still remember when my wife and I first came. It was the Deacon Lapp who became my first real friend and helped me to become established here. Of course he's passed on now but I know how difficult it can be to feel like an outsider."

"I've been blessed to have made a few friends already and I'm gradually getting to know the rest of the folks in the community. It takes time."

"*Ya* well I hope you will choose your friends wisely. I was lucky to have met the deacon. I hate to imagine what might have become of my soul if I had fallen under the wrong influence when I was so eager to establish myself in a new community," he says, shaking his head warily, "We are all known by the company we keep."

"I'll definitely keep that in mind Deacon Byler and *danki* for stopping by to *wilkom* me," I say dubiously, shaking his hand again.

"Feel free to call on me if you need me to make some introductions for you," he smiles, getting back into his buggy.

I bite my tongue and politely wave goodbye as he drives away.

I don't want to be disrespectful but I moved here almost four months ago and I know that it's probably *ne* coincidence that today is the first time he's bothered to say hello. If he saw my tractor at Sarah's it wouldn't take much to figure out who it belonged to. Either way, I resent the implication that I'm associating with the wrong people and what I believe to be the real motive for his visit.

Maybe Sarah has more serious opposition than I had originally thought. But it only strengthens my resolve to stand by her and my burning conviction to protect her from anyone who tries to hurt her or her standing in the community.

CHAPTER FOUR

Mamm and Hannah set the table for dinner. While Mark, Samuel and Josh groom and work the horses, since they'll be too busy with the rabbitat frolic to do it tomorrow.

"If we don't need anything else for tonight, I think I'll rest my feet," *mamm* smiles.

"Turkey, stuffing, sweet potato casserole and mulberry pie, I think that covers everything except for the spinach salad," I assure her. She has done quite a bit today and I can tell she's tired. "Why don't you go lie back on the couch for 30 or 40 minutes, I'll wake you when John arrives. You've had a long day."

Hannah helps her *mammi* to the couch and then I send her out to tell the boys to be quiet if they come in to wash up for dinner before John arrives.

I take the turkey out of the oven to let it rest, while I bake the sweet potato casserole and the pan of stuffing I prepared

Saturday. Mary prepares a large bowl of fresh spinach with chopped eggs, dried cranberries, toasted walnuts and goat cheese and I make the salad dressing.

"Which of *mammi*'s pies are we having tonight, the mulberry pie or the cheesecake?" she asks.

"I think we'll have the mulberry tonight; the cheesecake will go better with the fish tomorrow."

"Do you want me to whip the cream?" she asks.

"More practice for the bakery?" I chuckle.

"I can't help it, I'm so excited," she smiles.

"Take it out on the back porch so you don't disturb *mammi* and do it like I showed you so that you don't splatter it everywhere."

I smile to myself as she fills the bowl, grabs the whisk and goes outside. The bakery has always been a *gut* living for Ruth and her family and it wouldn't bother me in the least if either of my daughters chose to follow in her footsteps. I'm just thankful for Ruth's friendship and the opportunity for them to be mentored by her.

***

I arrive at Sarah's for dinner as the *kinner* are all chatting in front of the barn. "Hey, what's everyone doing?" I ask curiously.

"We're waiting until you get here to wash our hands," Hannah says.

"I see, well I'm here now so I think it's safe. See if you can do it without running through the house," I chuckle.

"I'll go wake *mammi*," Mary says, taking Hannah inside.

"Really we were just having a business meeting," Mark assures me following behind her.

"I hope you're still going to show us what's in the black box after dinner," Samuel adds.

"Me too," Josh says, trailing behind him.

I chuckle again, happy to see that they're excited about the surprise I promised them after dinner. I step inside the kitchen to find Sarah just taking a pan of stuffing out of the stove.

"Hi John," she smiles, "Your timing is perfect."

"Mmmm, it smells wonderful in here. I don't know how you feel about wine but my brother loved the banana bread you sent back with me and thought you might want to try the blackberry wine that he makes, it's really *gut*."

"I haven't had a glass of wine in a long time. This is the perfect night for it, *danki*," she says. "My *daed* used to make a wine with honey when I was growing up."

"I've never made it myself; my brother's neighbor got him interested in it a few years ago and he's taken up the hobby.

He's tried using different fruits but I think the blackberry is the best. Do you want to have it with dinner or after?"

"Let's have it with dessert, it'll be a nice relaxing end to our meal. I'll put it in the freezer to chill a bit."

"What's this I hear about wine?" Miriam asks, joining us in the kitchen.

"John's brother sent us a half-gallon jug of homemade blackberry wine," I smile, "I thought we would have it with dessert."

"You come from a *gut* family John Troyer," she smiles.

"I wasn't sure you would approve but maybe I should have him teach me how he makes it."

We all laugh as everyone gathers merrily around the table. We bow our heads in prayer before everyone digs in, chatting about the day and more ideas for the tours as I carve the turkey.

"I was thinking we could make a hay slide kind of like the one they had at the autumn festival a couple of years ago. It was lots of fun and it wouldn't take much to build it at all," Mark says.

"Wow, that's a really *gut* idea," I smile, "I can get all the hay we need from one of my brothers, he grows it and what he doesn't use he usually trades out with family and friends. In the winter time, you could even use it as a snow slide."

"That would be so cool!" Samuel agrees.

"*Ne* Samuel, that doesn't sound cool," she pauses, "That sounds freezing cold!" Sarah chuckles, "It's a wonderful idea."

"You're silly *mamm*," Hannah giggles as we all laugh.

"I'll bring back a load of bales each time I come back from Hopkinsville until we have enough. There's so much you can do with them for something like this, whether you use it to feed the animals or just use it for decoration, it'll come in handy."

"We went to a maze of hay one time, remember *mamm*?" Josh adds.

"*Ya* I remember, you were only three," she smiles, "A small hay maze might not be a bad idea for toddlers."

"I've been keeping a list of ideas for when we need them," Mark says, "There's nothing worse than having a great idea and not being able to remember it later," he sighs.

"*Gut* thinking Mark," I assure him, patting his shoulder.

Sarah looks at me and smiles and I have to remind myself not to gaze upon her too long. "This turkey is delicious, everything is…I even love the cranberries in the salad." I tell her.

She looks at Miriam and smiles knowingly. "*Danki*, I'm glad you like it."

"She has a secret way of cooking turkey," Mary informs me.

"It's not really a secret it's just a little unusual. My *Englisch* friend, the one with the store where I get my quilt orders from, she told me about it and I've been roasting poultry that way ever since."

"Okay, now I'm curious," I chuckle, "I don't know a lot about cooking but I don't even remember my *mamm*'s turkey being this moist and flavorful," I smile.

"I just mix my seasonings and push them up under the skin and then rub the whole bird in mayonnaise before I put it in the oven," she smiles, "After that, I don't even baste it or anything."

"Well your secret's safe with me but I might just have to bag a couple more turkeys for you this year," I chuckle.

"Ooooh, can I come? I've never been hunting," Mark says excitedly.

"Me too, I wanna go," Samuel adds.

"Well your *mamm* and I will have to discuss it first, but you can come with me to check on the pigs some time this week. They've been making themselves comfortable in the corral and it won't be long now."

"Why do you have to wait so long if they're already coming into it?" Samuel asks.

"Because I want to catch them all inside at the same time instead of just one or two. I'm letting them get used to the place and think it's safe. Some of them are too smart to go inside at first."

"Ohhhh," Samuel says.

"How do you lock them in once they're all inside?" Mary asks.

"I'll put out a nice feast for them and set the trigger. When they get ready to leave, the door will slide down and they'll be trapped inside," I explain.

"Then you'll have bacon!" Mark laughs.

"*Ya*, lot's of bacon for everyone," I chuckle, smiling at *mamm* and Sarah.

"I love bacon," Hannah says.

"Me too," Samuel agrees.

"Me five!" Josh smiles.

When we finish dinner, the *kinner* clear the table while Miriam pours three glasses of wine and Sarah serves the mulberry pie with whipped cream. I don't think I've ever had a more satisfying meal, not just because of the delicious food but because of the loving hands that prepared it and the fact that I helped provide for it. I feel a warm sense of satisfaction as I look at the happy faces around the table and as my eyes meet Sarah's I know that she does too.

"The wine is *gut* John, not too sweet and not too strong," Miriam says, taking another sip.

"It really is, be sure to thank your brother for us."

"Are you going to show us what's in the black box after you eat your pie?" Hannah asks curiously.

"*Och* ya, but I might have to sneak over there and eat a few bites of yours first – it's so yummy!" I tease.

She squeals and puts a big bite in her mouth as Josh does the same. Miriam, Sarah and I chuckle. "Don't forget how much he loves pie," Mary adds.

"And cookies," Josh laughs.

I start making an 'mmm, mmm' sound as I eat the last two bites on my plate and the *kinner* follow along as Miriam and Sarah giggle at us.

When the pie is gone, Sarah and Mary start on the dishes as everyone else tends to their chores. I slip out to the wagon to retrieve the black box that they've been curious about all day and take it out to the front porch to get everything set up. When Miriam finishes with Josh and Hannah in the chicken coop, she joins me with the jug of wine and refills our glasses.

"I sent Hannah in to help with the dishes and told the boys not to disturb us until we called for everyone," she smiles, sitting on the porch swing, and watches as I position the telescope and focus the lens.

"*Danki* John, for breathing a little life back into my family these past couple of weeks."

"It's funny that you should say that Miriam because that's exactly what you've all done for me," I chuckle, squinting into the eyepiece. "Hunting and fishing and just about everything I do lately has been a little more satisfying knowing that there's a purpose behind it greater than myself." I look over at her trying to be careful in what I say. "I just hope I'm not overstepping my boundaries."

"*Och ne* and I think your timing has been perfect," she smiles.

I take another sip of wine, wondering if she's referring to Sarah too but I don't want to let on in case she would be offended by my future plans to court her. It seems inappropriate to mention before she's even out of morning, "I'll have to take your word for it," I smile, sitting back in the rocker behind me.

"I've always found that God begins making preparations long before He puts a plan into motion…that includes preparing the hearts and minds of the people involved," she smiles. "Now are you going to give an old woman her first look into this contraption of yours?" she chuckles.

"Come on over and take a look," I say.

She steps over and peers through the lens as I show her how to adjust the focus. "*Och*, it's wonderful, I can see clear to the fields out behind the house across the main road," she marvels. "How did you ever find such a thing?" she asks, moving it slightly to look around.

"It's called a telescope, I took it in trade for some engine work I did a couple of years ago. My family back in Hopkinsville has spent hours looking through it. When it gets dark in a few minutes, you'll be able to see the moon and stars."

"It's like a scope on a rifle only you can see much further," she smiles.

"Why Miriam, I didn't know you had ever used a rifle," I chuckle.

"*Ya* my *daed* taught me when I was a girl. I was the oldest so I used to go hunting with him sometimes. When Sarah was little, I once used my husband's rifle to shoot a coyote on our property when he was gone."

"Maybe that explains why you're such a *gut* shot at horseshoes," I smile. "Take your time enjoying the view, I'm going to go get a couple of extra chairs and see if Sarah and the *kinner* are ready to join us."

I go into the kitchen where Sarah is putting away the clean dishes. "We're almost done," she says, as I grab the stack of plates from the counter.

I walk them over to where she's standing, putting away the salad bowl. She turns around just as I reach to put the plates on the shelf behind her. "I thought I'd grab a few chairs on our way out to the porch," I explain, looking into her eyes.

"*Danki*," she says just as Mary enters the room from the pantry, "I'll tell the boys and we'll be right out," she smiles, averting her gaze.

I grab two chairs from the dining table as Mary follows behind with another. Miriam's still busy looking through the telescope as she asks, "*Och* is that what was in the box?"

The rest of the *kinner* come galloping onto the porch with Sarah following behind. Miriam steps away from the telescope and refills our wine glasses as I get everyone situated. Then I explain to everyone how the telescope works.

She sits on the swing with Josh and Hannah while Mark, Mary and Samuel sit in the extra chairs. Sarah sits in the rocker next to mine as I show them how to focus and to move it around.

I decide to let the little ones go first so that I can sit them on my knee and help them point and focus while the others observe. They both giggle as they wonder at the moon and the stars. By the time it's Samuel's turn he knows exactly how to operate everything.

Miriam, Sarah and I chat and sip our wine as we watch the *kinner* take turns peering into the sky. Sarah takes a turn after the *kinner* have all gone and I can tell she's fascinated too. I can see the little girl in her as she slowly moves and observes the night sky with an awestruck face.

"Wow, it's so exciting to get a chance too see a part of God's amazing creation that we never get to see so closely. The colors are beautiful. What a wonderful surprise John."

"*Ya* John this is so cool!" Mark says excitedly.

As we talk about the wonders in the sky for the next hour or so, the *kinner* all take turns marveling at the stars while I look around at their seven happy faces, enjoying my own private Heaven right here on the ground.

CHAPTER FIVE

Tuesday, April 7

Today feels like the first day of a new life for my family and me. As I put on my kapp and apron, I thank God for the new beginning and for the people who have offered to support us in getting the tour business off the ground. I wonder if some of the businesses in town would allow me to put up a small sign.

At breakfast, I tell everyone about my idea.

"I know Ruthie will and probably the shoe store and the restaurant will too," Mary says.

"I bet Mr. Rupp will let us put a sign up at the butcher shop. A lot of *Englisch* from town go there too," Mark adds.

"What about Yoder's market? Lots of *Englisch* go there too," Samuel chimes in.

"*Ya*, I should probably pay a visit to Mrs. Yoder anyway to see how she's doing after her surgery," I smile, "Those are all *gut* places to start, now we just need to figure out what the signs should say."

"You should call Natalie. I'm sure she and her husband would put up signs there for you and it's not such a long drive for the *Englisch* in a car. How are you coming on her latest quilt order?"

"It's not due until August so I should be fine. That's a *gut* idea, maybe I'll give her a call later."

"I can talk to Aunt Ruthie today and we can work on some ideas for the signs after dinner tonight. They have lots of signs for the bakery," Mary says.

"Yeah we can ask John and Dan at lunch. I'll write down our ideas," Mark agrees.

"Are you going into town today?" *mamm* asks.

"Actually John is picking up the girls and meeting Dan at the bakery this morning and they're coming back together with the bakery case and Ben. Then they'll work on the rabbitat and John will go get the stove when he picks up the girls to bring them home. You and I will probably be busy making room for everything, cooking and cleaning so I thought we'd all just go into town together tomorrow."

"*Ya mamm*, maybe we can even put up the signs tomorrow," Mark says.

"We could break up into three teams and each team can put

up a few signs in different businesses. That would give us nine signs, not counting the bakery, and it wouldn't even take very long," Mary adds.

"We could probably get lots of business from nine signs," Samuel agrees.

"We'll make one *gut* sign and take it to the post office to copy on the machine. So let's plan to have it ready before we leave tomorrow. Maybe we'll even get some business by this Saturday."

The *kinner* all cheer happily as I put my plate in the sink and start the dishwater. *Mamm* grabs her egg basket just as I hear the tractor pulling down the drive. "John's here; finish your breakfast girls," I tell them.

The boys clear the table and head outside to start their chores as John helps the girls into the wagon. *Mamm* takes Josh to the chicken coop as I wave goodbye and head back into the kitchen to finish the dishes. She and Josh bring the eggs in to wash before heading back outside to pick some zucchini from the garden. I check the leftovers and premade items in the fridge to see what needs to be used up and what we still need to prepare for lunch and dinner.

There's only enough stuffing and sweet potato casserole left for one hearty serving, which I decide to send home with John tonight. I grab a divided plastic container and empty both pans into it along with some turkey meat and two deviled egg halves before putting it back in the fridge.

With the rest of the deboned turkey, ham and the loaf of bread that *mamm* made, I have enough for the sandwiches at lunch time. I'll serve them with the pea salad I didn't use last night, the rest of the salad mixture, the rest of the pickled beets, and the remaining deviled eggs which should make for a hearty meal. There's enough Easter cake left for the boys and two slices of *mamm*'s peach pie for Dan and John to have as an afternoon snack.

That leaves the fish I put in the fridge to thaw last night, the leftover pot of mashed potatoes and *Mamm*'s cheesecake for dinner. I think I'll fry some fresh, sliced zucchini to go with it.

Sine I expect us to be in town half of the day tomorrow, I decide to take a pot roast out of the freezer to thaw. That will give me an excuse to use up the rest of the carrots and celery in the fridge. I'll add a jar of new potatoes I canned last season and make a pan of cornbread to go with it. Maybe I'll make two pans so that we'll have some for tonight too. Leftover cornbread is never wasted in my house.

By tomorrow night, my fridge will be emptied out and it'll be time to start the whole process all over again. I chuckle to myself as *Mamm* and Josh return from the garden with a basket full of zucchini.

"We got a lot of zucchini," Josh smiles proudly, "*Mamm* says it wants to take over the garden but we won't let it."

"*Danki*, this is just what I need for dinner tonight."

"Can I go say hello to the bunnies now?" he asks.

"Go see if your brothers need any help with chores first and then you can all visit the bunnies when Ben gets here."

He heads outside while *mamm* pours us both another cup of coffee and sits down at the table.

"Are you feeling alright this morning *mamm*?" I ask.

"I'm okay, just a little tired from yesterday."

"Well today won't be as busy as I thought, maybe you can rest a little."

"What do we need to prepare today?"

"I just went through everything in the fridge and between the leftovers and the food we've made ahead, the cooking today is down to frying up some zucchini with the fish and baking some cornbread. I even took out a roast for tomorrow. I'll chop the carrots, onions and celery today so we can just throw it all in the oven when we get back from town tomorrow."

"That sounds like a *gut* plan. Set aside the zucchini you want to use tonight and I'll can the rest."

"Actually, I need to set aside some for my pineapple zucchini bread too. It freezes really well and that way we'll have some ready to sell for the tours. I want to pickle some too so you really don't have to can any today, it can wait until the next batch."

"Do you know where you're going to put the bakery case?" she asks.

"I was thinking we would put it just inside the side door of the barn for now. It's far enough away from the animals that people can access it from outside without disturbing them. We'll use the work counter behind it and the shelves in the corner to display things on if we need more room. We can bring people in through the side door, collect tour money at the long counter and hopefully people will shop the bakery case while they're there. I told Mark to sweep the area for when the case arrives and I'll move the tractor to the woodshop to open the space up and keep it out of the way from tourists for now."

"What about Jacob's tools and things?"

"We'll move them to the woodshop too. There are plenty of cabinets in there and it's not like I can use most of them anyway. I may have John and Dan sort through them to tell me what I should keep on hand and let them take anything they can use from what's left. It's the least we can offer them."

"As long as your comfortable with it, I think it's a very *gut* plan," she smiles.

"Really, it's okay *mamm*. Jacob's gone and there's *ne* sense in keeping his things in the barn like some shrine. He would want me to do whatever is necessary to keep this place running and I think with the tour business going, it will help us all to start living our new life together instead of hanging onto the old one."

"I think it's *gut*, I really do," she says, hugging me. "Since you don't need me here, I think I'll go get a couple of chores done at the *Daadi Haus* and take a little nap before lunch. Let me know if you need help with anything before then."

I go outside and get the boys to help me make room for the tractor in the woodshop then pull it inside just as John and Dan arrive with the bakery case. I sweep under where the tractor sat, just to make sure the area's clean before they unload it. When I finally see it sitting there in front of the work counter is when I start to realize that this is really happening.

"Wow it really looks official and everything," Mark marvels. "I can just see people lining up at the counter to pay," he chuckles.

"*Och* ya and you might even need Joker to help you count the money *mamm*," Samuel adds. We all laugh at the thought.

"Okay boys, take a few minutes to visit the bunnies until John and Dan are ready for you and keep the animals away from this area from now on. You'll have to use the back doors or the other side door when you take the animals in and out."

"Okay *mamm*," Mark calls out.

I tell John and Dan about the tractor in the woodshop and about looking through Jacob's old tools for anything they might need.

"Actually, I have my tools and Ruthie's *daed* left his behind too, so I'm set," Dan decides.

"I have plenty too but I'll help you sort through them soon after I get the plowing done. And we'll see if there's anything you could trade for any of the materials you might need for the business. You might want to think about letting me build a six or eight foot wall here to separate the animal side of the barn from the business side."

"Actually I might have another idea but I need to mull it over for. You guys go ahead and get started on the hutch and I'll bring out some tea."

I go inside, empty the ice into a cooler and set up a folding table near the kitchen door as a drink station so that the boys aren't running in and out all day. I carry the remaining three gallons or so of tea left in the large drink cooler out to the table next to the ice chest with a stack of plastic cups labeled with everyone's name just like we do at a real frolic.

When that's done, I go into my bedroom and pull Jacob's belongings from the wardrobe and dresser. I go downstairs and get an empty box from the basement and pack away his pocket knife, his pocket watch, the old pipe that belonged to his *daed*, his Bible, hat, winter coat, gloves, leather boots and suspenders. These are the things I plan to give to the boys someday to have something to remember their *daed* by. I label the box '*daed*'s keepsakes' and sit it in the hallway.

I don't know why I suddenly feel like doing this today but I decide to follow it through while I have the courage. I still have the wedding quilt that his *mamm* made for us and the wardrobe that he built for me, which I will probably pass on to the girls someday. I wrap the quilt in a plastic bag and store it on the top shelf of the wardrobe.

Finally, I bag up the remaining four pairs of pants, five shirts, four undershirts and six pairs of socks to give to Dan, who is about Jacob's size. There's just *ne* sense in seeing them go to waste and it will be seven to ten years before any of the boys can use them.

I put the bag on top of the box and go back into the kitchen to chop my vegetables. I start with the zucchini peeling and grating several until I have five cups of shredded zucchini for my bread. I dump the shreds into a clean tea towel and twist the towel over the sink to squeeze out the moisture. I won't have pineapple until I return from the store tomorrow so I put the drained shreds into a lidded glass container in the fridge. Next, I slice the rest of the zucchini with the skin on and put the slices in colanders to drain in the sink.

I rough chop the carrots, onion and celery for the roast tomorrow then dice up the rest of a second onion for pickling with the zucchini. As I work my knife, I imagine the bakery case in the barn filled with goodies and the corner shelves lined with jars of relishes, jams and pie fillings. I Imagine standing at the counter tallying purchases and collecting tour fees when I realize that I still have *ne* idea what to charge. I'll have to ask John and Dan what they think at lunch. It also occurs to me that *mamm* and I need to send a box of jams, relishes and pie fillings back to the bakery today so that he can set up the corner display.

I prepare my cornbread and get it baking in the oven while I boil the water to sterilize my jars and lids. While I'm waiting, I go downstairs and wash and wring a load of laundry, put it in the dryer and put a second load in to soak before returning to the kitchen.

I hand toss the zucchini in a little lemon juice, start my sugar, salt and vinegar mixture boiling in a saucepan, add my seasonings to the liquid and chop some garlic as it boils. When my jars are cool enough to handle, I load them with zucchini slices and pour the piping hot, seasoned pickling liquid over them into the jars. While they're cooling, I put the slices I plan to fry tonight in the fridge, take my cornbread out of the oven and head back downstairs to put the keepsake box away and to tend to the laundry.

By the time I make it back upstairs; it's time to prepare lunch and I'm starting to need a little break. Just as I finish setting the table for eight, *mamm* comes back from her nap.

"Feeling any better?" I ask as she sits at the table with her iced tea.

"*Ya*, much better, anything I can do to help?"

"I've only got one more load of laundry to put in the dryer, my jars are cooling, veggies are chopped for tomorrow and the cornbread's done. I just need to put the sandwiches together and put the food on the table."

"You've been busy," she smiles.

"I'll take a break at lunch," I assure her, "I put an empty box in the pantry; I just need you to choose the items you want to send back to the bakery with Dan so he can put them on display. I'll make a list of any other supplies we need to get tomorrow so that we can fill those shelves in the corner in the barn too."

"*Och* ya, *gut* idea, I took a peek at the bakery case on my way over. It's going to look like a miniature store in the barn once we get the case, shelves and counter filled," she chuckles.

"I know, it's hard to believe it's really happening but I'm so excited to see it starting to come together."

"Have you looked at the rabbitat?" she chuckles.

"*Ne*, I want to be surprised," I laugh, "I know they're working hard though."

"It's pretty impressive so far, I'm not sure how much help the younger boys have been but John and Dan make a *gut* team. Mark and Samuel are working right along with them," she says, from the pantry.

"I'm so glad they have this opportunity and I think I'm going to let him take them hunting. He thinks he can borrow some air rifles from his nephews to start them out with and the first few trips would be more about learning to spot tracks and things anyway. I trust John with them."

"I don't think you could find a better person to teach them," she says.

"He's definitely got a way with them and he's patient too. I want them to learn while it still interests them. They may have to be putting meat on the table before long," I say, slicing the bread.

"We only have three jars of my pumpkin pie filling left; do you want to save one for the family?"

"We always seem to want a pie before harvest time so leave them here and we'll put one in the barn to see if it sells. Ruth makes pumpkin pie at the bakery so we can do without there. We'll probably need to make lots in the fall though, especially once people get a sample of your recipe."

I hear jars clinking away in the pantry as she shuffles them around, making her selection. I dress the sandwiches, grabbing something from the fridge to put on the table each time I pass by. I stop to ring the old dinner bell on the porch so the men can wash up while I finish layering on the ham and turkey. Josh and Ben come in first.

"Go tell everyone to bring their tea inside and wash up while I get everything ready," I tell Josh as Ben heads for the bathroom sink.

Mamm calls me into the pantry, "The box is ready and I moved the jars to the corner that I think we should put on the shelves in the barn. You can see what that leaves us for the family before we move it and make sure you're happy with it."

"I'll double-check it later but it looks *gut*. We definitely need more jars though. We won't be getting these back," I chuckle.

The men finish washing their hands as I put the last of the sandwiches and the deviled eggs on the table. We bow our heads in prayer and dig in.

"It looks great Sarah," Dan smiles, helping Ben with his plate.

"*Danki*, I hope you all enjoy it."

"You should see the rabbitat *mamm* it's so cool," Mark says excitedly.

"I was tempted to look but I'm waiting to be surprised when it's finished."

"You're sure gonna be surprised at how much work we did," Samuel smiles.

"*Ya* I hear you boys have been really *gut* helpers."

"I think we'll be finished in a couple of hours, we should have plenty of time to get the stove in." John informs me.

"That's wonderful, now I just need to decide where to put it," I chuckle.

"How about putting it in the empty spot by the basement door in the pantry?" Mark asks.

"Well I know that would probably be the easiest place to put it, but I really don't want to heat up the pantry when I bake and I was kind of saving that spot for a freezer someday."

John looks at me with a strange smile, "I agree, you probably want it close to your counters and fridge anyway."

"Ruth is sending you some large sheet pans we don't use anymore with it," Dan informs me.

"*Mamm* has a box of canning goods to take back with you too. We're going to stop by tomorrow with some signs if you need help setting it up."

"I leave all of the decorating to her, but I'll be happy to take it too her."

"Do either of you have any idea what we should charge for the tours? For the two we've given so far, we just took what they offered. But I don't want to charge too much or too little."

"*Mamm* I remember reading the brochures in Marion and I think it was ten dollars for adults and eight dollars for kids; because I remember thinking it would take seventy dollars for all of us to go."

"How long ago was that?" John asks.

"A little over two years ago," I tell him, thinking back to when Jacob's *daed* was in the hospital.

"I think you should charge at least that and more if you're going to offer a corn maze and some of the other stuff you mentioned," Dan suggests.

"*Ya*, I would say at least twelve for adults and nine or ten for children," John agrees. "The one time I've been to a corn maze, I think they charged ten dollars per person and that was about nine years ago."

"Okay, so how about twelve dollars for anyone twelve and over, eight for children ages 4-11 and maybe three for children three and under?"

"As long as you have something each age group can enjoy, I think that's reasonable," Dan says.

"We should let the babies come for free," Josh giggles.

"He does have a point and really your target age group will probably be in the four to eleven range, I would charge nine dollars for them and let anyone three and under come free. It's simpler and it will probably even out in the long run."

"Okay, that sounds better; I don't want to make it too complicated."

"Have you decided what days and hours you're going to offer the tours? That was a big one for Ruth and I to decide when her parents retired," Dan asks.

"Definitely Saturdays but one day per week isn't enough to make all of these preparations worthwhile. *Ne* Sundays of course and I want the family to have at least one other day that isn't interrupted by tours."

"I know that Fridays tend to be one of our busier days at the bakery so you probably want to be open then too," he adds.

"Are you going to give the tours yourself while the *kinner* are in school?" John asks.

"When the *kinner* are in school, *mamm* and I will just have to find a way to work it into our day. I think maybe we'll start with Thursdays, Fridays and Saturdays and see how it goes. We still have a household to run," I decide.

"You'll probably have a better idea how busy it will be by the time summer's over. After that, you can always add days, cut back or hire help," Dan says.

"What hours are you going to be open?" John asks.

"Well, not before morning chores or breakfast and definitely not after dark. If the tours are going to take an hour or two, I guess that means we stop letting people in by 4:00 p.m., at least that way we can clean up and have dinner at a normal time. I'm willing to shuffle chores around and maybe even lunch but not morning and evening family time."

"Since this is your home too, I agree that you should keep the traffic as controlled as possible," Dan agrees.

"I agree," *Mamm* says.

"Me too," Mark adds.

"Me three," Samuel chuckles.

"Me five," Josh giggles.

"Who's four?" John laughs.

"Ben can be four," Josh tells him.

"But I'm six," Ben giggles.

"I guess that makes me four," John chuckles.

"Does anyone want more food?" I chuckle, "I have some dessert you can have now or you can have it for a snack later if you prefer."

"Oooooh I want dessert now," Mark says licking his lips.

"Me too," Dan adds.

"Me three," Samuel smiles.

John, Josh and Ben chime in with four, five and six as I slice the cake onto paper plates for the boys and warm the pie for a few minutes while I fix the adults some coffee.

"Boys you can feed and water the animals after cake while Dan and John have their pie and then you can all get back to your day."

"Okay *mamm*," Mark and Samuel say at the same time.

"So now you have days, times and rates. What else do you need to decide before you make the flyers?" *Mamm* asks.

"If you're going to make flyers, go to Mr. Albury three shops down from the bakery, he will copy fifty for less than two dollars. He's a *gut* customer of ours."

"*Ya* that's better than the post office, do you think he'll let us put up a sign there? We were going to see if we could find about ten places to put up signs tomorrow. I need to go to the grocery store and it will give the *kinner* something exciting to do in town."

"I don't see why not, he'll probably want to come for a tour himself, he's always asking me questions about the Amish when we have time to chat. I'll make a list of some people to ask in town and give it to you when you stop by tomorrow."

"I'll take a dozen of those flyers too, I know some places in Hopkinsville and two stores between here and there where I could probably put them," John says. "The tractor supply will probably let me put one there too, I just put some cards there for the repair shop."

I take the pie out of the oven and put it on plates with the last of the whipped cream. "*Danki*, both of you, with your help and my *Englisch* friend near the military base, we should generate some business."

"Any more word from the deacon?" Dan asks.

"*Ne* not yet but Bishop Graber gave me his blessing so I'm not going to let him discourage me."

"Well you let John or me know if he confronts you again, he can disagree all he wants but it wouldn't be wise for him to start interfering with your family's income," Dan assures me.

"You don't think he would go that far do you?" *Mamm* asks.

"I certainly hope not," Dan smiles.

"I'll probably be around quite a bit over the next few weeks, I'm going to plow next week and I promised to take the *kinner* to the corral. We have a hay slide and toddler maze to build and then it'll be time to plant and I want to see about taking the boys fishing one morning," he smiles. "I'll help keep an eye on things," John assures him.

"How are you planning to do all of that and work your farm too?" *Mamm* asks.

"I'm bringing Caleb back after church Sunday. He's serious about wanting to learn to work the land and my brother's being pretty supportive. He agreed to let him stay as long as I'm willing to keep him this time so we'll split the work and see how well he handles it."

"Well I feel a lot better knowing you'll be around but we'd better get back to that rabbitat so that I can make it back by the time the bakery closes or Ruth is liable to give my job to Mary and Hannah," Dan chuckles.

CHAPTER SIX

While the guys go back to working on the rabbitat, *mamm* and I wash dishes and tidy the kitchen as I try to decide where to put the new stove. I know that eventually, I may eliminate my wood stove completely but until I get used to the gas stove, I don't want to get rid of my wood stove or have to worry about sealing off the vent pipe. If business goes well who knows, I might need them both anyway.

Mamm and I move the fridge down the wall a bit and then move what we call the 'cutting table' on the other side of the fridge closer to the pantry door. It's a cabinet and countertop that matches the rest of my kitchen except that it's portable because of the casters and it has drop leaves on either side so that the counter top can extend from four feet wide to eight feet wide easily. Jacob built it for me years ago and we use it anytime we need extra counter space and for cutting out clothing patterns. It means we can put the stove on the same wall as the fridge close to the old hook up with the cutting table in between; we just won't be able to extend the countertop without moving it. I can live with that.

Once that's out of the way, I sweep and mop the kitchen and go back downstairs to finish the laundry. When the clean clothes are hung and folded, I fill a bucket with soapy bleach water, grab some cleaning rags and head out to the barn with *mamm* to clean the workspace. We tackle the shelves first and then the long countertop behind the bakery case. The case itself is spotless except for the handprints on the outside from moving it. I'll wait to clean that last. Next I move all of the tools and things inside the cabinets into the last three and clean out the inside of the two closest to the door. *Mamm* goes inside and fetches a few pens, a notepad and a calculator for money collecting while I carry out the canning goods we plan to sell and put them on the shelves.

"It really is starting to look like a mini store out here," I chuckle.

"We should put a lock on the cabinet drawer at the end because if you and I are giving the tours while the *kinner* are in school, we don't want the money we've collected sitting there in an unlocked drawer while we're off giving a buggy ride or something."

"*Gut* idea *mamm*, I'll see if John can handle that. You know, if this goes well this summer, I think I'm going to clear out the woodshop and move the bakery case and the items for sale out there like a little gift shop. It's already full of shelves, cabinets and counter space and we can put the tractor back in the barn where it belongs. The vent fans will help keep things cooler in the summer and we could even put an old fridge out there to sell cold drinks and things."

"*Ya* and people could park behind it too. What's stopping us from doing it now?" she asks.

"Well I only thought of it when I drove the tractor inside and the guys were already pulling in with the bakery case. I guess I've always just thought of it as Jacob's woodshop until today."

"Why don't you talk to John," she says.

"Talk to John about what?" his voice says from behind me. Startled, I turn as he wipes the sweat from his brow with a handkerchief.

Mamm chuckles, "I'll go check on the crew."

I tell him about my idea as he leans against the counter by the side door.

"I kind of had the same vision myself when Mark and I were in there looking around Saturday but I wasn't sure you were ready for the idea."

"It only occurred to me when I moved the tractor inside right before you arrived with the bakery case but I've been thinking about it all day. I think I'm ready to move on. Leaving the woodshop the way it is won't be of any use to us and it seems a shame to use it to store the tractor. Jacob's handiwork is in all of the cabinets and shelves and to the *kinner*, I think it will feel as if he's had a hand in this business too. I'm ready to let my new life begin without hanging on to some constant reminder of what will never be again."

He studies my face without saying a word for a few moments and then he puts his hands on the outside of my shoulders. "I think it's one of the best decisions you could make at this point and I'm proud of you for looking forward instead of backward. You should probably tell the boys what you've decided. Go over there and look at your new rabbitat while Dan and I load the bakery case back on the wagon and put the tractor back inside the barn. With Caleb here to help with the plowing, I'll be able to make some time to help you get the woodshop ready for business."

I throw my arms around him and hug him before I catch myself. I don't know if it's because I'm relieved to have his moral support, the excitement of the day or just because I'm so grateful for his help. All I know is that it feels *gut* to lean against his broad chest and feel the warmth of his big strong arms around me for those few seconds. My fears are laid to rest by his encouraging words and I feel a peaceful, safe feeling in his embrace. "*Danki* John," I say, pulling away slowly.

I walk toward the rear doors of the barn and glance back at him once more. He's still leaning against the counter, watching me as I go. I feel a warm, tingly feeling flutter in my chest and almost bump into the buggy as I walk. I pick up my pace a bit and join Dan, *mamm* and the boys at the rabbitat where the bunnies are already enjoying their new home.

Mamm looks at me curiously as I smile, "*Och* wow this is beautiful," I say, marveling at their handiwork. "These are the luckiest bunnies in the world!"

"All these nails *mamm*, Samuel and I hammered them in and John even let me saw with him too!" Mark says excitedly.

"You boys do *gut* quality work," I declare. "Now who put all of that cozy hay in the bottom and put the food inside?" I ask curiously.

"We did *mamm*," Josh and Ben smile.

"It looks so warm and snuggly in there I don't think the bunnies will ever want to come out," I chuckle.

"*Danki* so much Dan, I love it," I say sincerely. "I think John wants to see you in the barn, I want to talk to the boys for a moment," I say to him.

He grabs his tea and heads over to the barn as the boys look at me curiously.

"Boys this rabbitat is the first big project of our new business and I'm proud of what strong young men you've been today. I think it's time we start thinking about our next big project though."

"Just tell us what it is and we're ready!" Samuel says.

"*Ya mamm* what do you want us to do next?" Mark asks curiously.

“I was thinking that maybe we should use the woodshop for the tour headquarters instead of the barn.” I explain to them about the cabinetry, the parking, the space away from the animals and my concern about people traipsing around the animals and farm equipment unsupervised.

Mark ponders it for a moment. “That’s a *gut* idea, especially if we’re going to sell stuff,” Mark agrees, “We don’t want the goats chewing on things or trying to get the food in the case.”

I hadn’t even considered that but it’s true. I notice that Samuel is silent. “What about you Samuel?”

“Well I think it’s a *gut* idea but what about all of *daed*’s things?” he asks hesitantly.

“Do you think your *daed* would prefer for us to let it sit there all locked up and going to waste or would he prefer for us to put it to *gut* use?” I ask as *mamm* puts her hand on his shoulder.

“He would want us to use it to help the family,” he decides.

“Your *daed* made every cabinet and every shelf inside that woodshop. Wouldn’t it feel more like he’s with us in spirit if we used it instead of never going inside unless we need something?” I ask.

“*Ya* but what if we need the wood and tools he left in there to build something?”

“Well we probably will but we can store the leftover wood and the tools we don’t need somewhere else. Since none of us know how to make cabinets or furniture to sell like your *daed* did, I think the beautiful woodshop he made will just go to waste if we don't find a new purpose for it."

"*Ya* we got some supplies to build this rabbitat from there already and there's not a lot left, it doesn't make sense to keep it as a woodshop if we aren't building stuff all the time. It's not practical," Mark adds. I have to admit that I admire his grown-up perspective in times like these.

"I guess it's okay with me too," Samuel agrees. He's never been quite as independent as Mark and cleaved to Jacob a bit more, so I expected that he would be more sensitive to the idea. I'm just glad that he's as reasonable as he is emotional.

"We can give all the stuff to John, he probably needs it," Josh adds. Being only four when Jacob died, Josh spent very little time in the woodshop with his *daed*. So it's *ne* surprise that he's not quite as sentimental about it.

"We might still need some of it too but we can share with John if he needs something," I assure him.

I look at *mamm* and she gives me an approving smile.

"Okay so we'll have some work to do to get it ready but we now have an official headquarters and gift shop!" I say excitedly.

"Mary is going to be so excited," Mark says.

"I think she will too," I smile. In spite of their independent ways, I still have to remind myself sometimes that Mark and Mary are twins with a slightly deeper bond that didn't end in the womb. There isn't much one of them does without thinking of the other.

As we finish our conversation and walk back into the barn. John and Dan are already unloading the bakery case into the woodshop. I tell Mark to pull the tractor into the barn while I supervise. I can tell that he's overjoyed by the opportunity but handling it calmly, like a young man.

Ben and Josh go back to the bunnies so that Ben can tell them all goodbye. Dan, John and *mamm* come inside the house with me once the bakery case is unloaded.

I pull Dan aside as *mamm* and John chat about the rabbitat. I hand him the bag of Jacob's clothes. "I put aside keepsakes for the boys but we have *ne* use for these clothes. I know you're the same size and I don't want them to go to waste and neither would he. If you decide not to keep them, then please feel free to give them to someone who can get some use out of them," I tell him.

"Are you sure about this?"

"*Ya*, I'm sure," I smile.

"*Danki*, you know how Ruth hates to sew," he chuckles. "Really though, it means a lot to me."

"Are we ready to go get the stove?" John asks.

"I'm ready," Dan says as they both head for the door.

Mamm and I both plop down at the kitchen table, sigh, look at one another and chuckle.

"I guess there's *ne* turning back now," she sighs.

"It's okay," I smile, "We'll have a hard time longing for the past when we're all so excited to see what the future holds."

CHAPTER SEVEN

I drive the tractor back towards the bakery with Dan riding over the wheel as Ben sits in the wagon behind him.

He points to a small road in a thicket of trees with a barely visible street sign. "That's the turn-off there, then take your first right down to the end of the long dirt road," he tells me.

"*Och* ya, I never would have found this on my own," I tell him.

"Old man Sneed is a really nice man but he keeps to himself. He's *Englisch* but he lives a lot like an Amish and does most of his business with the Amish. The last time I was here, the trees were so grown over on both sides of the street that you couldn't see the road until you had already passed it."

"Sounds like my kind of guy," I chuckle.

We pull in through the old rusted gate and Dan closes it behind us.

"Hey Mr. Sneed," Dan says greeting the man as he steps onto the old wooden porch.

"Oh hey Daniel, I just dozed off in the porch swing, how ya been?"

"I'm *gut*; this is my friend John Troyer."

I shake his hand and give him a nod.

"He's looking for a *gut* working upright freezer," Dan explains to him.

"What color?" the old man asks.

"Preferably white but I'm more interested in how well it runs and how big it is," I tell him.

"Gotta big family 'eh?" he asks.

"It's for two widows and five *kinner*," I say, not wanting to get too personal.

"We were kind of hoping you'd be willing to barter for one," Dan explains.

"They Amish folks?" he asks stroking his whiskers.

"*Ya*, they are," I tell him.

"Come on around back and see what I've got. What were you thinking of trading?"

"Well I just set up my small engine repair shop, I moved into the old Schwartz place a few months back from

Hopkinsville. I also have tools of all kinds, I can do just about any kind of construction work and I've got four or five pigs I'm about to corral."

"Are you sure a freezer is all you need?" he chuckles.

"Depends on what else you've got," I laugh.

"Brother I have an entire barn and three sheds full of mowers, farm equipment, appliances and what not."

Just as we reach the edge of the barn dogs start barking loudly. "Don't mind them, I keep them behind the fence during the day but I wouldn't recommend stopping by at night unless you call first," he chuckles as he opens the barn door.

Dan stays behind with Ben as I venture inside. In spite of the old single-wide run down looking trailer he lives in, his barn is about five times larger with concrete floors and lots and lots of equipment in varying condition. He even has some old wood stoves and wringer washers.

"I see this is where some of the old Amish culture comes to die," I chuckle.

"You got it. Every once in a while though I find someone willing to pay a pretty penny for the stuff though, going off the grid is getting more and more fashionable these days. Here are the appliances in this section over here," he says, weaving through lawn mower handles, stacks of tires and various other findings.

“This one here works and has been checked for leaks but it’s a little on the small side,” he turns to look around behind him.

“What about that one over there?” I ask pointing to a newer looking large, white upright gas freezer near the side door. I recognize it because it looks just like my brother’s and I know he paid about $1000 for it used.

“I don’t know, I just got that one and the matching appliances next to it from an estate sale over in Marion on Saturday. I haven’t had time to look them over yet but they’re all gas,” he says.

“I’ve got a good running gas chest freezer over there if you’ve got to have gas.”

“I wouldn’t mind if it were for me but it’s probably not easy fishing frozen food out of a chest freezer when you’re only five feet, three or so,” I chuckle.

“I see your point,” he says, “Well I could look it over in a day or two and hold it for you if you’re sure you want it,” he offers.

“What would you take in trade?” I ask.

“I’ve got a mower and a tractor I could make a pretty penny off of if I could get them running, I can take the rest out in pork,” may as well make the wife happy every now and then,” he chuckles.

“Any idea what’s wrong with them?” I ask, following him

as he walks.

"Nah, I bought out a guys equipment to keep him out of foreclosure, you can crank them up and see what you think. Might not even be anything major but I don't fix engines, I fix appliances. I'm not so worried about haggling over price either, as long as we're both happy in the end that's all that matters."

I climb onto the tractor and listen carefully as it tries to crank. I ask him to close the barn door while I repeat the motion several times. Next, I climb onto the riding mower and from the age and brand I can almost predict what's wrong without even looking at it. I try to crank it and hear the familiar dry whizzing sound in the background and the blade scraping the cover.

"Do you think you could have the freezer ready by Saturday?" I ask.

"I could probably have it ready by Friday...I'd sure love to sell that tractor at auction next week." He opens the barn door as we walk outside.

"Well, I'm not sure how much longer before my pigs will be corralled but it shouldn't be more than a week."

"*Ne* matter, you get those engines running and I'll leave the amount of pork and the timing to your judgment. You just bring it by when it's ready and leave it with my wife if I'm not here."

"I'll bring my tools Friday morning and see if I can and try to get them going for you," I assure him.

"I'll be up at daylight and here all day unless I run to the store. Let me give you my card in case you need to call," he says, picking a business card out of his wallet.

"*Danki* sir," I tell him.

"Good to meet you son," he calls out as we climb onto the tractor.

"The things we do for women," Dan chuckles.

"*Ya* well, keep it under your hat," I chuckle, "I can't very well give the woman a hundred pounds of pork with *ne* place to put it."

"Your secret's safe with me, I promise," he laughs. "I've got to hand it to you though, I've known old man Sneed for about eight years and I've brought several people to meet him; I've never heard him tell someone it's good to meet them or call them 'son' before so you must be doing something right."

As we drive the rest of the way to the bakery, I think about how Dan and I had planned our little shopping trip this morning long before Sarah mentioned saving the spot in the pantry for a freezer someday. I felt like my heart would leap out of my chest with joy when I realized that once again, God had already put me on the path to help meet her needs. I park behind the bakery and follow Dan inside. I think it smells even better than it did this morning.

"Well look at you ladies," I say, marveling at Mary and Hannah in their little aprons smeared with powdered sugar, chocolate and floured fingerprints. “You look *gut* enough to eat and I smell chocolate!” I tease.

Hannah shrieks and giggles, “You can’t eat me, I’m a girl silly.”

“*Ya* but you’re a chocolate covered girl,” I laugh.

“We were drizzling chocolate on top of peanut butter chip brownies,” Mary informs me.

“Did you make a baker’s dozen?”

“I think we made 48,” she chuckles.

“Did you save me any?”

“They’re only for customers,” she laughs.

“We ate a whoopie pie after lunch,” Hannah giggles.

“I ate your *mamm*’s yummy peach pie after lunch but don’t tell Ruth because she gave me a peach fritter this morning and it was yummy too.”

“I think you really love sweets,” Mary concludes.

“I wonder if we’re having dessert tonight,” I say with a curious look.

“We are but I can’t tell you what it is, you’ll have to wait and see,” she laughs, “I don’t want you to get too excited and spoil your dinner.”

I chuckle. “You think we should go home and see if there

are any surprises for you ladies there?" I ask.

"Let me finish my job first and we can go," she tells me.

"*Ya* ma'am, just let me know when you're ready," I say very seriously.

I walk back toward the office looking for Dan as I hear the girls giggling while they work. Ruth says hello again and we chat for a moment while we wait for him to come back from the bathroom.

"Be sure to tell Sarah I said *danki* for lending me the girls, they were a big help. I'm going to go put these on the display," she says, grabbing the box of canning goods Sarah sent.

"I'll carry them," I offer, taking the box from her.

The girls giggle as we pass by.

"I hope your intentions are honorable John Troyer because those girls have talked about you all day," she chuckles.

I try to ignore the question but when I sit the box down for her, she looks at me with a serious look on her face, her eyebrows raised expectantly and she sort of has me backed into a corner in the front of the store.

"I would never knowingly or intentionally do anything to hurt Sarah or any member of her family," I smile sincerely. I realize this is not exactly the answer she's digging for but at the same time, I don't think it's fair to tell her how I feel before I've told Sarah and it's certainly not a *gut* time for that. I would hate for word to get out while Sarah is still in mourning, especially when I don't even know for sure how she feels.

Dan and I load the stove and his appliance dolly into the wagon with the girls beside it.

"Mind if I hang onto the dolly until next week?" I ask.

"Take your time," he says, closing the ramp gate.

We all wave goodbye and head for the farm. As we drive, I think what a great day it has been. I got to build something for people that I care about, I feel like I made two new friends in the community and I got to spend time with the boys, teaching them skills they can use for a lifetime. As if that weren't enough, I feel a greater sense of God's hand and purpose in my life and the woman I care about showed me that she's truly ready to move on with her life.

I think about holding her in the barn and how *gut* she felt in my arms for those few tiny moments. I wanted to kiss her, to protect her and to let her know how happy it makes me to see her so full of courage and excited about the future. I've known deep down that God has been getting me ready for something or someone but I felt a warm glow in my chest when I watched her walk away. I felt like God was saying, 'See, I've been getting her ready for you too.'

Even still, I can't help but feel a little presumptuous at the thought and pray that it isn't just friendly appreciation that she feels for me. I never thought I would find myself longing for the day when I would see the pale pinks and blues of the traditional Amish dress on a woman but that day has surely come.

When we arrive at the house, I park, lift the girls over the side of the wagon and tell Mary to let Sarah know I'm here and to prop the door open for me. I strap the stove to the dolly, back it down the ramp, up the step and over the threshold into the kitchen as the *kinner* watch excitedly.

Mark runs out to the barn to get my toolbox while I get the stove situated where she wants it. "Was there a stove here before?" I ask.

"*Ya*, the people we bought the farm from had a gas stove that they took with them but they never removed the wood stove which was fine with me at the time," Sarah explains. "You probably didn't see the connection before because the fridge used to be in front of it," she chuckles.

"Mind if I look at the pantry side of the wall?" I ask.

"Go right ahead, I'm going to take the girls for a little walk," she says with a knowing look.

I assume she's planning to show them the woodshop to get them comfortable with the idea of using it for tour headquarters. I open the freezer door and take a quick peek just to see how much meat she has or doesn't have because I doubt she would tell me if she were running out. I step into the pantry and pretend to look at the wall behind the connection but I'm really checking to see if the freezer spot already has a connection too. I look behind her dry erase board labeled 'Chore Chart' and I can't resist reading some of it.

As I stand there, fascinated by how neat and organized it all is with each child's name and assigned duties along with some sort of scoring system, I hear someone clear their throat. Startled, I almost knock the board off the wall as I look up to see Miriam watching me with an amused look on her face.

She puts some jars on the shelves and comes over next to me to admire it herself. "It's hard to imagine so much structure coming from one tiny woman isn't it?" she asks in a whisper.

"I'm a little speechless," I chuckle admittedly.

"Is that a *gut* kind of speechless or a bad kind?" she asks curiously.

"I think I'm slightly afraid and a little fascinated all at the same time," I smile at Sarah's industriousness.

"You're an honest man John Troyer," she chuckles, returning to the kitchen.

I double-check the wall and realize that this used to be a laundry room which explains the gas connection. I'm pleased that I won't have to install new gas lines tonight or when I bring the freezer.

"Do you have any other gas connections in the house?" I ask.

"*Ya*, down in the basement for the dryer," Miriam tells me.

I go downstairs and check the line, just making sure that everything's properly installed. I can't help but notice Sarah's small, dainty slips hanging on the drying rack next to it. I feel like I'm violating her privacy just by being in the same room with them. I notice that she still uses her old wringer washer too. Maybe that will be the next item to barter my services for, she probably won't have time for washing clothes this way for long.

Back upstairs I check to make sure I'm not interfering with anything by shutting off the main gas line outside and then install the stove before carefully checking my fittings for leaks. Sarah returns with the girls while I'm down on the floor, and I can't help but smile at how spotless it is in spite of ten or people running in and out of the kitchen multiple times today. Even my *mamm* would be impressed.

I check the time as the *kinner* chat excitedly about their plans for the woodshop. "I'm going to head on over to my place to feed and water the horses but I should be back in about an hour."

"Can I help?" Mark asks.

"If you don't mind hanging out with the horses while I run in and take a shower. I feel sawdust sticking to my skin," I chuckle.

"We can take care of the horses for you while you take a

shower," Samuel chimes in.

"If it's okay with your *mamm*," I tell them.

"Are you sure it's okay?" she asks.

"I think I could use a little help with the chores tonight," I smile.

"Go ahead, we'll have dinner ready when you get back," she chuckles.

CHAPTER EIGHT

While the boys are tending to John's horses, Mary and Hannah tell *mamm* and I all about their day at the bakery and all of the fun things they got to do.

I sit out two separate glass pans, one for dipping and one for dredging, as they talk. I put two large iron skillets on the stove and heat my oil, as Hannah dips and Mary dredges the zucchini slices. When the bottoms of both frying pans are covered, we chat as I wait to turn the slices.

We all talk about the gift shop and everyone agrees to help me clean it from top to bottom tomorrow. I'm relieved to see that they've handled the decision quite well. But I suppose that neither of them spent a lot of time there with their *daed*.

Mamm makes fresh tartar sauce for the fish as we continue dipping, dredging and frying enough zucchini for about ten people. When it's time to move on to the fish, I add a little more cornmeal and a little cayenne to the dredge mixture while Mary puts some mayonnaise in a cup. Hannah starts setting the table while *mamm* puts the mashed potatoes on the stove to heat.

“I think the mayonnaise will work great on the fish, it’ll make the batter stick nicely,” she says, slathering the fillets as I dredge and place them in the pan.

“Are we still having cheesecake for dessert?” Mary asks.

“*Ya*, we should probably take out a pint jar of strawberries to put on top,” I say to *Mamm*.

“John can’t wait for dessert,” Hannah giggles.

“He really loves sweets *mamm*,” Mary adds, “He doesn’t know what’s for dessert so don’t tell him until it’s time, he needs to eat his dinner first,” she explains.

Mamm and I chuckle. “I don’t think that will be a problem, he worked really hard today, I’m sure he’s hungry.” I put the cornbread and the zucchini in the oven so it’ll stay warm until the boys get back.

“He was going to eat me because I smelled like chocolate!” Hannah giggles.

“We better give him an extra piece of fish and cornbread,” Mary decides.

I know they’re my *kinner* but sometimes I still get tickled at their sense of reasoning.

The fish fries beautifully with the mayonnaise and John arrives with the boys just as I’m taking the last fillet out of the pan. We put the last of the food on the table as *Mamm* pours tea and the boys wash their hands.

John sits at the table and Hannah goes over and kisses him on the cheek, "You smell so *gut* that I have to give you a kiss," she laughs, "And if you eat all of your dinner you can have some dessert," she says, patting him on the shoulder.

We all chuckle but I'm still amazed at how she's been coming out of her shell around him. I suppose we all have. I smile to myself as we bow our heads to pray before everyone digs in.

We laugh and talk over dinner with the *kinner* still telling one another about their day while John recognizes each of them for something they did well today. I can see what a loving *daed* he would be someday. I love watching him with my *kinner* and the way they just soak up his praise, his kidding and even his instruction. I look over at *mamm* who catches me staring and looks back down at her plate. I can't help but wonder if she's watching me the same way that I watch them.

When everyone has finished dinner and dessert, everyone starts right into their chores as John asks me to join him on the porch to talk.

"Before you say anything, let me tell you a few things before I forget," I chuckle.

"Okay," he smiles curiously.

"Well for one, *Danki* for today and for being such a blessing to all of us," I say, feeling my cheeks flush a bit.

"I've enjoyed every minute of it and I hope to enjoy many more. You and your whole family have been a blessing to me too," he says looking at me with a gentle smile.

"I want you to promise to tell me if you need some space or don't have time to help us with whatever project we have going. I don't want to be a burden to you and I know you have your own farm and business to run."

"When I need to tend to my own responsibilities I will speak up. I don't think of anything you've asked for help with or anything I've done as a burden. I like what I'm doing and I thank the *gut* Lord for putting me in a position to do it. You're just going to have to trust me on that. By the same token, I don't want to overstay my *wilkom* or keep you and the *kinner* from the things you need to do so let's both promise to be open and honest about those things and let that be the end of it…unless you were planning on telling me I was already overstaying my *wilkom*," he smiles.

"*Ne*," I chuckle.

"*Gut*, so what else did you want to tell me?" he chuckles.

"That I would like it if you took Mark and Samuel hunting," I smile.

"*Ya* okay, I'll see what gear I can come up with by the time turkey season opens. That sure was some *gut* turkey you cooked."

"That brings me to my last item," I laugh, "I set aside some leftover turkey, stuffing and deviled eggs for you to take home and I'm sending you some leftovers from tonight too so that you'll have plenty of food for tomorrow. Promise you'll let me know when you need eggs and milk or even just feel like coming over for a meal because it's really *ne* trouble to cook another portion and sometimes I struggle to use up the milk and eggs."

"That I can do, if you promise to let me know anytime you want me to hunt a turkey or go fishing or even just bring over something to cook. I've got some deer meat, lots of ground beef and some pork in my freezer. I'm more than happy to provide as much as you need," he smiles. "It'll be like getting to do things I already enjoy with the added bonus of tasting the final results, in *gut* company with the hands that prepare it. You can even add me to the chore chart if it makes it easier for you," he snickers.

"John Troyer, you did not just make fun of my chore chart," I laugh incredulously.

"Something tells me that I'm not the first," he teases.

We both laugh heartily for several moments and it's hard not to start giggling as I think of the night Ruth and I were drunk with laughter over the very same thing.

"Just don't tell the *kinner*, they really look forward to it," I chuckle.

"I wouldn't even know what to say," he smiles.

We both catch our breath for a second. "Okay so now it's your turn," I say trying to get serious. "*Och*, one other thing, I wanted to ask you if you could put a lock on one of the drawers in the woodshop for us to keep the money in?" I smile.

"*Ya* I can definitely do that," he smiles, "Is it my turn now?"

"*Ya*, finally," I giggle.

"Well this is going to seem a little trivial after all of that," he chuckles, "I just wanted to ask you if you liked to fish," he smiles. "I thought I would invite the boys to go fishing Thursday but the whole family is *wilkom* to come unless you have other plans. We could even wait until Saturday if we need to."

"Let's do Thursday and unless something comes up we'll all go. Should I pack a picnic?"

"I'd like to go right after breakfast and morning chores," he chuckles, "The *kinner* will probably catch something every time they bait up which will be really encouraging for them."

"Well *Mamm* and I will enjoy it but Mary has never been too interested. I'll put her in charge of making a snack which will boost her enthusiasm. Hannah has never really been invited so she'll just enjoy being there if nothing else."

"*Gut* it's a date."

"You're probably the only man in the country who considers

taking two widow women and five *kinner* fishing as a date," I chuckle.

"*Och* those other guys don't know what they're missing," he smiles, looking at me intently.

"Is that all you wanted to talk to me about?" I ask curiously.

"Well I did want to offer to teach Mark to drive the tractor while we plow the fields. I know you said he needed to wait until fall but I think he's ready and I'll supervise him until he's ready to handle it on his own. He's a pretty responsible little guy."

"*Ya*, I'm okay with that," I smile.

"*Gut*, we'll start Thursday afternoon and should be able to finish Saturday. Caleb and I will get mine done next week but I want to get that maze planted as soon as possible."

"I'm making some ham and bean soup, some chicken and dumplings and I'm not sure what else this week, any particular cooking requests?" I ask, curious to know his favorite dishes.

"Both of those sound great to me."

"*Ya* but I want to know your favorite meal."

"I've never met a *gut* home-cooked meal that I didn't like and I love being surprised by what you cook. But that meatball casserole you made is pretty high on my list because I love meatloaf and I love Italian food. It was like the best of both worlds."

I chuckle to myself at the thought of *mamm*'s 'courtship meatloaf'. "I'm glad you liked it, I'll make it again soon."

"*Gut*, I'll bring you some frozen meat on Thursday and I was thinking I'd let the *kinner* come see the pig corral after we fish."

"It's a date," I chuckle.

CHAPTER NINE

Wednesday, April 8

As I stand in front of the mirror putting on my prayer kapp, I hear the *kinner* coming downstairs. I'm sure they're bright eyed and bushy-tailed, eager to spend the morning in town and the afternoon getting the woodshop ready for the tours.

With the promise of a fishing trip tomorrow, seeing the pig corral, plowing for the corn maze and John's involvement in general, they're probably excited about the entire rest of the week. It's a wonder they slept at all and I can't say that I blame them.

In preparation for our visit to Mrs. Yoder, I remember to take the last loaf of banana bread from the freezer on my way into the kitchen. Mark brings in some wood for the stove and gets it warming as *mamm* arrives from the *Daadi Haus*. Mary gets out the notepad and pen, knowing we usually finalize the grocery list before heading into town.

"What would you like to make as a snack for our fishing trip tomorrow?" I ask her as *mamm* sits the kettle on the stove.

"Are we making the pineapple zucchini bread today?"

"*Ya* I want to make at least four loaves to have ready for the tours or whatever else might come up."

"I think John will like it and he's probably never tried it," she decides. "I know we don't have room for two full batches in the freezer though, can we make six loaves and use one tomorrow and one for breakfast on Friday?"

"*Ya*, that will be fine, make sure we have six cans of pineapple on the list."

"I'm going to take the *kinner* to the coop while we wait for the stove," *mamm* says, grabbing her egg basket.

Josh and Hannah follow behind as the boys also head out to take care of their morning chores, in the hopes we can leave soon after breakfast.

"Want me to start writing down the menu too?" she asks.

Between the vegetable garden, our little herb garden, our supply of corn meal and the fresh eggs and milk everyday, it isn't likely that we'll ever completely starve to death but our way of life is hard work, which makes for hearty appetites for seven or eight people, three times a day.

With a limited income, it's impossible to do without planning ahead but that extra bit of forethought also keeps the kitchen running efficiently and prevents food from going to waste. Of course there are always things we find on sale that may alter the menu plan slightly but I usually plan meals *ne* less than two weeks in advance to make the most of our shopping trips.

"*Ya* let's plan for the next two weeks," I tell her.

"Are we going to make a pot of beans?"

When we have ham or any type of bone-in pork, she knows that a pot of beans will soon follow, even if we just end up canning them for later so that we can use the bones in the cooking.

"*Ya* I want to make some ham and beans but I'm not sure which day yet. I'll cook them on Friday though, because I plan to spend most of the day baking while they simmer. I already took out a roast for tonight but I think I'd rather wait until tomorrow so John can have some too."

"Okay so what about tonight?"

I pull out the deboned ham, the leftover cornbread and a dozen eggs from the fridge. "There's enough leftover fish and fried zucchini from last night for wraps and we have enough pea salad leftover too, let's have that tonight and avoid cooking since it will be a busy day. We'll pick some spinach too. Make sure we have tortillas on the list."

"Can we have tacos one night too?" she asks excitedly.

"*Ya*, put chicken tacos on the menu for Monday and add avocados to the grocery list, John will be back with Caleb and a load of hay for the slide from Hopkinsville and I want to make some guacamole," I chuckle.

"Okay," she smiles.

"Put ketchup, lemons and bananas on the list and sandwich cookies for pie crusts too," I tell her.

"Who's coming for visitation on Sunday?"

"The Shelters," I tell her, "Knowing Mrs. Shetler, I'm guessing she will bring some type of soup or stew but go ahead and put chicken and dumplings down for Friday night, I want to make a pot for John. I think we'll slaughter two chickens and divide it between three meals. You can put meatloaf down for Saturday night; John's bringing us some ground beef."

"He really must love your cooking," she chuckles.

"*Ya*, I think he likes having all of us around too," I smile. Thinking about him makes me lose track of where we are. "How far does that get us?" I ask as I put the cornbread in the oven to warm and start dicing the ham.

"We're on next Tuesday."

"Put the ham and beans for Tuesday, lasagna for Wednesday and chicken stir fry for Thursday. Make sure we have lasagna noodles on the list."

I give her a minute to catch up as I chop some green onions

and pull the whistling kettle off of the stove. *Mamm* returns with Josh and Hannah and I ask them to pick some spinach for dinner. *Mamm* washes the eggs, finishes making the coffee and takes a mug out to the garden with her.

"Since we'll be making beans already, how about hamburgers with baked beans one night?"

"Okay, put down chili for Friday and hamburgers for Saturday. Maybe we'll even cook them on the grill and eat outside if the weather's *gut*."

"Goodie," she giggles, "That only leaves Monday through Wednesday," she says as I get out my egg skillet.

I sit a clean bowl on the countertop, grab some cheese and milk from the fridge and start cracking the eggs as the boys come in to wash up.

I check the freezer, then think about the meat John mentioned last night and the fish we'll probably catch tomorrow, "Let's plan venison stew for Monday, pork chops on Tuesday and whatever we catch tomorrow for Wednesday," I chuckle.

"Okay," she giggles.

As the boys join us in the kitchen, *mamm* returns from the garden. "You guys get the table set, I'm starting the eggs," I tell them as I whisk the eggs, ham, green onions, cheese and milk together.

With the egg mixture in the pan, I take the cornbread out of the oven and slice it. *Mamm* washes and drains the spinach while I cook the eggs and Mary gets the butter and honey on the table. Once everything's plated and we share a moment in prayer, we discuss the plan for the day as we enjoy breakfast together.

***

Today while Sarah and the *kinner* are busy in town and transforming the woodshed, I have a couple of missions of my own to attend to. It occurred to me last night when Sarah told me that I could take the boys hunting that she was entrusting me with the lives of her *kinner*.

On the way home last night I thought about the day that Elizabeth had the seizure in the buggy and how helpless I was to call for an ambulance. In our community, we're permitted to have phones in the barn and in our place of business but I've decided to purchase a cell phone today in case of emergency.

If I'm questioned, I know that it's completely justified because my business is often mobile and I'm still transitioning back and forth between communities. I already know of a few people in both communities that rely on cell phones to operate their businesses and haven't had a conflict. I never thought I would embrace the idea personally but I don't ever want to be plowing, hunting or fishing with Miriam, Sarah or her *kinner* with *ne* way to call for help if something were to happen.

I also need to find a lock of some sort for her cash drawer

and to check on a couple of items I saw in old man Sneed's barn. I figure the sooner I get his equipment working, the more bargaining power I'll have with him – I can already tell that I'm going to need it.

I turn down the tree lined road toward his house, make the first right, let myself in through the gate and pull alongside his carport at the end of the drive.

He's out on his front porch sipping coffee in a fresh white t-shirt with Amish suspenders on over it.

"Hey Mr. Sneed," I say as I walk toward the porch.

"John, good to see you," he says shaking my hand, "It's not Friday is it?" he asks.

"*Ne* sir, I just had some free time this morning on my way into town and thought I would see if I could get that mower going and troubleshoot the problem with the tractor. I brought my tools and some parts from my shop."

"That's a relief; I thought I might have missed a day, it's been known to happen once or twice. Would you like a cup of coffee?"

"*Ne danki*, I've had mine," I smile.

"Well then, let's get started. I like a man who follows through on his promises," he says leading the way to the barn. "My son drops of a load of stuff every Thursday morning when he gets done at the auction but as soon as we get it unloaded,

I'll take a look at that freezer of yours."

"*Ne* problem, I though I might even shop for a couple of other items while I'm here if you have time."

He opens the double doors and smiles, "If you're as good with engines and motors as I suspect you are, there's nothing here that we couldn't work out a trade on," he assures me. "I hate taking things to that *Englisch*er in town for repairs; he doesn't make house calls and it's hard for me to make any money on used goods after I pay his rates."

I try not to chuckle at an *Englisch*er referring to another man as an *Englisch*er. "I had a shop in Hopkinsville for several years and I did a lot of bartering. I try to treat people I barter with the way I want to be treated; everybody has hard times but it all comes back around eventually."

"My son actually lives about five miles from Hopkinsville."

"I sold the business to my brother in November but I'm sure we could work something out if you ever need anything out that way."

"I'll probably take you up on that. What else were you interested in?"

"Well the whole barn looks like a candy shop to me," I laugh. "But I was thinking of the gas powered automatic washing machine that's over by the freezer and I thought I saw a trampoline folded up over there in the corner."

"You're kinda sweet on this widow woman aren't you?" he asks studying my face. I can tell there's *ne* point in trying to deny it.

"*Ya*, I am but she's still officially in mourning so I'd appreciate it if you didn't mention it to anyone."

"Nothing wrong with trying to be the first in line son," he chuckles, patting me on the shoulder. "You get these two running while I check out the washer and the freezer. I'll see what my son brings in and we'll work something out. The trampoline you can have, I got it for free. Why don't you come on over and look at what I've got in the sheds while I'm waiting on David?"

"I'd like that. This widow woman, her name is Sarah; well she's going to start giving farm tours to help support her family so that she can keep the farm. I'm trying to help her get it off the ground so I'm wide open to ideas."

"She sure picked a hard way to go, there's some people over there who I'm sure won't be too supportive."

"*Ya* but she has a widowed *mamm* and five *kinner* to think about, she can't do it making quilts or selling corn by the roadside."

"Well you just look out for old Deacon Byler; he's bound to come against anything that brings *Englisch* folks into the community, hell he barely gets along with the Amish. I know you people cast lots to choose deacons in the church, but I tell you there was sure something screwy going on in Heaven that day. I did some business with him a few years back and he took me for a pretty penny. Of course I have no way to prove it seeing as I do most of my business by the handshake but I'd be careful around him."

"He's already paid us both a warning visit."

"Yeah he likes to intimidate people," he says, shaking his head. "Boy, I'd do just about anything to piss that old snake in the grass off. You just let me know if you see anything you could use for these tours and I'll make it as easy on you as I can," he says, opening the first shed door.

"*Danki*, I'm grateful. Sarah and the *kinner* are putting out flyers today in town and I'm planting a corn maze, but it won't be ready until August. She's got chicks and bunnies to pet, buggy rides, pony rides and some baked goods and jams to sell but I feel like we need more activities to draw people in."

"I've got just the thing, let me see here," he says looking around the shed. When he doesn't see what he's looking for, he opens the next shed, "Ah, here we go," he says.

I step inside and see several painted sheets of plywood leaning against the side wall. The one in front looks like a giant mouse eating Swiss cheese with holes cut out of the board "What is it?" I ask, thinking it might be a corn-hole game.

"We got these from a guy over in Marion who bought an old miniature golf course that was in foreclosure. He was going to tear it all down to build a big parking lot and my son offered to haul it all away for free so he could keep a few things for himself. These are some of the old props for the course and I've got a big bag of putters and some balls to go with it. If she's got a farm, I'm sure you could set up a little course with a few obstacles. There's even a windmill somewhere. I doubt I'll ever sell any of it but I hate getting rid of stuff because you just never know."

"You sure don't do you," I say, already imagining the possibilities. I spot an old chest-style drink cooler with sliding doors and an old popcorn machine in the shed too. They both need a major cleaning but they would be perfect for the new headquarters.

"How about that old drink cooler and the popcorn machine?" I ask, "Do they work?"

"I never bothered to check but they came from the golf course too. I'll make sure the cooler's working for you and we'll work out a trade on that but the golf stuff and the popcorn maker you can have. Just tell Miss Sarah I want to bring my grandkids for a tour when she gets it all set up."

"Mr. Sneed, you've got yourself a deal," I smile shaking his hand, "The whole family's going to be so excited."

"You just show that Deacon Byler a thing or two," he snickers, slapping his knee, "I can't wait to hear all about it through the grapevine. Now pull on into the yard and let's load it up before my son gets here, we could use the space."

"You got it," I chuckle.

CHAPTER TEN

On the way into town we stop at the produce stand across the parking lot from Yoder's Market. Everyone gets out to stretch their legs while Mark and I buy a half-bushel of lemons, six avocados and some fresh bananas. He loads them into the back of the buggy while Mary and I go into Yoder's store to see how Mrs. Yoder is doing after her knee surgery. She's a little plump for her height and she took a fall in the store one afternoon while stocking some shelves from a step-ladder.

If she agrees, I'll bring one of our new flyers by on the way home for her to post in the window. The store is a bit crowded with narrow aisles and often busy with hurrying customers running in and out so *mamm* and Mark stay behind to enjoy the fresh air and watch the *kinner* in the parking lot.

"*Gut* morning Mrs. Yoder, I say cheerfully, "It's nice to see you up and walking again."

"*Danki*, I'm feeling much better but I've got to use this cane for two weeks and it's not easy getting around in here." She's always been one to complain *ne* matter how well things are going but she works hard and I can't imagine it's always enjoyable. I try not to let it discourage me.

I hand her the banana bread, "I thought this might cheer you up," I smile.

"You're a dear," she half-smiles, "Are you shopping today?" Her voice is a little cold but I assume it's because of her condition.

"If you need some help in the store this week-,"

She interrupts me, "*Ne*, I'm fine. I suppose I'll get used to it."

"Well I don't want to take up too much of your time but I wanted you to be one of the first to know. We're going to start giving tours of the farm and-,"

"*Ya*, we've heard. Deacon Byler was here this morning. I really don't have time to discuss it but I can tell you I don't want any problems. The Byler's are *gut* customers," she says with a cold look.

"*Och*, I'm sorry, I didn't realize," I say, taken aback by her disapproval.

"If you're not here to shop I'm afraid I have some work to do."

"Have a *gut* day Mrs. Yoder, I hope you're feeling better soon," I say grabbing Mary's hand and leaving the store.

"That was rude of her," Mary says once we're outside.

"I turn to face her, "This is not going to ruin our day, do you understand?" I ask her.

"But what are we going to do if people are going to get mad at us?" she asks.

I think about a passage from the Bible, "Mary, do you believe the tours are God's answer for us?" I ask her.

"*Ya*, I know they are."

I put my arm around her, "Well Jesus told his disciples in Matthew 10: 12-14 *'12* And when ye come into an house, salute it. *13* And if the house be worthy, let your peace come upon it: but if it be not worthy, let your peace return to you. *14* And whosoever shall not receive you, nor hear your words, when ye depart out of that house or city, shake off the dust of your feet.' Well that's what we're going to do liebchen; we're going to shake it off like Jesus said." I start to stomp my feet playfully all the way to the buggy, as she does the same, giggling.

Inside, I'm heartbroken that someone I've always considered a friend could take a stand against me without even talking to me about it but I can't let her stop me from providing for my family.

We climb into the buggy as *mamm*, Hannah and the boys look at us strangely. I click my tongue and head for the grocery store hoping that the distraction will help me get over my hurt feelings before we go to the bakery.

Most of the time, the items we buy in the store are limited to things that we can't grow, household staples, and things that are too troublesome to make from scratch or too cheap to bother.

With John's assurance last night, I'm confident that there will be some kind of meat on the table for a while and I can focus more of my budget on items we plan to make for the tours. Fortunately, I should be able to work in a few special things that I think he'll enjoy as my way of thanking him for all that he does for us.

Inside the grocery store, we load up the shopping cart with twelve cans of pineapple on sale, ten pounds of flour, a box of baking soda, four packages of sandwich crème cookies, a bag of shredded coconut, eight boxes of pudding on sale, a jar of vanilla extract, four bags of navy beans, a box of lasagna noodles, a box of tea bags, two jars of peanut butter and mayonnaise, both on sale and four packages of tortillas. By the time we leave, I'm mostly over my hurt but a little intimidated by the possibility of it happening again today. I look forward to going to the bakery and visiting with Ruth.

Once the *kinner* and groceries are loaded, I click my tongue and snap the reins. "Let's go see Aunt Ruthie," I say cheerfully, trying to keep a positive attitude about passing out the flyers. I really wish John were here with me. I think just seeing his handsome face and being around his calm, supportive demeanor would give me the strength I need to face the risk of rejection again this afternoon.

As the horses clop along toward town, the *kinner* play the alphabet game with *mamm* helping Josh to participate. As they look for signs that contain the letters from A to Z, it suddenly occurs to me that for the first time in thirteen years, the man I'm longing to see, the man I want to run to for comfort and assurance in my hour of need isn't Jacob…it's John.

I try to wrap my head around that for a moment as I steer the horses into the bakery parking lot. As we stop moving, I'm lost in my thoughts, mindlessly sliding the door back and stepping out of the buggy until I hear my name called. I look back at *mamm* who is motioning toward the building.

I turn to look as Deacon Byler marches straight for me. I hear *mamm* tell the *kinner* to stay in the buggy as he gets closer. Without a word from me, *mamm* gets out of the buggy and goes in through the back door as he comes around the horses and steps into my space. I do my best not to budge an inch even though my legs are trembling.

"I hear you're going through with this despicable tour business nonsense, flooding our community with *Englisch*ers to look at us like animals in a zoo," he says with a scowl on his face.

"Deacon Byler, please, I talked to the bishop and I'm not breaking any of our laws," I say in a pleading tone.

I notice the bakery door open quietly out of the corner of my eye as Dan steps out to see what's going on.

"You think you're so smart, talking to the bishop behind my back. But I can still call you before the council," he threatens as his face turns red.

"I'm just trying to provide for my family, what else am I supposed to do?"

"You sell the farm you can't possibly afford and you do something respectable. You might not care if you disgrace yourself and your family but I will see to it that you will not disgrace this community, Sarah Fisher!" He raises his hand as he yells at me and I flinch slightly, thinking he's going to slap me.

Dan hurries over, "Deacon Byler, I'm afraid I'm going to have to ask you to leave. This is not the time or place for this."

Deacon Byler looks around angrily to see who's watching him. Hannah is crying and there are a few *Englisch*ers getting out of their cars. "I'm warning you now, you have not heard the last of this," he says, pointing his chubby finger in my face as he walks past me.

Mamm grabs Hannah and calms her down while everyone gets out of the buggy.

"Please take them inside Dan," I say, trying to hold it together.

"I don't want to leave you out-,"

"Please," I ask, "I'll go sit down in the office I just need some time alone."

Dan walks over to the other side of the buggy, "It's okay everyone, he's gone, let's all go inside and I'll let you choose a mid-morning treat," he says, putting his arm around *mamm*'s shoulder and walking everyone inside as she holds Hannah's hand. I tie off the horses, go inside and straight to the back office, shutting the door behind me.

I'm hurt, I'm angry, I'm humiliated and after two incidents this morning, I'm afraid. I take a seat in the chair behind the door that faces the desk and try to calm down but *ne* matter how hard I try – I can't stop the tears from coming.

I put my elbows on the desk and bury my face in my forearms. As the tears stream down my cheeks, I pray for God's help. I think of the terrified faces of my poor *kinner* as Deacon Byler yelled at me and my chest burns with shame and sorrow. "Dear God, please show me that I'm doing the right thing, please give me the strength to stand up for my family in the face of adversity, please help me," I cry.

I sit there, sobbing for a few minutes and feeling defeated when I hear two quick taps on the door behind me before it opens. I don't even want Ruth to see me crying like this. I wipe my eyes and as I turn to look at her, I hear John's voice say, "Okay if I come in?"

I look up at him disbelieving. “John?” I ask.

He steps into the room and leans down to look at me. Our eyes meet and I see the concern on his face. He gently puts his hands around my shoulders and pulls me to my feet as I throw my arms around him.

“Hey, it’s okay, I’m here, don’t cry, everything’s going to be okay,” he says in a calm, gentle voice. He holds me close to him, rubbing my back to comfort me.

I say nothing for several moments just letting myself be comforted by his arms wrapped around me, the warmth of his touch and the slow, steady sound of his heartbeat against my cheek. I feel so small in his arms but not in a way that makes me feel insignificant. I feel safe, protected and cared for.

He brushes the back of his fingers against my cheek and cradles my face in his hand as my crying stops. He tilts my face to him and kisses my forehead. “Where did you come from?” I ask.

If he said that he had been sent from Heaven, it really wouldn’t surprise me at this point. Because from the moment I met him, he’s been rescuing me in one way or another like an Angel on a mission from God.

“I just finished running some errands in town and I thought I would stop by to see if you had been here yet, I was going to offer to help you put out flyers, what happened?”

In spite of how *gut* it feels to be in his arms, I pull myself away and sit down in the chair. "I went to see how Mrs. Yoder's doing after her surgery, hoping we could put a flyer there on the way back but she basically told Mary and I to leave if we weren't there to shop. She said that Deacon Byler had been there telling them about my plans to ruin the community with my tour business and that she didn't want any trouble because he's a *gut* customer. I was still okay at that point, a little hurt maybe – but handling it. And then I pull into the parking lot here and he just comes out of nowhere at me. My family was afraid, I was afraid, not to mention humiliated. I thought he was going to slap me. I need to see if the *kinner* are okay but I didn't want them to see me break down after just telling Mary we weren't going to let people's disapproval ruin our day."

"Okay, well first of all, the *kinner* are fine. When I walked in, they were sitting at a table with Miriam, eating doughnut holes. Secondly, what Deacon Byler did wasn't just a simple case of disapproval, he acted like a bully and he never should have approached you like that...not alone, not in front of the *kinner* or under any other circumstances. Of course you broke down. It was completely uncalled for and I will see that something is done about it. What I don't want you to do is beat yourself up over it, because it would be a shame to give him the satisfaction. That's exactly what he wants."

"I know you're right, it just took me by surprise, but I swear to you John, this is not going to stop me from doing what I think is right for my family," I assure him.

"That's my girl," he says rubbing my shoulder, "Now can you pull it together enough to check on the *kinner* while I talk to Dan and then we'll go see what surprises I have for everyone?"

I manage a smile, "I could use one of your surprises right about now."

He looks at me seriously and cradles my face in his hands. I feel his gaze reaching down inside of me and I want so much to feel his lips on mine but it's as if I can feel the blackness of my mourning dress swallow me whole.

He gives me a kind smile as he traces his thumb over my cheekbone, "Come on, let's get you home," he says, opening the door behind him.

CHAPTER ELEVEN

"Where's Ruth?" she asks as we walk toward the front.

"She was out delivering a cake when I got here and Dan was alone at the counter with a customer, so he just sent me to the back to check on you."

As we reach the front section of the bakery, Hannah and Josh hurry over to Sarah and hug her. I step over to the counter to talk to Dan while there are *ne* customers waiting.

"Is she okay?" he asks.

"She was just shaken up but I think she's got more resolve than you and I put together," I smile. "I think it was worsened by the fact that she had just come from Yoder's and they practically told her to leave the store. Deacon Byler had apparently been by there this morning."

"Knowing Mrs. Yoder, she's probably more concerned that whatever goods Sarah sells might take some of her precious business, than she is about what it will do to the community. Their store caters to the *Englisch* fascination with the Amish every day, heck most of the Amish can't even afford to shop there."

"Well I think Sarah's about to knock everybody's socks off. She's repurposing the woodshed as tour headquarters with a little gift shop to sell her wares. She doesn't know it yet but I got her an old fashioned popcorn machine, a drink cooler, a trampoline and a whole bunch of props from a miniature golf course from old man Sneed."

"You're kidding," he chuckles. "You've got it bad brother but you're right, that's going to be pretty incredible."

"Look, the whole reason I was coming by here in the first place is to get your number and give you my new cell phone number in case something like this happened."

"I didn't figure you for the cell phone type," he smiles, handing me a pen and his business card.

"Me either but I think it's the right thing to do considering the circumstances," I say, writing my number on a napkin.

"Well I feel a lot better knowing we can reach each other in a hurry," he says, "Maybe together we can stop Deacon Byler from turning the whole town against her."

"Did you make that list of business you think would let her put up flyers? I don't think she can handle any more rejection today."

"*Ya*, I gave it to Mary but maybe I should go with them. It might make a difference if they know that other people in the community are already behind her."

"I think that's a *gut* idea."

"Why don't you take the ladies home and when Ruth gets back, I'll take the boys around to put up flyers. I promised Ben I would take him for pizza at lunch time anyway. I'll bring them home later."

"That might work; I'll help the girls get things set up back at the house to surprise the boys, that'll get their spirits up."

"*Gut* idea. I'll see you later this afternoon then."

I pull Sarah aside and tell her the plan. She tells the boys that Dan and Ben are going to take them around to put up flyers and I can tell that Mark and Samuel are almost relieved knowing that he probably has more influence in town. It doesn't hurt that they probably don't want to imagine seeing their *mamm* confronted by anyone else.

Before we leave, Mary hugs Mark and I hear her tell him, "If anyone disapproves, just shake the dust off your feet like Jesus said, we know this is God's plan."

I'm actually kind of moved by it, not only because I know that it's probably something Sarah taught her at one point or another, but because I can see the special bond that they share as twins and how the same kindred, determined faith is woven through the entire family.

As soon as the girls see my wagon loaded down and covered with a tarp, they want to know what's back there. Mary and Hannah even try to bribe me with the promise of desserts but I stand my ground knowing it will be a much sweeter unveiling once they've spent an hour or so wondering about it.

Sarah leads the way in the buggy while I follow behind her. On the way there, I'm dreaming up ways to make the golf course work by building a sand trap and burying plastic pipe in the ground to make tunnels, cups and burrows around the different props.

As she turns onto the drive leading to the house, she stops the buggy and gets out. I pull behind her, watching to see what she's doing and I realize that someone has spray painted over her egg sign in black paint.

I step off of the tractor, put my hands around her shoulders and look her in the eyes to reassure her. "Shake the dust off your feet, whoever did this is just trying to intimidate you, don't let them rob you of your joy. You were going to need a new sign anyway and we'll make you an even better one," I promise her.

She nods her head and gets back into the buggy then pulls down in front of the barn. I know that she's upset by the fact that they've brought the fight to her home. I don't blame her and I'm enraged by the bullying tactic but she's trying to stand strong and the least I can do is try to contain my anger in her presence and just do what I need to in order to stop it. "God, show me the way," I pray as I shut off the engine.

Inside the house, Hannah sticks to me like glue, even hugging my legs and I can tell that she's still frightened.

Miriam starts the kettle while Sarah starts rifling through the fridge. "Come here girls," I say to Mary and Hannah, taking a seat at the table. Mary sits in the chair next to me and Hannah crawls into my lap.

"It's been a tough morning hasn't it?"

"I just don't like people getting mad at us when we didn't do anything wrong," Mary says.

"*Ya* and he scared me and he crossed out our sign," Hannah adds laying her head on my shoulder.

I take a deep breath to stop my outrage from reaching the surface in front of them because I know that's the last thing they need right now. "Sometimes just because people are grown-up it doesn't mean they always do the right thing but I promise he's not going to hurt you or your *mamm* or *mammi* or anyone here. I won't let him," I assure them.

"But what if you're not here?" Mary asks.

"Go get your notebook and a marker," I tell her.

She complies and comes back to the table.

I write my phone number on a piece of paper and fold it.

"Now Hannah you take this paper and Mary you take the

marker and run to the phone shack as fast as you can and call that number. Go on, I'm timing you."

They scramble to the door and run outside as I look at the clock.

"John, you didn't?" Sarah asks.

"I did and with everything that's happened today, I'm even more certain that it was the right decision. I wasn't going to be out hunting with the boys or even Caleb and not have a way to call for help in an emergency. Besides, I need it for the shop if I'm going to be running back and forth from here to my place to Hopkinsville."

"You're a wise man John Troyer," Miriam says, patting my shoulder as she brings me a cup of coffee.

My phone rings, "Hello?" I answer.

"This is your phone number? How long did it take us?" Mary asks.

"It took 21 seconds," I tell her, "Now write that number in the phone shack where everyone can see it and hide the paper there too, then come back."

"Okay," she says excitedly.

I write the number down three more times and tear the paper, handing two to Sarah and one to her *mamm*. "Make sure you each have it in your purse in case you're out somewhere and make sure there's one here at the house but you're still going to need to start locking the doors when you leave. I'll make you some extra keys if you need them."

"*Ya* we need to get into the habit anyway with strangers on the property," Sarah adds.

"Especially at the headquarters," Miriam agrees.

The girls make it back and promise to show the boys where the numbers are located.

"Okay so if something happens any of you can call my number anytime, even if it's on Sunday or in the middle of the night. I'm going to be here a lot while we get the tours going anyway but if you're too afraid to run to the phone shack you can always lock yourself in the house or the woodshop."

"You mean HQ, that's what we're calling it," Mary informs me.

"Ok well HQ will be a safe place too."

"Okay," they both agree.

"Can we see those big surprises on your wagon now?" Hannah asks.

At least I know that means she's feeling less traumatized by the day's events.

"Lunch is almost ready," Sarah says, "Go ahead and feed the animals and gather the eggs. We'll enjoy the surprise more after we eat, I'm hungry," she smiles.

"Okay!" the squeal, heading out the door.

"*Danki* John," Miriam says, "Those girls think a lot of you."

"I think a lot of them too."

"I'm going to go help them with the chores," she says, wiping her hands on a towel before she heads outside.

"Are you okay Sarah," I ask.

She drapes a towel over the cutting board she's working on, stirs the pot she has on the stove and sits down next to me. "*Ya*, I'm okay. I'm just angry that my *kinner* had to be affected by all of this."

"They're tough like their *mamm*, they'll be okay," I assure her, rubbing my hand over hers. All I want to do right now is to hold her and kiss away the hurt, but just being with her seems to calm the anger brewing inside of me. I know that I have to keep my head for her sake.

"I'm just glad you're here," she says curling her fingers around mine.

"I'm glad to hear you say that because we have a lot of work to do," I chuckle, trying to lighten the mood before I lose my self control.

"Look I suppose I should tell you one part of the surprise just so I don't get into trouble."

"Okay," she smiles suspiciously, going back to the stove to

stir the soup.

"It's a trampoline. I thought we could put hay around it to cover the metal frame and call it a hay bounce or something."

She's looking at me with a stunned look on her face.

"All kids love to jump around," I add trying to sell the idea. "I saw one the day I got the bunnies and yesterday, I just lucked upon it."

"Wait until surprise time to mention it to *mamm*," she tells me with a wary look.

"Should I be concerned?" I chuckle.

"*Ne* more than usual," she laughs and I suddenly feel like I'm the one in the dark.

I'm about to probe her for more information as Miriam and the *kinner* return from outside. The girls run to wash their hands in the bathroom while Miriam washes her hands and the eggs in the sink, before putting them in the fridge.

We sit down to a lunch of turkey wraps with a side of vegetable soup and all of us are now bubbling with anticipation. It's exciting and just the kind of distraction I need to quell my anger and forget about Deacon Byler, at least for today.

Once we finish, I take them all outside to the wagon, unfasten everything and pull back the tarp in one swift motion for the big reveal.

"Is that a popcorn machine?" *mamm* asks.

"It's like the one at the fall festival!" Mary squeals.

"What is all of the wood for?" Sarah asks.

I can't help but laugh as I lift one of the sheets out of the wagon and turn it around for her, "These are from a miniature golf course that shut down. I have clubs and balls and tees and lots of ideas for how we can set up a miniature golf course. We just have to decide where to put it," I chuckle.

"My goodness, I never would have imagined," Sarah says with a big smile, "What a great idea."

"I want to see the rest of it!" Mary giggles.

"Me too!" Hannah squeals.

"Me three," Miriam adds with a chuckle.

I unload all of the painted plywood and props one-by-one, lining them up against the side of the barn. There's the mouse, the top half of a windmill with spinning blades, a painted silo with a long plastic chute, a wooden bridge, a giant rubber pig where you have to stick your hand in its mouth to retrieve your ball, a giant bullfrog perched on a floating lily pad, a bull with legs that sway back and forth like he's bucking with his hind legs, what looks like a view of the inside of a hay loft, a hen sitting on a nest, and a cowboy riding a horse with a lasso over his head, painted horses in stalls and painted cows grazing in a pasture, and a teepee.

"I think it might have had a cowboy theme and I think some of these are just backgrounds because mini golf is usually just nine holes," I chuckle.

"It's amazing, we could make this work," Sarah says with her hand tucked under her chin as she walks back and forth looking at them.

"This must have cost a lot of money," Mary says.

"Actually, it didn't cost me anything. I'm doing some repair work for an *Englisch* man near town and we worked out some trades. When I told him about the tours, he threw in a lot of this especially for you for free; it was just sitting in his shed. He said to tell you he wants to bring his grandkids when you get it up and running."

"Of course, we'd be happy to!" Sarah chuckles.

"I wanna play!" Hannah says excitedly.

"Well we have to do the work to get it all set up first but I promise you'll get to be one of the first to test it out," I laugh.

"The boys are going to love this," Miriam says.

"I have a few other things too," I tell them, "I know it doesn't look like it now but that's a trampoline. I thought we could surround it with hay for safety."

I watch as Miriam looks at Sarah with a big smile and chuckles as the girls shriek with excitement.

"What?" I ask cluelessly.

"*Mamm* was just saying to me that we should try to find a used trampoline last night. She's always wanted to try one," Sarah says with a smile.

Miriam steps over to the wagon and runs her hand over the pile of parts. "You are an angel, John Troyer," she laughs, "My *daed* took us to a circus once when I was a teenager and the acrobats on the trampoline were my favorite, it looked like so much fun."

"Well then you have to be the first one to try it when we get it put together," I smile.

"Are you really going to do it *mammi*?" Mary asks curiously.

"You're darned right I am," she chuckles.

"I also have two tires for swings and a commercial cooler that we can put in the HQ so you can sell cold drinks. My *Englisch* friend is checking it over to make sure it's running properly. I'll bring it over after I work on his tractor Friday, but it's going to need a really *gut* cleaning."

"*Och* John, I just don't know what to say," she says as her eyes well with tears.

"Just tell me you won't let anyone stand in your way," I smile as Miriam hugs her.

"Well then, let's get started, we have lots of work to do,"

she laughs and comes over to hug me as the girls follow suit.

We leave the props alongside the barn for the boys to see and everyone pitches in to clear out the woodshed. Miriam and Mary start cleaning the popcorn machine while Sarah, Hannah and I start moving all of the tools into the cabinets and drawers in the barn and move the wood scraps, trims and veneers to the empty stall next to Joker. I store the stains and varnishes in the cabinets over the long counter and set aside a few of the bigger tools that I think she can sell.

Once there's nothing left but the cabinets, the bakery case and two tall swivel chairs, the girls start cleaning while I lay out the trampoline parts and try to figure out how to put it back together.

Sometime around 4:00 p.m., Dan arrives with the boys and we all gather near the barn as they head down the drive. Everyone climbs out and the boys rush over to see what's going on.

I give Dan a chance to take it all in and talk to Sarah for a few minutes before enlisting his help with the trampoline. The *kinner* talk excitedly about the endless golf course possibilities.

Sarah calms everyone down, sending Josh and Ben to tend to the rabbits as Mark and Samuel come over to help us.

"We put up fifteen flyers and we already had five people that said they would come for a tour!" Samuel tells me.

"Yeah Ruth's closing up the bakery tonight and bringing

dinner for everyone. She said that since we put up the sign, three of our customers have already told her that they were coming Saturday. She doesn't think that we have any time to waste."

I look at him and chuckle, "She's probably right."

"By the way, I brought a sign post we don't use anymore and two empty wooden barrels you can probably repurpose for something. There are three more at the bakery that Ruth's bringing with her; she's getting a ride from Mr. Albury."

"I'm sure they'll come in handy," I assure him.

In a little over an hour, we have the trampoline assembled. Since it's about fourteen feet in diameter and weighs about 200 pounds, we leave it right where it sits until we know for certain where it's going.

"Can we try it now?" Mark asks.

"*Ne* sir, I promised your *mammi* she could be first," I chuckle.

"Now that I have to see," Dan laughs.

We all walk back toward the barn as Josh, Ben and the women are all working like busy bees. Sarah comes out of the woodshed. "We're ready for the popcorn machine if you two want to bring it on over."

"We go inside the house where Miriam is taking four loaves of some kind of bread out of the oven with two more sitting on the counter. "Mmmm that smells *gut*," I tell her. "The trampoline's ready and we're going to take the popcorn machine over," I tell her.

"Okay I'm coming," she smiles.

We take the popcorn machine to the woodshed and marvel at how the place looks. There's a four foot counter along the side wall just inside the entrance with a swivel chair at each end and a four-foot span of cabinets and countertops across from it in the center of the room. The opposite wall is bare except for the two windows.

"I was thinking we would put the drink chest between the windows with maybe some kind of display on either side.

The bakery case is sitting in front of the shorter wall already filled with upper and lower cabinets and countertop and the cubby-hole shelves that span the opposing short wall are half-filled already with jars of jams, pie fillings, sauces and pickled goods. There's also a small corner closet with *ne* door which is still empty for the time being.

"Wow this is really a *gut* start," Dan says, "Is that so people can guess how many are in the jar?" he asks, pointing to a jar of candy corn on the counter next to a ceramic piggy bank shaped like a pig.

"It was Mary's idea; we thought we would charge a penny per guess or something."

"That's a *gut* idea," I chuckle, "How many are in there?"

"We can't tell you," Josh giggles.

"I counted them!" Hannah informs me.

We all chuckle just as a horn beeps outside. Sarah and the *kinner* run out to greet Ruth while Dan and I put the popcorn machine on top of the counter behind the bakery case. We unload the barrels and put one in each corner of the window wall, one on each side of the entrance and one in the closet area with the sign post until we figure out where we'll need them.

"*Ya*, I like it," Miriam says as Ruth joins us inside.

"*Och* wow, this is awesome," she says looking around.

"It's our tour HQ," Samuel informs her.

She chuckles, "I can just imagine it with gourds and straw decorations and all of your treats in the case, it's beautiful, I never realized how big it was but this is perfect and the golf course, that is going to be something else," she smiles hugging Sarah.

"Don't forget the trampoline!" Mark says, "Are you ready *mammi*?"

"*Ya* let's go," she laughs.

We go back outside and I help her onto the trampoline. We all watch her take the first few jumps before letting Hannah, Josh and Ben Join her. When they've had a *gut* fifteen minutes of jumping, Dan and I get the little ones down so they can play with the bunnies. Mark, Mary and Samuel take a turn while we show Ruth the golf props and toss around ideas on how to set it up.

"Should we postpone our fishing trip until Saturday morning and try to get this set up tomorrow instead?" Sarah asks.

"That's probably a *gut* idea if we want to have it in place by then, I have a tractor to work on Friday morning but we can still plow the corn field Friday afternoon," I tell her.

"I'll help for a few hours tomorrow too," Dan offers, "Ruth and I figured we should do what we can to be involved so that certain people around here know that you have our support too."

"I appreciate that, all of you, she smiles.

The women take the younger boys while Mark, Dan and I load up the props and drive around on the tractor to decide on a *gut* location for the golf course, the trampoline, the potential picnic area and the hay slide. Mark sketches it out on paper and makes notes as we make decisions and come up with a to-do list. Once we've determined the overall layout, we concentrate on the golf course, sitting out props as markers as we decide on the order and the set up of all nine holes.

When we're fairly confident in our plan, we tip the trampoline over onto the wagon and I very slowly drive it to our chosen spot with the two of them holding it in place to keep it from falling over. When we finally have it all set up, it's just about time for dinner.

CHAPTER TWELVE

Thursday, April 9

In spite of the discouragement we may have endured yesterday, the entire family was up by daylight and bubbling with excitement this morning.

The *kinner* head out to do their morning chores while *mamm* and I prepare a special breakfast. John sits at the table with his notes, working out details for the golf course while *mamm* fries the bacon he brought for us and I shred fresh carrots for my carrot-cake pancakes.

"I just want you both to know, Dan is going to talk to Bishop Graber today about the incident with Deacon Byler. I think it will help that he already knows the bishop pretty well and it did occur at his store," John explains, "I hope that it will give everyone a little peace of mind."

"*Danki* for letting us know but I don't want to mention it in front of the *kinner*. I think it will just upset them."

"I understand," he smiles.

"How's the golf course coming?" *mamm* asks.

"I just figured out a way to set up a ball tunnel for the hay loft and I'm trying to decide how to make something that looks like mud but isn't muddy," he chuckles.

"Is it for the big giant pig?" I chuckle.

"*Ya*, I think I can get some black sand from a guy in Hopkinsville for a few bucks. They use it for sandblasting."

That's a great idea and a lot cleaner than mud," *mamm* chuckles.

I stir my batter just as the bacon's finished frying and *mamm* calls Hannah in with the egg basket.

"She probably got distracted by the bunnies," she chuckles.

Mamm starts to cook the eggs and I start the pancakes. The girls come in to wash up and when they finish, Mary sets the table while Hannah starts counting black jellybeans for her second jar of 'Guess how many.'

A few minutes later, the boys come inside, wash their hands and unintentionally distract Hannah from her counting as they talk about how many golf balls and putters we have. She sighs heavily, puts all of the jellybeans back into the bag and decides to wait until later when she has a 'piece of quiet!'

I look at John and *mamm*, trying to resist the urge to laugh so that she doesn't feel made fun of but I'm too tickled to scold her.

When the pancakes and eggs are done, we gather around the table in prayer before digging in.

"I think I'm going to call Natalie today and ask her to make some new flyers on her computer. I want to include the golf course and trampoline and she can probably do it in less than twenty minutes. I was going to ask her to stop by sometime in the next few days anyway."

"That's *gut*, you'll probably spark more interest that way," John agrees.

"Can you ask her to put an Amish buggy on it like she did for the egg sign? Remember how the *Englisch*ers said that's how they knew we were Amish?" Mark asks.

"*Ya*, I will," I assure him, "Seeing the buggy might encourage people to read the flyer."

"I brought a load of hay from my place so that maybe you, Miriam, Josh and Hannah can start setting up the toddler maze. I'll get some to replace it on one of my trips back from Hopkinsville when I bring the rest, but it won't hurt to get a jump on it. We'll put it close to HQ so that *mamm*'s can shop while the kids play."

"*Gut* thinking," *mamm* says. "Are we going to do the same pattern as the cornfield?"

"Since it's for the little ones, let's see if there's an easier one in the coloring book," I tell her.

"I've got a plan for the corn maze too," John says. "We'll plow and then cross-seed in two different directions so that the walls of the maze will grow nice and dense. From there, we'll measure out the design by driving stakes into the ground and using string to mark our pathways. Then, in a month or so when the growth is ten or twelve inches high, we can mow-in the design and pull up our markers. We'll mow 60-inch paths so that there will be room for people to walk through side-by-side, with strollers or in wheelchairs. Anything that doesn't work, we'll just modify the next time we plant."

"Can I help?" Mark asks.

"Ask your *mamm*," John says, giving me a knowing smile.

"I've decided to let John teach you to drive the tractor so you'll help him do the plowing and mowing but only with his supervision."

"*Danki mamm*, I won't let you down I'll be very safe," he promises.

We finish our breakfast and help unload the hay near HQ. John, Mark, Mary and Samuel head out in the tractor to work on the golf course while the rest of us tidy up the kitchen. I assign Josh the job of tearing out the maze pages from the activity book so we can lay them out and compare them when we're done.

We choose a maze shaped like a barn because it has straight edges and a fairly simple design. I use a plastic ruler to measure the lines and plan the layout like I would for a quilt. I make little hatch marks to indicate each bale of hay so that the *kinner* can picture it better. "We might not have enough hay but we'll start with the outsides and fill in the inner walls later if we need to," I explain.

Outside, we start pushing bales onto the ground with the *kinner* rolling them to us as *mamm* and I line them up. Between the two of them, Josh and Hannah push about one bale for every two *mamm* and I carry but I don't mind because it keeps them involved and still divides the workload.

When we have all of the outside edges in place, we leave empty spaces representing the barn door and the hay loft to act as our entry and exit points. I'm still charged but I don't want to put too much stress on *mamm*.

We go back inside to get the beans on the stove with the ham and bones I already have prepped. I whip up a batch of cornbread and put the pan in the oven while *mamm* makes a peanut butter pie and the *kinner* work together on the jellybean jar.

She watches them along with the cornbread while I load the *kinner*'s wagon with three bales at a time from the barn and roll them over to the maze. I take my time and work on the inside walls until our hay supply is down to ten bales for the rabbits and horses. *Mamm* comes out to get me.

"*Och* Sarah, you shouldn't have done all of this by yourself," she scolds.

"It's okay *mamm*, I just had so much energy that I felt like getting as much as I could done with what we had available," I assure her.

"Well John and the *kinner* should be back for lunch at any minute, come and rest at least until after you eat or you won't be able to move tomorrow."

I know she's right but I feel satisfied and I think I worked out some of my pent up aggression and anger from yesterday. It's pretty cool looking if I do say so myself.

Back inside the house, we work together to put the fish wraps together since we didn't use them for dinner last night. *Mamm* already has the rest of the vegetable soup warmed on the stove and we still have the pea salad and a loaf of pineapple zucchini bread to go with it.

I hear the tractor just as I'm debating putting the wraps in the fridge. We decide to serve everything on paper plates to avoid a big cleanup. I look outside to see what's taking them so long to come inside as they walk toward the house.

"*Mamm*, we saw the maze! It's cool!" Samuel says.

"You guys really did a *gut* job; you must've robbed the hay from the barn," John smiles.

"You've got to see the golf course too," Mary adds

excitedly.

I chuckle, “We’ll all go look at it when you’re done, now come inside and get some food in your bellies.”

Shortly after lunch is over, Dan arrives with Ben and all of the boy head off to help with the golf course while *mamm*, Mary, Hannah and I decide to get busy with more canning and baking. Without more hay, there’s really little else we can do.

We start by emptying *mamm*’s freezer in the *Daadi Haus*, which we’ve always reserved for freezing fruit since she does most of the canning and pie baking. Our plan is to can everything inside into jam or pie filling, opening up the freezer space for our quick breads.

Mamm and Mary start working on a batch of strawberry rhubarb jam while Hannah and I mix the recipe for four loaves of banana bread. Once we get the loaves in the oven to bake, we set a timer to remind *mamm* and Mary to pull the bread out and head back over to the main house.

I stir the beans and prepare my cream cheese mixture which needs to sit overnight. Next, we mix the ingredients for my raisin spice loaves and get those four pans in my oven on a timer. While the bread is baking, we make a sheet pan of coconut macaroons and sit them in the fridge to set before I bake them.

As we mix a batch of oatmeal chocolate chip cookies, it occurs to me that I need to figure out the cost per item on everything we bake like Ruth does, so that I'll know what to charge and whether something is worth making or not. When we've finished spooning the cookies onto the sheet pan, I turn on the gas oven for the first time and put them in to bake with my macaroons on bottom.

By the time the cookies are in, it's just about time to start the roast for dinner. I put the hunk of beef in the pan, season it on both sides, surround it with the vegetables I pre-cut and watch carefully for the cookies to finish so that I can see how the gas oven compares to my wood stove. When they finish, I sit them out to cool and put my roast in right behind them while Hannah makes notes for me.

By dinner time, half of the baked goods have been cooled, flash-frozen, wrapped and labeled before storing them in *mamm*'s freezer compartment at the *Daadi Haus*. She and Mary made six jars of strawberry rhubarb jam, four quart jars of apple pie filling and two quart jars of peach.

The four of us load everything into the *kinner*'s wagon, pull it over to HQ and put them on display in the bakery case and the cubby shelves. Anything that doesn't sell can always be eaten or taken to frolics and Sunday church luncheons. But just seeing everything all set up is truly gratifying for all of us.

"It looks so beautiful in here. What else do we need to make?" Mary asks.

I chuckle. Undoubtedly she's running on sheer enthusiasm at this point just like her *mamm*. "That's enough for tonight, tomorrow we we'll try out the popcorn machine and make peanut butter caramel popcorn balls, which will probably fill half of the lower shelf and we'll candy some apples for the other half."

"*Ya* that would be perfect," *mamm* agrees, "We should probably make some tea and the lemonade too until we can afford to fill the cooler with sodas and bottled water."

"I want to help!" Hannah says as the boys return from the golf course. John gets them all tending to their evening chores while *mamm* and I set the table and warm the cornbread for dinner.

When everyone's work for the day is accomplished and our bellies full, *mamm* and I wash dishes while John takes the *kinner* to tend to chores at his house and to spy on the pig corral with binoculars. In spite of how completely worn out I feel by the time everyone's in bed for the night, I can't remember a more satisfying day.

CHAPTER THIRTEEN

Friday, April 10

By the time lunch is over and afternoon chores are done, the *kinner* are all anxiously awaiting John's arrival. We had a family arrive for a tour at 10:00 a.m. this morning and they're eager to tell him how it went. We also finished filling the bakery case with popcorn balls and caramel apples, made two gallons of fresh lemonade and five gallons of tea for the drink cooler.

I send the boys out to the garden to harvest peas, carrots, beets and celery while they wait. John promised to help them hang the tire swings in the picnic area before he and Mark plow the cornfield and they can barely contain their energy.

Mamm and Mary pluck two chickens, while Hannah and I bake an angel food cake for tonight's dessert. We'll top it with the last of the strawberries *mamm* emptied from her freezer yesterday and serve it with fresh whipped cream.

While the cake is in the oven, I walk over to the phone shack with my notes to call Natalie about making the updated flyers.

Natalie has been a dear and trusted friend since Mark and Mary were born. Back then, she was an obstetrics nurse who tended to me when I was hospitalized with complications from my pregnancy. She was the only nurse I encountered during my stay that didn't seem stand-offish because of my Amish roots and she was in the delivery room when the twins were born. She paid us a personal visit about a month later to check on everyone and we've been friends ever since. She still refers to Mark and Mary as 'The Miracle Twins.'

I eagerly tell her all about the tours and the preparations we've made as she cheers me on, asking questions and encouraging me.

"I'm so excited to know that all of you are working together to start the business. I just know it's going to be a success, in fact, I think I'm going to write about it in my blog," she chuckles.

"Is that the internet magazine you were telling me about?" I ask curiously.

"Yes, the one we started for the restaurant. People mention reading it when they come in, I never realized what a good marketing tool it would be."

"Well, that's part of the reason I called," I explain, "I made up a flyer by hand and had some copies made but that was before my friend John surprised us with the whole golf course idea and before we decided to make a gift shop out of the woodshop. I thought maybe I could give you some information and you could make up some flyers on your computer if it wouldn't be too much trouble. I owe all of this to you for putting that picture of the horse and buggy on our egg sign to begin with," I chuckle.

"Of course, I'll be happy to help, just tell me what you want on them," she says excitedly.

I give her the information from the old flyer and my notes on the things we want to add as she writes everything down, clarifying a few things here and there.

"I appreciate this so much; I've already encountered some opposition to the idea in the community. So, I'm thinking it wouldn't hurt to advertise outside of Hope Landing."

"Well bravo to you for not letting them intimidate you. Stephen and I will be happy to put up a flyer at the restaurant and in the store. I know a lot of the military moms around here would enjoy doing something like that with their kids. Are you giving tours tomorrow?" she asks.

"*Ya* we'll be here," I chuckle.

"I'll come by once the lunch crowd dies down, I'd love to see what you've done."

"Okay, I'll see you then!"

I hang up the phone and smile. *Englisch*er or not, I don't think there has ever been a time when I haven't felt supported and encouraged by Natalie's friendship.

As I walk back toward the house, I see the boys carry their buckets in from the garden as John pulls down the drive.

I watch as he parks in front of the kitchen door.

"How did your morning go?" I ask when he shuts off the engine.

"Quite well actually, I got the old man's tractor and another mower running. He's tickled pink and I'm ready to work out some other trades. He's got all kinds of useful stuff there, how was your morning?"

"Well we had a tour today. The *kinner* are eager to tell you all about it," I chuckle, "We still managed to get HQ stocked and ready to go except for the drink cooler and Natalie is coming tomorrow with new flyers."

"You'll probably have to help me get the cooler inside; I don't want to tip it on its side to put it on the dolly and I doubt Mark can lift as much as you can considering how you handled that hay yesterday," he chuckles.

"I can do that," I smile, "Come on inside, the boys just carried my vegetables in from the garden."

"Actually, could you send Mark outside for a minute?" he asks, unhooking the bungee cords from the blue tarp he has over the back half of the wagon.

I go inside and tell Mark to go outside while the other boys carry the laundry downstairs.

I take my cake out just in time to keep it from burning as *mamm* and Mary arrive with two plump, fresh chickens. I let them wash up while I get out my stock pots for boiling, deciding I may as well debone them at the same time.

Mary gasps, "*Mamm* look," just as I get the chickens washed and into the pots.

I dry my hands on the towel as I look over my shoulder at a big white freezer rolling through the kitchen door and over the threshold.

"What in the world?" I say, watching as John wheels it past the table and in through the pantry door.

Mamm, Mary, the boys and I all crowd around the door to see what's going on.

"John, you didn't?" I ask.

"Well, we're probably going to corral those pigs on Monday or Tuesday and hunt some turkey next week, you'll need the freezer space," he says, loosening the straps on the dolly.

I step over and hug him without thinking and before I know it *mamm* and all of the *kinner* are joining in.

"This is incredible, *danki*," I say as my eyes well with tears.

"John traded his *Englisch* friend for it *mamm*, maybe I should learn how to fix engines too," Mark says excitedly.

"You're a generous man John Troyer," *mamm* says affectionately.

My eyes are welled with tears. "If you only knew how long I've wanted a freezer," I say, trying not to cry as Mary and *mamm* marvel at how roomy it is.

"I'm so glad you like it," he smiles. "I wanted to get this and the cooler inside so that we can start plowing before it gets much later but I can install it after dark if I need to."

"I'm ready when you are," I smile, looking him in the eye.

We manage to get the cooler inside HQ and John sets off with the boys to put up the tire swings and work the cornfield. *Mamm* and Hannah prepare the biscuit dough for dumplings while Mary and I wash and chop vegetables, waiting for the chickens to boil.

"That was awfully nice of John to get us a freezer. We'll have plenty of room for our breads and things now," Mary says.

"Think of all that meat! We'll have to cook him nice dinners," *mamm* says.

"And bacon too," Hannah giggles.

"*Ya*, he has been very *gut* to us and I know the Lord is responsible for sending him," I smile, "We must all keep him in our prayers."

"Maybe you should marry him *mamm*," Hannah says.

"Hannah," *mamm* scolds.

"You don't marry someone just because they do nice things for you," Mary explains, "But John would probably make a really *gut daed* someday."

I turn to scrape the cut carrots into a bowl. *Mamm* smiles at me knowingly and I avert my gaze back to my cutting board.

Once the chicken is cooling and the vegetables are in the broth, Mary and I head to HQ with cleaning rags and buckets of bleach water to clean out the drink cooler. *Mamm* stays behind to debone the chickens and watch over dinner while Hannah makes a *danki* card for John.

***

Mrs. Byler answers the door for the final attendee of the private meeting that I've arranged. Once everyone is seated comfortably around the dining table, I commence with the business at hand.

"Mr. and Mrs. Glick; Mr. and Mrs. Shetler; Mr. Zug; Mr. and Mrs. Yoder, hello to you all and *danki* for coming," I smile warily, "I've asked you all here this evening because we have a serious cancer growing in Hope Landing that threatens the sanctity of our settlement, our *kinner*, our grandchildren and our friends and loved ones. I believe that it's our Godly duty to stop that cancer from infecting our community."

I take my seat at the head of the table and sigh, "I've chosen all of you because just like Mrs. Byler and me, you cleave the time-honored beliefs and traditions of our faith. We share the devout belief that separation from the *Englisch* is the most important way to preserve our values and the members of this community. I'm here to tell you that Sarah Fisher has been giving tours to *Englisch*ers and she intends to make an occupation of it!" I throw the flyers that I confiscated in town this afternoon onto the table for everyone to read.

"Now we've looked the other way at a few minor deviations from tradition because of the times we live in, but we mustn't allow our community to be overrun with *Englisch*ers – snapping pictures and gawking at us like zoo animals. Soon they'll be traipsing around at will, socializing with our *kinner*, coming into our homes and corrupting the minds of our youth. We all have a responsibility to protect the generations of faith and tradition that reside here. It is up to us to take a public stand against this nonsense before everything we've worked for our whole lives vanishes, leaving us driven out of the community and uprooted from our homes."

"What does the bishop intend to do about all of this Deacon Byler?" Mr. Glick asks.

"Bishop Graber is a busy man with the burden of the entire community on his shoulders, I couldn't possibly burden him with this too but the Word of God says in Matthew 5:30 that '*if thy right hand offend thee, cut it off, and cast it from thee: for it is profitable for thee that one of thy members should perish, and not that thy whole body should be cast into hell.'* I don't know about you Mr. Glick but I am offended and I will not let one insolent widow woman make a harlot of our humble, God fearing community. I will not trade my soul or the soul of my loved ones to the devil for her sake!" I wipe my brow with my handkerchief.

"Has she been letting the *Englisch* inside her home?" Mr. Zug asks incredulously.

"I can't prove it but I watched and waited from the roadway as she gave a tour and I never saw the *Englischers* outside. Whether she already has or not, how long before she is seduced by the way of the wicked?" I ask him, referring to Proverbs 12:26.

"All five of her *kinner* will be in school next year, right alongside mine and all of yours too. Her eldest son already struck Deacon Byler's grandson in the school yard last year and I don't want my *kinner* exposed to the violence of unruly children. Not to mention that farm…over forty acres for two widows to maintain…it's preposterous. How long does she expect to manage it? Her *mamm* is in poor health and none of her *kinner* more than ten years old," Mr. Yoder adds.

"Have they requested money from the widow's fund?" Mr. Zug asks.

"I'm sure it's only a matter of time, it's already recorded in the public record that she was late in paying her property taxes," I sigh.

"I don't begrudge a widow a reasonable amount of help as I'm sure none of you do but it's prideful and selfish to put us in this position, we're a small community with many struggling to support their own families, we just don't have those kinds of resources," Mr. Glick says.

"What do you suggest we do Deacon Byler?" Mr. Shetler asks.

"Sarah Fisher needs to be put in her place and reminded of the perils of disobedience. She needs to know that the esteemed members of this community will not support this tour nonsense and that we will not tolerate her careless, disgraceful behavior," I slap my hand on the table angrily to convey my outrage over this matter, "If my memory serves me correctly, Mrs. Shetler, you have visitation with her on Sunday," I say looking the woman in the eye.

"*Ya* Deacon Byler," Mrs. Shetler replies looking down at her hands in her lap. I doubt she possesses the fortitude to scold a child without her husband's permission but she's a dutiful wife.

"My own wife has already made our position clear to her," Mr. Yoder adds, "If we all make an effort to send the same message, maybe she will repent and learn to live within her means before the whole community is compromised."

"I've tried reasoning with her too but I'm afraid she seems rather insistent on going through with her plans. Either way, *ne* action that we could possibly take would be as detrimental to the as the consequences we all face if she isn't stopped."

"We're with you Deacon Byler," Mr. Glick announces.

I look around the table with horror as they all nod in agreement.

The End

AMISH COUNTRY TOURS 3

CHAPTER ONE

Monday, April 13

As Mamm and the *kinner* head outside to start their evening chores, John and I walk around to the front porch to talk. In spite of the difficult weekend, I feel comforted just being in his presence.

"I know you made light of the situation in front of the *kinner*, Sarah, but what really happened with Mrs. Shetler yesterday?"

"I suspected something was wrong when she came for visitation alone. Mr. Shetler and their *kinner* had stayed behind after church services and I didn't see them again until they stopped to pick her up after dinner."

I look down at my hands fidgeting in my lap. "The Shetlers

aren't exactly what you would describe as overly warm and friendly people, but from the moment she arrived, her manner was very cold and distant; I could tell she didn't want to be here at all."

"When the boys and I were unloading the hay today, Mark said that he thought you had been crying when Mr. Shetler arrived to take her home," he says looking at me intently.

I feel ashamed and as much as I want to, I find it difficult to look him in the eye for fear I will burst into tears. "After dinner, when Mamm and the *kinner* went outside to do their evening chores, she told me quite bluntly that she and Mr. Shetler believe that my tour business will be the downfall of our community and that they would not support the endeavor. She said that she hoped I would come to my senses and do what's right, but that we're all judged by the company we keep and she couldn't afford for her family to fall under the wrong influence. She told me not to come to the ladies' quilting frolic that's being held at her house next week unless I get over this foolish idea by then. And she said that it goes for Mamm too." I sigh and finally look over at him.

He meets my gaze with a slightly puzzled look, "What did you tell her?" he asks.

"I told her that I was sorry she felt that way but I have a family to provide for. I felt like such a fool for sitting there all evening and trying to make conversation. Mr. Shetler arrived to take her home before I could say anything more. She didn't give me a chance to describe the tours or to even talk about the situation, though I'm sure it wouldn't have made any difference, her mind was made up before she'd gotten here.

"I think I was more upset that we all had to sit through the whole awkward evening with her, not knowing what was wrong. I wasn't crying when the *kinner* came in, her soup felt like it was burning a hole in my stomach. I had just been ill in the trash bin and my eyes were still watery." I look down at the porch when I feel him place his hand on mine.

"I'm sorry," he says in his deep, soothing voice.

"I'm okay," I say, managing a half-smile, "Looking back, I don't know why I was so taken aback by it all in the first place; the Shetlers have always been conservative minded people. I guess I was just so excited about the turnout we'd had on Saturday that I wasn't even considering the possibility of her open disapproval, but I should have seen it coming."

"Well don't beat yourself up for hoping for the best, it's not in your nature to assume the worst about people before they disappoint you, and I, for one, like that about you," he says, squeezing my hand reassuringly.

I suppose he's right, I hate to think of what a miserable existence it would be to go around expecting the worst of everyone. "Maybe it's your fault for setting my expectations so high," I chuckle.

"*Danki* for the hay and for all the work you did today. The *kinner* had a wonderful time building the slide and finishing the toddler maze this afternoon," I tell him.

"I'm just glad to be part of it all. This place has really turned into something special. Even Caleb is excited, I think he wants to learn to play golf," he laughs.

"He's *wilkom* anytime," I smile, "You both are."

"Just don't tell him that until after we get the fields planted," he chuckles.

"What are you going to do with the harvest at your place?" I ask curiously.

"I'm planning on using most of the land for some specialty crops. We'll probably sell some at the farmer's market but I was thinking of letting Caleb run a produce stand out by the road in front of the shop. I'd like him to learn to run the business side of farming too."

"Well between the tours, my garden, the corn fields, the potato field and the pumpkin patch, I don't think we can handle any more farming projects. You're *wilkom* to use that back ten acres or so of our land for planting if you'd like."

"I appreciate that and I'll definitely give it some thought. In the meantime, I don't want you to worry. With the flyers you and your friend Natalie put out on Saturday, plus the ones I put up on my way into Hopkinsville, I imagine you may have your hands full sooner than you think."

"Don't forget we're on a blog now too," I chuckle.

"Don't laugh, you never know what might come of it," he smiles encouragingly and holds my gaze for a moment. It's all I can do to look away, but just as I open my mouth to ask about his family, Mamm joins us on the porch.

"Well the *kinner* are going for a ride with Caleb and I'm going to go write a letter before turning in for the night. I imagine we have lots of quilting to catch up on tomorrow now that we have everything in place for the tours."

"*Ya*, *Danki* again, Mamm, for your help; I'll see you in the morning," I smile.

"Good night you two."

She kisses my cheek as John stands, offering to walk her to the Daadi Haus. I watch as she steadies herself on his arm. She looks so fragile next to his broad shoulders and tall, sturdy frame and I'm grateful for how attentive he is to her…to my whole family.

It's only been two days since John and I sat on the porch alone talking after dinner, but I realize now just how much I've missed him in that short amount of time.

I look up at the evening sky and feel a sense of calm wash over me. As I take a deep breath and close my eyes, I feel as if my strength has been renewed. In spite of the things that have gone wrong, too much has gone right for this not to be God's plan for us.

"Sleepy?" John asks, startling me from my thoughts.

"Just enjoying the quiet," I smile as he sits back down in the rocking chair next to mine, "How about you?"

"Quiet is *gut*," he chuckles, "It's one of those things we long for when it's noisy, but if we get too much of it, we find ourselves longing for the noise."

"Are you speaking from experience?" I ask curiously.

"I am."

"Well if it's noise you're looking for, you're definitely in the right place," I chuckle.

"*Ya*, but it's the right kind of noise," he says fondly, "*Kinner* laughing and playing, dishes clanging, ladies chattering and chairs rocking. It always smells *gut* here too, something good's always cooking."

"When you put it that way, it seems so poetic," I smile.

"Maybe it is," he smiles.

"So how was your visit with your family in Hopkinsville?"

"It was *gut*, my brother's wife was a little sad to see Caleb go, but I think my brother is willing to do anything to keep him on the right path. They found out that he took a college entrance exam and they're both terrified that he might make the wrong choice and decide not to get baptized into the church."

"What does Caleb say?"

"He said he just wanted to know what his options were, but that he hasn't decided either way yet."

"How do you feel about it?"

"I don't know. I want the boy to have a future and I want him to be happy but I'd be lying if I said I didn't hope that he could find that happiness without having to be alienated by the people he loves."

He levels his gaze at me. "I do know that being involved with your family and the idea of the tour business has sparked a lot of interest in him, I think he sees it as a way to embrace his Amish roots in a way that will still feed his desire to learn new things and implement new ideas."

"I hope it goes without saying that we *wilkom* his involvement," I reassure him, "Just let me know how I can help."

"That means a lot to me, I'm hoping that as he and I spend the next week or so getting everything planted, we'll figure out a direction for the summer months. I think he's planning to make his decision before classes begin in the fall. If he gets involved in something he can see a future in, maybe his decision won't be so hard."

"Is that why you're planting specialty crops at your place?"

"Partly, I did some research last year when I first started

looking for a property. I didn't really have a desire to go back into farming in the traditional sense, but I knew that I wanted some land to tinker around with. At the time, I was more interested in building a new repair shop and the Schwartz farm offered the best of both worlds. Looking back now, I think it's going to work out better than I ever imagined a year ago."

"What do you mean?"

"Well it's thirty-two acres in total. The front plot consists of the house, the Daadi Haus, two barns and about ten acres of farmland, but the back plot has a small cabin and an old wooden barn on about three acres of farmland surrounded by fifteen acres of woods bordered by a creek. It was originally two plots of land. I think the Schwartz family bought the second plot from the old man that lived there to keep from ever having any rear neighbors, and they just used it to hunt.

He takes a sip of coffee, "I figured if I ever wanted to farm that land I could always clear what I needed, but having the wooded area seemed interesting. I want to try growing some bamboo and wild ginseng on it. On the cleared acreage, I plan to start a crop of elephant garlic and maybe avocados and I plan to use the old wooden barn for growing mushrooms. I may even grow some micro-greens. The ginseng will take ten years to really harvest but if it works, it will be well worth it."

"Where did you learn all of this?"

"It's funny, the mushrooms I just kind of got into because I love mushrooms and they're so expensive at the store. When

Elizabeth was in the hospital, I checked out a couple of books on growing them that were kind of vague. I learned a little about using a computer from one of the security guys that used to work the late shift, so one weekend before her last surgery, I did some research on the internet and found out basically all I needed to know.

"The security guy's wife worked in her family's restaurant and I sold my first mushroom harvest to her parents for $4.00 per pound. They referred me to some other folks in Marion who bought more. My mushrooms became kind of popular, which got me thinking outside of the box and researching other high-income crops."

"So the mushrooms you brought me today, you grew them?"

"They're part of the last harvest from my old barn in Hopkinsville. I have some growing here now but I plan to have a lot more."

"You amaze me sometimes," I chuckle. "Most of the time, actually," I smile.

"I hope that's a *gut* thing," he laughs.

I feel myself blush as I avert my eyes to the clatter of the tractor pulling alongside the house.

"Mamm, Caleb held Pumpkin Pie and she nibbled his ear," Hannah giggles, stepping onto the porch.

"*Ya*, Mamm it was so cute," Mary confirms.

"I think we saw a raccoon by the garden," Mark adds.

"*Ya*, we just saw a pair of eyes at first but it ran away when Josh screamed," Samuel says excitedly.

"It was going to eat Mamm's plants," Josh explained.

"Maybe we should set a trap for it," Caleb offers, hefting Josh down from his shoulders onto the porch.

"Ooooooh, I wanna help!" Mark says.

"Me too!" Samuel agrees.

"Not me," Josh says, shaking his head.

Everyone chuckles at his reluctance.

"We'll see. Right now, though, it's time for baths; you have school in the morning," I remind them.

"I don't have school and Caleb doesn't have school," Josh corrects.

"You still have to take a bath," Mark says authoritatively, "Come on, I'll let you put in the bubbles," he says, taking his hand.

"I'll be up to tuck you in when you're all squeaky clean," I reassure him.

"Come on Hannah," Mary says.

"Goodnight everyone," John says with a smile.

Hannah breaks away from Mary and hugs Caleb's legs, then hugs John. "Night Caleb, night John," she giggles.

They both tell her goodnight and they follow the boys into the house.

"I'm pretty sure you have the cleanest *kinner* on the planet," John chuckles.

"When the twins were little, I found that they slept through the night better on the nights they had a bath before bed. By the time Samuel came along, it just kind of became a routine. I think it helps them unwind," I sigh.

"It makes sense," Caleb agrees, "I miss taking baths sometimes."

"Just as long as you don't miss too many days in a row," John teases.

"Hey, I'm not the one with bath salts and a scrubbing mitt in my bathroom," he laughs.

"Those are Epsom salts and wait until you're over thirty and your muscles are aching from a sixteen-hour day, you'll be thinking about your old Uncle John's bath salts," he retorts.

"At least I know what to get you for Christmas," I grin.

"On that note, I think we'd better get back to the house," he chuckles. "We've got lots of planting to do tomorrow."

"*Danki* for dinner, Sarah," Caleb says.

"*Ya*, it was delicious as usual," John adds.

"Let me get you a quart of milk and some bread to take home," I offer.

"I'll go say goodnight to Pumpkin Pie and drive around to pick you up," Caleb says to John as he heads toward the barn.

"I thought for sure he would rename that bunny," I chuckle.

"Nah, he's a *gut* sport. I think he likes that the *kinner* named it especially for him."

"We're having ham and beans, fried squash and potatoes for dinner tomorrow if you guys want to join us," I say, stepping into the kitchen.

"That sounds great, I'm sure we'll both be ready for a *gut* hearty meal."

"I put some eggs and pineapple-zucchini bread in here for breakfast along with the plain bread and cheese. There's also some chicken salad that should get you guys through lunch for the next couple of days. I figured I would send you home with leftovers whenever possible so that you bachelors would have one less meal to worry about."

"As long as you're sure it's no extra trouble, I did kind of promise his *mamm* that I wouldn't let him live off of junk food," he smiles.

"Not at all, and thanks to you, we have plenty." I tuck the milk bottle into the basket and cover the whole thing with a tea towel before handing it to him.

"You're pretty amazing yourself you know," he says as our eyes meet again.

For a moment, I feel myself drawn to him as I did that day in the bakery office. I look at him curiously, wondering if he feels it too, but before either of us says anything more, I hear Mark trotting down the stairs.

"*Gut* night, Sarah," he says with a warm smile.

"Night John," I sigh, giving him a little wave as he steps out through the screen door.

"We're out of soap upstairs," Mark explains as he walks into the pantry and rustles around in the cupboard. "There's only one bar left after this. The boys are putting their pajamas on; I'm getting in the shower."

"I'll be up in a minute," I sigh as he bounds back up the stairs.

I'm not sure if I was reading John right or if I was completely out of line, but I feel like I just missed an opportunity to find out. I've been thinking about him a lot lately…especially when I'm alone at night with nothing but my thoughts surrounding me.

I glance across the kitchen and realize that I left the refrigerator door standing open. I shake my head as I close it. Whatever has come over me, the fridge door seems like proof positive that I must not be thinking clearly.

As I make my way upstairs to tuck the *kinner* into bed, I realize that I have to face my own feelings and see to it that I don't read more into John's kindness than what's really there. I shouldn't imagine that he thinks of me as anything more than a friend. I know that he's *gut*, thoughtful and kind, but even a man who enjoys our noisy household may not be ready for the responsibilities that go with it, and I would hate to ruin what we have over some girlish romantic notions that may never come around again.

CHAPTER TWO

Thursday, April 16

"They're here!" Mamm calls out from the kitchen.

I finish folding a bed sheet I just pulled out of the dryer and head upstairs.

Mamm watches through the kitchen window, putting on the teakettle as John and Caleb pull in front of the barn. "I'll put the leftover lasagna in the oven to warm," she assures me as I head outside to greet them.

"Wow, that's a lot of pork," I chuckle, looking at the load on the trailer.

"It's not just pork," Caleb smiles, hopping off the back as John climbs out of the driver's seat. I can tell by the look on Caleb's face that they have something up their sleeve.

"We made a little trade on our way back from the butcher this morning," John explains.

“One of your surprises?” I smile curiously as Mamm joins us outside.

“*Och, Gut* Heavens,” Mamm says as John removes the tarp.

“Is that—?” I start to ask, marveling at the heavy-duty extra-large capacity, gas-powered washing machine.

“It is,” John smirks proudly.

“If this is your clever way of getting me to do your laundry John Troyer, all you had to do was ask,” I chuckle.

“You owe me ten bucks,” Caleb says. “I told him if he gave you a washing machine you would think he wanted you to do our laundry.” He laughs.

“You’re a practical man, John Troyer,” Mamm says patting him on the shoulder.

“For the record, I don’t want you to do my laundry,” he chuckles, elbowing Caleb, “I just thought that with the tours and all of the extra baking and cooking, having an automatic washing machine might make things a little easier and I was able to make a trade for it. I guess I could sell it if you don’t want it,” he sighs.

“Don’t you dare!” I laugh.

“Good, then let’s get it inside and get it hooked up. I’m starving and we still have to pick up the rest of our pork and deliver it this afternoon.” He smiles.

"The *kinner* said there were five pigs trapped in the corral last night," I say, propping the screen door open.

"*Ya*, I had him butcher one for you and I put as much as I could fit in my freezer until we need it, I traded some to Mr. Sneed this morning and to the butcher for his services. When I pick up the rest, I'm going to take some to Dan at the bakery and to the Lapp family. I'll give one to my brother when I take the trailer back in the morning, and probably sell one to a friend in Hopkinsville," he says as he and Caleb grab the first cooler full of neatly labeled packages.

They sit the large cooler in front of my new freezer and go back to fetch the second one as I start to put everything away. By the time I get everything organized, they're wheeling the washing machine inside on the appliance dolly.

"John I've never seen so much meat in one household at the same time and I feel overwhelmingly blessed, *Danki*."

"I'm not even sure we got all of them; we'll walk the property again and look for signs, but either way, I plan to move the corral closer to the creek and try it again just to make sure. I was thinking that Mark and Samuel could come along as their first lesson in hunting. We should finish our planting next week; we could do it next Wednesday after school and have the boys back in time for dinner, that way it won't interrupt the tours."

"I'm sure they'll be on the edge of their seats until then just thinking about it."

"Let me get my laundry out of the way while you bring that downstairs," I say, opening the basement door and flipping on the light.

"I'm going to show Caleb how to turn off the gas, we'll be right down."

I wash my hands in the utility sink and quickly pull my unmentionables from the drying rack, tossing them into a laundry basket to fold later. I finish folding the sheets and pillowcases from the dryer and put them on top of the basket as I hear them wrestling the dolly down the steps.

Once the washer is installed, Caleb goes back upstairs to turn on the gas while I load the washer with the last load of laundry. John shows me how to operate it and how to clean the filter. He holds my gaze for a moment before pulling out the knob to test it.

"Are you okay?" he asks in a concerned voice.

I hesitate, lost in the moment again. "I—what do you mean?" I ask, unable to look away.

"You've been a little distracted these past few days, is everything alright?"

"I'm good; I've just been trying to stay on top of everything. I feel so blessed, it's like my feet aren't touching the ground sometimes."

"Are you enjoying it?" he chuckles.

"How could I not? I mean it's crazy and busy but it's exciting too."

"Let me know when you're ready," Caleb calls out from the side of the house.

John smiles, "I almost forgot that he's waiting for my signal. Go ahead!" he yells before turning his attention back to me.

"I'm just so grateful," I say, hugging him.

"I'm so glad that you're happy but remember our deal. You don't owe me anything, Sarah, I'm enjoying this as much as you are," he says, brushing his hand against my cheek.

The truth is that I've been longing to feel his arms around me since Mrs. Shetler left Sunday night.

"I know, it's silly, I'm sorry if I made you uncomfortable."

"It's not—"

"Is it working?" Caleb calls out.

I avert my gaze and pull away a bit embarrassed as he pulls the washer knob and checks the connection for leaks.

"It's working, come on inside!" he calls out.

"Come on upstairs, I'm sure Mamm has the table all set," I chuckle, trying to lighten the mood. "We're having pork stir-fry tonight with fresh mushrooms, zucchini, sugar snap peas and carrots; you guys need to get going soon so you can be back in time for dinner."

I hear Caleb's footsteps on the stairs, "I'll just go put this in my room." I grab the laundry basket and start making my way upstairs.

"We'll meet you in the kitchen," John replies, gathering his tools.

In my room, I put the laundry basket on the floor next to the bed, use the restroom and wash my hands. As I look at myself in the mirror, I feel obscured by the black of my mourning dress, and it reminds me that John probably has a hard time seeing past it as well.

How could any man be expected to see beyond the man who came before him with a dark reminder staring him in the face every time he looks at me? Then again, I suppose that's the whole point. Maybe I am out of line. I smooth my kapp and apron and join everyone in the kitchen for lunch.

"Forgive me, I don't get up and down the stairs much anymore with my arthritis, but the new washer will save so much time on laundry days, *Danki*, both of you," Mamm says with her hand on John's arm.

"It's my pleasure," John smiles, looking at me tentatively.

I smile at him and we bow our heads in prayer before digging in.

"So the corn field is seeded and cross-seeded and my potatoes are planted, I'm going to plant some summer squash, lettuce and cucumbers in the garden, what's left to plant at your place?" I ask Caleb.

"I'm planting sweet potatoes, beans, cucumbers, lettuce and garlic while John gets the mushrooms and some micro greens going in the small barn. Once that's done we're going to work on the back of the property planting some bamboo and ginseng in and around the woods. We might have a whole different plan by fall, but I'm just getting my feet wet and we're doing a little experimenting."

"Are you thinking of opening a produce stand this summer?"

"We haven't really decided, I want to, but I don't want to sit out by the road every day waiting on customers to show up. If we get the mushrooms, garlic and micro greens going, I could be out delivering to restaurants in bulk a couple of days a week and probably make more money."

"You know, you could always set up your stand here and help manage tour HQ on Thursdays, Fridays and Saturdays. I'm sure we can come to some kind of arrangement. We haven't been getting much business on Thursdays so far but that will probably change when school gets out in a few weeks. Maybe we can attract business for each other. Of course it's up to you and John, you should probably talk it over before you decide." I smile.

"That's an interesting idea," John agrees. "I think it could work with a little planning, we'll talk it over."

Just as I put the last bite of lasagna in my mouth, I hear a car pulling into the drive. I get up from the table and look out the window. "Someone must be here for a tour."

"Caleb, why don't you go open HQ and help Sarah do the tour so you can see what it's like. I'll finish our errands in town and be back as soon as I'm done," John says, stepping outside with me as I hand Caleb the keys.

Mamm follows us outside just as a woman, a man with a camera around his neck and two children step out of a shiny blue van.

"Hello," I say, "I'm Sarah Fisher, are you here for a tour?"

"Well sort of," the woman smiles, "My name is Elise Fullerton and I write for the entertainment section of the county *Gazette*. I'm good friends with Natalie Ramsey and she told me about your farm and the tours you're offering. I write articles about family-oriented places to visit in the county and I wondered if you would let us do a piece featuring your farm tours.

"Well, I—" I start to protest nervously but she continues.

"As far as I know, Ms. Fisher, you're the first to offer something like this in the whole county. Our paper has a great reputation for sparking the community's interest in places like yours. We would just take a casual tour like anyone else, get a few photos of the children having fun and you'll be able to read all about it in next Saturday's issue. I assure you, we will show you the utmost respect. We did an article on Natalie's restaurant when they first opened, that's how we met."

The idea of real publicity frightens me but I know that Natalie wouldn't have recommended her if she didn't trust her. "There would be no photos of any Amish, just the children?" I clarify.

"Yes ma'am that's correct, just the children, and maybe the facilities if you're comfortable with that. We even pay for the tour just like any other customer. Shane had to take his kids out of school for a check-up at the dentist today and we thought we would make the most of it and check out your farm while we had the kids to come and experience it with us. This is my camera man Shane, his son Jarred and his daughter Leslie."

"Natalie said that today would probably be your slowest day which is perfect for us, but she didn't have a way to warn you that we might be coming on such short notice," Shane adds.

"*Och ne*, we're getting used to people just stopping by, nice to meet you," I say, shaking their hands. "Come on over to the store and we'll get everything started. This is my *mamm*, Miriam, my youngest son Josh and my neighbor Caleb; he and his uncle helped us put everything together for the tours."

"Natalie said that you're a widow with five children, all under the age of eleven; what a great idea to build a family business right here at home. I really must commend you."

"*Danki*, it isn't something we entered into lightly."

"I respect that and I assure you, I'm honored that you've agreed to let us take a peek."

. "This is our gift shop; the tours begin here so that everyone can check in while we get the horses and the buggy ready."

"Pay the lady, Shane," she chuckles.

Mamm takes Josh inside and Caleb takes his cue to go hitch up the buggy as I collect the fees and give them a flyer to take with them.

"This is great; did you make everything that you have for sale here?"

"*Ya*, we bake the breads, make the popcorn balls, can the jams and everything you see here. We might also be adding a produce stand and some Amish crafts this summer."

She flips through the quilt binder lying on the counter. Natalie made a copy for me with color printed photos of my finished quilts.

"You can buy raffle tickets for a handmade custom quilt if you'd like, those are pictures of my work. Natalie takes them for me when I complete an order."

"Oh yes, I've seen this portfolio at Natalie's store, you do beautiful work, I definitely want ten of those tickets for myself."

I roll off ten tickets and have her print her name and phone number on the back before sticking them in the gallon jar while the cameraman browses.

"Dad can we get a snack?" Jarred asks, peering into the bakery case.

"I want a popcorn ball," Leslie says, looking up at her father.

"Those are peanut-butter caramel popcorn balls, my very own recipe," I tell her.

"I'll take three waters and two—"

"Ahem," Elise interrupts.

"Make that four waters and four popcorn balls," he chuckles.

"Kids you have to wait until we get to the picnic area to eat them," he warns as I hand them the popcorn balls wrapped in plastic.

"Everything in here looks scrumptious, we might have to stop back by on the way out," Elise smiles.

Shane snaps a few photos of the wall of canned goods and the bakery case. "The buggy should be ready if you are," I tell her, trying not to appear nervous about the camera.

"Lead the way!" she smiles, writing notes on her notepad as we walk toward the barn.

Once we're inside, I tell the children about the goats and let them pet and feed them a handful of grain before introducing the horses. I do my best to give them the show the way that

Samuel does, letting Joker shake his head *'Ya'* and *'ne'* to silly questions and showing them that he can count to three and six. Even Caleb seems pretty impressed as he observes.

We pile into the buggy, and I narrate for them the way that Mark does as we tour the property, this time pointing out the miniature golf range, the hay bounce, the hay slide and the picnic areas for them to use later if they wish.

"Okay, we are definitely hitting that trampoline and playing a few holes of golf," Shane says as his children cheer excitedly.

I tell them a little more about our Amish lifestyle and take them by the old crapper/phone shack, which of course, they photograph before we head back to the barn. Caleb gets Waffles saddled up for pony rides while Mamm and Josh let the children pet the bunnies and the baby chicks as Shane takes photos.

Once the children are seated on the pony, Caleb fetches some putters and golf balls and together, we walk them out to the hay slide where they take a few photos of the children playing before heading to the picnic area.

I answer a few more questions and talk with Elise as the children play and enjoy their snack, and then lead them to the golf course. "There's a bell post here on the first hole; if you need us for anything, just ring it several times. Otherwise, feel free to play at your own pace and then bring your putters and balls back to the gift shop on your way out." I smile.

"Thank you Sarah, we'll let you know when we're done," Elise says.

Back at HQ, Caleb gets busy making some notes of his own as he mans the gift shop while Mamm, Josh and I go inside to tidy up the kitchen. As I wash the dishes, I decide that we probably need to fence in the open end of the golf course to keep people from wandering off into the fields and we need a better system of overseeing that area and communicating back and forth. It will be easier when the *kinner* are here, but still not as controlled as I would like it to be. I'll definitely need to see if John has any ideas to make it run more smoothly.

"Are you going to tell me what's going on?" Mamm asks.

"I'm just thinking about how to make the tours run more smoothly."

"That's not what I'm talking about; you've been a little distant these past few days, like you have a heavy heart. Something's bothering you, I can tell."

"It's nothing, I just embarrassed myself, I'm fine," I say reassuringly.

"Well, if you need to talk about it, I'm here for you liebchen," she says, patting me on the back. In the meantime, maybe you should go pay Ruthie a visit or do something to take your mind off of everything for a few hours. You've been so focused on the tours and trying to keep the household on schedule that you haven't given yourself any time to breathe."

"I promised Mary that we would have a picnic dinner tomorrow, if we don't have any tours. We'll spend the whole evening outdoors, maybe play some horseshoes or try some golf. It'll be something everyone can look forward to; I'll be fine, Mamm."

She gives me a wary look, but I smile and hope that will suffice for now because I really don't feel like talking about it… I'm not even sure there's anything to talk about.

Once the dishes are dried and put away, I go downstairs to put the first load of laundry from my new washer into the dryer. I can't help but admire such a practical and thoughtful gift and I thank God for John's kindness and generosity.

I think about the look in his eyes earlier today and I know that I felt something real between us. Even in that one tiny moment, it was as if I could feel his heart reaching out to me, but I probably made him think that I embraced him out of some sense of obligatory gratitude rather than my burning desire to feel closer to him in my joy.

I've never been good at concealing my emotions. "Lord let him see my true heart in your timing, not mine," I pray.

Back upstairs, Mamm is busy stitching some of our quilting pieces together while Josh plays with his toys.

"I'm going to head over to HQ to talk to Caleb while we wait for our guests to return, it's been over an hour since I left them."

"Take your time; I'll just work on this until the *kinner* get home from school." She smiles.

When I arrive, Caleb is hunched over his notepad deep in thought. "So what do you think of the tour?" I ask.

"I really like it; I think it's going to get pretty busy around here once more people find out about it." He smiles. "I just think we need a little fine tuning."

"*Ya*, I agree. You have some ideas?"

"I'm working on it; we should probably talk to John."

"The *kinner* will be home from school at any minute and I want to say goodbye to our guests, so go ahead and pull your thoughts together and we'll all talk later," I say, spotting the Englischers walking toward us.

"That was fun!" young Jarred exclaims, skipping his way over to me excitedly.

"I'm so glad you had a good time," I chuckle.

"To tell you the truth, we could have stayed all afternoon, but I've got to get back to the office and Shane has to get his kids to their swimming lessons."

"My wife would really enjoy this too, maybe we'll come back when the corn maze is ready." He smiles.

"Yeah, we want to come again!" Leslie cheers.

"*Ya* please, we would love to have you," I assure them.

"We're a little new at doing these tours, do either of you have any suggestions?" I ask curiously as Elise browses the wall of canned goods.

"I think you've got a really great thing going here. It's welcoming and relaxed with the right mix of activities to really give your visitor's their money's worth," she says, pulling a jar of pear honey from the shelf. "You might even want to consider raising your prices a bit. We never expected that you had so much to offer."

"I agree and I think that corn maze will add just the right element to round it out nicely," Shane adds. "Most people would pay more for the golfing. That's usually an outing all in itself."

"I'll take that under advisement," I chuckle.

"It's amazing to me how much you've accomplished and that you had the time to do all of this yourself," Elise says, grabbing a jar of pumpkin pie filling from the shelf.

Just as I'm about to reply, the *kinner* come peeking into the doorway.

"I had lots of help," I chuckle. "Come on inside *kinner*, this is Elise, she's a friend of Natalie's, and she's writing a newspaper article about our tours for the entertainment section."

The *kinner* all come inside and say hello as I introduce them one by one.

“Did you guys take the tour?” Samuel asks her.

“We certainly did and we had a great time,” she assures him.

“Did Mamm tell you about the quilt raffle?” Mary asks.

“Got myself ten tickets; I sure hope I win,” she chuckles.

“Did you pet the bunnies?” Hannah asks Jarred and Leslie.

“They were so soft and cuddly, so were the baby chicks,” Leslie tells her.

“Did you go through the maze?” Josh asks.

“Josh and Hannah, why don’t you show the children the hay maze while we talk,” I suggest. “He helped build the toddler maze, they’re probably too old for it, but it will give them something to do for a few minutes.” I smile.

“What’s your article going to say?” Mark asks Elise studiously.

“Well, I’ll tell my readers about all of the activities there are to do here and how much fun we had. I could make sure you get a few copies when the article comes out next Saturday if you’d like,” she tells him.

“That would be great; Mary can put one in her scrapbook,” he replies.

“Did you help bake all of these breads? I can’t decide which one to try,” she asks Mary.

"*Ya*, we made everything here, my favorite would probably be the banana bread, everyone loves my *mamm*'s recipe but I don't know anyone else who makes the raisin spice loaf. It's really good too, especially if you want to try something new."

"You are quite the salesman, little lady, I think I'm going to take a loaf of each," she chuckles.

"Are these for you too?" Mary asks, picking up the jars on the counter.

"Yes ma'am, and I think I'll take another bottle of water for the road."

"You're lucky, this is the last jar of pumpkin pie filling we have available; it's my *mammi*'s recipe. Did you need some eggs too?" she asks.

"Oh, I almost forgot about the eggs, I'll take a dozen, it'll save me from stopping at the store for my wife on the way home," Shane replies.

"You go gather the eggs, I'll bag everything up," Caleb tells her.

Mary heads out to the coop while Caleb writes everything down and tallies the order.

"My editor will probably bring his family here as soon as he reviews my article; he's fascinated with the Amish community. I really think you're going to get a lot of business from this story, it will not only be in the paper, but it'll be featured online as well," Elise informs me.

"I admit that I'm a little apprehensive about the attention, but I know it's a necessary part of running a business. Thank you for taking the time to come, I'm really glad you enjoyed it."

"Don't you worry; I'll treat this opportunity with the utmost respect. I'm a big supporter of female business owners, and your children are all so adorable, you make a wonderful team; it was a great experience."

When Mary returns with the eggs, they pay for their purchases and we all say goodbye just as John pulls into the drive. I'm brimming with excitement but a little nervous too. I can't wait to see what he thinks.

"Okay *kinner*, time for everyone to get started on afternoon chores while I talk to John," I announce.

"I'll go help with the horses," Caleb says, leading the way.

John pulls the tractor in front of HQ and comes inside. "How did it go?" he asks.

"They were reporters," I say, wanting to see his reaction.

"What?" he asks with a puzzled look.

"My friend Natalie sent them. Apparently they did a story about her restaurant after it first opened and she called them and told them about us. They're doing a feature story about the tours in the entertainment section of the *Gazette* on Saturday.

They said it will be online too."

"That's wonderful!" he says, hugging me excitedly.

"I'm so glad you approve."

He puts his hands on my shoulders and looks at me intently. "Of course I approve, I want the best for you Sarah," he says in a comforting tone.

"I—" he stops me before I can say anything.

"And about earlier, I just wanted to say that I love your cooking and spending time with you and your family, but that's only a small part of why I do the things I've done. It makes me happy to see you happy and I just want to make sure you understand that."

"It makes me happy that you're in our lives, John, my gratitude for the things you've done for us doesn't define that, it only enhances it."

"Good, because I think we make a pretty good team." He smiles, gently letting go of my shoulders.

I may not know where things are going, but at least now I know that I'm not just some charitable cause that he's devoted his time to.

Part of me is terrified by my own feelings, but I'm so relieved that we've cleared the air between us that it's all I can do to resist the urge to throw myself into his arms and kiss him.

Deep down, I would love nothing more than to get lost in the moment with him, but I know that in spite of my romantic instincts, I need to honor myself and my husband's memory by being faithful to my heritage and Amish customs.

I do my best to change the subject. "Caleb was pretty encouraged about the tours today; we both have some ideas to discuss with you and I also need to know what your plans are for tomorrow."

"In the morning, I plan to take the trailer I borrowed for the hay back to my brother in Hopkinsville along with the pork I have for him. I've got three coolers packed that the butcher's holding for me in his freezer. I talked to the Lapp brothers when I stopped by this afternoon and they're coming to help Caleb plant the fields tomorrow. That should ensure that we'll have all of the planting done by Monday night or Tuesday. Why, what's going on?"

"I promised Mary that we would have a picnic dinner. I thought maybe we would grill hot dogs and hamburgers and spend a little time trying out the golf course. We've all been so busy planning and putting everything together that none of us have had time to enjoy it ourselves. I'm afraid things might get so busy in the weeks to come that we might not have the opportunity. The Lapp brothers are *wilkom* to come."

"That's a really good idea, I'm sure they'll enjoy that. I've got to meet a customer at the repair shop at 3:00 p.m. but I can come by after and work the grill with Mark and Samuel if you ladies will take care of the rest. I'll tell Caleb and the boys to be here by 5:00 p.m. Any tours you have should be wrapped up by then and we'll still have time to eat and play around until dark."

"Sounds like a good plan to me." I smile. "I know the *kinner* will be excited too."

"Let's go over your tour ideas at dinner; I've got some timbers for landscaping border that I want to install around our black sand pit. I'll get the boys to help me and we should be able to get it installed before dinner. It'll keep the sand from getting scattered all over the course."

"They should be done with their chores at any moment; I'll have the girls help me work on dinner and restocking the bakery case for the weekend in the meantime. That way I'll be free to get the rest of our signs painted tomorrow while the *kinner* are in school."

"You paint them and we'll install them," he chuckles. "I'll go grab the rake and shovels while the boys are finishing up," he says as we walk toward the barn.

"See you at dinner," I say, heading toward the house.

Once inside the kitchen, I tell Mamm, Mary and Hannah about our plans for the picnic tomorrow as they put away the eggs and milk.

"I'll go take out the ground beef and the hot dogs from the freezer," Mary offers.

"That's good, grab some bacon too," I tell her.

"I'll get some bread dough going so that it can be rising," Mamm adds.

"Holy mackerel!" Mary says, standing in the pantry with the freezer door open, "Is this all of the pork from the pig corral?"

Hannah runs over to look too. "Lot's and lots of it." She giggles as Mary rifles around for the bacon.

"*Och*! *Ya*, I forgot that you weren't here when he brought it over," I chuckle.

"Don't forget the basement," Mamm reminds me.

"What about the basement?" Hannah asks curiously.

"Come on ladies, I'll show you." I smile.

Mary sets the meat in the fridge to thaw and they both bound down the steps excitedly. As soon as they reach the bottom step, Mary squeals instantly.

"*Och* Mamm, it's an automatic washing machine! Where did you get it?"

"John brought it for us," I explain.

"You mean it's ours to keep?" Hannah giggles.

"*Ya* it's ours. It washes a lot at one time too," I marvel.

"Now I can't wait to do laundry," Mary smiles, looking at

the dials.

"I'm so glad to hear you say that, you two can fold the last load in the dryer and bring it upstairs with you, I'll show you how to work the machine on Saturday when we have washing to do," I chuckle.

"Mamm, that wasn't really what I meant," Mary says, shaking her head.

"I have another project for you when you finish," I say, giving them a little wave as I head back upstairs.

"I could hear the excitement from here," Mamm says as she measures out her flour.

"*Ya*, they're overjoyed. I have to admit, it does make things a lot easier. I couldn't believe it when I saw it."

"John's a thoughtful man and very resourceful too," Mamm smiles.

"*Ya*, he is," I sigh, thinking about his smile as I start slicing lemons in half.

The girls put away the laundry and come back to the kitchen.

"Okay, what's the next project?" Mary asks.

"Hannah, you help Mamm, Mary, you come with me," I tell them.

Mary follows me into my bedroom and puts the bedding away for me while I fold and put away my slips and other unmentionables. When that's done, I lay my folded quilt across the bed.

"Mary, when I gave the tour today, I realized what a good idea you had about the quilt raffle. Our very first customer paid ten dollars just for a chance to win. I was thinking though, the portfolio doesn't really replace seeing an actual quilt and I was thinking that I would like to hang this quilt that you and I made together in the closet opening and set the jar of raffle tickets next to it. It would also be a beautiful decoration, hanging there for everyone to see, but I didn't want to do it without checking with you first since we made this together."

"I think it's a *gut* idea but what will you sleep with?"

"I thought maybe I'd just use my blankets until you and I complete a new one for my bed."

"As long as we get to make a new one together, it's okay with me if it's okay with you," she agrees. "Maybe it will even help us get some new orders."

"I really can't wait to see how much the raffle will bring. Who knows, it might even bring more than a normal order would."

"I'll be sure to sell lots of tickets," she smiles.

"How about helping me put it on display? You grab some push pins from the desk and I'll bring the step stool," I say as we head to HQ together.

The closet itself is just an empty space about four feet wide, paneled in wood to match the cabinetry. Jacob had at one time debated about filling it with shelves, but for the most part, it served as storage space for trim pieces standing on end. Since it has no door, it makes the perfect area to display the quilt without being in the main traffic area of the store. Hopefully, the recessed area will help deter dirty hands from being tempted to soil the display.

"How are we going to hang it?"

"Go down to the basement and get the roll of clothesline lying on the shelf next to the washer, I'll go get a hammer and some nails."

When she returns, I hammer the first nail into the sidewall of the closet and tie the clothesline securely around it, then beat the nail toward the ceiling so that it forms a hook to keep the line from slipping loose. I hammer the second nail into the opposing wall and tie a slipknot around it, pulling it as tight as we can before repeating the process and securing it with a second knot.

Once that's finished, we hang the quilt over the line and spread it from end to end. I step down to look at it but it needs something more.

"Help me roll that barrel over here," I tell her, pointing to the extra wooden barrel that Dan brought us from the bakery.

We set the barrel in the corner, use the pushpins to drape the quilt and put the portfolio binder on top of it for people to look through.

"That looks so much better, and now people won't be in the way of the bakery case while they look through the book," Mary says.

"We'll still keep the roll of tickets Natalie gave us locked in the drawer and set the jar on the counter behind the case so that nobody bothers it."

"*Gut* idea, Mamm," she says admiring our handiwork.

"I think so too," I chuckle. "Now let's restock the breads you sold today in the bakery case and make some lemonade for our picnic dinner tomorrow."

"I'll go grab two loaves from the freezer; we probably need to make some more raisin spice loaf, I think that was our last one."

"*Ya*, we'll do that too," I assure her. I put my arm around her as we walk back toward the house. It's gratifying to see my *kinner* taking part in the business and enjoying it at the same time.

In the kitchen, Hannah is covering four large mounds of bread dough with tea towels as they rise while Mamm cleans up the floury mess on the counter.

I finish slicing lemons in half while Mary starts juicing. "We put a quilt up for display at HQ; Mamm already sold ten dollars in raffle tickets, you should see how pretty it looks Mammi," Mary says.

"I'll take a look at it the next time I'm over there, liebchen, in the meantime, I need to get some dessert made for tonight," Mamm assures her. "What's on the menu for the picnic besides hamburgers and hot dogs?"

"Baked beans and broccoli slaw for sure, we need to use up the rest of the broccoli in the fridge," I tell her.

"How about deviled eggs? John loves them," Hannah says.

"*Gut* idea Hannah," Mamm agrees.

"It doesn't hurt that Hannah loves them too," I chuckle.

"I'll put a pot of water on to boil," Mamm laughs.

"Make it a big pot and I'll make enough egg salad for the *kinner* and to send some home with John and Caleb for lunch too."

"He sure loves your cooking, Mamm," Mary smiles, shaking her head.

Mamm smiles too, but I pretend not to notice. "We could make creamy potato salad," I offer.

"Hamburgers, hot dogs, baked beans, broccoli slaw, deviled eggs and potato salad, that sounds like the perfect cookout," Mary says.

"*Ya*, we still need to decide what we're going to make for

dessert though, there will be eleven of us if the Lapp boys come and we still need a dessert for tonight," Mamm reminds us.

"What about the German chocolate cake with that gooey coconut-pecan frosting?" I ask, "We could just make two 9x13 cakes and have one for tonight too. We haven't had that in a long time and I still need to make some raisin spice bread tonight."

"Mmmm, that sounds good," Mary agrees.

"John loves sweets, he'll love any kind of cake," Hannah agrees.

"German chocolate cake it is," Mamm chuckles, "I'm going to need some crumbled pecans," she says to Hannah, knowing how she loves to crush the nuts for her.

"Okay!" she giggles, grabbing the meat mallet and a plastic baggie from the cupboard before getting the bag of pecans out of the freezer.

Mamm shakes her head and laughs, "Find the recipe for me in the binder so I don't forget anything."

Hannah puts her tools aside, gets out the binder and starts thumbing through the desserts while I rinse the pork and start chopping it into strips for stir-fry.

"I'll prep dinner while you guys work on that, I want the meat to marinate. I'll make the spice bread while the cakes are baking and put them in right after so we don't have to heat both ovens."

"It's really nice to have two ovens when we need it isn't it, Mamm?" Mary asks.

"*Ya*, we've been very blessed this year haven't we?"

"God blesses us and John blesses us and even Caleb blesses us," Hannah giggles.

"Don't forget Aunt Ruthie and Uncle Dan," Mary adds.

"And Mammi," Hannah agrees.

I look at Mamm and smile, "*Ya*, and Mammi too."

"Don't forget everyone in your nightly prayers," Mamm says.

"I think Mamm should marry John, and Mary should get married to Caleb," Hannah says.

"Hannah!" Mary shrieks in protest.

Mamm chuckles quietly as I try not to blush. "Hannah, that's enough," I scold. I realize that she's probably just imagining marriage as a way to keep the people she cares about close to her, but this is the second time she's said it and I don't want her to repeat it in mixed company, making anyone else uncomfortable. Not to mention that I don't even want to think of Mary getting married and leaving home someday.

I put the pork strips in the soy marinade mixture, put the bowl in the fridge and then put the eggs into the boiling water as Mamm mixes her cake batter.

Once the cakes are baking, Mamm and Hannah start making the frosting while I start peeling potatoes. Between the boiling water, Hannah pounding the pecans, Mamm opening and closing cabinets and Mary grunting as she squeezes the lemons in the juicer, the kitchen is noisier than ever. I smile to myself wondering if John would find it comforting.

***

As soon as the landscaping border is installed around the pit, we spread the rest of the sand, drop the boys off at the house and head to my place to feed the horses and get cleaned up.

"You taking the trailer back in the morning?" Caleb asks.

"*Ya*, and dropping off the pork. John Miller and his brother are buying eighty pounds; I'm giving the rest to Jake and your *daed*. Do you need anything while I'm there?"

"Naomi Miller's *daed*?"

"*Ya*, I think he has a daughter named Naomi, why?"

"Just curious." He smiles.

"Oh *Ya*?" I chuckle, "Someone you're thinking about courting?" I tease. "I had no idea."

"Are you thinking about courting Sarah Fisher?" he asks with his brow raised knowingly.

"Point taken," I sigh. "Look, it's your private business but I think it's good that you might have someone you're interested in, what you do in life isn't nearly as important as having someone to share it with."

"Then how come you've been single for so long? There are plenty of ladies interested in you back in Hopkinsville."

"I'm not single, I'm a widower, there's a difference, and never you mind about those ladies in Hopkinsville," I say dismissively.

"I just meant that—"

"Look, I'm sorry; I didn't mean to snap at you. It's just that most people don't understand what it's like to lose a spouse. I'm not saying I handled it all that well, it took me a long time to be willing to move on, but it doesn't change the fact that without someone in my life, the things I've done, the places I've seen, the people I've met and all the money I made didn't really matter much…I had no purpose, no one to share it with, the good or the bad."

"*Ya*, but you did what you wanted, traveled around a bit, tried new things—you got out and experienced life."

"*Ya*, that I did, which is why I can tell you from experience that without a wife and family to come home to at the end of the day, it is a lonely, empty life…a life that I'm done with. I'm not trying to rush you into anything Caleb; you're like a son to me. I want the best for you, but more than anything, I want to make sure that you see the bigger picture and know what really matters when you make decisions that could affect the rest of your life."

"I respect you Uncle John, I always have. Your advice means a lot to me and I promise to take it into consideration. I can see how much happier you've been lately and I hope you do court Sarah—she's great, her whole family is great. I'm just not sure that I know enough about life or even myself to choose the right woman to spend it with. In the meantime, I'm just keeping my options open."

"Just remember that with women, sometimes not deciding means missing your chance altogether. I think you'll know when the right one comes along. Maybe it's Naomi and maybe it's not, but if I were you, with what I know now, I'd give the idea of finding out a little more of my attention."

"Look, if you see her while you're there, just tell her I'll be back for church next Sunday; it's her birthday." He gives me a half-smile, "Just don't mention anything to anyone else…if you don't see her, I'll just surprise her."

"You've got it." I smile. "Now we'd better get cleaned up, we can't very well show up for dinner covered in dirt. We're having stir-fry and I'm pretty sure they were frosting a cake when we dropped the boys off."

"Well, you might have found the only woman in town you can't even court yet, but at least she can cook," he chuckles.

“You just make sure that little bit of information stays between us,” I say, slapping his shoulder as I head for the shower.

“Which part?!” he calls out teasingly.

CHAPTER THREE

Saturday, April 18

I awake around 11:30 p.m. to a big thud against my bedroom wall. I dart out of bed, tie my robe around my waist and grab Jacob's hunting rifle along with the flashlight hidden behind the crown molding on top of my wardrobe. I slide my feet into my slippers next to the door and make my way through the kitchen in the dark.

I have no idea what I expect to find or what I intend to do about it, but I have an uneasy feeling in the pit of my stomach. I've heard tales of coyotes and other predatory animals lurking about the neighboring farms at night but we've never had one on the property that I know of. Besides, the thudding sounded like it was on the outside wall of the house right above my bed. Whatever it is, it's way too tall to be a four-legged creature.

As I quietly open the kitchen door and step outside, I'm wide-awake with every nerve in my body on high alert. The night air is cool and damp as it sends a chill up my spine and I shiver involuntarily. I stand in silence to let my eyes adjust for a moment as I listen carefully for any more sounds coming from the darkness.

I click on the flashlight but nothing happens…the batteries must be dead. I suppose it doesn't surprise me seeing as I haven't used it since Jacob died, but the timing couldn't be worse. I walk past the house and creep alongside the barn when I hear another thudding sound. I gasp and try not to make a sound but my heart feels like it's going to leap out of my chest.

When I reach the corner of the barn, I creep past the rabbitat and peer around the open area in the moonlight to see if I detect any movement. I hear another thud, this one much closer.

"Who's there?" I call out in a low whisper, gripping the rifle in my hand.

There's no reply but I hear rustling and the sound of footsteps. I'm in such a panic that I can't tell if they're coming toward me, moving toward the house or running in the opposite direction. Under the dim moonlight, I can see a clear path to the phone shack in the distance and I remember about John's cell phone.

I grasp the rifle in my hand tightly and break into a run, almost tripping in the grass as I lunge for the door handle. I step inside and latch the door behind me as I try to catch my breath. I lift the phone off the receiver, thankful for the dim yellow glow that shines around the buttons. I'm pretty sure that

I remember John's phone number, but I hold it up to the wall and see where Mary had written it on the wall.

My hands are shaking as I get a dial tone and punch in his number. I force myself to breathe in and out slowly to calm myself as I pray for him to answer. I feel like a sitting duck.

"Hello?" he says in a groggy voice.

"John, there's someone here, my flashlight's not working but they were outside the house and I heard them running, I'm locked in the phone shack."

"Okay, don't move, keep the door locked I'm on my way, just keep talking to me," he says, "Can you hear anything?"

I listen carefully for a moment, "I can't hear anything."

"I'm starting the tractor," he assures me, "Just stay where you are."

"John, I'm worried about Mamm and the *kinner*!" I say emphatically, trying to keep my voice down.

"Sarah, I'm on my way do you hear me? I'm pulling out onto the road, just stay there…tell me what happened."

"I heard something hit the outside of the house right above my bed. I got up, grabbed the rifle and the flashlight and came outside to see what was going on. I was already out by the barn when I heard the sound again and realized that the batteries in the flashlight are dead. I heard the sound again followed by the footsteps, I just ran for the phone shack as fast as I could, oh

God John, I should have gone back to the house!"

"No Sarah, you did the right thing, just calm down; I'm almost there. Have you heard the sound again?"

"No," I say, fighting back the tears.

"Take a deep breath and tell me what it sounded like," he says in a soothing voice.

"It sounded like someone kicking the side of the house only it was high up the wall."

"And when you heard it the last time, was it the same?"

"*Ya*, only it sounded like someone kicking the outside of the gift shop, it was coming from that direction."

"Can you tell which direction the footsteps were moving?"

"I was standing in the clearing between the barn and the rabbitat, it sounded like they were in front of me but something disturbed the chickens and then I wasn't sure if they were in front of me or behind me."

"Did you check the door to the chicken coop?"

My mouth is dry and my stomach is in knots as I try to answer his questions. "No, I just remembered your phone and ran for the phone shack because I couldn't really see much else. I panicked."

"It's okay, I'm turning down your drive right now, I'll come straight to you and we'll check everything together okay?"

"John if anything has happened to Mamm or the *kinner* I'll never be able to live with myself."

"It's okay, I'm here and I'm right outside. Do you see my lights?"

I peer through the old wooden slats and unlatch the door as he pulls it open from the other side. I feel like I'm going to pass out as he reaches out his arms and pulls me to him.

"Let me have the rifle, I'm not going to let anything happen to you," he says, holding me tightly against him.

I loosen my grip on the rifle and he lifts me into his arms. He puts the rifle and me in the wagon and then gets back onto the tractor and heads for the house.

"I'm going to go inside, turn on the porch light and check the house, do you want to wait here or come with me?"

"I want to come," I assure him, climbing out of the wagon with the rifle in my hand.

"Just stay behind me; let's try not to frighten the *kinner* if we don't have to."

Inside the house, we creep quietly up the stairs and check each bedroom. I feel a bit calmer as we close each door behind us. The *kinner* are all sleeping soundly in their beds.

Back downstairs, we check the rest of the house together from my bedroom and bathroom to the hall bath, the living room and finally, the pantry.

"You stay here," he says flipping on the light.

I wait patiently, my legs still shaking until he re-emerges from the basement door.

"Everything's fine down there too, I'm going to go check the Daadi Haus and the rest of the property. Take my phone, keep the door locked until I get back and call 911 if anything happens," he says, walking me across the kitchen.

"But what about you?" I protest, taking the phone from is hand.

"I'll be on the tractor, I have my rifle and a working flashlight; I'll be okay. I promise I'll be back as soon as I can."

"Please hurry," I plead.

"I will," he assures me with his hand in the small of my back. "How about making us some coffee?"

I can't help but notice how intensely blue his eyes are. "Okay," I assure him, grateful just to have some task to distract me at the moment.

***

At the Daadi Haus, I try the door quietly, which I'm glad to find locked, and then take a careful walk around the perimeter. From there I check the chicken coop, the rabbitat and the barn but don't find anyone or anything lurking on the grounds. I climb back onto the tractor and drive around behind the barn, past HQ, down the fence line toward the golf course and back again, looking for any signs of movement but find nothing.

As I drive back toward the house, I decide to take one last walk around the main house before going inside.

I walk past the porch, guided by the beam of my flashlight until I reach the backside of the house behind Sarah's bedroom. I remember her telling me that she heard the first sound on the wall above her bed. I can smell the odor as I approach. I shine my flashlight and realize that the wall is smeared with what appears and smells like cow dung.

I curse under my breath and finish the walk around the perimeter. When I'm satisfied that the pranksters have gone, I check my shoes with the flashlight before heading back inside to check on Sarah.

"Did you see anything?" she asks, closing the door behind us.

"Your *mamm*'s door was locked and I didn't see anyone anywhere on the property; you probably frightened them off earlier."

She pours us both a cup of coffee as I wash my hands and sit down at the table. "I think it might have been teenagers pulling a prank," I tell her, running my hands through my hair, realizing that I don't have my hat on.

She sits across from me and looks at me curiously. God, she's beautiful. Her wavy brown hair falls loosely around her delicate face and over her shoulders; her dark eyebrows frame her intense blue eyes while everything is softened somehow by her warm pink, full lips and the gentle curve of her cheekbones. I would give anything to touch her, to kiss her and to make her feel safe in my arms.

"What makes you think so?" she asks.

"What?" I say, realizing that I've been so lost in my own thoughts that I wasn't paying attention.

"What makes you think it was some kind of prank? Are you sure everything's okay?"

I clear my throat uncomfortably, "Cow dung."

"What?"

"Someone threw cow dung against the house. I didn't see it until I made a final walk around the house and inspected the wall outside of your bedroom before coming inside. There's really no way to tell how bad it is until daylight."

"Who would do such a thing?" she asks incredulously.

"There's no telling, what time did you say it was when you first heard the noise?"

"It was right around 11:30 p.m. I know because the clock beside my bed was the first thing I saw when I woke up."

"I'm going to go out on a limb and say that the culprits were probably Amish."

“Why is that?”

“Well, for starters, the only people upset with you right now are Amish, and Englischers would have been more likely to pull a stunt like this later at night to ensure that the victims are sound asleep. Maybe it’s just a hunch but something tells me that these pranksters were trying to accomplish their dirty deed as late as possible but still before midnight, because of the Sabbath. They’re probably expecting that you’re too devout to clean it up until Monday.”

“That’s a disturbing thought.”

“Which part, the fact that someone in the community could have done this, the possibility that they planned it around the Sabbath or the idea of waiting until Monday to clean it up?”

“All of them. The fact that anyone would do this at all knowing that there are five *kinner* in the house is terrifying to me John. If they could do this and frighten us half to death, what will they do next? What if I had shot someone in the dark? What if I weren’t the first one to wake up and go outside?”

“I know it was frightening, and something definitely needs to be done about it, but let’s just be grateful that it wasn’t worse—that none of those things happened and that you’re safe.”

“This is really going to upset Mamm and the *kinner*,” she says, propping her elbows on the table and resting her head against her fists.

It's difficult to watch and I can't resist the urge to comfort her. I gently brush a long tress of hair from her cheek and tuck it behind her ear. "I understand your wanting to shield them from all of this, but it happened. I think it would be better for them to know. It will make them more cautious and watchful than they would if they were kept in the dark and possibly caught off guard if it happens again."

"You saw how upset the girls were when Deacon Byler confronted me in the parking lot that day, this is something that happened right at home where they're supposed to feel the safest, how can I tell them about this?"

"I know that Hannah was the most upset until I gave her a plan of action. Your *kinner* are smart and mature for their ages, I think you should educate them on what to do if they hear someone outside in the middle of the night or if someone on a tour makes them uncomfortable—Amish or Englisch. This incident might help them understand the importance of keeping doors and cash drawers locked and knowing what to do if they need help. It's unfortunate that it happened, but they'll most likely take their cues from how you handle it. If you fold, they'll fold, if you gird yourself up, they will too. All of those *'what ifs'* you just mentioned will still be a possibility if you keep them in the dark and pretend it never happened."

"I know you're right. I guess I just don't want to accept that it has come to this," she says, looking at me and then closing her eyes.

"Tell me what I can do to help," I say encouragingly. "I'll get out there with a water hose before daylight if you want me to," I offer.

"I appreciate your coming over in the middle of the night, and I don't know what I would have done without you," she says, squeezing my hand. "I think I just need to rest for a little while. It was a really busy day with four tours and I had only been asleep for about an hour when it happened. I'm not even thinking clearly."

"Will you be able to rest?"

"I don't know, but what else can I do?"

"Look, if you're still afraid, I could sleep on the couch for a few hours, set the alarm on my phone and be up before the *kinner* if that would help you to get some rest. I'm sure that if anyone finds out, they'll understand once you explain what happened."

"I don't really want to be alone but I hate to ask you to do that."

"As long as you don't ask me to sleep in the barn I don't mind," I chuckle.

She goes into the hallway under the stairs and grabs a blanket and pillow from the closet. "The *kinner* aren't usually up before six. Mamm's usually here a few minutes after. If I could just get a few hours of sleep before then, I'll be fine. Are you sure you'll be okay?"

"I'll be fine, just wake me up if you get frightened, I'm a light sleeper," I assure her, taking the bedding from her, "Go get some rest."

"Good night, John."

She steps into her bedroom and closes the door behind her. I tuck my rifle under the couch and put my shoes in front of it before crawling under the blanket. I set the alarm on my phone for 5:30 a.m. and tuck it into my pocket.

The pillow she gave me smells like her. I must be a glutton for punishment offering to sleep in the next room from a beautiful woman that I can't get out of my head, let alone touch or kiss or even tell how I feel about her. Still, I could never forgive myself if I left her here alone with the *kinner* and anything bad was to happen.

As I lay here, my thoughts keep drifting back to the first time I ever saw this house. Not the day that I met Sarah, but the day that my real estate agent drove me by the place while we were out looking at properties in the area. I think I'll call her in the morning and see if she's heard anything lately. Something just doesn't feel right about this situation, and for an Englischer, she certainly seemed to know a lot about the goings on in the community. In the meantime, at least the couch is comfortable, the people I care about are safe and I've got a few ideas about how to handle the situation from here.

CHAPTER FOUR

Sunday, April 19

I awake to my phone vibrating in my pocket and a dim glow pouring into the room. I sit up and fumble to put my shoes on, fold the blanket, grab the pillow and my rifle and follow the light into the kitchen.

"Hi," Samuel says casually, sitting his glass of milk on the table, unsurprised by my presence.

"Hey buddy, what are you doing up this early, you couldn't sleep?"

"I just needed a glass of milk. Sorry if I woke you up."

"No, I didn't even hear you come downstairs," I say awkwardly.

"Are you going hunting this morning?"

I suddenly remember the rifle in my hand and decide to just

follow my own advice and tell him what happened, "No, your *mamm* heard something outside and called me from the phone shack. She was a little frightened but I think she's okay now, she just needed to get some sleep."

"Was it a coyote or something? One of the older boys at school said he shot a coyote in the woods behind their pasture but I'm pretty sure his *daed* was really the one who shot it. He lies all the time."

"I'm not sure what it was, I checked the property and didn't find anything roaming around. I was planning to wait until daylight and check it again to see if anything had been disturbed." I sit the rifle by the door and put the bedding back in the closet before joining him at the table.

"Well I'm glad you came, my *mamm* probably feels a lot safer with a grown man in the house. She's pretty brave, but girls get scared easier and I don't even think she knows how to use a rifle."

"Your *mamm* has a lot of people to look after; it's probably not easy doing it alone."

"*Ya*, she's got a lot more responsibilities with my *daed* gone, that's why Mark and I want to learn to plow and hunt and do our tours. That way, we can make a lot of money for the family and bring food into the house."

"Well it looks like your plan is starting to work; I heard you had four tours yesterday."

"*Ya*, and you're giving us our first real hunting lesson on Wednesday, Mamm already told us." He smiles.

"*Ya*, I'll show you a little about tracking and trapping in the woods and you'll learn how to set up a pig corral. Then in a week or two, we'll go bag ourselves another turkey. After that, you'll get plenty of practice during squirrel season."

"Awesome."

"What's awesome?" Sarah asks, standing in the doorway.

"Good morning," I say with a knowing grin, "Samuel and I were just talking about our hunting plans. I hope we didn't wake you."

"*Ya* Mamm, maybe you should learn to use *daed*'s rifle," he says.

"Samuel, go upstairs, brush your teeth and get yourself dressed without waking your brothers and sisters. It's not even daylight yet."

"*Ya* ma'am," he says, putting his glass in the sink.

"I should probably run home and grab my hat and a shirt, I kind of left in a hurry." I smile self-consciously as he tiptoes up the stairs. "When I get back, it should be light enough to ride around and check the property."

"What did Samuel say about your being here?" she asks in a whisper.

"He was sitting in the kitchen drinking a glass of milk when my alarm went off. I pretty much had to tell him that I came over because you heard something outside and you were frightened. He said that he was glad that I was here and I told him that I stayed to let you sleep and so I could check the property again at daylight."

She sighs and takes a deep breath. "I'm sorry; he isn't usually up this early,"

"It's not like we did anything wrong Sarah," I remind her, "Now you're going to do your morning routine and make us a fabulous breakfast. I'll go get Caleb and meet you back here when we're both properly dressed…not that I don't love seeing you with your hair down." I smile. "After I'm able to drive the property and see what we're dealing with, we'll all pitch in to clean it up and have a family meeting to talk about everything. It will be fine, just trust me."

"Breakfast will be ready in an hour," she says, giving in to my plan.

"That should give me plenty of time," I assure her with a smile. I grab my rifle as I head out to the tractor, "I'll see you then," I chuckle.

I start the tractor and head for the road. The sun will be up in a few minutes and I'm anxious to get back and see just exactly what happened last night.

On my way out of the drive, it occurs to me to check the new sign at the property entrance. I stop the tractor and shine my flashlight on it. Sure enough, it's splattered with cow dung, which almost assures me that this whole thing was meant as some sort of declaration against the tours and that the culprits were more than likely our very own Amish neighbors. My blood is boiling as I drive, but by the time I get to my house, I've at least calmed down enough to think rationally.

Before going inside the house, I open the shop and start digging through the few remaining boxes of old equipment I have stored in the back. I find the radio base and all four handsets along with a spool of telephone wire and a high-pressure nozzle for the garden hose.

I also load the empty five-gallon buckets I have, all of the empty pallets I was storing to use for the produce stand, the canopy and the folding tables. I'm not exactly sure how we'll incorporate everything yet, but I know that Caleb agrees with Sarah about setting up the produce stand at her place, and I'll feel better knowing that he'll be there. We may as well get what we can set up so that we can see what we lack.

By the time I've got the stuff from the shop loaded, I meet Caleb walking toward the barn to feed the horses.

"Where did you go dressed like that?" he asks curiously, eyeing my t-shirt.

"I left in a rush last night. Sarah called me from the phone shack. Someone pelted the house with cow dung although we didn't know that until later. She was terrified. Go ahead and take care of the horses, I'm going to go get dressed and we'll head over there. It was still dark when I left and I don't know how bad it is, but she's making breakfast."

"I'll grab the shovels and a rake too," he assures me.

"Load the big hose reel and a bucket of water too. We'll probably need it."

I realize that today's the Sabbath, but under the circumstances, I think the good Lord will understand. I've been spending a lot more time thinking like a father myself these past few weeks, and I can't imagine that He would want his *kinner* disgraced on the Sabbath either.

Once I get a quick shower, change, put on my old work boots and hat, I grab my old straw broom and some gloves and we head over to Sarah's to assess the damage, starting with the entrance sign.

I let the trailer idle at the top of the drive while I snap a photo of the defaced sign with my phone. Next, I sweep off the debris and Caleb rinses it down with the bucket of water before we head toward the far end of the property.

The fencing all looks like it's intact and the rear acreage appears undisturbed. We move past the clusters of pear and apple trees that lead to the picnic area and that section looks fine too. Of course there isn't much to destroy, but I don't see any tracks or signs that anyone was even back here since our picnic Friday evening.

We check the cornfield, which looks fine and then the golf course. We find some props down, several backboards are splattered with random cow dung, and there are several small tire tracks scattered about, leading to the open area that borders the fields.

I drive over to the side gate and check the lock. The chain has been cut with the padlock lying on the ground outside the gate. "They must've come in through here, hit the golf course first and then traveled toward the house."

We both stand and survey the neighboring landscape. "There," Caleb says, pointing to some tracks in the grass.

We walk over to take a closer look. "They're too small to be a tractor and too randomly spaced to be a buggy. It looks like bicycle tires and there were at least two of them."

"They had to cut across that field because that hill behind it would be too rough to travel at night loaded down with crap. One random fall and someone's doing the walk of shame all the way home," Caleb says with a chuckle.

"Good point," I agree. "Let's see what else they hit," I say, climbing back onto the tractor.

We head back toward the house and find heavier rutted tracks behind the hay slide which doesn't appear to have been damaged.

"I'm guessing they used this for cover and to park their bikes," I say, "I have a feeling they intended to focus their mayhem on HQ and the house."

As we pull in front of tour HQ, my worst fears are confirmed. In front of the door is a wad of tour flyers lying on the ground covered in cow dung. The front and side walls are splattered in it, but fortunately, the window isn't broken and the door is still locked.

"Well they may have gotten their message across and made it very uninviting, but at least they didn't break in or destroy anything," I sigh.

"If the people who did this were Amish, how would they know about HQ? Even I didn't know about it until I came back this time because you guys didn't put it together until after I left."

"I don't know, but that's a good point and one we'll have to dig into a little deeper. Let's check the rest of the property on foot as we walk toward the house."

We check the outbuildings from the chicken coop to the rabbitat to the barn and do a quick walk around the house before heading inside.

"Let me talk to Sarah in private before we mention anything to the *kinner*," I assure him before we enter the kitchen.

"Good morning everyone," I say as Hannah runs up to hug me, and then Caleb.

"Good morning," they all say randomly.

"I'll make you some coffee," Miriam says. "Caleb do you want some too?"

"*Ya*, ma'am, *Danki*," he says, taking a seat next to Mark and Samuel.

I step over to the stove as Sarah flips the eggs in her pan, "Let's talk for a moment," I whisper. "Mmmm, that bacon sure smells good," I say, mostly for the *kinner*'s benefit.

"I'm toasting some banana bread too," Mary says cheerfully.

"I can't wait," I chuckle.

"Mamm would you watch the eggs? I need to speak to John for a minute," Sarah says, following me outside.

I relay to her what we found minus the questions we have and the clues. "I brought back some equipment and I don't think it'll take too long to clean up. I think we should just tell them about it after breakfast. Once the cleanup is done, we'll implement some new safety precautions and I'll put their minds at ease."

"I trust you John, we'll handle it the way you feel is best," she says grasping my forearm momentarily as she looks into my eyes.

"That means a lot to me, I really think this is the right way to handle it." It feels good to know that she has faith in me, but I still can't stop thinking about kissing her. "I could really go for that cup of coffee right about now," I smile, changing the subject before I take her into my arms right here and now.

Back inside the kitchen the buzz of activity begins to settle as Miriam and Mary bring the food to the table and everyone gathers around. I take another swig of coffee before we say grace and dig in.

"I was thinking about the discussion we had last night about separating the golf course from the rest of the tour and also about your idea to set up the produce stand here," I announce, "I think they're both great ideas."

"Me too, and I'd be happy to help out, at least through summer," Caleb adds.

"Awesome," Samuel says.

"That's great, we'll really need someone to keep an eye out back there and especially after the corn maze is ready," Mark adds.

"I'll feel a lot better knowing you're around, Caleb," Sarah says.

"Me too, and I'm good at sales. I'll sell your produce for you when you're working the golf course," Mary offers.

"There are a couple of conditions," I interject, "We need better communications so I want to start by running a phone line to the barn and to HQ," I say, leveling my gaze at Sarah knowingly.

"*Ya* okay, I think that's a good idea," she agrees.

"And the second one is that I brought over some walkie-talkies that we used to use with my *daed*'s construction business. I kept them when they switched to cell phones, I wasn't even sure why at the time, but they'll enable everyone to communicate more efficiently no matter where they are on the property. They're supposed to have a five-mile range, so they may even work as far as my house but we'll have to test it."

"Oooohh cool, walkie-talkies!" Mark cheers happily.

"You're a wise man, John Troyer," Miriam smiles, "Maybe God knew you would find the perfect use for them someday."

"I suppose that will solve our communication problem," Sarah agrees.

"Good, now can someone pass the bacon?" I chuckle.

"Do I get a walkie-talkie too?" Josh asks.

"Everyone here is going to learn to use them, but they're mainly for when one of you is working somewhere out on the property and you need to communicate with HQ or the house."

"Or when we need Caleb to come help us?" Hannah asks.

"*Ya*, if you need any kind of help," I assure her.

"When are we going to learn to use them?" Mary asks.

"Well, I know it's the Sabbath, but I have a lot of work to

do this week and I want you to all practice in the afternoons before the next tour, so I was planning to show you today. First, your *mamm* and I have some things we need to talk to you about and the handsets have to charge for a few hours."

"We'll still spend the day together and you'll have some time to play and relax. Dan and Ruthie are coming for visitation this afternoon too but this is important," Sarah explains.

"I'd rather work on the tours than play anyway, it's more fun," Mark says.

"Me too," Mary agrees, "Besides, this will make the whole week run smoother."

"After last night it's probably a really good idea," Samuel adds.

Everyone looks at him for a moment, probably because he's already spilled the beans to the rest of the *kinner*, but I decide to keep him out of trouble with his *mamm*. "Your *mamm* and I will explain to everyone what happened after breakfast, but not before I finish this banana bread toast. I think this really is the best banana bread I've ever had."

"This is the last of it, we put out samples yesterday and I sold four loaves," Mary informs me, "It was Samuel's idea."

We make it through breakfast and Sarah nominates me to explain what happened last night to everyone before they start asking questions. I tell them what happened and answer their questions before assuring everyone that we're going to implement some new safety rules starting today.

I head out to HQ to get the radios set up on the charger while the *kinner* do their morning chores. Once the *'operation cow-dung-cleanup'* is finished, I gather the whole family around the toddler maze and lay some ground rules for what to do if they hear something in the night, how to handle it if someone makes them feel uncomfortable, the importance of keeping the doors and cash drawer locked, where to go and what to do if they feel scared and so on.

By the time we finish and everyone's on the same page, I give them all a couple of basic self-defense tips.

"Okay so no matter who it is, man or woman, Amish or Englisch, what do we do if someone tries to grab you or make you go somewhere or do something you don't want to?"

"Scream and tell people to call 9-1-1," Mary answers.

"Very good and if someone grabs you, there are four places you can hit them to try to get away."

"You mean in the nuts?" Hannah asks.

"*Ya*, she accidentally kicked Mark in the nuts when we were playing once, we know all about it," Samuel explains.

"*Ya* okay," I say looking at Sarah and Miriam but neither of them offer any help, "So *Ya*, you can knee them or kick them between the legs as hard as you can, you can kick their shins, right here on this bone," I say, showing them the shin bone,

"You can hit them right here in the throat, or you can poke your fingers in their eyes."

"That's gonna hurt a lot," Josh says.

"I know it all sounds very painful, but if someone is trying to grab you, you want it to be painful so that they'll let go of you and focus on the pain while you run and get help."

"Nuts, shins, throat and eyes," Mary recites.

"Very good, now everyone tell me those four places again one at a time," I say expectantly.

They answer one by one until everyone has it down. It may be very basic, but at least this lesson might come to them if they're ever in danger.

I have them spend the next hour practicing their screaming and their moves while Caleb and I attempt to lure and grab them, making sure they only pretend to kick, punch and gouge our body parts.

"John can you teach us to swim?" Samuel asks.

"Who doesn't know how to swim?" I ask.

To my surprise, they all raise their hands.

"Well, I'll teach you all how to swim this summer if it's okay with your *mamm*. In the meantime, Caleb's going to help me run the phone line and we'll have the lesson on how to use the radios right after lunch."

“You guys can relax and play until then,” Sarah announces.

“That was some lesson,” Miriam says, patting me on the shoulder.

“I know it was a bit crude but I’d rather they be informed than taken by surprise, especially with strangers on the property three days a week.”

“He’s right, I don’t think it would come naturally to Josh or Hannah to scream if someone grabbed them, but now I think they would if they were ever in danger. I was apprehensive in the beginning, but I think it was necessary,” Sarah says with a smile.

I walk away feeling a bit more confident that not only do the *kinner* feel more empowered, but Sarah does too.

Caleb and I spend the next two hours running the phone lines to HQ and the barn. I make myself a note to get two wall plates and phones the next time I’m in town. Until then, they’ll have the radios. I just hope last night’s anti-tourists are planning to observe the Sabbath and take the night off.

***

Between our picnic lunch, the radio lessons and dinnertime, John and Caleb wired the phone lines, replaced the chain on the back fence and have the canopy up for the produce stand. We set up two long folding tables and some empty buckets for displaying the goods.

For dinner, Dan and Ruthie brought shepherd's pie, dinner rolls, a cheesecake and a huge box of donut holes. As the *kinner* finish up their evening chores, pet the bunnies and take a ride with Caleb in the wagon, we all sit on the porch, talking about the days events.

"I know it must have been terrifying Sarah, I'm just glad John was able to get here," Ruthie says with a concerned look, "I've often worried about you, Mamm and the *kinner* out here all alone."

"I've heard things in the night before, but I've never been afraid like I was last night. I'm just glad that they didn't try to break in or do any serious damage."

"I'm with you John, it sounds like someone's trying to frighten Sarah out of doing the tours, and as much as I hate to imagine it, they had to be Amish," Dan says, shaking his head.

"Do either of you recall anyone you vaguely recognized or anyone who could have been Amish, dressed in Englisch clothes taking the tour in the past couple of days?" John asks. "Maybe teenagers even?"

"Not that I recall, most of the people who have been coming are families with younger children."

"I didn't recognize anyone either," Mamm agrees, "Why do you ask?"

"Well Caleb made a good point earlier: most of the vandalism was directed at HQ and that's where we found the crumbled up flyers. He pointed out that HQ didn't even exist as part of the tours until recently, so it had to be someone who knew about it. Even Deacon Byler doesn't know that—he hasn't been here to see how the tours operate."

I get a bad feeling in the pit of my stomach thinking about last Sunday night, "The Shetlers know and they definitely disapprove."

"Do the Shetlers have bicycles?" John asks.

"Their *kinner* might, but I really don't know."

"They've always been followers, this doesn't sound like something they would do on their own," Dan says.

"Don't forget the Yoders, their *kinner* definitely have bikes, they ride them in town all of the time," Ruthie adds.

"*Ya,* but when Sarah told me what Mrs. Shetler said, those were Deacon Byler's words; I know because he said almost the exact words to me the day he visited my place. I'm sorry I didn't tell you about it Sarah, I didn't want you to worry about his attempt to sway me from helping you," John explains.

"Well, he obviously does have a lot of influence in Hope Landing," I sigh.

"I think I should go to the bishop again, just to keep him informed. We might not be able to prove who did it, but I don't think even he will question who's behind it," Dan offers.

"I agree and I have pictures of the whole mess on my phone

if that helps," John agrees.

"I still worry about you guys being here alone," Ruthie says.

"We're going to test the radios tonight and I'll have a phone in the barn tomorrow," I smile at John, "Caleb's also going to run his produce stand here through the summer and help with the tours while he's here. We won't be alone," I say, squeezing her hand.

"For what it's worth, I don't think these culprits are violent. They didn't even break out any windows last night, but I'll be around as much as I can too," John assures her.

"How's the produce stand going to work?" Dan asks, lightening the mood. "The canopy looks good."

"The plan is that we'll put out a sampling of what we both grow and Caleb will be here on the days we're open for tours. He'll oversee the golf course and make a weekly trip to the farmer's market on Thursday mornings to supplement our produce supply until we have enough variety of our own to sell. It will give us both a chance to see if it goes over well enough to keep doing," I explain.

"It really does sound like you guys have it under control, I'm really proud of you, this has turned into much more than I ever imagined," Ruthie says encouragingly.

"*Ya*, for us too," I laugh.

Everyone laughs along with me, and in spite of the setbacks

and the discouragement from last night, we have made lots of progress. I think about the verse in Romans 8:28 that says: '*And we know that all things work together for good to them that love God, to them who are the called according to his purpose.*' I think verse 31 also says: '*If God be for us, who can be against us?*'

In my heart, I know that God has certainly worked things out for our good, and I'm increasingly grateful for the wonderful people I have in my life…those who are against us don't have a chance.

CHAPTER FIVE

Thursday, April 30

As the last group of tourists leaves for the day, the *kinner* and I are all heading back toward the house together when I spot Deacon Byler's buggy at the bottom of the drive. He's standing by the roadway, stopping the last two families as they leave.

"Everyone inside the house, John should be here soon," I tell them as I march angrily toward him.

"I'm coming with you," Caleb protests.

"Just let me do the talking," I tell him.

As we approach, the expression on his face is somewhere between a scowl and the look of a kid caught with his hand in the cookie jar.

"I warned you Sarah Fisher, you'll not make a mockery of this community," he huffs. "I doubt your guests will be visiting again anytime soon," he says with a smirk.

"Deacon Byler, you have no right to interfere! We have done nothing wrong. Now I'm telling you to leave. You are not *wilkom* on this property ever again," I say defiantly, looking him in the eye.

"You're a foolish woman, Sarah Fisher, just remember that you've been warned!" he huffs angrily as he wrestles his round frame back into his buggy.

We watch as he drives away and I don't think I've ever been so outwardly angry in all my life. I stand there for a moment, frozen, unaware that I have my fists clenched at my sides until Caleb puts his arm comfortingly around my shoulder.

"So that's Deacon Byler," he says, lightening the mood, "I can't believe you didn't introduce me."

I feel myself relax at his strange timing to share his sense of humor. "Maybe next time," I chuckle.

"Uh *Ya*, I really doubt there will be a next time after that." He smiles as we walk back to the house, "You were pretty fierce."

"Fierce, huh?" I ask.

"Borderline frightening," he assures me.

"Think I could scare you into helping Mark and Samuel dig up a sack of potatoes while I get dinner ready?"

"That all depends," he smiles.

"On what?" I ask curiously.

"On whether there's a meatball casserole anywhere in my future," he chuckles.

"I'll see what I can do," I laugh.

CHAPTER SIX

Saturday, May 2

I take a seat at the head of the table and greet our guests to begin the meeting. "Mr. and Mrs. Wyse, glad you could join us this evening, Mr. Zug, Mr. and Mrs. Glick, Mr. and Mrs. Shetler, Mr. and Mrs. Yoder, good to see you all again. By now, you're all aware of why we're here. We have a parasite in our community that threatens to infect us all. We've tried reasoning, we've tried warning and thus far, we've used a light hand to try to remind Sarah Fisher of her place, but I'm afraid it's more out of hand than ever.

"The missus and I rode by there this afternoon like you suggested Deacon Byler and you were right, the place was crawling with Englischers," Mrs. Wyse informs us.

"*Ya*, and I'm afraid after seeing this disturbing article in last week's paper," I say, sliding the folded newspaper across the table, "There's no way she's going to stop these tours voluntarily. I even went over there on Thursday to try to reason with her and even thanked a few of her guests for coming to the last of her tours but she defied me and ordered me off the property." I watch as they gasp at her insolent display.

"This article says that she has a gift shop and a golf course. How in the world did two widows and five *kinner* get the kind of resources for that?" Mr. Glick asks.

"I think it's obvious that she's had help. I know that she's very close friends with the owners of Kaufmann's Bakery and I think this John Troyer fellow helped her get this whole disturbing thing off the ground. I tried talking to him, too, for what little good it did," I explain, "I think it's time that we take our efforts to the next level. We have got to send our message loud and clear before this tour business becomes a permanent fixture in our community."

"What do you suggest we do? Everything we've tried so far doesn't seem to be getting through to her," Mr. Yoder asks.

I look around to the men in the room one by one, "I don't think we need to have an open discussion on the specifics. Each man in this room will have to take responsibility for his own actions just as I do. I think it's more important that we rally the community to take a stand against her and show her that this insolence will not be tolerated. If these tours aren't over and done with by May 17th, she will *ne* longer be able to hide behind her status as a widow and we will discuss bringing her before the council."

I watch as everyone processes the seriousness of the matter.

"What does Bishop Graber say about all of this?" Mr. Zug asks.

"As I've said before, I don't think it's necessary to involve the bishop in this matter with the weight of the entire community resting on his shoulders, but maybe she's become too defiant for her Amish brothers and sisters to save," I say, rubbing my beard, letting them weigh the implication.

"If I may, Deacon Byler," Mrs. Wyse interjects, "Maybe we shouldn't involve anyone on an official level just yet, I don't agree with what Sarah's doing but maybe we should follow your instincts and try to address the problem privately first."

"I think it's too late for reasoning, we need to root out the cancer before it spreads," Mr. Shetler argues.

"I agree with the deacon. Let's do what we can on our own until the 17th and then meet again before involving the bishop or calling her before the council," Mr. Glick agrees, "Church services are being held at our house that Sabbath, we can all stay behind after everyone leaves and meet then."

"Then it's settled. Just remember that it's up to each of you to play a part in putting an end to this before this disgraceful behavior is brought before the officials, now is not the time for polite deterrence," I remind them.

CHAPTER SEVEN

Thursday, May 7

I awake around 2:40 a.m. to rustling and screeching sounds right outside of my bedroom window, soon followed by the sound of Joker neighing in his stall. I hurry out of bed, pull on my robe and slippers and fetch the rifle and flashlight from the top of the wardrobe like before. This time, I know that my batteries are working and I have a plan.

I creep quietly into the kitchen, turn on the porch lights, confirm that the door is still locked then grab the radio handset from the kitchen counter.

"John, are you there?" I whisper into the handset,

After a few moments, he comes on the line, "I'm here, what's going on?"

"Something's wrong with the animals, I think someone's here."

"Okay turn on the outside lights like we talked about and stay inside, I'm on my way. I'll call the phone in the barn, standby."

We agreed that he would call on the phone and hang up after a few rings so that any prowlers outside would hear the ringing and possibly be frightened off or suspect that we're still awake in the house.

I put the saucepan of water on the stove and watch the clock for the next seven minutes as I wait for it to boil, knowing that's how long it takes him to get here in a hurry. It seems like the longest seven minutes of my life next to the ones I spent locked in the phone shack a couple of weeks ago. At least this time, I can breathe and I don't feel nearly as vulnerable.

I set the can of wasp spray out on the counter and let the water boil like we planned until he comes to the door. If someone forces their way in, we have a blinded, scalded intruder; if it's a false alarm, John and I have coffee. Needless to say, I'm praying for coffee, even at this hour.

A few minutes later, I see the headlights of the tractor pass in front of the kitchen window and stop.

I listen and wait for him to give me the *'all clear'* before unlocking the door. It's funny how all of these details seemed so unnecessary when we first discussed them but in the heat of the moment, they're the only thing keeping my family and me from harm. My heart is pounding and my hands are shaking.

"It's me Sarah, we're all clear," I hear him say through the door.

"Thank God," I say, opening it to let him in.

"There's no sign of anyone outside but I'm afraid they let two of the horses out and opened the rabbitat. I'm going to need you to come with me to help round them up. Bring your flashlight but I don't think you'll need the rifle."

I turn off the stove burner and hurry to put the rifle back in its place before following John outside.

"Oh John, the *kinner* will be devastated," I say, swallowing hard to fight back the tears.

"I'm sorry, I should have brought Caleb too; I just wanted to get here as quickly as I could. I didn't expect this," he says in a frustrated tone.

I can hear in his voice that he feels responsible and that he let us down. I hug him, "You didn't know, and I doubt the horses will go far; let's focus on the bunnies first. We'll find them," I assure him.

He looks at me for a moment and I'm sure it surprises him as much as it does me that I'm the one comforting him. "Let's figure out which ones are missing," he says.

We reach the rabbitat and find that Lammie and Licorice are still huddled safely in the back corner.

"Well that's no surprise; those two are the shyest of the

bunch."

"*Ya*, two down, seven to go," he sighs, creeping toward the garden, watching the ground beneath him.

"John, there's Cinnamon!" I whisper, "Right behind your left foot."

He crouches down, grabs Josh's bunny by the fur of the neck and sticks it back in the cage. I see a flash of white in the grass out of the corner of my eye and take a few steps to the left.

"I've got Patches, I whisper, creeping through the plants to put him back in the cage with the rest. "I'm going to check by my window, I heard something there, that's what woke me."

"I think I see Mary's bunny with the long ears, I'll be right back," he assures me.

I step over to the corner of the house and peer down the sidewall. I spot a blonde lump of fur in the grass, "Oh no," I say under my breath, shining my flashlight onto it. It's Cookie and she looks like she's been scratched up. I grab her gently, cupping my hands beneath her, but before I even pick her up to examine her more closely, her little head flops over my fingertips and I know that she's dead.

I sigh and try not to cry as I lay her tattered body by the corner of the house. I work my way toward the chicken coop to keep looking for the others. As a grown-up, I may not be as emotionally attached to my bunny as the *kinner* are, but I know that it will break their hearts just the same and it saddens me to have to tell them.

I continue around the coop looking everywhere, but I don't find any more stray bunnies, so I start looking for John. In the beam of my flashlight, I spot him just ahead, walking toward me with a ball of fur in each hand. I feel a sense of relief and gratitude wash over me.

"I found the two gray ones stuck in the toddler maze. Which ones are still missing?" he asks, carrying them over to the rabbitat.

"That only leaves Pumpkin Pie; Cookie's dead," I tell him.

He stops and looks at me for a moment. I'm sure he can see the disappointment on my face in spite of my attempt to be strong and focus on the task at hand. "I'm sorry Sarah," he says, smoothing his hand gently over the crown of my head.

"At least it wasn't one of the *kinner*'s bunnies," I sigh.

"I think I saw Waffles over by the hay slide, I don't think she's going anywhere, why don't you see if you can bring her in while I keep looking for Pumpkin Pie. After that, we'll get on the tractor and go look for Jonah."

I head off in the direction of the hay slide, and sure enough, Waffles is enjoying a midnight snack. I scold her for eating the slide as I walk her back over to the barn and put her in her stall.

I stop for a minute to look at the buggy and the other equipment in the barn but nothing else appears to be disturbed.

I check on the goats but they're still secured in the pen.

Joker's neighing protest; the porch lights, the phone call or a combination of those things must have scared the prowlers off before they could finish the job. "You're a smart horse, good boy Joker" I say, stroking his neck. I grab a lead for Jonah and walk toward the tractor to meet John.

"No sign of Pumpkin?" I ask when he returns empty handed.

"No, we'll have to look again in the daylight, I doubt she'll survive the night without shelter, but I'd hate for one of the *kinner* to find her."

"I'll keep an eye out while we look for that mule of a horse," I tell him, "He's stubborn, so let's hope he's in a good mood."

We drive the property, both of us seated in the driver's seat which is a pretty tight fit but I feel safe and it's sort of nice being so close to him in spite of the circumstances. I try to focus my attention on watching for Pumpkin Pie instead of his muscular frame, slightly rumpled hair and perfectly shaped lips in the moonlight, but it's not easy.

I take turns shining my flashlight beam to the right and left of the tractor as we drive but I don't see any sign of her orange and white fur hopping around. We find Jonah out near the pear trees and after about ten minutes of coaxing, John finally takes over and gets him to walk toward the barn.

Once he's safely back in his stall, we make our way inside the house. "I'll start some coffee." I reach for the coffee press from the cupboard and when I turn around, John's standing right in front of me.

"Are you sure you're okay?" he asks knowingly.

I sigh. "I just feel like every time we think we're safe and begin to enjoy that feeling for even a moment, something bad happens."

I fight back the tears that I've managed to keep at bay throughout this whole ordeal but I can't stop them now. "I'm grateful that we didn't lose more than we did tonight, and I'm trying to focus on that, but I'm afraid of what these people will do next. I really don't know how much more of this I can handle."

He pulls me to him and puts his arms around me. I'm amazed at how much safer and more relaxed I feel in his embrace even though the circumstances haven't changed. More than anything, I wish that I could stay right here indefinitely, safely tucked away from the evils of the world in his arms.

"Look at how well you handled all of this tonight," he says, rubbing his hand over my back comfortingly. "You followed the plan, you were prepared and you kept your head. You probably even frightened them away before they could do something worse. We're going to get to the bottom of this Sarah but I want you to know that I'm so incredibly proud of you."

"Thank you for being here," I tell him, trying to compose myself, "I don't know what I would have done without you."

"I'm going to the bishop today. If Dan and I both put a little pressure on him, he's got to intervene. In the meantime, how about making us a cup of coffee while I go bury Cookie? It doesn't look like we're going to get any more sleep tonight and I don't want the *kinner* to see her. I'll be back in a few minutes."

I look at the clock as he kisses my forehead and heads back outside. It's after 4:00 a.m. I have to be ready to face a busy day in less than two hours and I feel like I could sleep for two days.

***

As I dig the grave for Cookie, all I can think about is Sarah and the painfully sweet, tortured feeling I have every time I'm in her presence. I try to keep my distance emotionally but I keep finding myself in situations where I'm swept up with her until her joy and pain become my own.

'Just dig,' I say to myself under my breath, hoping to blow off some steam from the wellspring of feelings for her that are resonating deep in my soul. I push my boot against the shovel again as it sinks into the soil and I think about how beautiful she is and how frustrating it is not to be able to kiss her. *'Love is patient,'* I recite to myself, *'Dig.'*

All of the other women I've encountered in the years since

Elizabeth's death were easily put out of my mind by a hard day's work but no, not Sarah. The harder I work, the more I think of her and how I want to build a life for us together, *'Dig,'* the more I do, the more I want to do for her, with her…and to her, *'Dig.'* The way she looks at me sometimes makes my knees feel like rubber, *'Dig.'* According to Dan it's only a couple of weeks before she's finally out of her mourning dress. I try to remember how long ago he told me that, but either way, it feels like the longest two weeks of my life, *'Dig.'* I have to let her know how I feel *'Dig.'* I just pray that she feels the same way about me, *'Dig.'* Then again, women are complicated, *'Dig,'* what if it's too soon for her and she sees me like some sort of big brother? *'Dig.'* What if I—

I stop the shoveling, and more importantly, stop this vicious, never-ending circle of thought when I realize that Cookie's grave is already about five feet deep. I lay the shovel down, put the bunny into the hole and decide to stop chasing my tail. I sit on the ground next to the grave for a moment to catch my breath.

I decide that I'm going to march right in there, take her in my arms and kiss her. She's not the only one who has reached the limit of what she can endure. I cover the grave, return the shovel to the barn and head toward the house, full of steam.

On the way there, I calm down a bit and my practical, maybe even levelheaded, side begins to take over. I would hate to cause any awkwardness between us by acting inappropriately, and I can't risk offending her and having her avoid me with all of this going on in her life. I would never forgive myself if something happened to her or the family because she was too ashamed or put off by my advances to call on me for help.

Like it or not, I'm stuck…at least for the time being. I'll just have to focus my energy on talking to the bishop, replacing the barn latch and building that golf hut to store the equipment in. I sigh heavily as I tuck my shirt back in and put my hat on. It's going to be a really long day.

CHAPTER EIGHT

Monday, May 11

John helps me into the buggy and walks around to the other side to get in.

"I'm perfectly capable of driving myself you know," I say, not wanting to be a burden.

"*Ya*, but we both have errands to run today; we may as well do them together. Besides, you'll need help with the heavy stuff and we both wanted to stop by the bakery."

"You just don't want me putting the new flyers out by myself," I chuckle.

"Is that such a bad thing?" he asks, clicking his tongue as he snaps the reigns.

"*Ne*, it's sweet of you. I suppose I'm a little nervous about it too considering how alienated I felt at church last Sabbath. Even Mrs. Wyse snubbed her nose at me."

"I'm sorry I wasn't there with you, Caleb had a prior commitment in Hopkinsville that he didn't mention until after I brought him back last time. I'm afraid we won't be here next service either."

"Was it a female prior commitment by any chance?" I ask curiously.

"One of his friend's birthday." He smiles, but the look on his face has girlfriend written all over it.

"Good for him," I chuckle.

"Do I even want to know what's in that folder?" he asks curiously.

"Just a copy of the newest flyer that Natalie brought by on Saturday which includes the separate pricing for miniature golf, along with a few copies of the newspaper article about the tours that I wanted to get laminated, my errands list, my shopping list and the menu plan for the next couple of weeks so I can change things around if I see any good sales at the store," I smile, "Oh *Ya*, and a picture that Hannah colored for Ruthie."

He looks at me knowingly but makes no comments about my organizational skills even though I can tell that he's tempted. "Where do you need to go besides the bakery, the printer and the grocery store?"

I look at my notes, "I need to switch out the flyers at the shoe store, the butcher, the glass shop, the tractor supply, the pawn shop and the library. Ruthie agreed to switch out the other two near her house on the way home."

"I was thinking maybe we would stop and have lunch, you know, one you didn't have to prepare and serve yourself," he smiles.

I give him a bit of a curious look. "Is there something in particular you're hungry for?"

"Not particularly."

"A meal with no *kinner*, no tours, no laundry going, no cooking required and someone else to clean up afterwards?" I chuckle. "I'm not sure I'd know how to act."

"Then let's find out," he laughs.

"Okay but we should stop at the printer's first so we'll have the new flyers on hand, and then we can work our way around town and end at the bakery. I prefer to hit the grocery store on our way home in case we get anything that has to be refrigerated."

"That'll work," he assures me.

We talk as we ride into town and it's nice to be out in the buggy on such a beautiful day together. I'm so used to seeing him zip around on that tractor of his that this outing seems much more leisurely in spite of our big to-do list. We stop at the printer's and get copies of the flyers from the teenager at the counter while we wait for the owner to laminate the newspaper clippings.

He replaces the old flyers with the new and tells me that he's looking forward to bringing his family for a tour when school gets out for summer break. I assure him that we'd love to have him and say goodbye, grateful for his support.

We replace the flyers at the shoe store, the butcher and the glass shop and then make our way over to the library.

"You switch out your flyers, I want to check something," he says, heading toward the computer desk.

When I'm finished, I browse the shelves while I wait for him near the entrance. We move on to the pawn shop where he browses the merchandise while I talk to the owner, and then finally to the tractor supply where he picks up some parts, chats with the clerks and switches out my flyers for me.

He helps me back into the buggy with a strange smile on his face.

"What's that look about?" I ask curiously.

"The cashier at the tractor supply said you were the prettiest Amish woman he had ever seen."

I look down at my hands self-consciously and then gaze out the side window. I don't suppose I'm used to being privy to what men think of me. Jacob had courted me for almost two years before we married and I hadn't been exposed to many Englisch before then. Aside from overhearing an occasional rude comment, they seem put off by my Amish clothing, which has always suited me just fine.

"I'm sorry if that makes you uncomfortable but I couldn't exactly argue with him."

I find myself blushing a bit but it pleases me to hear it from John. God knows I think he's quite handsome.

"Are you ready for lunch?" he asks.

"*Ya*, I could eat," I smile.

We turn off on one of the side roads in the middle of town and park the buggy behind an old brick building that has a hitching post. He helps me out of the buggy and we walk around to the front. He opens the door for me and follows me inside as we wait to be seated.

I'm impressed at how comfortable and easygoing he is when he's surrounded by Englischers. He's personable and people seem to like him instantly, Englisch or Amish. I admire that about him and it always puts me at ease when we're together.

The waitress seats us and fills the empty glasses on the table with water while we look over the menu.

"I don't know about you, but I'm having the steak platter. I think we have plenty of pork in our future," he chuckles.

"*Ya*, and turkey too, Samuel still hasn't stopped talking about your hunting trip."

I look over the menu and, like him, I want something I don't usually cook at home. "Steak sounds *gut* but the fried shrimp does too."

"We could get both and share," he offers. "But only if you like your steak medium rare."

"*Ya*, that sounds perfect, with sweet potato fries, I don't deep fry that often."

"Good, you deserve something a little different to just enjoy yourself now and then. You spend a lot of time taking care of a lot of people."

"Look who's talking," I chuckle.

"*Ya*, okay maybe it's what we both enjoy doing but you have to admit that it makes times like this, when we can just enjoy the moment, that much sweeter."

"*Ya*, I'm enjoying it, *Danki*." I look down at my hands as I feel myself blushing again and think of the many sweet moments I've enjoyed with him, whether he's been aware of it or not.

The waitress returns and he places our order, asking for extra fries instead of salads on both plates.

"I don't think I can eat all of those fries," I laugh.

"What we don't eat I'll take home to Caleb. That boy is an eating machine. He never gains a pound though."

"He's going to be taller than you, I think."

"*Ya*, maybe, all that food has to go somewhere," he laughs.

"Just think what it would be like to have three boys."

"*Ya*, but your boys are already prepared to hunt and fish and work the fields, at least they'll probably be able to bring in enough food to feed themselves by the time they get to be teenagers."

"Did you have a big appetite as a teenager?"

"*Ya*, but not quite like my eldest brother. He could always eat twice as much as me even though he's tall and lanky like Caleb."

"How is your family doing?"

"They're all doing fine; it was *gut* seeing them last Sunday. How about you; have you heard from your brother?"

"*Ya*, Mamm got a letter from him, he's worried about my uncle's health, but other than that he's keeping busy with the farm in Maryland.

"When is the last time you saw him?"

"He came for a visit last year after Jacob's funeral, but before that it had been about three years."

"You should know that it meant a lot to me the day that we met and you shared with me about being widowed."

"I wondered at the time if I had been too forward," I say, briefly looking down at my hands again.

"No, Sarah," he says looking into my eyes, "It was refreshing to talk so openly and honestly with someone who had been through what I had, and I admired that you didn't let your modesty stand in the way of sharing your valuable experience," he assures me.

"I remember there were things that I admired about you as well," I smile.

"Oh *Ya*? I'm not sure I should ask," he chuckles.

"You were just so calm and easygoing in spite of the rain and the threat of being hit by a car while you were helping me with my bicycle. Then you got out and opened the door for me in spite of getting soaked. You took care of me that day, like you've pretty much done ever since."

I never thought I would see it from such a quietly confident man, but as I sit here right across from him, I watch as he blushes a little. It's sweet to see his vulnerable side and I don't feel so embarrassed about my own.

Just as he is about to say something, the waitress brings our order to the table. He asks for a side of mayonnaise to mix with his ketchup for his fries and divides the steak between us as I put some fried shrimp on his plate.

We share a moment in silent prayer and dig in the way we do at home. "Mmmm, the steak is cooked perfectly," I say, happy to be able to rave about someone else's cooking for a change.

"*Ya*, the shrimp too," he agrees, "One of my *daed*'s friends goes to Florida for the winter every year. He tells stories about catching buckets of jumbo shrimp with his buddies down there. I'd like to go someday."

"Ruthie loved Florida. I think I'd like the beach and I definitely want to drive a golf cart," I chuckle.

"You don't have to go to Florida to drive one; I've even worked on a few for a guy over in Marion."

"I think it would be ideal to have on a farm. How is your business doing anyway?"

"It's going well, but then I never wanted to be a high-volume shop. I get too claustrophobic being there all day, every day."

"You seem to thrive in an environment where you have several different types of irons in the fire at once."

"*Ya*, a lot like you," he smirks.

"Maybe so, I never grew up wanting to be one specific thing. I knew that I wanted to be a wife and a mother, and I'm devoted to that, but my hobbies seem to vary. I like quilting, sewing, cooking and gardening. I like to read although I don't get a lot of time to devote to it and I like to try little crafts with the girls but I get bored if it gets too routine."

"I think we're a lot alike in that way," he smiles.

"*Ya*, but you're much more of a people person than I am."

"That reminds me; I wanted to tell you my idea for the back acreage on your farm. I was thinking about something low-maintenance with a high yield, but something that would also tie in with the tours. I think you should plant fir trees. It will take seven years or so for them to mature, but they would be very low maintenance in the meantime. When they do mature, you can get fifty dollars and up per tree; not to mention that you can probably make that on one decorated Christmas wreath, which I'm sure is an activity the girls would enjoy doing. Plus a Christmas-tree farm would give you a viable winter attraction for the tours. Even if you never harvested the trees, you could decorate it like some winter wonderland or something, but the trees would increase the overall value of your land."

"That's a really good idea. The land is just sitting there, and for as long as I have a *mamm* and five *kinner* to take care of, I can't see ever being able to manage farming it all with fruits and vegetables."

"I think you should also plant a few cold-hardy avocados. Since you cook, you can always use what you don't sell, but you know how expensive they are."

"I love avocados too, they're both good ideas. How much would I need to invest to get started?"

"Well, two-year seedlings are much more expensive than starting from scratch, but I'm assuming you want to see the return on your investment by the time the *kinner* are eighteen."

"*Ya*, that would be ideal."

"You can probably plant about 200 trees per acre, and I know where you can get the seedlings for around $2.50 each if you buy 100 or more at a time, but I need to shop around and make sure that's the best price. I think we can do better."

"See what you can find out and I'll try to do at least a hundred this season. I can always add more as we go."

"I'll look into it, and I'll get a price on the avocados too. We may as well take advantage of having Caleb around to help get everything planted when he's not working the golf course."

"*Ya*, I'm much happier with our plan to have him work back there while Mary sells the produce from the gift shop. He can also watch over the corn maze from there and make sure that nobody gets lost. We still need to find a hand stamp for the customers who pay for miniature golf so he'll know that they've already paid."

"The printer can order that, we'll stop back by there on the way to the bakery."

"Here we are, talking about work," I chuckle.

"I know, but it's exciting to watch it unfold. You're beautiful when you're in planning mode," he laughs.

"Okay, now you're just trying to make me blush," I say, trying to keep from getting lost in his eyes, which look so green today.

Before he can embarrass me any further, the waitress brings him the check. He puts some money in the leather binder on the table and escorts me back to the buggy. We take the short ride back to the center of town and park near the hitching post in the bakery lot. We walk around to the printer and order a specialty hand stamp before stopping at the bakery for a visit with Dan and Ruthie.

"Hi! Good to see you both," Ruthie says from behind the counter.

"I wanted to bring by the updated flyers I mentioned, but I also have a little keepsake for you." I smile, handing her the laminated article from last week's *Gazette* along with a stack of flyers and the picture from Hannah.

She stops to read through it, "Wow this is a really well-done article. You're going to be so busy this summer; I'm going to hang this on the wall over by your canned goods. Tell Mamm I'm out of strawberry-rhubarb jam and pear honey. Dan has some money for you from the stuff we've sold."

"She's working on the pear honey as we speak and I'm picking up strawberries today," I chuckle.

"Is Dan around?" John asks.

"He just went to take the trash out; we don't have a helper today. He'll be right back."

"So what are you two out doing today?" she asks.

"We've been replacing flyers, running errands and having lunch. We're going to stop by the grocery store on the way home. I need to restock HQ too."

"You went to a sit-down lunch?" she asks curiously.

"*Ya*, over at Saddler's," John explains.

"Well that was sweet of you," she smiles at John, "She needs to get out more."

I know by the look on her face that she's dying to know the details but she can't ask in front of him, which is perfectly fine with me.

A bakery customer enters just as Dan walks in from the back. We sit at a table and look at the new flyers while he makes his way over to us. "Natalie did an even better job this time," I say, admiring how professional it looks.

"It's very impressive. Even though I've watched it all come together, it still amazes me seeing it like this; between the article and this flyer, you've got quite an impressive sales package," John says.

"Hi guys," Dan says, approaching the table.

"Hey Dan," I say as they shake hands.

"Have you heard anything from the bishop about my visit with him on Friday?" John asks.

"Nothing yet, he usually comes in on Mondays but we haven't seen him today. Did you find the last bunny?"

"No, not yet," I sigh.

"We're still hoping that's a good sign," John adds.

"I just can't believe someone would stoop that low. I have heard that Deacon Byler's been forming a group of disgruntled community members, but I still think they'll be sadly outnumbered by the people who would support you," Dan offers.

"I can't believe he doesn't have anything better to do," I say, frustrated at the revelation.

"Well the church isn't going to stand by and let him interfere with your ability to make an income for your family if you aren't violating the Ordnung, which you aren't. I know it's tough, but I think he's just trying to bully you. Hang in there and let us know if you need anything at all," Dan reassures me. "In the meantime, I think this guy's been doing a pretty stellar job of looking out for you," he says, slapping John's shoulder.

"*Ya*, he has," I smile, "*Danki* again Dan. Your support means a lot to me."

"Go ahead and talk to Ruthie while John and I get those baskets for your produce stand loaded into the buggy before it gets busy in here. I'll see you soon," he says, leading John toward the back of the store.

I walk over to the counter as Ruth makes change for a customer.

"So, he took you out to lunch today?" she asks in a hushed tone.

"*Ya*, we had a really good time."

"You two seem to be getting pretty close," she says observantly.

"We have a lot in common, he's been protective of me and the *kinner* and he's been so generous with his time and his resources, it's impossible not to feel close to him."

"Sarah, this is me you're talking to," she says with a raised eyebrow. "How do you feel about him?"

"I'm a little nervous that he doesn't know what it's like to be a full-time parent and a little worried that he'll get bored with the idea."

"Nobody knows what it's like to be a full-time parent until you are one, but I've seen him with your *kinner* and believe me, he's got what it takes, you should know that better than me."

"Maybe so, but going from being a bachelor to becoming a father of five is a huge leap. I'm not saying he couldn't handle it but I have no idea that he wants to…it's hard to imagine any man wanting to."

"*Ya*, but John isn't just any man and the more I see of him when you're together, the more I think he's in love with you…all of you," she says in a serious tone.

"I just don't know if I can handle finding out that you're wrong."

"Look, you've told me all of your doubts and fears but you haven't said one word about how you feel about him. I think you're letting those things stand between you and your feelings for him. I understand that you have a family to think about, but I still say you owe it to yourself to see where your heart leads and let God worry about the rest."

Before I can say anything, another customer comes in. She quickly jots down a note for me on a scrap of paper and hands it to me. It simply says: *'Read Psalms 37, I love you.'*

I smile at her and tuck it into my wallet as John returns.

"Are you ready to go?" he asks.

"*Ya*, I think she's going to be a while."

CHAPTER NINE

We finish the grocery shopping, and to my surprise, John was quite helpful and even a little fun to shop with. I think he enjoyed discovering what was on the menu before everyone else and seeing what was on sale to coincide with it. The *kinner* would certainly have enjoyed the outing, but it's nice to spend some time with him alone as I get to know him better. I keep thinking about our lunch and what Ruthie said and she's right, he's not just any man.

I find myself being more observant of his actions and seeing the person underneath. He wouldn't even let me help load the buggy which is the first time I've experienced that in a very long time. Even when Jacob was alive, the *kinner* and I usually shopped while he was busy working. I can't help but feel a little pampered and a little more aware of who he is.

We talk more on the drive home and he tells me a little about his travels and experiences. Though our pasts are very different, it's obvious to me that God, family, and community have always been the driving constants in his life and I respect him for that.

Back at the house, he helps me out of the buggy and I go to unlock the door for us but my key won't turn in the lock. I think about paying my taxes late and feel a sudden surge of panic as if the house had been auctioned out from under me.

I remember receiving the receipt for my payment, so logically, I know that isn't the case. but it doesn't help my state of mind. I fidget with it for a minute but the key seems to be stuck.

John steps over to the door with me and sets the armload of groceries down to try it himself but he can't unlock it either.

"Is this the same key that opens the front door?" he asks.

I nod *'yes'* and I know he realizes that I'm worried. "Let's try it," he says walking around to the front porch as I follow behind.

He starts to put the key into the lock and then stops. "Hang on a second," he says, crouching down in front of the doorknob.

"Do you have a hair pin?"

I hand him a bobby pin from the bottom of my kapp and he proceeds to bite the tip off, straighten it and probe inside of the lock. After a minute or two of fiddling with it, he tries the key but the same thing happens.

"Okay, don't panic," he says in a wary tone, "But I think someone jammed something inside your door locks," he sighs, "Let's check HQ."

I follow him over to HQ where we run into the same problem. I don't know what comes over me but I kick the bottom of the door a few times in frustration before he grabs me by the shoulders and pulls me to him. "Hey, it's okay, I can fix this," he chuckles.

"I just hate feeling like I constantly have to look over my shoulder!" I say angrily.

"I know you're frustrated and you have a right to be, but you're going to hurt yourself or the poor door and that wouldn't solve anything. Let's go get the cold items out of your grocery bags and take them over to the Daadi Haus while I get it straightened out."

"*Ya*, okay," I sigh warily.

We rifle through the bags sorting out the cold items and John carries them over to Mamm's for me. I knock on the door and explain what's happened before Josh comes to greet us. "Did you look before you opened the door just now?" I ask, knowing by the look on her face that she didn't. "Mamm, someone was prowling around here today."

"We were working in the kitchen, I didn't hear anything," she explains.

"Sarah, it only takes two seconds to jam a lock," John

reminds me.

"Sorry, I'm just annoyed," I say, trying to adjust my attitude.

"Let's get this stuff inside and focus on fixing the problem," John says motioning toward the kitchen, "You probably shouldn't lock the door right now in case yours is jammed too," he tells Mamm, setting the bags on the counter.

"I can't believe someone did this while we were here," she whispers.

"I know, that's why we have to be more careful," I say, grabbing her hand.

"Josh, are you and Mammi making pies?" John asks excitedly as I put the groceries in Mamm's fridge.

"*Ya* and jam," he smiles proudly, his shirt covered in flour.

"I sure hope I get to try one," he says.

"You can have three, John, but the rest are for custobers."

We all chuckle at his mispronunciation but at least he's on the right track.

"Feel better?" John asks me under his breath.

"*Ya*, I'm okay."

"I'm going to go check the other locks and go get some tools and stuff, do you want to come with me?"

"I want to know a secret too," Josh says, hearing us whisper.

John goes over and whispers in his ear to which, he giggles, "*Ya*, okay."

"Mamm, I'm going to help John get the locks straightened out, we'll be back in a little while. Can you guys stay inside until we get back?"

"*Ya*, go ahead, we have plenty to do; we'll be fine," she assures me.

"Go ahead and lock it behind us, I'm going to take the whole thing off when I get back."

We head over to the chicken coop, the rabbitat and the barn with my keys but all of the locks are jammed.

"That's a really rotten thing to do."

"*Ya*, it's also illegal, you could always call the police and file a report. There isn't much they can do about it but they would probably go and question anyone you named as a potential culprit and it might send a message back to his little group."

"Who would I name? We know Deacon Byler is probably behind it but he probably convinced someone else that they'd be saving the community if they did it. It could have been any number of people."

"We could go to the bishop together this time."

"I'd like that if you have time. Maybe I'll ask him if he thinks I should call the police. If nothing else, the very mention of it should get some wheels turning in one direction or another."

"Since the buggy is already hitched, let's go see the bishop first and we'll stop at my shop on the way back. That way we'll be back here by the time the *kinner* get home."

He helps me back into the buggy and we set out toward the bishop's house together. Although this ordeal has derailed my plans for the afternoon, I can't help but feel grateful for John's support and the opportunity to spend a little more time with him without a lot of distractions.

***

I look over at her as we pull out of the drive and think about how strong and beautiful she is. Her little tantrum at HQ shows me just how much all of this is getting to her, but she bounced back and focused herself of the solution. She's definitely a force of determination when she needs to be…and just a little scary when provoked to anger, I smile to myself.

"Do we need to go back to town to buy new locks while we're out or do you think you can fix the old ones?" she asks.

"I have some spare padlocks to replace the ones on the coop and the rabbitat. I also have the four doorknobs and deadbolts that used to be on my house when I bought the place. It's probably quicker and easier to replace yours with those than it is to fix the jammed ones. I don't have a lock like the one on the barn door but I can see if I can improvise. I have a key maker in the shop so I can make sure you have enough keys to everything while we're there. I should be able to get it all taken care of in a few hours."

"Do you think we should make everyone a set of keys? I don't think Josh and Hannah are ready for the responsibility, but in light of everything that's been going on, I would hate for them to be out on the property and unable to get inside the house."

"Actually I have a solution for that," I smile as she looks at me intently, "When my house was on the market, the front door to the Daadi Haus had one of those coded door locks. You just punch in the four-digit code and it unlocks. I'm pretty sure I wrote the old code on a piece of tape when I changed all of the locks. We can put that one on the house and at least nobody will ever be able to jam that lock again. We'll just have to program a code that the *kinner* will be sure to remember."

"It sounds pretty handy. Why didn't you use it on your house?"

"I already had new locksets for everything and I didn't want to take the time to figure out how to reprogram it at the time. I'll have to call my friend over at the tractor supply, have him look up the model number online and tell me how to reprogram it but it shouldn't be a problem, he looks up part numbers for me sometimes."

"It makes me feel a lot safer knowing we'll never be locked out again and it's perfect for the little ones, *Danki*."

"As far as the keys go, I think you need to make a complete set for you, Miriam and all of the older *kinner* because it's plausible that any one of them might need to access a locked area on any given day."

"Won't that be a lot to keep up with?"

"No, four keys at the most. I can make sure the padlocks use the same key and the old locksets from my place are all on the same key; that only leaves the barn key and the cash drawer key, which everyone doesn't need. Besides, your *kinner* are pretty responsible. We just need to set up a system and teach them how to use it. Maybe even put the keys on a lan*Ya*rd they can wear around their necks, tucked under their clothes."

"*Ya*, they respond to structured systems very well," she agrees.

"I wonder who they got that from," I chuckle as she blushes a bit.

CHAPTER TEN

Bishop Graber steps out of the barn to greet us as I help Sarah out of the buggy. I can tell by the look on his face that he knows we aren't here for a social call.

"Hello John, hello Sarah," he says, shaking my hand. "Come on inside the barn, I'm just grooming the horses."

"We apologize for just dropping in like this but there was another incident today at Sarah's place and we felt you needed to know about it right away."

"What happened this time?"

"When I got home from town this afternoon, all of the locks on all of the doors on the property had been jammed. I can't even get into my house," Sarah says.

"What do you mean jammed?" he asks curiously.

"I suspect they've all been jammed with a toothpick or something similar. Something has been broken off inside of all nine locks so that the keys no longer turn when you try to use them," I explain, "I'll probably have to break in somehow to open the doors."

"And this happened today?" he asks.

"*Ya*, sometime between 8:00 a.m. and 2:00 p.m. Bishop Graber my *mamm* was right there in the Daadi Haus with my youngest boy and they jammed the locks on her doors too."

"If what you suspect is true, I suppose it wouldn't take much to walk up to a door and jam a toothpick in the lock."

"Someone could easily have been on and off of the property in under ten minutes," I add, "I know we can't prove who's doing these things but this particular attack is actually a criminal offense and the word around town is that Deacon Byler has formed a group of supporters who are opposed to the tours and they're trying to put Sarah out of business. She's already suffered a loss from these pranks, and today she'll have to have all of her locks rekeyed or replaced. It's not only costing her time and money and affecting her family's business, but it's frightening all of them and it has to stop."

"Out of respect for you and our Amish ways, Bishop Graber, I wanted to come to you about this again before going to the police, but I have to protect my family and all that we've worked for, our survival depends on it," she explains tactfully.

He sits on a stool next to the barn door and sighs. "I knew there would be some grumbling opposition to the idea of these tours in the community but I never expected that it would go this far."

"I'm constantly afraid of what they'll do next," she pleads.

"I don't know what disciplinary action I can take without some sort of proof of the parties involved in this mess but I can talk to the suspected participants individually and see if that will put an end to these shenanigans. You are well within your rights as part of this community to provide for your family and I will stand behind my decision to allow the tours to go on. If you find yourself in another predicament, I can't stop you from involving the police but I won't hold it against you. I'm just sorry that I can't offer a better solution."

"One thing I'd like to add, Bishop Graber, is that Deacon Byler has personally confronted Sarah twice at her home and once in public, all three times in front of plenty of witnesses. The last time he stopped her customers as they were leaving and told them not to come back. She made it clear to him that he was not *wilkom* on the property again and I cannot be responsible for what happens if he violates that warning. I love and respect this community and our ways but I will not hesitate to forcefully remove him or have him arrested if he confronts her again. I respectfully suggest that you make certain he understands that before his bullying embarrasses the whole church in the eyes of the community."

"I will handle this a bit more sternly this time. Please keep me posted if anything else happens, I promise you that I will do what I can to put an end to this," he assures us.

"*Danki*, Bishop Graber," Sarah says kindly.

I escort her back to the buggy and we head for the shop. She's silent for a few minutes, probably concerned about me offending the bishop but I felt it needed to be said.

"I know I was a little harsh back there but the soft approach hasn't exactly been very effective thus far."

"No, you handled it well. I think that Bishop Graber probably wanted to believe that these attacks weren't being done by someone in our community but I think you made a believer out of him."

"I guess we'll find out soon enough."

Once we arrive at the shop I set an empty box on the counter and head back into the storage area to find the locksets. I locate a working key and sit it out on the counter for copying as I load the parts into the box. I peruse the shop looking for anything with a lock that I can use for the barn but I don't find anything suitable. What I do find is my softball equipment bag leaning in the corner. I empty it and find two whistles and three I.D. lan*Ya*rds leftover from a softball tournament that I organized for my *daed*'s company in Hopkinsville.

I put them in the box along with a few other tools and set out to find some window locks since I'll probably have to break in to HQ and the main house through a window, "I'm going to leave the softball gear here for now but it's available if you ever feel like playing," I smile.

"*Ya*, I like softball, the *kinner* do too," she smiles, looking at the whistles. "These might be handy for the tours too."

"I was bringing them for the lan*Ya*rds but I'm sure we could incorporate them into the communications system," I tease.

"You laugh, John Troyer, but you can't deny that it works," she scoffs.

"I'm not denying, just admiring," I smile, playfully.

"You know, you're a lot more organized than I imagined," she says, looking around while I try to find two padlocks already keyed the same, "I can't help but notice how nicely labeled all of your boxes and bins are; even that tool chest over there that's taller than me is labeled meticulously."

I smile to myself before poking my head around the corner to look at the expression on her face. I've always been pretty organized, just maybe not to the extreme that she is. Still, she looks impressed; maybe I'm scoring points right now.

"Does it meet your approval?" I laugh.

"Oh *Ya*; maybe we aren't as different as I thought, this is very eye opening."

"Oh we're very different in some ways," I say, sneaking up behind her, "But a certain amount of *'different'* is good," I smile as she turns to face me. "Come over here, I've got a job for you," I tell her, grabbing the stool behind the counter.

"You like sneaking up on me don't you?" she asks.

"You're not going to kick me are you?" I tease.

"I should," she laughs.

She sits on the stool and I stand behind her with my arms on either side of her as I demonstrate. "Here are the keys we need to copy and these are the blanks we'll use. You just put the original key here and clamp it in, then load the blank and clamp it here," I say, locking the clamp.

"You want me to make them?" she asks incredulously.

"*Ya*, put these on," I say, handing her a pair of safety glasses.

She puts them on and I show her how to set and run the machine by making three copies of the first key together with my hands guiding hers. We test them in one of the doorknobs to make sure our cuts are accurate.

"Cool," she chuckles.

"Good, because we need three more of these, and six of those. I'm going to drive to the back property and get a lock for your barn. I should be back by the time you finish."

***

John worked on replacing all of the locks, securing the windows and reprogramming the automatic lock right up until dinnertime. We didn't explain to the *kinner* about the jammed locks. We told them that it was all part of our new security regimen and that we would have a family meeting after evening chores were done.

I take a seat in the porch rocker next to John, preparing the key rings while we wait for everyone to join us.

"*Danki*, John, for everything today," I tell him.

"I just want to make sure you're safe in your own home," he says casually.

"*Ya*, and I appreciate that too, but I was referring to the whole day. Going into town with me, taking me to lunch, going to the bishop with me…I enjoyed it and the parts that I didn't enjoy, you turned into positives."

He looks at me for a moment. "I enjoyed it too Sarah, maybe we should do it again soon," he says, working a set of keys onto a key ring.

"I'd like that," I say, slipping the colored rubber caps over the keys as I hand them to him. He takes one from me—holding my hand and squeezing for a moment before letting go.

"I'll be gone most of the day tomorrow but Caleb will be on the radio. On Wednesday we'll start plotting out the maze design so that we can get a good solid day in with two of us working on it. He and Mark can help finish Thursday, Friday and even Saturday for a couple of hours if needed, but I want to get that design mowed in on Monday morning."

"I can help too if you need me," I offer.

"You mean between the essentials of cooking, cleaning, laundry, baking, quilting, gardening and helping with the tours?" he chuckles.

"I'm busy but I can make time to help," I assure him.

He raises his eyebrows to protest but Mamm, Josh and Hannah arrive for the meeting with the rest of the *kinner* not far behind.

Once everyone is gathered on the porch, I feed the key rings onto the lan*Ya*rds while he talks.

"Okay *kinner*, today, we installed new locks on every door and now they all work with just three keys. The gold keys with the yellow key guards around them are the *'Home'* keys because they're gold and that's the most treasured color. The home key opens HQ and all of the house doors; the front door, the kitchen door and both doors at the Daadi Haus—so it's your main key," he says, holding up the brass key.

"The *'Barn'* key has a red key guard around it because the barn is red. It only opens the locks on the barn doors and nothing else, he says, showing them the key with the red-colored guard."

"The *'Animal'* key has a black key guard around it because animals are often black. This key only unlocks the rabbitat and the chicken coop."

"Pumpkin Pie!" Hannah shrieks.

"Oh my gosh, there she is!" Mary says excitedly, pointing to the rust-speckled bunny nestled next to the porch steps.

John steps down and grabs her by the fur and hands her to Caleb. We all laugh and cheer excitedly as Josh gives Caleb a congratulatory hug.

"Okay, you can all spend time with her in just a few minutes but let's finish our meeting," John says, getting everyone's attention back on the business at hand.

"What color is the animal key, Samuel?" he asks.

"Black," Samuels replies.

"Very good, what color is the barn key, Hannah?"

"Red!" she giggles.

"Good and what color is the home key, Josh?"

"Umm, gold," he smiles.

"Very good and what doors does the home key open, Mary?"

All of the doors on both houses and HQ," she answers.

"Perfect, and Mark, can you guess what these small keys with no key guards are for?"

He thinks about it for a second, "Ooooh, the cash drawer!" he says decidedly.

"Very good, the little keys are for the cash drawer and only

Mamm, Mary and Caleb have one on their ring, but I'm going to give all of the older *kinner* a key chain to wear around your neck. You need to wear them on tour days the whole time. Be careful not to take them off or lay them down somewhere while you're working because then strangers will have the keys to everything—the houses, the barn, HQ and the cash."

"Can we wear them when we aren't working?" Mark asks.

"Only under your clothes, in your pocket or somewhere out of sight; you don't want to advertise that you have your keys to everyone because some bad person could hurt you and take them from you…everyone needs to be careful. If someone does get them from you, come and tell Mamm or me right away, don't put up a fight and get hurt over them. We can always replace locks and cash but we can't replace you. Is that clear to everyone?"

"*Ya*," we all reply in unison.

"Now, one more thing about the keys: the kitchen door has a new kind of lock with a regular hole for the key but it also has a keypad on it. This is very important, especially for Josh and Hannah so listen up. If you don't have a key to get in or if you try your key and it doesn't work, you can punch in a special code on the keypad and the door will unlock for you. Everyone needs to memorize the code but we made it simple for you. Since all of you have already memorized my phone number, we made the code to the door the first four digits of my phone number, Josh tell me what that is."

"2-5-5-0," he says proudly.

"Very good, let's go try it."

We all follow him to the door where Josh types in the code and opens the door successfully. He has Hannah repeat the process as the other *kinner* marvel at the technology.

"Does anyone have questions?" he asks.

"Can I make my own key necklace?" Mary asks.

"As long as it's nice and strong and won't accidentally come untied, *Ya* you can."

"Okay, so for the last part of the meeting, since Josh and Hannah don't get key rings, we have something else for you. These whistles are for you to wear on tour days around your neck just like the older *kinner* but this is not a toy. This is only for you to use if you need help. If anyone else hears the whistle sound," he demonstrates blowing several times, "Come and find Josh and Hannah right away. They will NOT blow their whistles as a prank or a joke because they know how important this is, right guys?"

They both nod their heads very seriously.

"Very good, you can also use them in practice drills like when you practice after school with the radios. Does anyone have any questions?"

Nobody speaks up so he concludes the meeting. The *kinner* all follow Caleb to the rabbitat to put Pumpkin Pie away.

"That was good John, *Danki*," I tell him.

"You're a very good teacher, John Troyer," Mamm chuckles. "I'm going to go write a letter and take a bath, you two enjoy your visit," Mamm says, patting me on the hand.

We both tell her good night and stroll over toward the willow tree as the *kinner* pile into the wagon for a ride.

"You're about to lose a button," I say, noticing the second button of his shirt holding on by a thread. "I know we joked about not doing your laundry when you brought the washer but it really is no trouble to throw it in with the rest. You spend so much time doing for us, I can at least keep things washed and mended for you to free up some of your time."

"We get by, but it has gotten a little more cumbersome with two of us here. I don't really sew either so I might just take you up on that offer," he chuckles.

"Just bring it over and we'll see that it gets done," I assure him.

"This guy I'm working for tomorrow, he buys out random items from businesses that are closing and people that get foreclosed on, I told him a couple of weeks ago to keep an eye out for some picnic tables for you. He says he might be getting two from a taco stand that's closing down and he's willing to trade for them."

"That's great; I was thinking we should try to find some tables when we had that cookout with the Lapp brothers. Are you sure you wouldn't rather trade for something for yourself?"

"I would if I needed something but he doesn't really have anything I need right now. I like strengthening my working relationship with him and his *daed* though; it gives me lots of bargaining power so I really don't mind doing the work. We both usually come out ahead in the end."

He's so handsome when he's strategizing. Much like me, once he gets on a mission to do something, there's no turning back until it's done. I think about my conversation with Ruthie earlier and I hope that the same determination applies to his personal relationships as well because it's suddenly clear to me that I'm hopelessly and madly in love with him.

CHAPTER ELEVEN

Monday, May 18

I awoke this morning with a feeling I can't describe. I spent the Sabbath yesterday wearing my mourning dress for the last time. I thought about Jacob a lot on the anniversary of his death with Dan and Ruthie by my side for our last widow's visitation, but the pain of losing him is much different now. Even the kinner were able to talk freely about fond memories of their daed without any sullen moments or bouts of tears last night, and I know in my heart that John's presence in our lives is partly responsible for that.

In the past couple of months, we've all grown a little wiser, become a little stronger and healed a little faster because of him. Just the things we've been through in getting the tour business up and running has been enough to thicken anyone's skin, but more importantly, we witnessed God's loving hand in bringing someone into our lives that we could all turn to for the caring guidance and support that we had lost.

I put on my lavender dress, carefully fastening the pins in place the way I have so many times before, but as I look in the mirror today, I see a different woman. I see someone filled with new hope, a new sense of purpose and a heart filled with new desires.

For the past year, I've been content with just surviving, but today I'm looking forward to starting over. I have a new dream of a thriving business, a family with a renewed zest for life and a desire to share the love that I still have left to give with John. I only hope that he's ready too. I put on my white kapp for the first time in a year and say a prayer before joining everyone in the kitchen.

"Good morning everyone," I smile, kissing Hannah on the top of the head as she wriggles into her chair at the table.

"You look beautiful, Mamm," Samuel says as I pour myself a cup of coffee.

"*Ya*, Mamm, you really do," Mark agrees.

"*Danki*, boys," I say, trying not to blush.

I kiss Mamm on the cheek as I hover over the stove to see what's for breakfast, "*Danki* for cooking this morning."

"It's good for you to sleep in once in a while," she smiles knowingly.

"We did our chores already too," Mary informs me.

"How in the world did I get so lucky to be blessed with such wonderful *kinner*?" I smile, ruffling Josh's hair.

"Because God made us," Josh explains.

"Oh *Ya*, that must be it," I say kissing his cheek.

"God made me too!" Hannah adds.

"Oh He did? Well then where are my kisses? I think I need some proof," I chuckle as she kisses my cheek.

"I'm pretty sure that God made everyone, but some people are just better at showing it than others," Samuel explains.

We all have a chuckle. "Out of the mouths of babes," Mamm says.

We finish our breakfast and spend a few minutes talking about the week ahead before the *kinner* head off to school. It's a twelve-minute walk from our doorstep and they're usually met by some of the other *kinner* at the top of the drive. I wave and go back inside to help Mamm tidy up before starting the laundry.

"I noticed the ground beef and sausage thawing in the fridge, what's on the menu tonight?" Mamm asks casually.

"I thought I'd make a meatball casserole, Caleb requested it several days ago and it's one of John's favorites. Did you have something else in mind?"

"No, I think it's the perfect choice. What's John doing today?"

“He wanted to get the corn maze mowed this morning but he had to drop off some motor he’s been working on and he has some appointment in town. He and Caleb are picking up the picnic tables and mowing the maze this afternoon instead. They’ll be finished by dinner time,” I assure her.

“I’ll get started on the bread and bake a pecan pie for dessert tonight. After that I think I’ll take Josh over and spend the rest of the day catching up on a few things at the Daadi Haus unless you need us for something,” she offers.

“I’ll be fine, are you feeling okay?” I ask curiously.

“I feel good, I just want to clip some coupons, peel the big batch of pears that Caleb picked on Saturday and do some canning. I’ll make sure he gets lunch, don’t worry.”

“Well then I’m going to go down and start the laundry. Maybe I’ll be able to get some serious quilting done while the house is quiet today,” I chuckle.

***

We stop at the real estate office on the way back to town with the picnic tables in the wagon. “Watch the tractor, I tell Caleb as we park in the lot, “I shouldn’t be long.”

Nancy Edgerton is standing in the reception area waiting for me when I arrive. “Good to see you again, Mr. Troyer, and I apologize about the mix up when you first called, we had just left for vacation and my new assistant didn’t recognize your name. How are you liking it in Hope Landing?"

"It's good; I think I'm finally all settled in. I wanted to ask you about some of the other properties in the area," I explain.

"Ah, well I'm afraid there isn't anything else available out there right now. I sold the old Beller property, and of course you scooped up the Schwartz property before anyone else even knew it was back on the market after the title issues, but there haven't been any new listings in months. About the closest you're going to get with over an acre is on the other side of town. I've been selling farms in Hope Landing for twenty years and I don't even have a whiff of anything coming available anytime soon."

"I wanted to ask about that farm we drove by just north of the school—the Fisher place."

"Ah yes, Sarah Fisher, well if she were willing to sell, which doesn't seem to be the case, Deacon Byler has had his eye on that property for some time. Of course I have a tendency to look out for my lo*Ya*l clients first," she whispers conspiratorially.

"I didn't know the deacon was looking to move," I say, hoping she'll go on.

"Oh it's not for him; he's looking for a place for his eldest son and his family."

"I didn't know he had a son either," I smile.

"Oh yes, Deacon Byler's first wife died when his son was about twenty. He stayed behind in Ohio when the deacon got re-married and moved to Hope Landing about twenty years ago. Between you and me, I think there was a bit of bad blood between them, but apparently they've moved past all of that and he wants to relocate closer to the family. Grandparents make wonderful babysitters," she chuckles.

"He must be a farmer," I say casually.

"He runs a small Amish restaurant geared for tourists and he's got a separate Christmas tree farm somewhere else. The Fisher place would be an ideal spot for him to combine both businesses on one property but it doesn't look like Ms. Fisher is willing. I took her his cash offer in February and she turned it down flat, without even looking at it. I can't say that I blame her; she's raised a family there. She's smart too because all of the big properties along the main road will be worth a fortune someday, including yours."

"Well, *Danki* for the information—here's my new number," I say, handing her a card. "Be sure to call me if you hear of anything coming available," I tell her.

"Between you and me, John, you'll be the first one I call," she assures me.

"I appreciate that Nancy," I say shaking her hand, "Have a nice day."

We head toward Sarah's and I'm on the edge of my seat to

tell her what I've just learned though I'm not sure what good it will do. I turn into her drive and head back to the picnic area to unload while I give it some thought.

Once the wagon's empty, I make a quick call to Dan to talk it over with him.

"Hey Dan, it's John."

"Hey John, man you should have attended church in Hope Landing yesterday. Bishop Graber pretty much made a public statement supporting tourism and new business ideas that support our fellow Amish families during the announcements. Then, his sermon was from Matthew 7:1 *'Judge not, that ye be not judged,'* and from James 4:11 *'Speak not evil one of another, brethren,'* and all of that. He pretty much built the whole service around her and I didn't see any of the suspected cohorts socializing with Deacon Byler after church. I think his supporters might be starting to realize that he's in the wrong."

"That's great, I wish I had been there to see it but I found out some pretty damning information about what's really behind this whole scheme and it's not good."

"You mean the deacon's not really trying to save the whole community by wiping out Sarah's business?" he asks in a sarcastic tone.

"Oh it's more self-serving and money grubbing than any of us imagined," I say, relaying everything Nancy told me.

"I knew there had to be more to it," he says. "You know who

else might have some inside info?" he asks.

"Mr. Sneed?"

"You guessed it, I'm going over to the print shop to use the computer and do a little digging about this restaurant in Ohio, you talk to old man Sneed and I'll call you later."

I hang up and climb back onto the tractor. I promised Caleb I'd take him over to Mr. Sneed's sometime this week anyway. We may as well go now so that I can be back in time to get the mowing done before dinner.

We pull up in front of Mr. Sneed's and I introduce him to Caleb as he walks us around to the back of the property.

"I promised my nephew I'd bring him out to look around but I also wanted to talk if you've got a few minutes," I explain.

"Sure, what are you in the market for young fella?" he asks Caleb.

"I'm gonna be working the golf course for the tours and I'm selling some produce there. I don't know…I just wanted to see what else you might have."

"Well you look until your heart's content, I'm pretty fond of your uncle here, I'll make you a good deal on whatever you find," he says opening the shed doors.

"*Danki*," Caleb says as he starts to browse.

"I hear your widow friend's been catching a little hell from the old-order die-hards in the community, how's she holding up?"

"She's a trooper; she's been accosted in public, alienated at church, had cow dung thrown at her house, her animals let loose in the middle of the night, her locks all jammed with toothpicks and there's a rumor that Deacon Byler has formed a secret committee to put her out of business. That's what I came to talk to you about; you seem to keep pretty good tabs on what's happening in the community."

"I've been here longer than anyone in Hope Landing, I do lots of business with the Amish in these parts but I didn't know all of that. I love the Amish, don't get me wrong, but I have nothing good to say about Deacon Byler or the Shetlers and that would be my first guess as to who's behind it."

"Do you know anything about Deacon Byler's son from Ohio?"

"I heard he had a son that was shunned from the community before the deacon moved here but that's about all I know. I will tell you this; when he screwed me over, I was boiling mad and ran my mouth about it to about anyone who cared to listen. I found out from Mr. Beller, who used to be his neighbor, that the deacon is quite a drinker; that's why he's always so gruff and red in the face. Old man Beller said the deacon was always playing little pranks on his property because old man Beller's dog used to crap in Mrs. Byler's garden. I can't say I blame the pooch on that one, I've considered it myself."

"My real estate agent told me that his son wants to buy Sarah's property and I think that's his real reason for trying to shut her business down. He thinks that if he destroys her ability to support herself and the *kinner*, she'll be forced to sell."

"Ah, but you're not going to let that happen are you?" he smiles knowingly.

"No sir, I'm not."

"Have you gone to the bishop?"

"*Ya*, and he has openly given her his blessing but so far that hasn't stopped the attacks."

"Tell me how I can help. I'll be dipped in boiling oil before I stand by and let Deacon Byler get away with something like this."

"Well you've already done a lot; the golf course is a big hit. I just need to put a stop to these attacks somehow, if you can find out anything about who's behind them or you can spread the word about what's been going on to anyone who would likely support her, please let me know. All five of her *kinner* are eleven and under and this is really frightening for them."

"I'll keep my ears open and my mouth too, you can count on that. You let me know if you think of anything else I can do and I'll do the same."

"You wouldn't happen to know where I can get some fir tree seedlings pretty cheap do you?"

"My son does, did you trade out on those picnic tables today?"

"*Ya*, I did, but I was so preoccupied with this whole mess that I forgot to ask him. I'll give him a call."

"What did you find?" he asks Caleb as he emerges from one of the sheds.

"A crossbow set I'd like to have and maybe this air rifle for one of Sarah's boys."

"You're still ahead if you want the crossbow, take the rifle to the boy for free, I've got another big mower that needs some work too when you get a chance."

"*Ya*, I'll take it and I'll stop by on Thursday to take a look at the mower. Keep your eyes open for a golf cart and any other kind of hunting equipment for young boys," I tell him.

"I sure will."

I drop Caleb off past the cornfield so he can play around with his new crossbow while I go talk to Sarah and get the mower ready.

I pull alongside the barn and walk up to the house. I can smell the aroma of fresh bread wafting through the screen door as I approach. I tap on the frame. "It's John," I call out.

"Come on in," she says, emerging from the pantry door with a basket of laundry in her arms.

I open the door and step over to help her.

"*Danki*," she says, closing the door behind her.

I set the basket on a chair and stand there for a moment, unable to take my eyes off of her.

"Everything okay?" she says with a concerned look.

She's dressed in lavender with a white kapp on and a million thoughts are racing through my mind, but mostly I can't believe how absolutely beautiful she looks. "That's a pretty color on you," I say, trying to contain my excitement.

"Oh *Ya*, yesterday was the last day for mourning," she smiles, "I thought you knew."

"I knew that the day was coming sometime soon from our talks but I didn't know the exact day. How do you feel?"

"Honestly? I feel rejuvenated."

"Where are Mamm and Josh?"

"She wanted to spend the afternoon at the Daadi Haus canning pears. I thought I would get some quilting done."

God help me, I'm alone in the house with her on the day I can finally be open about my feelings for her and I have to deliver bad news? I take a deep breath and sigh as I try to collect my thoughts, which I'm finding rather challenging at the moment. I put my hat on the hook near the door, run my hands through my hair and take a seat at the table.

"What's gotten into you? Is something wrong?" she asks curiously.

"Maybe I could use something to drink," I say, feeling my mouth getting dry.

"Oh sorry, where are my manners?" she chuckles, "Lemonade, tea, coffee or water?" she asks.

Wherever her manners went, I'm pretty sure my self-control isn't far behind them.

"Lemonade," I decide, finally getting my wits about me. "I do need to talk if you have time," I tell her, trying not to be obvious about watching intently as she moves around the kitchen.

She sits the glass in front of me and I can smell her familiar smell as she walks past me to sit in the chair adjacent to mine. It's a mild lavender smell, probably from her shampoo or some kind of lotion but it has a delicately sweet note to it that I swear I can almost taste.

"Something is wrong isn't it?" she asks, putting her small hand gently on my forearm.

At this point, I'm seriously considering not telling her because I can tell by just being around her for a few minutes that she's having a really good day. It's as if she's lighter, freer…softer somehow…or maybe it's just my imagination because she isn't weighted down from head to toe in black.

Then again, maybe I'm wavering because I'm so taken with her that I don't want to be the bearer of any bad news on this happy day, which is selfish of me. She deserves to know the truth; my feelings will have to wait.

I look into her pretty blue eyes as I explain. "I talked to a couple of people in town today, trying to dig a little deeper into this whole thing with Deacon Byler, and what I've learned so far is kind of disturbing," I say, telling her everything the real estate agent said and most of what Mr. Sneed said.

She sits there silently for a moment, staring at her hands on the table in front of her but I can't really tell whether she's angry, hurt or just processing everything. I give her a few more seconds before I try getting her to open up.

She gets up and pours herself a glass of iced tea, moving calmly but purposely across the room. As she sort of paces back and forth between the edge of the table next to me and the counter, she tells me about breaking Deacon Byler's window when she was twelve and how she's always felt his unspoken dislike for her.

"What really makes me angry about all of this is knowing that he's been hovering over me like some hungry vulture since Jacob's death, waiting to pick the bones dry for his own self-serving purpose and now that I'm finally starting to stand on my own two feet and have hope for my family's future, he makes me feel like some kind of filthy harlot who sold out her community for a few pieces of silver and all the time he's just some hypocrite whose precious son—that nobody ever even speaks of—plans to bring just as many Englischers into the community as I am."

Her blood is boiling and yet she's incredibly mesmerizing all at the same time. I don't blame her one bit for her anger and yet all I want to do is make it go away. I stand right in her path, timing it perfectly as I pull her to me for a long, slow, burning, passionate kiss.

As our lips and tongues move together, I can feel the anger and tension drain from her body. I moan softly as I feel her surrender, slipping my hands gently around her delicate face as I revel in the sweet smell of her hair, the softness of her skin and the taste of her lips.

As I feel her desire meeting mine, a feeling of relief washes over me. I wrap my arms around her to hold her against me while the wellspring of emotions that I've harbored for her flow through my mind.

As her lips respond to mine, she clasps her hands around my neck. I close my eyes and feel my heart's journey from my initial curiosity about this brave and beautiful woman to the fondness that has grown with every passing day. I feel the pendulum sway from the confident revelation that she was ready to love again, to the uncertain worry that she wouldn't feel that love for me. I've feared for her safety and been brought to my knees before God by my desire to hold her, to kiss her and to know her heart.

As my mouth explores hers, every doubt and fear is finally laid to rest in this very moment, with her safely in my arms and her lips pressed against mine. It feel's like Heaven has descended upon me.

As we sink deeper into the moment, I want to tell her that I love her but my phone rings in my pocket and I pull away slightly, kissing her softly several times before letting her stop to catch her breath. I could have kissed her for hours.

I stand in front of her, my heart pounding in my chest as I study her face. Her cheeks are flushed, her lips darkened by the friction against mine, her eyes wide and captivating. I can almost feel her pulse racing as I watch her chest rise and fall with every shallow breath.

She looks down at the table next to her and rests her hand to steady herself as the ringing phone stops. She brushes her fingertips across her lips modestly. As I look at her, drinking in her radiance, I feel whole again for the first time in a very long time.

I reach out to her and caress her cheek in my hand as she leans into me. She places her hand on mine as she closes her eyes and it's beautiful to watch her savor my affection as she nuzzles her face against my fingertips.

I pull her to me and hold her in my arms, kissing the top of her head as she puts her arms around my waist and let's herself bask in this peaceful moment with me. I don't think I've ever felt as close to anyone as I do to her right now. I pull away enough to tilt her face to mine and kiss her again as I feel her sigh contentedly against my lips.

“I hope this means you’ll be letting me court you, Sarah Fisher, otherwise I’m going to feel pretty silly.”

She chuckles, “Well we couldn’t have that now could we?”

CHAPTER TWELVE

By the time my phone rings a second time; I decide that I probably need to answer it. I recognize the number on the display as Mr. Sneed's number.

"This is John," I answer.

"Albert Sneed here; I have someone here that needs to talk to you and it's pretty important. I called and we drove by your place but you weren't there."

"I'm at Sarah's but if it's important, I can meet you at my shop."

"We'll be along in about ten minutes, I've got to stop for gas," he says, disconnecting the call.

I kiss Sarah again. "As much as I would rather spend the rest of the afternoon alone with you, Mr. Sneed is on his way over to the shop to talk to me. He says it's important and I'm guessing that it's concerning the situation with Deacon Byler."

“I’ll be okay, I need to get some sauce on the stove and finish the laundry. I’ll be here when you get back,” she says, as I grab my hat.

“I promise, I’ll be back as soon as I can, just don’t forget where we left off,” I smile, kissing her forehead.

I walk back to the tractor and drive around to get Caleb.

“I was just about to come see if you needed my help with the mower.”

“Something’s come up; I’ve got to meet Mr. Sneed at the shop. Do you think you could check the fluids and get it ready by yourself?”

“I do it at home all the time,” he says putting his crossbow in the wagon.

“I’ll drop you at the house, tell Sarah what you’re doing, everything you need should be in the cabinets along the side wall of the barn.”

I arrive at the shop to find Mr. Sneed and another man sitting in his truck in the driveway. I unlock the shop door as they follow me inside.

“John this is Tim Zug; Tim, this is John Troyer, he’s the partner I mentioned.”

Mr. Sneed winks at me as I shake the man’s hand so I play along, curious to see what’s going on.

"Mr. Zug came to my place not long after you left today. His gas freezer quit this morning and he desperately needs to work out a trade on a new one," he explains.

"My food will be ruined in a few hours; my freezer's full of beef that I just butchered and I just paid my taxes, I can't even afford a used one right now," Mr. Zug adds.

"Mr. Zug has been a friend and neighbor of Deacon Byler's for say, fifteen years now?"

"Well I wouldn't say friend exactly, but I've known him about that long, *Ya*," Mr. Zug says nervously.

"I assured Mr. Zug that we might be willing to consider working out a sweetheart of a trade on that large capacity gas-powered chest freezer you and I bought from that estate sale a couple of weeks ago if he might be able to offer us some real help with the problem you've been having."

I've got to hand it to my buddy Sneed; he's an ingenious old coot with a heart of gold. I cross my arms and lean back against the counter casually, "Is that so?"

"I was there for Deacon Byler's last three secret meetings and I asked him outright what the bishop thought of his plan to persuade Sarah Fisher to quit giving these tours. He said he didn't want to burden the bishop and that he wanted Sarah to have a chance to repent on her own but after that talk the bishop gave in church yesterday, I realized that the bishop doesn't mind what Sarah's doing at all."

"You're not telling me anything I don't already know Mr. Zug, the bishop told me himself that he gave Sarah his blessing weeks ago and we know all about Deacon Byler's terrorist-like methods of persuasion, he's got two widows and five small children frightened half to death."

"I didn't do any of those things; I promise you that on my wife's grave. I didn't agree with the deacon from the start but he got on this crusade and kind of bullied me into going to the meetings. I went along because I didn't want to be on his bad side but I never acted on it."

"Who else is participating in this *'crusade'* of his?" I ask.

He looks at Mr. Sneed nervously and back at me.

I decide to bluff, "Well, *Danki* for coming by Mr. Zug but if you can't be more helpful, I—"

"The Yoders, the Shetlers, the Glicks and now Mr. and Mrs. Wyse are in on it too, but I don't know who did what. The deacon didn't want us to know, he said every man had to be responsible for his own actions. I do know for a fact that Deacon Byler hired a teenager to put toothpicks in her locks because he bought the toothpicks at Yoder's and I heard him telling the kid what to do in the parking lot. I was smoking a cigarette outside the store and I ducked behind the ice machine when the deacon pulled in."

"Are you willing to go to the bishop with everything you've just told me?" I ask.

"Look, I'm really sorry for everything that's been happening to Sarah Fisher, she's always been kind to me and I never wanted to be involved in any of this. Deacon Byler pretty much told everyone to shun her, that she and her Mamm would bankrupt the community if they started requesting money from the widow's fund and that her tour business is some kind of cancer that's going to corrupt the whole community."

He fidgets with his hands nervously. "The deacon said her sons were violent and even tried to make us think she was letting Englischers into her home but I never believed any of it, I'm just afraid to go against him. Deacon Byler is not an enemy you want to have in this community, especially when he's your neighbor; he practically drove the Beller family out of Hope Landing with his bullying and pranks just because their dog pooped in his *Ya*rd."

"Do you know what these people are planning to do to Sarah next?"

"Deacon Byler said if she didn't stop the tours by the seventeenth, he was going to call her before the council and he told us to rally the community against her but after the sermon yesterday, I think the Glick's got cold feet; they were supposed to do something tonight but they didn't stay for the meeting. I think Deacon Byler's going to do something himself, he was pretty angry."

"Does Deacon Byler have a drinking problem that you know of?"

"*Ya*, we used to play cards together a lot after my wife died, he's drunk by about 9:00 p.m. most nights, I try never to be around him when he's liquored up."

"I appreciate you coming to me about this but I don't see how it's very useful if you're not willing to go to the bishop. I'm trying to stop him from terrorizing a widow with five *kinner* who's just trying to provide for her family. Deacon Byler's not going to end his crusade just because someone accuses him of wrongdoing. The bishop has already received complaints and warned him at least once already, yet according to you, he's as determined as ever. I need proof Mr. Zug, give me something I can work with here," I say emphatically, "Stand up and stop him from destroying a woman who has done nothing wrong."

I take my hat off, sigh and run my hands through my hair in frustration. I'm so close to putting and end to this but I don't know if what he has will be enough. I look over at Mr. Sneed who's still leaning against the counter with a knowing half-smile on his face. I look at him curiously as I pace back and forth a few times.

"If that's all you've got Mr. Zug, I'm afraid I'm going to have to confer with my partner," I tell him, hoping he'll cough up anything he may have left out.

When he doesn't respond, I walk into the back room I use as an office. Mr. Sneed grabs his phone and keys from the counter and follows me.

“I really think he’s holding out on telling me everything he knows,” I say.

“Doesn’t really matter, I’m just enjoying your whole interrogation technique, you would have made an excellent cop,” he says.

“I appreciate that but now is not the time—” I stop myself mid sentence when it occurs to me that he’s been recording the whole thing on his phone.

“I could kiss you right now old man but that would be a little weird,” I chuckle, “So what’s the deal on the freezer?”

“My son would like to see the Deacon arrested and he’s got friends in the local police department if we need them but I suppose if we can’t find a way to catch him in the act, I’m willing to do a good deed and eat the cost of the freezer to get the Deacon at least some of what he deserves. I figure maybe we’ll get some beef out of the deal, maybe enough cash to take our ladies out to dinner, a free tour for my grandkids, my mower fixed and call it even.”

“I’m okay with that, let me give it one more try before we throw him under the bus, we can always use the recording as a last resort,” I tell him.

I go back into the front of the shop, pull up a stool and sit across from Mr. Zug.

“Look, Mr. Zug, don’t you ultimately want to be free of Deacon Byler’s tactics? I mean it can’t be easy living so close to him, being bullied by him and seeing him undermine every good thing that this community is founded on."

"*Ya*, he's a disgrace to our Amish faith and he abuses his power in the community but he has a way of getting people to do things and I don't want to be next on his list."

"Okay so tell me how I can do that for you, for everyone he's ever bullied or taken advantage of. If he were caught in the act, doing something he shouldn't, I could use that to see that he never does this to another Amish family again. I don't care if I have to go to the bishop, stand before the council, call the police or hide in the bushes and take pictures, but I think you know things that can put him out of his position of authority for good. I will take responsibility; nobody ever has to know it came from you if that's the way you want it but I think that in fifteen years of knowing him, you've dreamed about seeing him stopped and you know exactly how it can be done."

"He's after you too now, for helping Sarah, he said as much in the meeting last night."

"Mr. Zug, he has to be stopped and I'm willing to do what everyone else is afraid to do in order to make that happen. You can help me or cower in the corner and watch with the rest of your friends but if you do nothing, who will fight for you when it's your turn on his list?"

He studies my face in silence for several moments as he weighs his options. "What kind of deal are we talking on the freezer?"

"We'll take it out in beef; I can bring it over this afternoon."

"Would fifty pounds be enough?"

"That's a $1000.00 freezer plus delivery; give John the help he needs, throw in a hundred bucks with the beef and you've got a deal," Mr. Sneed interjects, though I personally would have settled for just the information at this point.

"Okay," he sighs heavily, "You've got a deal."

CHAPTER THIRTEEN

Once my meatballs are ready, I brown them slightly before dropping them in the sauce to finish cooking. As I wash my hands, I see John pulling into the drive. My heart begins to race, partly because of my excitement to see him and partly because I'm anxious to know what happened with Mr. Sneed.

I take off my kitchen apron and hang it on the back of the pantry door before unlatching the screen door.

"Mmmm, it smells good in here," he says with a playful smile, "Meatball casserole?"

"*Ya*, the meatballs are cooking in the sauce. I just have to assemble it and bake it about forty minutes before dinner time," I chuckle.

He puts his arms around me as I stir the sauce and I love how affectionate he can be. It's not exactly typical Amish behavior, especially for Amish men, but I want that in my life and I want my *kinner* to have that too.

"Sorry it took me so long, I had to interrogate someone, plan a strategy, deliver a freezer and pick up a couple of surprises," he says casually as I put the lid back on the pot.

"You've had a busy afternoon, are you going to share what happened in your meeting with Mr. Sneed?" I ask, turning to face him.

"There's nothing I won't share with you," he says softly, as he cradles my face in his hand and kisses me.

"But first, I have 25 pounds of beef to bring in and I'm going to need you to make me a promise."

"You never cease to amaze me John Troyer," I chuckle. "I'll help you put it away while you tell me about this promise."

He goes outside to retrieve the cooler while I shuffle a few things around to make room in the freezer. As we unload the cooler he tells me that he and Mr. Sneed worked a trade with Mr. Zug for the beef and that was the reason he went to deliver the freezer.

"We certainly are blessed," I say marveling at the fully stocked freezer.

"More than ever before," he says kissing me again, "Come and I'll tell you the rest."

I take the meatballs and sauce off the stove and sit at the table with him.

"I found out more about this situation with Deacon Byler

today, but before I tell you I want you to promise me that you'll trust my judgment in how to handle this situation, knowing that I won't let any harm come to you, your *mamm* or the *kinner*."

"*Ya*, of course I trust you John," I say, putting my hand on his.

He tells me about his interrogation of Mr. Zug, and then about the secret meetings, the people who participated, lies that were told against me and about the Deacon being behind the toothpicks in my locks. He tells me about Mr. Sneed's help, the recording of the conversation and how Mr. Zug finally agreed to come forward to the bishop as long as he wasn't alone.

"Okay, so we know what was done, who was doing it and why, but even if Bishop Graber punishes him, that doesn't mean it will stop him and I'm sure he'll be on a warpath."

"I know and that's why I need you to trust me because there's more. First of all, the deacon is a drunk and Mr. Zug can testify to that, secondly, as deacon, he's in charge of the widow's fund. Well last night, he showed Mr. Zug a ledger showing that he gave you money from the widow's fund."

"He did no such thing," I say emphatically.

"I know, which begs the question as to where that money went."

"Probably right in his pocket," I say, trying to contain my anger.

"Exactly, but the deacon doesn't think you'll ever find out that he supposedly gave you the money so there would never be a reason to question it."

"Except I do know, and I will testify that I never received a dime from the widow's fund."

"You and your *mamm*," he says.

"Oh that dirty thief," I say angrily.

"I know," he says, "Just bear with me," he says, squeezing my hand in his, "The Glicks were supposed to pull a prank tonight, they were going to throw bricks through your windows. Deacon Byler even told them specifically to make sure they threw one through the woodshop window behind the barn."

"How do you know?"

"Because Mr. Zug and I went to their house after I dropped off the freezer and we convinced them to testify too. They didn't stay for Deacon Byler's meeting last night after church so Mr. Zug figured out that they got cold feet."

"Still, what's to stop him from doing it anyway?"

"That's what I'm counting on…because you and I, along with Mr. Sneed and two policemen will be watching and waiting for him to do it. He'll be arrested, probably drunk and with all of the testimony we have, plus the missing money, it should be enough to have him removed as deacon and possibly excommunicated."

"I don't want the *kinner* to see all of that, and what if something goes wrong?"

"Dan is coming to get them after dinner, they'll stay the night at Ruthie's and he'll drop them at school in the morning. Caleb will stay with your *mamm* at the Daadi Haus until it's over and I'll stay here. Mr. Sneed is going to park his truck near the side gate so when it happens, he'll block the deacon in and be the one to call the police. They're friends of his sons and they'll be parked at the school waiting. You don't even have to take the blame for involving them."

"I don't know what to say, I just hope it works."

"Well, Dan and I both agree that unless he's removed as deacon, he'll just continue to abuse his power over the community. The only way to make sure that happens is if he threatens to publicly bring shame upon the church. Getting arrested will accomplish that. If it doesn't happen, we'll take our chances with the bishop on the evidence we have so far. There's certainly enough of it, but Bishop Graber is a kind man and if he's lenient with the deacon, it may only make things worse for his victims."

CHAPTER FOURTEEN

I wave goodbye to Dan, Ruthie and the *kinner* as they pull out of the drive. Mamm gets out the cards for a game of rummy with Caleb, "Are you two going to play?" she asks, happy to have someone as interested in the game as she is to play with.

"Actually, I have something I want to show Sarah before it gets dark, I think we'll go for a little ride if that's okay."

"*Ya*, you two go ahead, we'll be fine," she assures him.

"Why do I feel as if you had this planned all evening?" I chuckle.

"Maybe I just wanted some time alone with you," he smiles, getting on the tractor and holding out his hand to help me in the seat next to him.

We drive out to the picnic area, and planted in the clearing between the clusters of pear and apple trees, are two cherry trees standing almost five feet tall with beautiful white blossoms in bloom and a single lavender bow tied around both trunks.

"Oh John, they're beautiful," I say, touching the leaves and leaning in to smell the blossoms.

"It's my courtship gift to you," he smiles, sitting in one of the tire swings.

"Is that why there are two?" I ask leaning back against him as he puts his arm around me and pulls me into his lap.

"Well in doing all of this plant research, I read that cherry trees symbolize awakenings and new romance," he says as we sway gently together, "The blooms of the cherry tree are also symbols of good fortune, love and affection. I just thought that it described us perfectly."

"That's one of the most beautiful things anyone's ever said to me." I say, looking into his eyes.

He leans in and kisses me softly as he brushes his hand against my cheek, "I love you, Sarah, and I know in my heart that God brought us together. I don't know what the social rules are for second marriages but we're not teenagers. We both know what it takes to make a marriage work and I know that I've found what I've been waiting for. We can court for as long as you want or have the shortest courtship in Amish history; either way, it won't change the way I feel. I want to be your husband, a father to your children and even a son to your *mamm*. You take as long as you need but I plan to marry you,

Sarah Fisher."

I look at him as his words sink into my soul and warm my heart. I've spent most of my life content to live by the rules and I've abstained from letting my feelings get in the way of tradition, but I know first-hand how short life can be. I too believe that God brought us together and with His loving hand, He laid the groundwork in our hearts long before we got here, to this moment.

"I love you too, John, and I can think of nothing that would bring me more honor and joy than to be your wife."

He kisses me passionately and pushes his foot against the tree. As we sway together, laughing and kissing in the tire swing with the glow of the sun setting on the horizon, it's as if all of Heaven is rejoicing with us.

CHAPTER FIFTEEN

Wednesday, May 22

My stomach is in knots as I sit in the entryway with Mamm, John, Dan, Ruthie, Mr. and Mrs. Glick and Mr. Zug.

As the victims and witnesses to the corruption in our community, we all await our turn to give individual testimony to the accusations against Deacon Byler. Each person will be questioned, charges will be recorded, Deacon Byler will be called in alone to refute any accusations for the record and the leadership will confer before making a decision as to how severely he will be punished.

Even in light of everything the deacon has done, not only to us, but to the whole community, I can't help but feel sadness for him and what this will do to his family.

I take comfort in the fact that no matter what happens there will be no more secret committees to destroy what my family and our loved ones have worked so hard to build, there will be no more vicious lies, or attacks on our home and no more corrupted authority being wielded over us.

This experience has only made us stronger and wiser, binding us together in the face of adversity, teaching us new ways to live, how to support one another in our strengths and weaknesses and to appreciate the many blessings bestowed on us…for that, I am eternally grateful.

***

After three hours of testimony, an hour of refute, another hour of corroboration and ten minutes of deliberation, I look around the table to both Minister Oyer and Minister Eicher, "I think we're all in agreement, let's bring him back in."

Deacon Byler takes a seat at the table across from us as we reconvene the private hearing.

"Have you anything else to say on your behalf before punishment is administered?" I ask, hoping for some sign of a humbled, repentant heart.

"No, I do not Bishop Graver," he says curtly.

"The good people in this community depended on you Amos Byler. A deacon's calling is to minister to the widows and the poor, yet you repeatedly threatened them, stole from them and conspired to destroy them. You've made a drunken mockery of your position, publically shamed the church, and caused a division in this peaceful community by turning families against one another to satisfy your own selfish and covetous agenda. You have repeatedly abused your position and ignored several previous warnings, and I am punishing you to the full extent of my authority."

"I'm revoking your position as deacon and excommunicating you from Hope Landing for good. If I even suspect that you've uttered a single word or act of retaliation against anyone in this district, or committed one minor infraction of the Ordnung, I will call you before a public hearing where I will play the recorded evidence and provide detailed witness accounts of your sins before the district council and the members of this community where they will vote on whether to ban you from the Amish church forever. You will also be excluded from all communion services until you repent by confessing your sins before the congregation. This hearing is adjourned."

***

Once we've enjoyed a quiet afternoon picnic together, John sits back and pulls me to him, kissing my forehead as I nestle myself in his arms. I look around us and feel a sense of awe and wonder at the beautiful day, grateful that we could spend a couple of hours together before the house is buzzing with activity again.

I watch as a handful of blossoms from the cherry tree are carried away by the wind like faded memories before they fall to the ground and I think about how much our lives really are like that tree. Our biggest achievements begin with a tiny seed rooted in a solid foundation, every season has a purpose, every blossom has a time for glory and every fruit has a time to harvest, but none of it would be possible without the beauty of starting over.

The End.

Thank You for Reading!

And thank you for supporting me as an independent author. I hope you enjoyed reading this as much as I loved writing it! I hope you enjoyed reading this as much as I enjoyed writing it! If so, I hope you also enjoy the sample in the next chapter of my other work.

Lastly, if you enjoyed this book and want to continue to support my writing, please leave me a review to let everyone know what you thought of my work. It's the best thing you can do to keep indie authors like me writing. (And if you find something in the book that – YIKES – makes you think it deserves less than 5-stars, drop me a line at (Rachel.stoltzfus@globagrafxpress.com)

I'll try to fix it if I can!

All the best,

Rachel

FALSE WORSHIP – BOOK 1

When Beth Zook's *daed* starts courting a widow with a mysterious past, will Beth uncover this new family's secrets before she loses everything?

Sixteen-year-old Beth Zook has already lost so much -- first her sister in a tragic accident and then her *mamm* a year later to cancer. As Beth and her *daed* Marcus struggle to rebuild their lives in the Amish community of Indianasburg, Marcus finds love awakening in his heart when a new family -- a widow and her two sons -- move into their quiet community. But things are not as they seem, and the more Beth learns about this new family, the more reason she has to fear. Will Beth uncover this new family's secrets before she loses everything? Find out in Rachel Stoltzfus' False Worship series.

CHAPTER ONE

I'm running, my heart pounding in my chest, veins swollen with rushing blood. The faster I run, the faster it courses through me, threatening to rupture my arteries and leave me to a slow bleed-out, before I have the chance to escape.

I look back, but I can't see who (or what) is chasing me.

I turn just in time to avoid running face-first into the sturdy trunk of a northern red oak, and I twist my ankle on one of its upraised roots as I run past. I trip, hands reaching out to protect me as I fall into the thorny ground, a thick carpet of mulch and broken twigs, little rocks and littler bugs.

Feet and hands scrambling, I'm back up and running, after missing only a beat.

But I'm afraid it's enough to make all the difference; just a quick moment, a second or two, is all the margin my pursuer needs to gain the ground that separates us. I can imagine myself in the predator's sight: his feeble prey, bent forward and awkwardly pushing through this maze of fallen logs and low-lying branches, prickly shrubs and flittering birds, crying out in panic as I continue my futile flight.

I can feel the heartbeat of my pursuer as the distance between us closes. I can hear the feet pounding the earth behind me, almost as loud as my own strained breath, in the deepest crevices of my ears.

And I know, with the silent inner voice of doom, that I won't make it.

I almost want to stop running, to finally succumb to the cruelty of nature and the casualness of nurture. Nothing could have prepared me for this: only God, and He seems to have deserted me.

I start praying, my mind desperately launching pleas and promises: for delivery, and for eternal debt.

Please, God, spare me from the hellfire I can't outrun, from the pain which I know is craving the taste of my soul in its putrid belly. Please, God, don't let me die.

No answer comes, no lightning bolt from On High, no great hand to reach down from the clouds and lift me to safety, high above the bramble and brush.

My nose fills with the stench of wood rot and mold, and my own sweat, dripping down the sides of my face, collecting in the nape of my neck, retreating down the crevice of my spine.

I keep running, even as the predator's panting gets louder behind me. I can almost feel the hot snarl of that churning hatred, frothing over with a desire to end my life, in a way most swift and terrible.

At least, I hope it will be swift.

Something grabs me from behind, but I slip free; fingers or talons or claws, I can't be sure. But it doesn't matter, because with the second strike, I am captured and knocked to the ground, that murderous weight about to fall upon me from behind, and finish me off.

I bolt up with a start, looking around my quiet, dark bedroom. All is well. I am alone and unhurt, sheltered in the place of my childhood. *Just a dream,* I tell myself, heart pounding in my chest, skin clammy with sweat. *Thank God, it was just a dream.*

***

The quilt slowly takes shape beneath my sure and steady fingers. I've often wondered how many little stitches it takes to create one of these cozy and colorful quilts. *A hundred thousand?* I silently wonder once more. *A million?*

Does it matter?

It doesn't matter to the *Englisch*ers who buy them, souvenirs from their weekends among us, ornaments for their homes, gifts for their friends. They don't care how much work these quilts require, but they can certainly appreciate it.

We usually sew in quilting bees, and mine includes Greta and a few older ladies. But I don't always wait for them to collect in our quiet, somber home. There's work to be done, and it helps take my mind off of how quiet the house has become in these last few, terrible years.

When I'm focusing on the intricate diamonds and fine lines

of the quilt, I don't have to think about *Mamm*: those awful months she spent in bed, getting weaker and smaller, until, finally, there was nothing left of her at all. When I'm dipping that sharp needle into the cotton, making sure the line is straight and the weaves are even, I'm distracted from thinking about Margaret, struck down by a carriage, just a year before *Mamm* took ill. I knew then (and I always will be sure of this) that *Mamm* didn't die from cancer, but from a broken heart, over the death of my kid sister. I'm not a doctor, and I have to admit that even those *Englisch*er doctors may have been right about the tumors growing in her stomach, preventing her from eating. But the cancer was only God's way of answering *Mamm*'s own prayers for death. She didn't want to live after what happened to Margaret.

All prayers are heard, I remind myself, even the horrible ones.

I stop and pray that my *daed* won't turn himself over to the same sorrowful resolution. He's always been steady; a calm surface over a deep, still sea. But even the seas themselves can part, even the bowels of the Earth can rip apart and swallow us whole, especially if we ask God to make it so.

So I ask God to prevent it, to give his servant Marcus Zook (and his sole surviving daughter Beth) the strength to endure our losses, and enjoy our blessings. We still have each other, I remind myself, and our friends here in Indianasburg, and Aunt Sarah in Clarion, just a few counties away.

Maybe it's time we brought Aunt Sarah here to live with us, it occurs to me. She can't be very happy since her own husband died, and that was years before our family tragedy turned its attention to our own household.

What did this family ever do to invite such heartache? I ask God, not for the first time. *Daed* is a good man, even-tempered, and reasonable. Doesn't he deserve to be happy? Won't you turn your loving light upon him, Lord? I don't care for myself; but for his happiness, I'd offer any sacrifice.

No answer, at least not in the form of a lightning bolt or a burning bush; just silence, thick and cold and heavy.

All prayers are heard, and they are answered.

But not all answers are what they appear to be…

THANK YOU FOR READING!

And thank you for supporting me as an independent author. I hope you enjoyed reading this as much as I loved writing it!

If so, look for this book in eBook or Paperback format at your favorite online book distributors. Also, when a series is complete, we usually put out a discounted collection. If you'd rather read the entire series at once and save a few bucks doing it, we recommend looking for the collection.

Lastly, if you enjoyed this book and want to continue to support my writing, please leave me a review to let everyone know what you thought of my work. It's the best thing you can do to keep indie authors like me writing. (And if you find something in the book that – YIKES – makes you think it deserves less than 5-stars, drop me a line at Rachel.stoltzfus@globagrafxpress.com, and I'll fix it if I can.)

All the best,

Rachel

ABOUT THE AUTHOR

Rachel was born and raised in Lancaster, Pennsylvania. Being a neighbor of the Mennonite community, she started writing Amish romance fiction as a way of looking at the Amish community. She wanted to present a fair and honest representation of a love that is both romantic and sweet. She hopes her readers enjoy her efforts.

CPSIA information can be obtained
at www.ICGtesting.com
Printed in the USA
LVHW080355140920
665937LV00017B/1192

9 781522 978411